THE TRAITOR'S EMBLEM

Juan Gómez-Jurado is an award-winning journalist and bestselling author. His debut novel, *God's Spy*, was an instant bestseller, with rights sold in 42 countries. *The Traitor's Emblem* won Spain's second biggest literary award, the Premio de Novela Ciudad de Torrvieja. He lives in Spain with his wife and two children.

Also by Juan Gómez-Jurado

God's Spy
Contract with God

THE TRAITOR'S EMBLEM

Juan Gómez-Jurado

Translated by Daniel Hahn

First published in Great Britain in 2011 by Orion Fiction
An imprint of the Orion Publishing Group
Orion House, 5 Upper St Martin's Lane
London WC2H 9EA

An Hachette UK company

© Juan Gómez-Jurado 2008
© Random House Mondadori, S.A. 2008
Translation © Daniel Hahn 2011

The rights of Juan Gómez-Jurado and Daniel Hahn, to be identified
as the author and translator of this work respectively, have been asserted
in accordance with the Copyright, Designs and Patents Act 1988.

This book is a work of fiction. Names, characters, places and
incidents either are the product of the author's imagination or are
used fictitiously, and any resemblance to actual persons living or
dead, events or locales is entirely coincidental.

A CIP catalogue record for this book
is available from the British Library

978 1 4091 0078 2 (hardback)
978 1 4091 0079 9 (trade paperback)

Typeset by Input Data Services, Bridgwater Somerset

Printed and bound in the UK
by CPI Mackays, Chatham, Kent

The Orion Publishing Group's policy is to use papers
that are natural, renewable and recyclable products and
made from wood grown in sustainable forests. The logging
and manufacturing processes are expected to conform to
the environmental regulations of the country of origin.

www.orionbooks.co.uk

Treason and murder ever kept together,
As two yoke-devils sworn to either's purpose,
Working so grossly in a natural cause,
That admiration did not whoop at them:
But thou, 'gainst all proportion, didst bring in
Wonder to wait on treason and on murder:
And whatsoever cunning fiend it was
That wrought upon thee so preposterously
Hath got the voice in hell for excellence . . .

William Shakespeare, *Henry V* – Act II, scene ii

Prologue

The Straits of Gibraltar
12 March 1940

When the wave threw him against the gunwale, it was pure instinct that made Captain González grab at the wood, scraping the skin all the way down his hand. Decades later – by which time he'd become the most distinguished bookseller in Vigo – he would shudder as he remembered that night, the most terrifying and extraordinary of his life. As he sat in his armchair as an old, grey-haired man, his mouth would recall the taste of blood, saltpetre and fear. His ears would remember the thundering of what they called the 'toppler of fools', the treacherous swell that takes less than twenty minutes to rise and that seamen on the Straits – and their widows – had learned to fear; and his astonished eyes would glimpse again something that, quite simply, could not have been there.

When he saw it, Captain González quite forgot that the engine was already struggling, that his crew was no more than seven men when there should have been at least eleven, that among them he was the only one who, just six months earlier, hadn't got seasick in the shower. He quite forgot that he had contemplated knocking them to the deck for not having awoken him when all the pitching and rolling began.

He held fast to a porthole in order to turn his body round and haul himself on to the bridge, bursting in to it with a blast of rain and wind that drenched the navigator.

'Get away from my wheel, Roca,' he shouted, giving the navigator a hard push. 'You're no earthly use to anyone.'

'Captain, I . . . You said we weren't to disturb you unless we were about to go down, sir.' His voice trembled.

Which is precisely what's about to happen, thought the captain, shaking his head. Most of his crew was made up of the tottering leftovers of a war that had devastated the country. He couldn't blame them for not having sensed the arrival of the great swell, just as nobody could blame him now for concentrating his attention on turning the boat around and bringing it to safety. The most sensible thing would have been to pay no attention to what he'd just seen, because the alternative was suicide. Something only a fool would attempt.

And I am that fool, thought González.

The navigator watched him, mouth wide open, as he steered, holding the boat firm and cutting in towards the waves. The gunboat *Esperanza* had been built at the end of the previous century, and the wood and steel of its hull creaked savagely.

'Captain!' yelled the navigator. 'What the hell are you doing? We'll capsize!'

'Eyes to port, Roca,' the captain replied. He was afraid too, though he couldn't allow the slightest trace of that fear to show.

The navigator obeyed, thinking the captain had gone completely mad.

A few seconds later, it was his own judgement that he'd begun to doubt.

No more than thirty swimming-strokes away, a little raft was rolling between two crests, its keel at a precarious angle. It seemed to be on the brink of capsizing; in fact, it was a miracle it hadn't gone over already. There was a flash of lightning, and suddenly the navigator understood why the captain was gambling eight lives on such a poor hand.

'Sir, there are people over there!'

'I know, Roca. Tell Castillo and Pascual. They should leave the pumps, come on deck with two ropes and hang on to those gunwales like a whore hangs on to her money.'

'Aye-aye, Captain.'

'No . . . wait . . .' said the captain, grabbing Roca's arm before he could leave the bridge.

The captain hesitated for a moment. He couldn't supervise the rescue and steer the boat at the same time. If the prow could just be held perpendicular to the waves they could make it. But if it didn't come down in time, one of his boys would end up at the bottom of the sea.

To hell with it.

'Leave it, Roca, I'll do it myself. You take the wheel and keep it steady, like this.'

'We won't be able to hold out long, Captain.'

'The moment we get those poor devils out of there, head straight into the first wave you see, but a moment before we reach the highest point, pull the wheel to starboard as hard as you can. And pray!'

Castillo and Pascual appeared on deck, their jaws set and bodies tense, the look on their faces attempting to mask two bodies filled with fear. The captain positioned himself between them, ready to direct the perilous dance.

'At my signal, cast out the gaffs. Now!'

The steel teeth dug into the edge of the raft; the cables tensed.

'Pull!'

As they hauled the raft closer, the captain thought he could hear shouts, see arms waving.

'Hold her tight, but don't get too close!' He bent over and picked up a boathook twice as tall as he was. 'If they hit us it will destroy them!'

And quite possibly it would open a breach in our boat too, the captain thought. Beneath the slippery deck, he could feel the hull creaking more and more as they were tossed about by each new wave.

He manoeuvred the boathook and managed to catch one end of the raft. The pole was long and would help him keep the small craft at a fixed distance. He gave orders to tie the lines to the bitts and for a rope-ladder to be dropped, while he did his best to cling to the boathook, which bucked in his hands, threatening to split open his skull.

Another flash of lightning lit up the inside of the craft and Captain González could now see that there were four people on board. He could also finally understand how they had managed to remain on the floating soup dish as it leaped about between the waves.

Damned lunatics – they've tied themselves to the boat.

A figure wearing a dark waterproof was leaning across the other occupants, waving a knife and frantically cutting the ropes that bound them to the raft, slashed ropes trailing from his own wrists.

'Go on! Climb up before this thing sinks!'

The figures approached the side of the boat, their outstretched arms reaching towards the ladder. The man with the knife managed to grab hold of it and urged the others to go on ahead of him. González's crew helped them up. Finally there was no one left but the man with the

3

knife. He took hold of the ladder but as he leaned against the side of the boat to push himself up, the boathook suddenly slipped. The captain tried to hook it in again but then a wave that was higher than the rest raised the keel of the raft, hurling it against the side of the *Esperanza*.

There was a crunch, then a shout.

Horrified, the captain let go of the boathook. The side of the raft had struck the man's leg, and he was hanging from the ladder with one hand, his back against the hull. The raft was moving away, but it would only be a matter of seconds before the waves hurled it back towards the *Esperanza*.

'The lines!' the captain shouted to his men – 'for God's sake, cut them!'

The sailor closest to the gunwale searched in his belt for a knife and then began to cut the ropes. The other tried to lead the rescued men to the hatch that led to the hold before a wave hit them head-on and swept them out to sea.

His heart in his mouth, the captain searched under the gunwale for the axe that he knew had been rusting away there for many years.

'Out of the way, Pascual!'

Blue sparks flew from the steel, but the axe-blows could barely be heard above the growing clamour of the storm. For a moment, nothing happened.

Then there was a crash.

The deck shook as the raft, freed from its moorings, rose up and splintered against the prow of the *Esperanza*. The captain leaned over the gunwale, certain that all he'd find would be the dancing end of the ladder. But he was wrong.

The shipwrecked man was still there, his left hand flailing, trying to regain its grip on the rungs of the ladder. The captain reached down to him, but the desperate man was still more than two metres away.

There was only one thing for it.

He put one leg over the side and grabbed the ladder with his injured hand, simultaneously praying to and cursing that God who was so determined to drown them. For a moment he almost fell, but the sailor Pascual caught him just in time. He descended three rungs, just enough to be able to reach Pascual's hands in case he lost his grip. He didn't dare go any farther.

'Take my hand!'

The man tried to turn his body round to reach González, but he couldn't make it. One of the fingers with which he was clinging to the ladder slipped.

The captain forgot all about his prayers and concentrated on his curses. Albeit quietly. After all, he wasn't so unhinged as to taunt God at a moment like that. He was, however, mad enough to take one step farther down, and grab the poor fellow by the front of his waterproof.

For a second that seemed eternal, all that held those two men to the swinging rope-ladder were nine fingers, the worn sole of a boot and a mountain of willpower.

Then the shipwrecked man managed to turn himself around enough to cling on to the captain's body. He hooked his feet on to the rungs, and the two men began their ascent.

Six minutes later, bent over his own vomit in the hold, the captain could scarcely believe their luck. He was struggling to calm down. He still wasn't quite sure how the useless Roca had managed to see off the storm, but already the waves were beating less insistently against the hull, and it seemed clear that this time the *Esperanza* was going to make it.

The sailors stared at him, a semicircle of faces filled with exhaustion and strain. One of them held out a towel. González waved it away.

'Clean up this mess,' he said as he straightened up, gesturing towards the floor.

The dripping castaways huddled in the darkest corner of the hold. It was scarcely possible to make out their faces in the trembling light of the cabin's only lamp.

González took three steps towards them.

One of them came forward, and held out his hand.

'*Danke schön.*'

Like his companions he was covered from head to toe in a hooded black waterproof. Only one thing distinguished him from the others – a belt round his waist. And shining in the belt was the red-handled knife he had used to cut the ropes that had secured his friends to the raft.

The captain couldn't contain himself.

'Damned son of a bitch! We could all be dead!'

González swung his arm back and struck the man on the head,

5

knocking him down. His hood fell back, revealing a head of fair hair and a face with angular features. One cold blue eye. Where the other should have been there was only a stretch of wrinkled skin.

The shipwrecked man got up and repositioned a patch that must have been displaced by the blow over the socket. Then he put his hand on his knife. Two of the sailors stepped forward, fearing he would rip the captain apart there and then, but he merely drew it out gently and threw it on to the floor. He held his hand out again.

'*Danke schön.*'

In spite of himself, the captain smiled. That damned Kraut had balls of steel. Shaking his head, González held out his hand.

'Where the devil did you come from?'

The other man shrugged. It was clear he didn't understand a word of Spanish. González studied him, slowly. He must have been thirty-five to forty years old, and under his black waterproof he wore dark clothes and heavy boots.

The captain took a step towards the man's companions, eager to know who he'd gambled his boat and crew for, but the other man held out his arms and moved to the side, blocking his way. He planted his feet firmly, or at least he tried to, as he found it difficult to remain standing and the expression on his face was pleading.

He doesn't want to challenge my authority in front of my men, but he's not prepared to let me get too close to his mysterious friends. Very well, then, have it your way, damn you. They'll deal with you back at headquarters, thought González.

'Pascual.'

'Sir?'

'Tell the navigator to make for Cadiz.'

'Aye-aye, Captain,' said the sailor, disappearing through the hatch. The captain was about to follow him, heading back towards his own cabin, when the German's voice stopped him.

'*Nein. Bitte. Nicht Cadis.*'

The German's face had altered completely when he heard the city's name.

What is it you're so terrified of, Fritz?

'*Komm. Komm. Bitte,*' said the German, gesturing that he should approach. The captain leaned in and the other man began begging in his ear. '*Nicht Cadis. Portugal. Bitte, Kapitän.*'

6

González drew back from the German, contemplating him for over a minute. He was sure he wouldn't be able to get any more out of the man, since his own grasp of German was limited to yes, no, please and thank you. Again he faced a dilemma where the easiest solution was the one that appealed to him the least. He decided that he had already done enough by saving their lives.

What are you hiding, Fritz? Who are your friends? What are four citizens of the most powerful nation in the world, with the biggest army, doing crossing the Straits on a little old raft? Were you hoping to get to Gibraltar on that thing? No, I don't think so. Gibraltar is full of the English, your enemies. And why not come to Spain? Judging by the tone of our glorious Generalíssimo, we'll all be crossing the Pyrenees before long to give you a hand killing the Frogs, chucking stones at them most likely. If we really are as thick as thieves with your Führer . . . Unless you're not so keen on him yourself, of course.

Damn it.

'Watch these men,' he said, turning to the crew. 'Otero, give them some blankets and get something hot inside them.'

The captain returned to the bridge, where Roca was plotting a course for Cadiz, avoiding the storm that was now blowing into the Mediterranean.

'Captain,' said the navigator, standing to attention. 'May I just say how much I admire what . . .'

'Yes, yes, Roca. Thank you very much. Is there any coffee?'

Roca poured him a cup and the captain sat down to savour the brew. He took off his waterproof cape and the sweater he was wearing underneath, which was soaking. Fortunately it wasn't cold in the cabin.

'There's been a change of plan, Roca. One of the Bosch we rescued has given me a tip-off. Seems there's a band of smugglers at the mouth of the Guadiana. We'll go to Ayamonte instead, see if we can steer clear of them.'

'Whatever you say, Captain,' said the navigator, a little put out at having to plot a new course. González fixed his gaze on the back of the young man's neck, slightly concerned. There were certain people you couldn't talk to about certain matters, and he wondered whether Roca might be an informer. What the captain was proposing was illegal. It would be enough to get him sent to prison, or worse. But he couldn't do it without his second-in-command.

7

Between sips of coffee, he decided that he could trust Roca. His father had killed *nacionales* after the fall of Barcelona a couple of years earlier.

'Ever been to Ayamonte, Roca?'

'No, sir,' said the young man, without turning round.

'It's a charming place, three miles up the Guadiana. The wine is good, and in April it smells of orange blossom. And on the other bank of the river, that's where Portugal starts.'

He took another sip.

'A stone's throw, as they say.'

Roca turned, surprised. The captain gave him a tired smile.

Fifteen hours later, the deck of the *Esperanza* was deserted. Laughter rose from the mess where the sailors were enjoying an early dinner. The captain had promised that after they'd eaten they would drop anchor at the port of Ayamonte, and many of them could already feel the sawdust of the tavernas under their feet. Supposedly the captain was minding the bridge himself, while Roca guarded the four shipwrecked passengers.

'You're sure this is necessary, sir?' asked the navigator, unconvinced.

'It will just be the tiniest bruise. Don't be so cowardly, man. It has to look real. Stay down on the floor for a bit.'

There was a dry thud and then a head appeared through the hatch, quickly followed by the castaways. Night was beginning to fall.

The captain and the German lowered the lifeboat into the water, to port, the side farthest from the mess. His companions climbed in and waited for their one-eyed leader, who had covered his head with his hood once more.

'Two hundred metres in a straight line,' the captain told him, gesturing towards Portugal. 'Leave the lifeboat on the beach – I'll need it. I'll fetch it back later.'

The German shrugged.

'Look, I know you don't understand a word. Here . . .' said González, giving him back his knife.

The man tucked it away in his belt with one hand, while he fumbled under his waterproof with his other. He took out a small object and placed it in the captain's hand.

'*Verrat*,' he said, touching his index finger to his chest. '*Rettung*,' he said, touching the chest of the Spaniard.

8

González studied the gift carefully. It was a sort of medal, very heavy. He held it closer to the lamp hanging in the cabin; the object gave off an unmistakable glow.

It was made of solid gold.

'Look, I can't accept ...'

But he was talking to himself. The boat was moving away already, and none of its occupants looked back.

To the end of his days, Manuel González Pereira, former captain in the Spanish navy, dedicated every minute he could spare away from his bookshop to the study of that gold emblem. It was a double-headed eagle set on an iron cross. The eagle was holding a sword, there was a number 32 above its head and an enormous diamond encrusted in its chest.

He discovered that it was a Masonic symbol of the highest rank, but every expert he spoke to told him that it had to be a fake, especially since it was made of gold. The German Masons never used noble metals for the emblems of their Grand Masters. The size of the diamond – as far as the jeweller was able to ascertain without taking the piece apart – made it possible to date the stone approximately to the turn of the century.

Often, as he sat up late into the night, the bookseller thought back to the conversation he'd had with 'The One-Eyed Mystery Man', as his little son, Juan Carlos, liked to call him.

The boy never tired of hearing the story, and he invented far-fetched theories about the identity of the castaways. But what excited him most were those parting words. He had deciphered them with the help of a German dictionary, and he repeated them slowly, as though by doing so he might better understand.

'*Verrat* – treachery. *Rettung* – salvation.'

The bookseller died without ever having solved the mystery hidden in his emblem. His son Juan Carlos inherited the piece, and became a bookseller in his turn. One September afternoon in 2002, an obscure old writer came by the bookshop to give a talk about his new work on Freemasonry. Nobody turned up, so Juan Carlos decided, in order to kill time and lessen his guest's obvious discomfort, to show him a photo of the emblem. On seeing it, the writer's face changed.

'Where did you get this photo?'

'It's an old medal that belonged to my father.'

'Do you still have it?'

'Yes. Because of the triangle containing the number thirty-two we worked out that it was . . .'

'A Masonic symbol. Obviously a fake, because of the shape of the cross, and the diamond. Have you had it valued?'

'Yes. The materials are worth about three thousand euros. I don't know if it has any additional historical value.'

The writer looked at the piece for several seconds before replying. His lower lip trembled.

'No. Definitely not. Perhaps as a curiosity . . . but I doubt it. Still, I'd like to buy it. You know . . . for my research. I'll give you four thousand euros for it.'

Juan Carlos politely refused the offer, and the writer left, offended. He started coming to the bookshop on a daily basis, even though he didn't live in the city. He pretended to rummage among the books, though in reality he spent most of the time watching Juan Carlos over the thick plastic frames of his glasses. The bookseller began to feel harassed. One winter night, on his way home, he thought he heard footsteps behind him. Juan Carlos hid in a doorway and waited. Moments later the writer appeared, an elusive shadow shivering in a threadbare raincoat. Juan Carlos emerged from the doorway and cornered the man, holding him up against the wall.

'This has to stop, do you understand?'

The old man started to cry and fell babbling to the ground, hugging his knees.

'You don't understand, I have to have it . . .'

Juan Carlos softened. He accompanied the old man to a bar and set a glass of brandy in front of him.

'Right, now tell me the truth. It's very valuable, isn't it?'

The writer took his time before replying, studying the bookseller, who was thirty years his junior and six inches taller. Finally he gave up.

'Its value is incalculable. Though that's not the reason I want it,' he said, with a dismissive gesture.

'Why, then?'

'For the glory. The glory of discovery. It would form the basis for my next book.'

'On the piece?'

'On its owner. I've managed to reconstruct his life after years of research, digging around in fragments of diaries, newspaper archives, private libraries ... the sewers of history. As few as ten very uncommunicative men in the world know his story. All of them Grand Masters, and I'm the only one with all the pieces. Though no one would believe me if I told them.'

'Try me.'

'Only if you'll promise me one thing. That you'll let me see it. Touch it. Just once.'

Juan Carlos sighed.

'All right. On the condition you have a good story to tell.'

The old man leaned over the table and began to whisper a story that had, till that moment, been passed from mouth to mouth between men who had sworn never to repeat it. A story of lies, of an impossible love, of a forgotten hero, of the murder of thousands of innocent people at the hands of one man. The story of the traitor's emblem ...

THE PROFANE
1919–21

Where understanding never goes beyond one's own self

The symbol of the Profane is a hand held out, open, solitary but capable of grasping hold of knowledge.

1

There was blood on the steps of the Schroeders' mansion.

When he saw it, Paul Reiner shuddered. It wasn't the first time he'd seen blood, of course. Between early April and May 1919, Munich's inhabitants had experienced in thirty days all the horror they'd managed to avoid in four years of war. In the uncertain months between the end of the empire and the proclamation of the Weimar Republic, countless groups had attempted to impose their agendas. The communists had taken the city, and declared Bavaria a Soviet republic. Lootings and murders had become widespread as the Freikorps narrowed the gap between Berlin and Munich. The rebels, knowing their days were numbered, tried to get rid of as many political enemies as they could. Mostly civilians, executed in the dead of night.

Which meant that Paul had already seen traces of blood, but never at the entrance to the house where he lived. And although there wasn't much, it was coming from beneath the big oak door.

With any luck Jürgen has fallen on his face and knocked out all his teeth, thought Paul. *Maybe that way he'll give me a few days' peace.* He shook his head sadly. He didn't have that kind of luck.

He was only fifteen, but already a bitter shadow had been cast over his heart, like clouds blocking the sluggish mid-May sun. Half an hour earlier, Paul had been lazing around among the bushes of the Englischer Garten, glad to be back at school after the revolution, though not so much for the lessons. Paul was always ahead of his classmates, and of Professor Wirth, too, who bored him immensely. Paul read everything he could get his hands on, gulping it down like a drunk on payday. He only feigned attention during lessons, but always ended up top of the class.

Paul didn't have friends, however hard he tried with his classmates. But in spite of everything, he did enjoy school, because the hours of lessons were hours spent away from Jürgen, who attended an academy where the floors weren't made of linoleum and the edges of the desks weren't chipped.

On his way home Paul always took a turn around the Garten, the largest park in Europe, which that afternoon seemed almost deserted, even by the ubiquitous red-jacketed guards who would reprimand him whenever he strayed off the path. Paul made the most of this opportunity, and took off his shabby shoes. He liked to walk barefoot on the grass, and bent down distractedly as he went, picking up a few of the thousands of yellow pamphlets that the Freikorps planes had dropped over Munich the previous week, demanding the communists' unconditional surrender. He threw them in the bin. He would gladly have stayed to clear up the whole park, but it was Thursday, and he had to polish the floor of the fourth storey of the mansion, a task that would occupy him until dinner-time.

If only he weren't there . . . thought Paul. *Last time he locked me in the broom cupboard and poured a bucket of dirty water on to the marble. Good thing Mama heard me shouting and unlocked the cupboard before Brunhilda found out.*

Paul wanted to remember a time when his cousin hadn't behaved like that. Years ago, when they were both very small and Eduard would hold their hands and take them to the Garten, Jürgen used to smile at him. It was a fleeting memory, almost the only fond memory of his cousin that remained. Then came the Great War, with its orchestras and parades. And off marched Eduard, waving and smiling as the lorry that carried him away gathered speed and Paul ran alongside it, wanting to march with his big cousin, wishing he were sitting beside him sporting that impressive uniform.

For Paul, the war had consisted of the news he read each morning posted on the police station wall, which was on his way to school. Frequently he had to slip through a thicket of legs – something he never found difficult as he was as thin as a rake. There he read delightedly about the advances of the Kaiser's army, which daily took thousands of prisoners, occupied cities, and expanded the borders of the empire. Then in class he would draw a map of Europe and amuse himself by imagining where the next great battle would take place, and wondering whether Eduard would be there. Suddenly, and quite without warning, the 'victories' started happening ever closer to home, and the war dispatches almost always announced 'a return to the position of security originally envisaged'. Until one day a huge poster announced that Germany had lost the war. Underneath was a list detailing the price that would have to be paid, and it was a very long list indeed.

Reading that list and the poster, Paul had felt as if he'd been deceived, cheated. Suddenly there was no cushion of fantasy to mitigate the pain of the increasing number of thrashings he received from Jürgen. The glorious war would not wait for Paul to grow up and join Eduard at the front.

And there was certainly nothing glorious about it at all.

Paul stood there for a while, looking at the blood at the entrance. In his mind he rejected the possibility that the revolution had started again. Freikorps squads were patrolling the whole of Munich. This puddle seemed fresh, however, a small anomaly on the great stone whose steps were large enough to fit two men lying end to end.

I'd better hurry. If I'm late again, Aunt Brunhilda will kill me.

He debated a little longer between fear of the unknown and fear of his aunt, and the latter prevailed. He took the little key to the service entrance from his pocket and let himself into the mansion. Inside, everything seemed quiet enough. He was approaching the staircase when he heard voices from the main living quarters of the house.

'He slipped as we were climbing the steps, madam. It's not easy to hold him up, and we're all very weak. It's been months and his wounds keep reopening.'

'Incompetent fools. No wonder we lost the war.'

Paul crept across the main entrance hall, trying to make as little noise as possible. The long bloodstain that ran under the door narrowed into a series of drips that led towards the largest room in the mansion. Inside, his aunt Brunhilda and two soldiers were leaning over a sofa. She kept rubbing her hands together until she realised what she was doing and then hid them in the folds of her dress. Even though he was hidden behind the door, Paul couldn't help quaking with fear when he saw his aunt like this. Her eyes were like two thin grey streaks, her mouth was twisted into a question mark, and her authoritative voice trembled with rage.

'Look at the state of the upholstery. Marlis!'

'Baroness,' said the servant, approaching.

'Go and fetch a blanket, quickly. Call the gardener. His clothes will have to be burned, they're covered in lice. And someone tell the baron.'

'And Master Jürgen, Madam Baroness?'

'No! Especially not him, you understand? Is he back from school?'

'He has fencing today, Madam Baroness.'

'He'll be here any moment. I want this catastrophe sorted out before he returns,' Brunhilda ordered. 'Go!'

The servant rushed past Paul, her skirts swishing, but he still didn't move, because he had spotted Eduard's face behind the legs of the soldiers. His heart began to beat faster. So that was who the soldiers had carried in and laid down on the sofa.

Good God, it was his blood.

'Who is responsible for this?'

'A mortar shell, madam.'

'I know that much already. I'm asking why you've only brought my son to me now, and in this state. It has been seven months since the war ended, and not a word of news. Do you know who his father is?'

'Yes, he's a baron. And Ludwig here is a bricklayer, and I'm a grocer's assistant. But shrapnel has no respect for titles, madam. And the road from Turkey was a long one. You're lucky he's back at all; my brother won't be coming back.'

Brunhilda's face turned livid.

'Get out!' she hissed.

'That's nice, madam. We return your son to you and you throw us out into the street without so much as a glass of beer.'

A glimmer of remorse might perhaps have crossed Brunhilda's face, but it was overshadowed by rage. Speechless, she raised a trembling finger and pointed towards the door.

'Piece of aristo shit,' said one of the soldiers, spitting on the carpet.

Reluctantly they turned to leave, their heads down. Their sunken eyes filled with weariness and disgust, but not surprise. There was nothing, thought Paul, that could shock these men now. And when the two men in large grey greatcoats moved out of the way, Paul finally understood the scene.

Eduard, Baron von Schroeder's firstborn son, was lying unconscious on the sofa at an odd angle. His left arm was propped up on some cushions. Where his right should have been, there was only a badly sewn fold in his jacket. Where he should have had legs, there were two stumps covered in dirty bandages, one of which was seeping blood. The surgeon had not cut them in the same place – the left was severed above the knee, the right just below.

Asymmetric mutilation, thought Paul, remembering that morning's art history class, and his teacher discussing the Venus de Milo. He realised he was crying.

When she heard the sobbing, Brunhilda raised her head and hurled herself towards Paul. The look of contempt and disdain she usually reserved for him had been replaced by one of hatred and shame. For a moment Paul thought she was going to strike him and jumped away, falling backwards and covering his face with his arms. There was a tremendous crash.

The doors to the hall had been slammed shut.

2

Eduard von Schroeder was not the only child to return home that day, a week after the government had declared the city of Munich secure and begun to bury the more than twelve hundred communist dead.

But unlike that of Eduard von Schroeder, this homecoming had been prepared for in minute detail. For Alys and Manfred Tannenbaum, the return journey had begun on the *Macedonia*, from New Jersey to Hamburg. It continued in a luxurious first-class compartment on a train to Berlin, where they found a telegram from their father ordering them to take up residence at the Esplanade until they received further instructions. This, for Manfred, was the happiest coincidence of the ten years of his life, because Charlie Chaplin happened to be staying in the room next door. The actor gave the boy one of his famous bamboo canes, and even accompanied him and his sister to the taxi the day they finally received the telegram saying it was now safe to undertake the last leg of their journey.

So it was that on 13 May 1919, more than five years after their father had sent them off to the United States to escape the impending war, the children of Germany's most important Jewish industrialist set foot on platform 3 of the Hauptbahnhof station.

Even then, Alys knew that things were not going to end well.

'Hurry up with that, will you, Doris? Oh, just leave it, I'll take it myself,' she said, snatching the hatbox from the hands of the servant her father had sent to meet them and placing it on top of the trolley. This she had commandeered from one of the young station assistants who buzzed around her like flies, trying to take charge of the luggage. Alys shooed them all away. She couldn't bear people trying to control her, or even worse, treating her as if she were incapable.

'I'll race you, Alys!' said Manfred, breaking into a run. The boy didn't share his sister's concerns, and worried only about clinging on to his precious walking-stick.

'Just you wait, you little squirt!' shouted Alys, launching the trolley in front of her. 'Don't get left behind, Doris.'

'Miss, your father wouldn't approve of you carrying your own luggage. Please . . .' begged the servant, trying unsuccessfully to keep up with the girl while glaring at the young men who were nudging each other mischievously and pointing at Alys.

It was precisely the problem Alys had with her father: he programmed every aspect of her life. Although Josef Tannenbaum was a man of flesh and bone, Alys's mother had always maintained that he had gears and springs instead of organs.

'You could set your watch by your father, my dear,' she'd whisper in her daughter's ear, and the two of them would laugh – quietly, because Mr Tannenbaum didn't like jokes.

Then, in December 1913, influenza took her mother. Alys did not emerge from her shock and sadness until she and her brother were on their way to Columbus, Ohio, four months later. They lodged with the Bushes, an upper-middle-class Episcopalian family. The patriarch, Samuel, was director-general of Buckeye Steel Castings, an establishment with which Josef Tannenbaum had many lucrative contracts. In 1914, Samuel Bush became the government official in charge of Arms and Munitions, and the products he acquired from Alys's father began to take a different form. To be precise, they took the form of millions of bullets that travelled across the Atlantic. They travelled westwards in crates while the United States was still supposedly neutral, then in the cartridge-belts of the soldiers travelling east in 1917, when President Wilson decided to spread democracy across Europe.

In 1918, Bush and Tannenbaum exchanged friendly letters, bemoaning the fact that 'owing to political inconveniences' their dealings would have to be suspended temporarily. Trade resumed fifteen months later, coinciding with the return of the young Tannenbaums to Germany.

The day the letter arrived in which Josef reclaimed his children, Alys thought she would die. Only a girl of fifteen, who is secretly in love with one of the sons of her host family, and who discovers that she will have to leave for ever, can be so fully convinced that her life is coming to an end.

Prescott, she wept in her cabin as she headed home. *If only I'd spoken to him more ... If I'd made more of a fuss of him when he came back from Yale for his birthday, instead of showing off like all the other girls at the party ...*

Despite her own prognosis Alys did in fact survive, and she swore into the drenched pillows of her cabin that she would never again allow a man to make her suffer. From that moment she would take all the decisions in her life, no matter what anyone said. Even her father.

I'll find work. No, Papa will never allow it. It would be better if I asked him to give me a job at one of the factories, until I've saved up enough for a ticket back to the United States. And when I set foot in Ohio again, I'll grab Prescott by the throat and squeeze him until he asks me to marry him. That's what I'll do, and no one can stop me.

However, by the time the Mercedes had come to a stop on Prinzregentenplatz, Alys's resolve had deflated like a cheap balloon. She was finding it difficult to breathe and her brother was jumping about nervously on his seat. It seemed extraordinary that she'd carried her decision with her over four thousand kilometres – halfway across the Atlantic – only to see it fall apart during the four-thousand-metre journey from the station to this luxurious building. A porter in uniform opened the car door for her, and before Alys knew it they were on their way up in the lift.

'Do you think Papa has arranged a party, Alys? I'm starving!'

'Your father has been very busy, young Master Manfred. But I took it upon myself to buy cream buns for tea.'

'Thank you, Doris,' mumbled Alys, as the lift stopped with a metallic crunch.

'It's going to be strange living in an apartment after the big house in Columbus. I hope no one's touched my things,' said Manfred.

'Well, if they have, you're not likely to remember, shrimp,' replied his sister, momentarily forgetting her fear of seeing her father and ruffling Manfred's hair.

'Don't call me that. I remember everything!'

'Everything?'

'That's what I said. The wall had blue boats painted on it. And there was a chimpanzee playing cymbals at the end of the bed. Papa wouldn't let me take it with me because he said it would drive Mr Bush mad. I'll go and get it!' he shouted, slipping between the legs of the butler as he opened the door.

'Wait, Master Manfred!' shouted Doris to no effect. The boy was already running up the hallway.

The Tannenbaums' residence occupied the top floor of the building, a nine-room apartment of more than three hundred and twenty square metres that was tiny in comparison to the house in which the brother and sister had lived in America. To Alys, the dimensions seemed to have changed completely. She hadn't been much older than Manfred was now when she'd left in 1914, and somehow she was seeing it all from that perspective, as though she had shrunk thirty centimetres.

'... Fräulein?'

'Sorry, Doris. What were you saying?'

'The master will receive you in his study. He did have a visitor with him, but I think he's leaving.'

Someone was coming down the hallway towards them. A tall, solid man, wrapped in an elegant black frock coat. Alys did not recognise him, but behind him was Herr Tannenbaum. When they reached the entrance, the man in the frock coat stopped – so abruptly that Alys's father almost bumped into him – and stood staring at her through a monocle on a gold chain.

'Ah, and here's my daughter! What perfect timing!' said Tannenbaum, giving his companion a complicit glance. 'Herr Baron, allow me to introduce to you my daughter Alys, who has just arrived with her brother from America. Alys, this is Baron von Schroeder.'

'A pleasure,' said Alys, coldly. She omitted to give the polite curtsy that was almost compulsory when faced with members of the nobility. She didn't like the baron's haughty bearing.

'A very pretty girl. Though I fear she may have caught some of the American manners.'

Tannenbaum shot his daughter a look of outrage. The girl was sad to see that her father had barely changed in five years. Physically he was still thickset and short-legged, with hair in conspicuous retreat. And in his manner he remained as obliging towards those in power as he was firm with those under him.

'You can't imagine how much I regret that. Her mother died very young, and she has not had much of a social life. I'm sure you

23

understand. If only she could spend some time in the company of people her own age, well-bred people . . .'

The baron gave a resigned sigh.

'Why don't you and your daughter join us at our house on Tuesday around six? We'll be celebrating my son Jürgen's birthday.'

From the knowing look the men exchanged, Alys got the sense that this had all been arranged in advance.

'By all means, Your Excellency. It's such a lovely gesture on your part to invite us. Allow me to accompany you to the door.'

'But how could you be so inconsiderate?'

'I'm sorry, Papa.'

They were sitting in his study. One wall was covered with bookcases that Tannenbaum had filled with books bought by the metre, based on the colour of their bindings.

'You're sorry? A "sorry" doesn't fix anything, Alys. You need to understand I'm doing some very important business with Baron Schroeder.'

'Steel and metals?' she asked, using her mother's old trick of taking an interest in Josef's business whenever he flew into one of his rages. If he started talking about money he could go on for hours, and by the time he had finished he'd have forgotten why he'd been angry in the first place. But this time it didn't work.

'No, land. Land . . . and other things. You'll find out when the time is right. Anyway, I hope you have a pretty dress for the party.'

'I've only just arrived, Papa. I don't really feel like going to a party where I don't know anyone.'

'Don't feel like it? For the love of God, it's a party at the house of Baron Schroeder!'

When she heard him say that, Alys flinched slightly. It wasn't normal for a Jew to take the name of God in vain. Then she remembered a small detail she had missed when she came in. There was no mezuzah on the door. She looked around, surprised, and saw a crucifix hanging on the wall, beside a picture of her mother. She was struck dumb. She wasn't particularly religious – she was going through that stage of adolescence in which she sometimes questioned the existence of a divinity – but her mother had been. Alys saw that cross beside her picture as an unbearable insult to her memory.

24

Josef followed the direction of her gaze and momentarily had the decency to look embarrassed.

'It's the times we live in, Alys. It's hard to do business with the Christians if you're not one of them.'

'You were doing enough business before, Papa. And I think you were doing well,' she said, gesturing to the room.

'Things have turned ugly for our people while you've been away. And they'll get worse, you'll see.'

'So bad that you'd give up everything, Father? Converted for . . . for money?'

'It's not about money, you insolent child!' said Tannenbaum, no longer sounding ashamed and thumping his fist on the desk. 'A man in my position has responsibilities. You know how many workers I'm in charge of? These idiotic wretches who sign up to ridiculous communist unions and think Moscow is heaven on earth! Every day I have to tie myself in knots to pay their wages, and all they can do is complain. So don't even think about throwing in my face all the things I do to keep a roof over your head.'

Alys took a deep breath, and again succumbed to her favourite fault: saying exactly what she thought at the most inopportune moment.

'You needn't worry about that, Papa. I mean to leave very soon. I want to return to America and make my life there.'

When he heard this, Tannenbaum's face turned scarlet. He waved a chubby finger under Alys's nose.

'Don't you dare say that, you hear me? You'll go to this party and you'll behave like a polite young lady, understand? I have plans for you, and I won't have them ruined by the whims of a badly behaved girl. You hear me?'

'I hate you,' said Alys, looking straight at him.

Her father's expression didn't change.

'That doesn't bother me, as long as you do what I say.'

Alys ran out of the study, tears welling in her eyes.

We'll see about that. Oh, yes, we'll see.

3

'Are you asleep?'

Ilse Reiner turned over on the mattress.

'Not any more. What is it, Paul?'

'I was wondering what we're going to do.'

'It's half past eleven. How about getting some sleep?'

'I was talking about the future.'

'The future,' his mother repeated, almost spitting out the word.

'I mean, it's not as if you really have to work here, at Aunt Brunhilda's, do you, Mama?'

'In the future I see you going to university, which happens to be just around the corner, and coming home to eat the tasty food I have prepared for you. Now good night.'

'This isn't our home.'

'We live here, we work here, and we thank heaven for it.'

'As if we should . . .' whispered Paul.

'I heard that, young man.'

'Sorry, Mama.'

'What's up with you? Have you had another fight with Jürgen? Is that why you came back all wet today?'

'It wasn't a fight. He and two of his friends followed me to the Englischer Garten.'

'They were just playing.'

'They threw my trousers in the lake, Mama.'

'And you hadn't done anything to upset them?'

Paul snorted loudly, but said nothing. This was typical of his mother. Whenever he had a problem, she would try to find a way to make it his fault.

'Best go to sleep, Paul. We have a big day tomorrow.'

'Ah yes, Jürgen's birthday ...'

'There will be cakes.'

'That other people will eat.'

'I don't know why you always have to react like this.'

Paul thought it was outrageous that a hundred people should celebrate a party on the ground floor, while Eduard – whom he hadn't yet been allowed to see – languished on the fourth, but he kept this to himself.

'There will be a lot of work tomorrow,' Ilse concluded, turning over.

The boy watched his mother's back for some time. The bedrooms in the service wing were at the back of the house, down in a sort of basement. Living there instead of in the family quarters didn't bother Paul that much, because he'd never known any other home. Ever since he was born, he'd accepted as normal the strange sight of watching Ilse wash her sister Brunhilda's dishes.

A thin rectangle of light filtered through a little window just beneath the ceiling, the yellow echo of a street lamp that melded with the flutter of the candle Paul always kept beside his bed, as he was terrified of the dark. The Reiners shared one of the smaller bedrooms, which contained only two beds, a wardrobe and a table over which Paul's homework was strewn.

Paul felt oppressed by the lack of space. It wasn't as though there was a shortage of spare rooms. Even before the war, the baron's fortune had begun to dwindle and Paul had watched it melt away with the inevitability of a tin can rusting in the middle of a field. It was a process that happened over many years, but it was unstoppable.

The cards, the servants whispered, shaking their heads as though speaking of some contagious disease, *it's because of the cards*. As a child, these comments terrified Paul, to the point that when a boy came to school with a French deck he'd found at home, Paul ran out of the class and locked himself in a bathroom. It was a while before he finally understood the extent of his uncle's problem: a problem that was not contagious, but deadly all the same.

When the servants' unpaid wages began to mount up, they started to quit. Now, of the ten bedrooms in the servants' quarters, only three were occupied: the maid's, the cook's, and the one Paul shared with his mother. The boy sometimes had trouble sleeping, because Ilse always got up an hour before dawn. Before the other servants had left, she had been only the housekeeper, tasked with ensuring that everything was in its place. Now she had had to take on their work too.

That life, his mother's exhausting duties, and the tasks he'd carried out himself for as long as he could remember, had seemed normal to Paul at first. But at school he discussed his situation with his classmates, and soon he began to draw comparisons, to notice what was going on around him, and to realise how strange it was that the sister of a baroness should sleep in the staff quarters.

Time and again he'd hear the same three words used to define his family, slipping by him as he passed between desks at school, or slamming shut behind his back like a secret door.

Orphan.

Servant.

Deserter. That was the worst of them all, because it was aimed at his father. The person he'd never known, about whom his mother never spoke, and about whom Paul knew little more than his name. Hans Reiner.

And so, it was through piecing together tears with fragments of conversations Paul overheard that he learned his father had done something terrible,

(over in the African colonies, they say)

that he had lost everything

(lost his shirt, ruined)

and that his mother lived on the charity

(a skivvy in her own brother-in-law's house – a baron, no less! – can you believe it?)

of his aunt Brunhilda. Which didn't seem to be any more honourable for the fact that Ilse didn't charge her a single Deutschmark for her work. Or that during the war she should have been obliged to work in a munitions factory, 'in order to contribute to supporting the household'. The factory was in Dachau, sixteen kilometres from Munich, and his mother had to wake two hours before sunrise, do her share of the household chores, and then take a train to her ten-hour shift.

It was just after she'd arrived back from the factory one day, her hair and fingers green with dust, her eyes dazed after a whole day of inhaling chemicals, that Paul asked his mother for the first time why they didn't find somewhere else to live. A place where they weren't both being constantly humiliated.

'You don't understand, Paul.'

She had given him the same response many times, always looking away or leaving the room or rolling over to sleep, just as she had done a few minutes ago.

Paul watched his mother's back for a few moments. She seemed to be breathing deeply and regularly, but the boy knew that she was only pretending to be asleep and wondered what ghosts would assail her in the middle of the night.

He looked away, and fixed his gaze on the ceiling. If his eyes could have bored through the plaster, the square of ceiling immediately above Paul's pillow would have caved in long ago. That was where he focused all his fantasies about his father on the nights when he had trouble reconciling himself to sleep. All Paul knew was that he'd been a captain in the Kaiser's fleet and that he'd commanded a frigate in South-West Africa. He had died when Paul was two years old, and the only thing he had left of him was a faded photo of his father in uniform, with a large moustache, his dark eyes looking straight at the camera, proud.

Ilse tucked the photo under her pillow every night and the greatest anguish Paul had caused his mother wasn't the day Jürgen pushed him down the stairs and broke his hand; it was the day he stole the photo, took it to school and showed it to everyone who had called him an orphan behind his back. By the time he returned home, Ilse had turned the room upside down looking for it. When he took it out tentatively from between the pages of his maths book, Ilse gave him a slap, and then began to cry.

'It's the only one I have. The only one.'

She hugged him, of course. But she grabbed the photograph back first.

Paul had tried to imagine what this impressive man must have been like. Under the grubby whiteness of the ceiling, by the light of the street lamp, his mind's eye conjured the outline of the *Kiel*, the frigate in which Hans Reiner had 'sunk in the Atlantic along with all his crew'. He invented hundreds of possible scenarios to explain those nine words, the only information about his death that Ilse had given her son. Pirates, reefs, a mutiny ... However it began, Paul's fantasy always ended the same way, with Hans clinging to the rudder, waving goodbye as the waters closed over his head.

When he reached this point, Paul always fell asleep.

4

'Honestly, Otto, I can't bear the Jew a moment longer. Just look at him, stuffing himself with *dampfnudels*. He's got custard down the front of his shirt.'

'Please, Brunhilda, keep your voice down, and try to stay calm. You know as well as I do how much we need Tannenbaum. We've spend our last pfennig on this party. Which was your idea, by the way . . .'

'Jürgen deserves the best. You know how confused he's been since his brother came back . . .'

'Then don't complain about the Jew.'

'You have no idea what it's like playing hostess to him, with his endless chatter, those ridiculous compliments, as if he doesn't know he's the one holding all the cards. A while ago he even had the cheek to suggest that his daughter and Jürgen should marry,' said Brunhilda, expecting a contemptuous response from Otto.

'It might put an end to all our problems.'

The tiniest crack opened in Brunhilda's granite smile, as she looked at the baron in shock.

They were standing at the entrance to the hall, their tense conversation muttered between clenched teeth, and interrupted only when they paused to receive guests. Brunhilda was about to respond but was forced instead to paint a grimace of welcome on her face once more:

'Good evening, Frau Gerngross, Frau Sagebiel! How good of you to come.'

'Sorry we're late, Brunhilda dear.'

'The bridges, oh, the bridges.'

'Yes, the traffic is just *dreadful*. Really, *atrocious*.'

'When are you going to give up this cold old mansion and come over to the east bank, my dear?'

The baroness smiled with pleasure at their darts of envy. Any one of the many nouveaux riches at the party would have killed for the class and power that exuded from her husband's coat of arms.

'Do please help yourselves to a glass of punch, it's delicious,' said Brunhilda, gesturing towards the centre of the room, where an enormous table surrounded by people was overflowing with food and drink. An ice horse, a metre high, was poised over the punch bowl, and at the back of the room a string quartet added Bavarian popular songs to the general hubbub.

When she was sure that the new arrivals were out of earshot, the countess turned towards Otto and said in a steely tone which very few ladies of Munich's high society would have deemed acceptable:

'You've done a deal on our son's wedding without even telling me, Otto? Over my dead body.'

The baron didn't blink. A quarter of a century of marriage had taught him how his wife would react when she felt undermined. But on this occasion she would have to yield, because there was much more at stake than her foolish pride.

'Brunhilda, dear, don't tell me you didn't see this Jew coming from the very beginning. With his supposedly elegant suits, going to the same church as us every Sunday, pretending that he doesn't hear every time he's called "the convert", sidling up towards our seats . . .'

'Of course I've noticed, I'm not stupid.'

'Of course you aren't, *Baroness*. You're perfectly capable of putting two and two together. And we don't have a penny to our name. The bank accounts are completely empty.'

The colour drained from Brunhilda's cheeks. She had to reach out to the alabaster wall mouldings to stop herself falling.

'Damn you, Otto.'

'That red dress you're wearing . . . The dressmaker insisted on being paid for it in cash. The word is out, and when rumours start there's no stopping them until you find yourself in the gutter.'

'You think I don't know that? You think I haven't noticed the way they look at us, the way they take little nibbles from their cakes and smirk at each other when they realise they aren't from Casa Popp? I can hear what those old ladies are muttering about as clearly as if they were shouting in my ear, Otto. But to go from that to allowing my son, my Jürgen, to marry a dirty Jew . . .'

'There's no other solution. All we have left is the house and our land, which I put in Eduard's name the day he was born. If I can't get Tannenbaum to lend me the capital to set up a factory on that land, we might as well give up. One morning the police will come for me, and then I'll have to act like a good Christian gentleman and blow my brains out. And you'll end up like your sister, doing someone else's sewing. Is that what you want?'

Brunhilda removed her hand from the wall. She took advantage of the pause necessitated by the arrival of new guests to gather her rage and then hurl it at Otto like a stone.

'You and your gambling are what got us into this mess, what devastated the family fortune. Sort it out, Otto, the same way you sorted things out with Hans thirteen years ago.'

The baron took a step back, shocked.

'Don't you dare mention that name again!'

'You were the one who dared to do something back then. And what good did it do us? I've had to put up with my sister living in this house for fifteen years.'

'I still haven't found the letter. And the boy's growing up. Perhaps now...'

Brunhilda leaned in towards him. Otto was almost a head taller, but he still looked small standing next to his wife.

'There's a limit to my patience.'

With an elegant wave, Brunhilda dived into the throng of guests, leaving the baron with a smile frozen on his face, struggling not to scream.

On the other side of the room, Jürgen von Schroeder set aside his third glass of champagne to open the present one of his friends was holding out to him.

'I didn't want to put it with the others,' he said, pointing to a table behind him, which was stacked with brightly coloured packages. 'This one's special.'

'What do you say, lads? Shall I open Krohn's present first?'

Half a dozen adolescents huddled round him, all of them dressed in the stylish blue blazers that bore the crest of Metzingen Academy. They all came from good German families, and were all uglier than Jürgen, shorter than Jürgen and laughed at every single joke Jürgen made. The baron's young son had a gift for surrounding himself with people who wouldn't overshadow him, and in front of whom he could show off.

'Open it, but only if you then open mine, too!'

'And mine!' chorused the others.

They're fighting for me to open their presents, thought Jürgen. *They worship me.*

'Now don't worry,' he said, raising his hands in what he thought was a gesture of impartiality. 'We'll depart from tradition and I'll open your presents first, then those from the rest of the guests after the toasts.'

'Excellent idea, Jürgen!'

'Well then, whatever could this be, Krohn?' he continued, opening the small box and lifting its contents to eye level.

In his fingers Jürgen held a gold chain with a strange cross made up of two intersecting black lines, the bent arms of which formed a pattern that was almost a square.

'It's a swastika. An anti-Semitic symbol. My father says they're in fashion.'

'You're mistaken, my friend,' said Jürgen, putting it round his neck. '*Now* they are. Here's hoping we'll be seeing a lot of these.'

'Definitely!'

'Here, Jürgen, open mine. Though best not show this one off in public . . .'

Jürgen unwrapped a parcel about the size of a packet of tobacco, and found himself looking at a small leather box. He opened it with a flourish. His chorus of admirers laughed nervously when they saw what was inside: a sort of cylindrical hood of vulcanised rubber.

'Hey, hey . . . that looks big!'

'I've never seen one before!'

'A present of the most personal kind, eh, Jürgen?'

'Is that some kind of proposal?'

For a few moments Jürgen felt he was losing control over them, that they had suddenly begun to laugh at him. *It's not fair. It's not fair at all, and I won't allow it.* He felt the rage growing inside him, and turned to the one who'd made the last comment. He put the sole of his right foot on top of the other's left, and leaned his full weight on it. His victim turned white, but gritted his teeth.

'I'm sure you'd like to apologise for that unfortunate joke?'

34

'Of course, Jürgen ... I'm sorry ... I wouldn't think of questioning your manhood.'

'Just as I thought,' Jürgen said, slowly lifting his foot. The huddle of boys had fallen silent, a silence accentuated by the noise of the party. 'Well, I don't want you to think I have no sense of humour. Actually, this ... thing will be extremely useful to me,' he said, with a wink. 'With her, for example.'

He was pointing at a tall dark girl with dreamy eyes who was holding a glass of punch in the middle of the crowd.

'Nice tits,' whispered one of his acolytes.

'Any of you want to bet I can premiere this thing and get back in time for the toasts?'

'I'll bet fifty marks on Jürgen,' the one with the trodden foot felt compelled to say.

'I'll take the bet,' said another behind him.

'Well, gents, you just wait here and watch – you might learn something.'

Jürgen swallowed softly, hoping the others wouldn't notice. He hated talking to girls, as they always made him feel awkward and inferior. Although he was good looking, his only contact with the opposite sex had been in a brothel in Schwabing, where he'd experienced more shame than excitement. He'd been taken there by his father a few months before, dressed in a discreet black overcoat and hat. While he did his business, his father had waited downstairs drinking cognac. When it was over, he gave his son a slap on the back and told him that he was now a man. This was the beginning and the end of Jürgen von Schroeder's education on the subject of women and love.

I'll show them how a real man behaves, the boy thought, feeling his companions' eyes on the back of his neck.

'Hello, Fräulein. Are you enjoying yourself?'

She turned her head but didn't smile.

'Not really. Do we know each other?'

'I can see why you're not enjoying yourself. My name's Jürgen von Schroeder.'

'Alys Tannenbaum,' she said, holding out her hand without much enthusiasm.

'Do you want to dance, Alys?'

'No.'

The girl's brusque response startled Jürgen.

'You know I'm hosting this party? It's my birthday today.'

'Congratulations,' she said sarcastically; 'no doubt there are plenty of girls in this room desperate for you to ask them to dance. I wouldn't want to take up too much of your time.'

'But you have to dance with me at least once.'

'Oh, really? And why is that?'

'Good breeding dictates it. When a gentleman asks a lady . . .'

'You know what annoys me most about arrogant people, Jürgen? The number of things you take for granted. Well, you should know this: the world isn't the way you see it. By the way, your friends are giggling and they can't seem to take their eyes off you.'

Jürgen glanced round. He couldn't fail, couldn't allow this ill-mannered girl to humiliate him.

She's playing hard to get because really she likes me. She must be one of those girls who thinks the best way to excite a man is to push him away until he goes crazy. Well, I know how to deal with her sort, he thought.

Jürgen took a step forward, taking the girl by the waist and drawing her towards him.

'What the hell do you think you're doing?' she gasped.

'Teaching you to dance.'

'If you don't let me go right now I'll scream.'

'You wouldn't want to make a scene, now, would you, Alys?'

The young woman tried to force her arms between her body and Jürgen's, but she was no match for his strength. The baron's son squeezed her to him even more closely, feeling her breasts through her dress and his growing erection against her stomach. He began to move to the rhythm of the music, a smile on his lips, knowing that Alys would not scream. Creating a fuss at a party like this would only harm her reputation and that of her family. He saw the young woman's eyes crystallising into a cold hatred, and suddenly toying with her seemed a lot of fun, much more satisfying than if she'd simply agreed to dance with him.

'Would you like a drink, miss?'

Jürgen stopped with a jolt. Paul was at his side, holding a tray with several glasses of champagne, and his lips firmly pursed.

'Hey, it's my cousin the waiter. Get lost, you cretin,' barked Jürgen.

'First I'd like to know if the young lady is thirsty,' said Paul, advancing the tray towards him.

'Yes,' Alys said hurriedly, 'that champagne looks marvellous.'

Jürgen half-closed his eyes, trying to work out what to do. If he let go of her right hand to allow her to take a glass from the tray, she would be able to detach herself completely. He slightly weakened the pressure on her back, allowing her to free her left arm, but squeezing the right even harder. The girl's fingertips were turning purple.

'Come on, then, Alys, take a glass. They say it brings happiness,' he added, feigning good humour.

Alys leaned towards the tray, trying to free herself, but it was useless. There was nothing for it but to take the champagne with her left hand.

'Thank you,' she said, weakly.

'Perhaps the young lady would like a napkin,' said Paul, raising his other hand, in which he held a saucer with small squares of fabric. He had moved around so that he was now on the other side of the couple.

'That would be marvellous,' said Alys, staring intently at the baron's son.

For a few seconds, no one moved. Jürgen studied the situation. With the glass in her left hand, the only way she could take a napkin would be with her right. At last, boiling with rage, he had to give the battle up for lost. He released Alys's hand, and she stepped back, taking the napkin.

'I think I'll get some air,' she said with remarkable poise.

Jürgen, as though spurning her, turned his back to return to his friends. Passing by Paul, he gripped his shoulder and whispered:

'You'll pay for that.'

Somehow Paul managed to keep the champagne glasses balanced on the tray – they clinked but didn't topple. His inner balance was another matter entirely, and at that precise moment he felt like a cat trapped in a barrel of nails.

How could I have been so stupid?

There was only one rule in life: stay as far away from Jürgen as possible. It wasn't easy to do, since they both lived under the same roof, but it was simple, at least. There wouldn't be much he could do if his cousin decided to make his life impossible, but he could certainly avoid crossing his path, still less humiliating him in public. This would cost him dear.

'Thank you.'

Paul lifted his eyes and, for a few moments, he forgot absolutely everything: his fear of Jürgen, the heavy tray, the pain in the soles of his feet from having worked twelve hours straight in preparation for the party. Everything disappeared, because she was smiling at him.

Alys wasn't the sort of woman who could take a man's breath away at first sight. But were you to give her a second glance, it would probably be a long one. The sound of her voice was attractive. And if she smiled at you the way she smiled at Paul that moment . . .

There was no way that Paul could not fall in love with her.

'Ah . . . it was nothing.'

For the rest of his life Paul would curse that moment, that conversation and the smile that would cause him so many problems. But back then he was oblivious, as was she. She was sincerely grateful to the skinny little boy with the intelligent blue eyes. Then of course, Alys went back to being Alys.

'Don't think I couldn't have got rid of him on my own.'

'Of course,' said Paul, still reeling.

Alys blinked; she wasn't used to such an easy victory, so she changed the subject.

'We can't talk here. Wait for a minute then meet me in the cloakroom.'

'With great pleasure, Fräulein.'

Paul did a circuit of the hall, trying to empty the tray as quickly as possible so he would have an excuse to disappear. At the start of the party he'd been eavesdropping on conversations, and was surprised to discover how little attention people paid him. It really was as though he was invisible, which was why he found it strange when the last guest to take a glass smiled and said: 'Well done, son.'

'I beg your pardon?'

He was an older man, with white hair, a goatee and prominent ears. He gave Paul a strange, meaningful look.

'"Never has a gentleman saved a lady with such gallantry and discretion." That's Chrétien de Troyes. Apologies. My name is Sebastian Keller, bookseller.'

'Delighted to meet you.'

The man gestured towards the door with his thumb.

'You'd better hurry. She'll be waiting.'

Surprised, Paul tucked the tray under his arm and left the room. The cloakroom had been set up in the entrance, and consisted of a high table and two enormous hanging-rails on wheels that held the hundreds of overcoats belonging to the guests. The girl had retrieved hers from one of the servants the baroness had hired for the party, and was waiting for him by the door. She didn't hold out her hand when she introduced herself.

'Alys Tannenbaum.'

'Paul Reiner.'

'Is he really your cousin?'

'Unfortunately he is.'

'It's just that you don't seem like . . .'

'The nephew of a baron?' said Paul, pointing to his apron. 'This is the latest fashion from Paris.'

'I mean, you don't seem like *him.*'

'That's because I'm not like him.'

'I'm glad to hear it. I just wanted to thank you again. Take care, Paul Reiner.'

'Of course.'

She put her hand on the door, but before opening it she turned quickly and kissed Paul on the cheek. Then she ran down the steps and disappeared. For a few moments he scanned the street anxiously, as though she would return, retracing her steps. Then finally he shut the door, rested his forehead on the frame and sighed.

His heart and stomach felt heavy and strange. He couldn't give the feeling a name, so for want of anything better he decided – correctly – that it was love, and he felt happy.

'So, the knight in shining armour has received his reward, isn't that right, boys?'

On hearing the voice he knew so well, Paul turned as fast as he could. The feeling changed instantly from happiness to fear.

5

There they were, seven of them.

They stood in a broad semicircle in the entrance, blocking the way into the main room. Jürgen was at the centre of the group, slightly to the fore, as though he couldn't wait to get his hands on Paul.

'This time you've gone too far, cousin. I don't like people who don't know their place in life.'

Paul didn't reply, knowing that nothing he said would make any difference. If there was one thing Jürgen couldn't abide, it was humiliation. That it should have happened in public, and in front of all his friends, at the hands of his poor dumb cousin, the servant, the black sheep of the family, was inconceivable. He had resolved to cause Paul a lot of pain. The more – and the more visible – the better.

'After this you'll never want to play the knight again, you piece of shit.'

Paul looked around desperately. The woman in charge of the cloakroom had disappeared, no doubt on the orders of the birthday boy. Jürgen's friends had spaced themselves out across the middle of the entrance hall, removing any escape route, and were advancing towards him slowly. If he turned and tried to open the door to the street they'd grab him from behind and throw him to the ground.

'You're *trem*-bling,' chanted Jürgen.

Paul ruled out the corridor that led to the servants' quarters, which was practically a dead end, and the only route they'd left open to him. Although he'd never gone hunting in his life, Paul had heard all too often the story of how his uncle had bagged each of the specimens that hung on his study wall. Jürgen wanted to force him in that direction because down there, no one would be able to hear his cries.

There was only one option.

Without another moment's thought, he ran straight at them.

Jürgen was so surprised to see Paul speeding towards them that he simply turned his head as he passed. Krohn, who was two metres behind, had a little more time to react. He planted both feet firmly on the floor and prepared himself to thump the boy who was running towards him, but before Krohn could punch him in the face, Paul launched himself on to the floor. He fell on his left hip – which gave him a bruise he'd have for two weeks – but the momentum allowed him to slide across the polished marble tiles like hot butter on a mirror, finally coming to rest at the foot of the staircase.

'What are you waiting for, idiots? Get him!' shouted Jürgen, exasperated.

Without stopping to look back, Paul got to his feet and raced up the stairs. He'd run out of ideas, and it was only survival instinct that kept his legs moving. His feet, which had been bothering him all day, were beginning to hurt terribly. Halfway up the stairs to the second floor he almost tripped and rolled down but managed to get his balance back just in time as the hands of one of Jürgen's friends brushed his heels. Grabbing the bronze banister, he continued up and up until, on the last flight between the third and fourth floors, he slipped suddenly on one of the steps, and fell, his arms sprawled in front of him, almost knocking his teeth out on the edge of the staircase.

The first of his pursuers had caught up with him, but he in turn tripped at the crucial moment, and was only just able to grab hold of the edge of Paul's apron.

'I've got him! Quick!' said his captor, gripping the banister with his other hand.

Paul tried to get to his feet, but the other boy pulled on the apron, and Paul slid down a step, banging his head. He kicked out blindly, striking the boy, but he didn't manage to free himself. Paul struggled for what seemed an eternity with the knot of his apron, hearing the others closing in on him.

Damn it, why did I have to do it up so tight, he thought as he struggled.

Suddenly his fingers found the exact spot to pull, and the apron came undone. Paul fled and reached the fourth and final floor of the house. With nowhere else to go, he ran through the first door he saw and closed it, fastening the bolt.

*

'Where's he gone?' Jürgen screamed when he reached the landing. The boy who'd grabbed Paul's apron was now clutching his injured knee. He gestured to the left of the corridor.

'Let's go!' said Jürgen to the others, who had stopped a few steps below.

They didn't move.

'What the hell are you ...'

He stopped abruptly. His mother was watching him from farther down the stairs.

'I'm disappointed in you, Jürgen,' she said, icily. 'We've gathered together the best of Munich in order to celebrate your birthday, and then you disappear in the middle of the party to mess around on the stairs with your friends.'

'But ...'

'Enough. I want you all to go down at once and rejoin the guests. We'll talk later.'

'Yes, Mother,' said Jürgen, humiliated in front of his friends for the second time that day. Gritting his teeth, he set off down the stairs.

That isn't the only thing that will happen later. You'll pay for this one too, Paul.

6

'It's good to see you again.'

Paul was concentrating on calming down and recovering his breath. It took him a few moments to realise where the voice was coming from. He was sitting on the floor, his back against the door, afraid that any moment Jürgen might fight his way through. But when he heard those words Paul jumped to his feet.

'Eduard!'

Without realising it, he'd gone into his elder cousin's room, a place he hadn't visited in months. It all looked the same as it had before Eduard left, an organised, tranquil space, but one that reflected its owner's personality. There were film posters on the wall, Eduard's collection of rocks, and above all books – books everywhere. Paul had already read most of them. Spy novels, Westerns, fantasy, books on philosophy and history ... They occupied the bookcases, the desk and even the floor beside the bed. Eduard had to rest the volume he was reading on the mattress in order to turn the pages with his only hand. A number of cushions were stacked under his body to allow him to sit up, and a sad smile floated on his pale face.

'Don't feel sorry for me, Paul. I couldn't bear it.'

Paul looked him in the eye and understood that Eduard had been watching carefully for his reaction, and had found it strange when Paul hadn't been surprised to see him like this.

'I've seen you before, Eduard. The day you came back.'

'So how come you never visited me? I've seen almost no one but your mother since the day I got back. Your mother and my friends May, Salgari and Verne,' he said, raising the book he was reading so that Paul could see the title. It was *The Count of Monte Cristo*.

'They forbade me to come.'

Paul bowed his head, ashamed. Of course Brunhilda and his mother had forbidden him to see Eduard, but he could at least have tried. In truth, he had been afraid of seeing Eduard like this again, after the horrible experience of that afternoon when he had returned from the war. Eduard looked at him bitterly, no doubt aware of what Paul was thinking.

'I know how ashamed my mother is. Haven't you noticed?' he said, gesturing towards a tray of cakes from the party that sat untouched. 'It wouldn't do to let my stumps spoil Jürgen's birthday, so I wasn't invited. How's the party going, by the way?'

'There's a band, people are drinking, talking about politics and criticising the military for losing a war we were winning.'

Eduard gave a snort.

'It's easy to criticise from where they're standing. What else are they saying?'

'Everyone's talking about the Versailles negotiations. They're pleased we're rejecting the terms.'

'Damned fools,' said Eduard, bitterly. 'Since no one fired a shot on German soil, they can't believe we've lost the war. Still, I suppose it's always the same. Are you going to tell me who you were running away from?'

'The birthday boy.'

'Your mother's told me you haven't been getting along very well.'

Paul nodded.

'You haven't touched the cakes.'

'I don't need much food these days. There's a lot less of me. Take them, go on, you look hungry. And come closer, I want to see you better. God, how you've grown.'

Paul sat on the edge of the bed and began to wolf down the food. He hadn't eaten since breakfast; he had even missed school so he could prepare for the party. He knew his mother would be looking for him, but Paul didn't care. Now he'd overcome his fear, he couldn't pass up this chance to be with Eduard, the cousin he'd missed so much.

'Eduard, I want to ... I'm sorry I haven't been to see you. I could have snuck in, in the afternoons when Aunt Brunhilda goes out for a walk ...'

'It's OK, Paul. You're here, and that's what matters. You are the one who has to forgive me, for not having written. I promised I would.'

44

'What stopped you?'

'I could tell you I was too busy shooting the English, but I'd be lying. A wise man once said that war is seven parts boredom to one part horror. In the trenches we had plenty of time, until we started killing each other.'

'So?'

'I couldn't do it, simple as that. Not even at the start of this absurd war. The only people who've come back from it are a handful of cowards.'

'What are you talking about, Eduard? You're a hero! You volunteered to go to the front, one of the first!'

Eduard gave an inhuman cackle that made Paul's hair stand on end.

'A hero ... Do you know who decides for you whether you'll sign up as a volunteer? Your schoolmaster, when he talks to you about the glories of the Fatherland, the empire and the Kaiser. Your father, who tells you to be a man. Your friends, the same friends who, not that long ago, were arguing with you in gym class over whose was biggest. They all hurl the word "coward" in your face if you betray the smallest doubt and blame you for the defeat. No, cousin, there are no volunteers in war, only those who are stupid and those who are cruel. The latter stay at home.'

Paul was dumbstruck. Suddenly his fantasies about the war, the maps he'd drawn in his exercise books, the newspaper reports he'd loved to read, all this seemed ridiculous and childish. He considered telling his cousin this but feared he would laugh at him and throw him out of the room. For at that moment Paul could see the war, right there in front of him. The war wasn't a bald list of advances towards enemy lines, nor the dreadful stumps hidden below the bedsheets. The war was in Eduard's empty, devastated eyes.

'You could ... have resisted. Stayed at home.'

'No, I could not,' he said, turning his face away. 'I've told you a lie, Paul – at least it's partly a lie. I also went to get away from them. So I wouldn't turn out like them.'

'Like who?'

'You know who did this to me? It was around five weeks before the end of the war and already we knew we'd lost. We knew that at any moment they'd call on us to go home. And we were more confident than ever. We didn't bother about the people falling beside us because we knew that it wouldn't be long before we'd be going back. Then one day, in the middle of a retreat, a shell fell too close.'

Eduard's voice was quiet; so quiet that Paul had to lean in to hear what he was saying.

'I've asked myself a thousand times what would have happened if I'd run two metres to the right. Or if I'd stopped to tap my helmet twice, like we always did before leaving the trench' – he rapped on Paul's forehead with his knuckles. 'Doing that made us feel invincible. I didn't do it that day, you see?'

'I wish you'd never gone.'

'No, cousin, believe me. I went because I didn't want to be a von Schroeder, and if I came back it was only to reassure myself that I was right to leave.'

'I don't understand, Eduard.'

'My dear Paul, you should understand better than anyone. After what they've done to you. What they did to your father.'

This last phrase fixed itself in Paul's heart like a rusty hook.

'What are you talking about, Eduard?'

His cousin looked at him, in silence, biting his lower lip. Finally he shook his head and closed his eyes.

'Forget what I said. Sorry.'

'I can't forget it! I never knew him, no one ever talks to me about him, though they mutter things behind my back. All I know is what my mother's told me, that he went down with his boat on the way back from Africa. So tell me, please, what did they do to my father?'

There was another silence, this time much longer. So long that Paul wondered whether Eduard had fallen asleep. Suddenly his eyes opened again.

'I'll burn in hell for this, but I have no choice. First I want you to do me a favour.'

'Anything you say.'

'Go to my father's study, and open the second drawer on the right. If it's locked, the key used to be kept in the middle drawer. You'll find a black leather bag, it's rectangular with a flap folded over it. Bring it to me.'

Paul did as he was told. He tiptoed down to the study, scared that he might meet someone on the way, but the party was still in full swing.

The drawer was locked, and it took him a few moments to find the key. It wasn't where Eduard had said, but finally he found it in a little wooden box. The drawer was filled with papers. Paul found a piece of black felt at the back, with a strange symbol etched in gold. A square and a compass, with a letter G inside. The leather bag lay underneath.

The boy put it under his shirt and returned to Eduard's room. He could feel the weight of the bag against his stomach, and trembled just imagining what would happen if someone were to find him with this object that wasn't his hidden beneath his clothes. He felt immense relief as he entered the room.

'Have you got it?'

Paul took out the leather bag and walked towards the bed, but on the way he tripped over one of the piles of books that were strewn across the room. The books scattered and the bag fell on to the floor.

'No,' cried Eduard and Paul at the same time.

The bag had fallen between a copy of May's *The Blood Revenge* and Hoffman's *The Elixirs of the Devil*, revealing its contents – a mother-of-pearl reflection on the black leather.

It was a pistol.

'Why do you want a gun, cousin?' said Paul, his voice trembling.

'You know what I want it for.' He raised the stump of his arm in case Paul was in any doubt.

'Well, I won't give it to you.'

'Listen carefully, Paul. Sooner or later, I'll manage because the only thing I want to do in this world is to leave it. You can turn your back on me today, put it back where you got it, and force me to go through the terrible indignity of having to drag myself on this ruined arm in the dead of night to my father's study. But then you'd never find out what I have to tell you.'

'No!'

'Or you can leave it on the bed, listen to what I have to say, then give me the dignity of choosing how I'm to go. You decide, Paul, but whatever happens I will get what I want. What I need.'

Paul sat, or rather collapsed, on to the floor, clutching the leather bag. For a long while the only sound in the room was the metallic tick of Eduard's alarm clock. Eduard closed his eyes until he felt a movement on his bed.

His cousin had dropped the leather bag within reach of his hand.

'God forgive me,' said Paul. He was crying, standing at Eduard's bedside, but not daring to look at him directly.

'Oh, He doesn't give a damn what we do,' said Eduard, caressing the delicate leather with his fingers. 'Thank you, cousin.'

'Tell me, Eduard. Tell me what you know.'

The wounded man cleared his throat before beginning. He talked slowly, as though each of the words had to be dragged out of his lungs rather than being spoken.

'It happened in 1905, which is what they've told you, and up to that point what you know is not so far from the truth. I remember clearly that Uncle Hans was on a mission in South-West Africa, because I loved the sound of those words and used to say them again and again as I tried to find the place on the map. One night, when I was ten years old, I heard shouting in the library and went down to see what was happening. I was very surprised to see that your father had called on us at that time of night. He was in discussion with my father, the two of them sitting at a round table. There were two other people in the room. I could see one of them, a short man with delicate features like a girl's, who was saying nothing. I couldn't see the other one from the door but I could hear him. I was about to go in and greet your father – he always brought me presents from his travels – but just before I entered, my mother grabbed me by the ear and dragged me to my room. "Did they see you?" she asked. And I said no, over and over. "Well, you're not to say a word about this, not ever, do you hear me?" And I . . . I swore I'd never tell . . .'

Eduard's voice trailed off. Paul grabbed his arm. He wanted him to continue the story whatever it took, though he was aware of the suffering that it was causing his cousin.

'You and your mother came to live with us two weeks later. You weren't much more than a baby, and I was pleased, because that meant I had my own platoon of brave soldiers to play with. I didn't even think about the obvious lie my parents told me, that Uncle Hans's frigate had gone down. People were saying other things, spreading rumours that your father was a deserter who'd gambled everything away and had disappeared in Africa. Those rumours were just as untrue, but I didn't think about them either, and eventually I forgot. Just as I forgot what I heard soon after my mother left my bedroom. Or rather, I pretended that I'd made a mistake, in spite of the fact that no mistake was possible, given the excellent acoustics in this house. Watching you grow up was easy, watching your happy smile as we played hide-and-seek, and I lied to myself. Then you started getting older, old enough to understand. Soon you were as old as I'd been that night. And I went off to war.'

'So tell me what you heard,' said Paul in a whisper.

'That night, cousin, I heard a shot.'

7

Paul's understanding of himself and his place in the world had been teetering on the edge for some time, like a porcelain vase at the top of a ladder. That last sentence was the final kick, and the imaginary vase tumbled, shattering into pieces. Paul heard the crash it made as it broke, and Eduard saw it in his face, too.

'Forgive me, Paul. Christ help me. You should go now.'

Paul got up and leaned over the bed. His cousin's skin was cold, and when he kissed his forehead it was like kissing a mirror. He walked to the door, not quite in control of his own legs, only vaguely aware of having left the bedroom door open or of having slumped down on the floor outside.

When the shot rang out, he barely heard it.

But as Eduard had said, the mansion's acoustics were excellent. The first guests to leave the party, busy exchanging air-kisses and empty promises as they collected their overcoats, heard a bang that was muffled but unmistakable. They'd heard too many in the preceding weeks to fail to recognise the sound. Their conversations had all ceased by the time the second and third echoes of the report rebounded through the stairwell.

In her role as the perfect hostess, Brunhilda had been saying goodbye to a doctor and his wife whom she couldn't stand. She identified the sound, but automatically activated her defence mechanism.

'The boys must be playing with firecrackers.'

Disbelieving faces popped up around her like mushrooms after a rainstorm. At first there were only a dozen people, but soon more emerged into the hallway. It wouldn't be long before all the guests knew that something had happened in her house.

In my house!

Within two hours it would be the talk of all Munich if she didn't do something about it.

'Stay here, I'm sure it's nothing.'

Brunhilda picked up the pace when she began to smell gunpowder halfway up the stairs. Some of the braver guests were looking up, perhaps hoping she would confirm that they had been mistaken, but not one set foot on the staircase; the social taboo against entering the bedroom area during a party was too strong. The murmuring grew, however, and the baroness hoped Otto would not be so foolish as to follow her, as someone would inevitably want to accompany him.

When she reached the top and saw Paul sobbing in the corridor, she knew what had happened without putting her head round Eduard's door.

But she did anyway.

A spasm of bile rose to her throat. She was gripped by horror and by another incongruous feeling that she would recognise only later, disgusted, as relief. Or at least the disappearance of the oppressive feeling she'd been carrying in her breast ever since her son had returned, maimed, from the war.

'What have you done?' she cried, looking at Paul. 'I'm asking you, what have you done?'

The boy didn't raise his head from his hands.

'What did you do to my father, bitch?'

Brunhilda took a step back. For the second time that night, someone had recoiled at the mention of Hans Reiner, but ironically the person doing it now was the same one who had used his name as a threat earlier.

How much do you know, child? How much did he tell you before ...?

She wanted to scream, but she couldn't, she didn't dare.

Instead she squeezed her hands into fists until her nails stuck into her palms, trying to calm herself and decide what to do, just as she had done that night fourteen years earlier. And when she had managed to recover a minimum of composure, she went back downstairs. On the first floor she poked her head over the banister and smiled down into the entrance hall. She didn't dare go any farther, because she didn't think she could keep up the pretence for long in front of that sea of tense faces.

'You'll have to excuse us. Friends of my son have been playing with firecrackers, just as I thought. If you don't mind I'll deal with the chaos they've caused up there' – she gestured to Paul's mother – 'Ilse, my dear.'

The faces softened when they heard this, and the guests relaxed when they saw the housekeeper following their hostess up the stairs as though nothing was wrong. They already had plenty of gossip about the party, and could hardly wait to get home to bore their families with it.

'Don't even think about screaming,' was the only thing Brunhilda said.

Ilse had been expecting some childish mischief, but when she saw Paul in the corridor she was afraid. Then, when she half-opened Eduard's door, she had to bite her fist to stop herself from screaming. Her reaction was not so very different to that of the baroness, except that with Ilse there were tears as well as horror.

'Poor boy,' she said, wringing her hands.

Brunhilda watched her sister, her own hands poised on her hips.

'Your son was the one who gave Eduard the gun.'

'Oh, Holy God, tell me that's not true, Paul.'

It sounded like an entreaty, but her words contained no hope. Her son didn't reply. Brunhilda approached him, exasperated, waving her index finger.

'I'm going to call the magistrate. You'll rot in prison for giving a gun to an invalid.'

'What did you do to my father, bitch?' Paul repeated, slowly getting up to face his aunt. She didn't step back this time, even though she was scared.

'Hans died in the colonies,' she replied, lacking conviction.

'That's not true. My father was in this house before he disappeared, your own son told me.'

'Eduard was sick and confused, he was making up all kinds of stories because of the injuries he suffered at the front. And in spite of the fact that the doctor forbade him visitors you've been in here, making him agitated, and then you go and give him a gun!'

'You're lying!'

'You killed him.'

'That's a lie,' said the boy. Nonetheless he felt a chill of doubt.

'Paul, that's enough!'

'Get out of my house.'

'We're not going anywhere,' said Paul.

'You decide,' said Brunhilda, turning to Ilse. 'Judge Strohmeyer is still downstairs. In two minutes I will go down and inform him what's happened. If you don't want your son to spend tonight at Stadelheim, you'll leave straight away.'

Ilse paled in terror at the mention of the prison. Strohmeyer was a good friend of the baron's, and it wouldn't take much to convince him to charge Paul with murder. She grabbed her son by the arm.

'Paul, let's go!'

'Not until . . .'

She slapped him so hard that it hurt her fingers. Paul's lip began to bleed but he stood watching his mother, refusing to move.

Then, finally, he followed her.

Ilse didn't allow her son to pack a suitcase, they didn't even go by his room. They went down the service staircase and left the mansion through the back door, skulking along the alleys to avoid being seen.

Like criminals.

8

'And may I ask where the hell you've been?'

The baron appeared, furious and tired, the edges of his frock coat creased, his moustache dishevelled and his monocle hanging loose. An hour had passed since Ilse and Paul had left, and the party had only just ended.

Only when the very last guest had left did the baron go and look for his wife. He found her sitting on a chair she'd brought out into the fourth-floor corridor. The door to Eduard's room was closed. Even with her immense will, Brunhilda couldn't manage to bring herself to return to the party. When her husband appeared, she explained to him what lay inside the room, and Otto felt his own share of pain and remorse.

'You're calling the judge in the morning,' said Brunhilda, her voice dispassionate. 'We'll say we found him like this when we came to give him his breakfast. That way we can keep the scandal to a minimum. It might not even get out.'

Otto nodded. He drew his hand back from the door handle. He didn't dare to go in, nor would he ever. Not even after the traces of the tragedy had been scrubbed from the walls and the floor.

'The judge owes me a favour. I think he'll be able to sort it out. But I wonder how Eduard got hold of the gun. He can't have got it on his own.'

When Brunhilda told him Paul's role and that she had thrown the Reiners out of the house, the baron was livid.

'Do you realise what you've done?'

'They were a threat, Otto.'

'And have you by any chance forgotten what's at stake here? Why we've had them in this house all these years?'

'To humiliate me and ease your conscience,' said Brunhilda, with a bitterness she'd been holding in for years.

Otto didn't bother to reply, since he knew what she said was true.

'Eduard talked to your nephew.'

'Oh, God. Do you have any idea what he might have told him?'

'That doesn't matter. After leaving tonight they've become suspects, even if we don't turn them in tomorrow. They won't dare speak out, and they have no proof of anything. Unless the boy finds something.'

'Do you think I'm worried about them finding out the truth? For that they'd have to find Clovis Nagel. And Nagel hasn't been in Germany for a long time. But that doesn't solve our problem. Your sister is the only one who knows where Hans Reiner's letter is.'

'Keep an eye on them, then. From a distance.'

Otto reflected for a few moments.

'I've got just the man for the job.'

Someone else was present during that conversation, though he was hidden in a corner of the corridor. He had listened without understanding. Much later, when Baron von Schroeder retired to their bedroom, he went into Eduard's room.

When he saw what was inside, he sank to his knees. By the time he rose, what was left of the innocence his mother had not been able to burn away, the parts of his soul that she hadn't been able to sow with hatred and envy towards his cousin over many years, were dead, turned to ashes.

I'll kill Paul Reiner for this.

Now I am the heir; but I will be the baron.

He couldn't make out which of the two competing thoughts excited him the most.

9

Paul Reiner was shivering in the light May rain. His mother had stopped dragging him, and now walked by his side through Schwabing, the Bohemian district at the heart of Munich, where thieves and poets sat side by side with painters and whores in the taverns until the early hours. Few of the taverns were open now, however, and they didn't go into any that were, as they didn't have a pfennig.

'Let's take shelter in this doorway,' said Paul.

'The nightwatchman will throw us out, it's happened three times already.'

'You can't go on like this, Mama. You'll catch pneumonia.'

They squeezed into the narrow doorway of a building that had seen better days. At least an overhang protected them from the rain that drenched the deserted pavements and uneven flagstones. The weak light of the street lamps cast strange reflections on the wet surfaces – it was unlike anything Paul had ever seen.

Paul was afraid and pressed even closer to his mother.

'You're still wearing your father's wristwatch, aren't you?'

'Yes,' said Paul, alarmed.

She had asked him this question three times in the past hour. His mother was drained and empty, as though slapping her son and hauling him through the alleys far from the von Schroeders' mansion had used up a reserve of energy even she hadn't known she possessed, and which was now lost for ever. Her eyes were sunken and her hands trembled.

'Tomorrow we'll pawn it and everything will be all right.'

The wristwatch was nothing special, it wasn't even made of gold. Paul wondered whether it would pay for any more than one night in a boarding-house, and a hot dinner if they were lucky.

'That's a great plan,' he forced himself to say.

'We need a place to stay, and then I'll ask for my old job back, at the gunpowder factory.'

'But, Mother . . . the gunpowder factory doesn't exist any more. They demolished it when the war ended.'

And you were the one who told me that, thought Paul, now extremely concerned.

'The sun will soon be up,' said his mother.

Paul didn't reply. He craned his neck, alert to the rhythmic steps of the nightwatchman's boots. Paul wished he would stay away long enough to allow him to shut his eyes for a moment.

I'm so tired . . . And I don't understand any of what's happened tonight. She's behaving so strangely . . . perhaps now she'll tell me the truth.

'Mama, what do you know about what happened to Papa?'

For a few moments Ilse seemed to wake from her lethargy. A spark of light burned deep in her eyes, like the last embers of a bonfire. She held Paul's chin and stroked his face gently.

'Paul, please. Forget it, forget everything you've heard tonight. Your father was a good man who died tragically, in a shipwreck. Promise me that you'll cling to that, that you won't go looking for a truth that doesn't exist, because I couldn't bear to lose you. You're all I have left. My boy Paul.'

The first glimmers of dawn cast long shadows on the Munich streets, carrying away the rain.

'Promise me,' she insisted, her voice fading.

Paul hesitated before answering.

'I promise.'

10

'Whooooah!'

The coal merchant's cart screeched to a halt on Rheinstrasse. The two horses stamped restlessly, their eyes covered by blinkers and their hindquarters blackened by sweat and soot. The coal merchant jumped to the ground and distractedly ran his hand along the side of the cart, which bore his name, Klaus Graf, even though only the first two letters were still legible.

'Clean this, Willi! I like my customers to know who is bringing them their raw material,' he said, almost amiably.

The man in the driver's seat removed his hat, pulled out a rag still bearing distant memories of the original colour of the cloth, and set about working on the wood, whistling. This was his only way of express-ing himself, as he was a mute. The melody was gentle and swift: he, too, seemed happy.

It was the perfect moment.

Paul had been following them all morning, ever since they came out of the stables Graf kept in Lehel. He'd also observed them the previous day, and understood that the best time to ask for a job would be just before one in the afternoon, after the coalman's midday rest. Both he and the mute had polished off large sandwiches and a couple of litres of beer. Left behind was the bad-tempered drowsiness of early morning, when the dew accumulated on the cart as they waited for the coal store to open. Not yet apparent was the irritable tiredness at the end of the day, when they'd drink their final beer in silence, the dust constricting their throats.

If I can't do it, God help us, thought Paul, desperately.

*

He and his mother had spent two days trying to find work and had eaten nothing whatsoever in that time. Pawning the watch had given them enough money for two nights in a boarding-house and a breakfast of bread and beer. His mother had persevered looking for work, but they'd soon learned that a job was a pipe dream in those days. Women had been thrown out of the positions they'd occupied during the war when the men returned from the front. Not because the employers wanted this, naturally.

'Damn this government and its directives,' a baker had said to them, when they'd asked him for the impossible. 'They've been forcing us to hire war veterans, when women do the work just as well and charge much less.'

'Did women really do the work as well as men?' Paul asked him, insolently. He was in a bad mood. His stomach was growling and the smell of bread baking in the ovens was making matters worse.

'Better sometimes. I had one woman who could work the dough better than anybody.'

'So why'd you pay them less?'

'Well, it's obvious,' said the baker, shrugging his shoulders. 'They're women.'

If there was any logic to this, Paul couldn't understand it, even though his mother and the employees in the workroom nodded in agreement.

'You'll understand when you're older,' one said, as Paul and his mother left. Then they all burst out laughing.

Paul's luck hadn't been better. The first thing he was always asked, before the potential employer found out if he knew how to do anything, was whether he was a war veteran. He had suffered many disappointments in the space of a few hours, so he decided to confront the problem as rationally as he could. Trusting to fortune, he decided to follow the coalman, to study him and approach him in the best way possible. He and his mother had managed to stay in the boarding-house for a third night on promise of paying the following day, and because the landlady felt sorry for them. She even gave them a dish of thick soup, with bits of potato floating in it, and a piece of black bread.

So there was Paul, crossing Rheinstrasse. A bustling and happy place, filled with peddlers, newspaper-sellers and knife-grinders, who hawked their boxes of matches, the latest news or the benefits of getting your knives well sharpened. The smell of the bakeries mixed with the dung of horses, which were much more common in Schwabing than cars.

Paul took advantage of the moment when the coalman's assistant left to fetch the doorman of the building they were going to supply, to get him to open the door to the cellar. Meanwhile, the coalman prepared the enormous birchwood baskets in which they transported their wares.

Maybe if he's alone he'll be friendlier. People react to strangers differently in front of their juniors, Paul thought as he approached.

'Good afternoon, sir.'

'What the hell do you want, lad?'

'I need a job.'

'Get lost. I don't need anyone.'

'I'm strong, sir, and I could help you unload this cart really fast.'

The coalman deigned to glance at Paul for the first time, looking him up and down. Paul was wearing his black trousers, white shirt and sweater, and still looked like a waiter. Compared to the corpulent bulk of the big man in front of him, Paul felt like a wimp.

'How old are you, lad?'

'Seventeen, sir,' lied Paul.

'Even my Aunt Bertha, who was terrible at guessing people's ages, poor thing, wouldn't put you at any more than fifteen. Besides, you're too scrawny. Scarper.'

'I turn sixteen on May twenty-second,' said Paul, sounding offended.

'In any case, you're no use to me.'

'I can lug a basket of coal perfectly well, sir.'

He climbed up on to the cart with great agility, took a shovel and filled up one of the baskets. Then, trying not to let the effort show, he put the straps over his shoulder. He could tell that the fifty kilos were destroying his shoulders and lower back, but he managed a smile.

'See?' he said, using all his willpower to keep his legs from buckling.

'Kid, there's more to it than picking up a basket,' said the coalman, taking a packet of tobacco out of his pocket and lighting a battered pipe. 'My old Aunt Lotta could pick up that basket up with less fuss than you. You need to be able to carry it down steps that are as damp and slippery as a showgirl's crotch. The cellars we go down to almost never have any light, because the building administrators don't give a damn if we smash our heads open. And maybe you could get one down, maybe two, but by the third . . .'

Paul's knees and shoulders could no longer take the weight and the boy fell face down on to the pile of coal.

'. . . you'll tumble over, as you've just done. And if that were to happen to you on those narrow stairs, yours wouldn't be the only skull to get broken.'

The lad clambered up on stiff legs.

'But . . .'

'There's no "but" that'll make me change my mind, kid. Get off my cart.'

'I . . . could tell you a way of making your business better.'

'Just what I need . . . And what would that be?' asked the coalman, with a mocking laugh.

'You lose a lot of time between finishing one delivery and beginning the next because you have to go to the warehouse to collect more coal. If you bought a second cart . . .'

'That's your bright idea, eh? A good cart with steel axles to take all the weight we carry costs at least seven thousand marks, not counting the harnesses and horses. Have you got seven thousand marks in those tatty trousers? I'd guess not.'

'But you . . .'

'I make enough to pay for the coal and keep my family. You don't think I've thought about getting another cart? I'm sorry, kid,' he said, his tone softening as he noticed the dejection in Paul's eyes, 'but I can't help you.'

Paul bowed his head, defeated. He'd have to find work somewhere else, and quickly, because the landlady's patience wouldn't last much longer. He was getting down from the cart when a group of people approached them.

'What's this then, Klaus! A new recruit?'

Klaus's assistant was returning with the doorman. But it was another, older man, short and bald, with round glasses and a leather briefcase, who had addressed the coalman.

'No, Herr Finken, it's just a kid who came looking for work, but he's just on his way.'

'Well, he has the mark of your trade on his face.'

'He seemed determined to prove himself, sir. What can I do for you?'

'Look, Klaus, I have another engagement to get to, and I thought of settling up this month's coal. Is that the whole lot?'

'Yes, sir, the two tonnes you ordered, every ounce.'

'I trust you absolutely, Klaus.'

Paul turned on hearing those words. He'd just understood where the coalman's real capital lay.

Trust. And he'd be damned if he couldn't convert that into money. If only they'll listen to me, he thought, returning to the group.

'Well, if you don't mind . . .' Klaus was saying.

'Just a moment!'

'Might I enquire what exactly you're doing here, kid? I've told you I don't need you.'

'You'd need me if you had another cart, sir.'

'Are you stupid? I don't have another cart! Excuse me, Herr Finken, I can't shake this lunatic off.'

The coalman's assistant, who'd been giving Paul suspicious looks for a while, made a move towards him, but his boss gestured for him to stay back. He didn't want to make a scene in front of the customer.

'If I could supply you with the means to buy another cart,' said Paul, moving away from the assistant while trying to maintain his dignity, 'would you hire me?'

Klaus scratched his head.

'Well, yes, I suppose I would,' he conceded.

'All right. Would you be so good as to tell me what margin you get for bringing the coal?'

'The same as everyone else. A respectable eight per cent.'

Paul did some quick calculations.

'Herr Finken, would you agree to pay Herr Graf a thousand marks as a down payment in exchange for a discount of four per cent on the price of coal for a year?'

'That's an awful lot of money, lad,' said Finken.

'But what are you saying? I wouldn't take money in advance from my customers.'

'The truth is, it's a very tempting offer, Klaus. It would mean a big saving for the estate,' said the administrator.

'You see?' Paul was delighted. 'All you have to do is offer the same to six other customers. They'll all accept, sir. I've noticed that people trust you.'

'That's true, Klaus.'

For a moment the coalman's chest inflated like a turkey's, but the complaints soon followed.

'But if we reduce the margins,' said the coalman, not yet seeing it all clearly, 'what will I live on?'

'With a second cart you'll work twice as fast. You'll make your money back straight away. And there will be two carts with your name painted on them going through Munich.'

'Two carts with my name ...'

'Of course, it'll be a bit tight to begin with. After all, you'll have one more salary to pay.'

The coalman looked at the administrator, who smiled.

'For God's sake hire this boy, or I'll hire him myself. He has quite a business head on him.'

Paul went around with Klaus for the rest of the day, speaking to the estate administrators. Of the first ten, seven accepted, and only four insisted on a written guarantee.

'It seems you've got your cart, Herr Graf.'

'Now we're going to have a hell of a lot of work. And you'll need to find new customers.'

'I'd thought that you ...'

'No way, kid. You get along with people, though you're a little shy, like my dear old Aunt Irmuska. I think you'll be good at it.'

The lad remained silent a few moments, contemplating the day's successes, then addressed the coalman again.

'Before I accept, sir, I'd like to ask you a question.'

'What the hell do you want?' asked Klaus, impatient.

'Do you really have that many aunts?'

The coalman gave an enormous laugh.

'My mother had fourteen sisters, kid. Believe it or not.'

With Paul in charge of collecting the coal and finding new customers, the business began to prosper. He drove a full cart from the stores on the banks of the Isar to the house where Klaus and Hulbert – for that is what the mute assistant was called – were finishing their unloading. First he would rub the horses down and give them water in a bucket. Then he'd change the team, and harness up the relief animals to the cart he had just brought.

Then he would give his companions a hand so they could dispatch the empty cart as quickly as possible. It was difficult to begin with, but as he got used to it and as his shoulders broadened, Paul was able to haul the enormous baskets around. Once each particular estate was done with he'd gee up the horses and head back to the stores, humming happily, as the others made their way to another house.

Ilse, meanwhile, had found some chores to do in the boarding-house where they were lodged, and in exchange the landlady gave them a small discount on their rent, which was just as well since Paul's wage was barely enough for the two of them.

'I wish I could make it lower, Herr Reiner,' the landlady would say, 'but it's not like I really need that much help.'

Paul would nod. He knew that his mother wasn't helping all that much. Other tenants in the boarding-house had whispered that some-times Ilse would stop, lost in thought, halfway through sweeping a corridor, or peeling a potato, holding on to the broom or the knife and staring into the void.

Concerned, Paul spoke to his mother, who denied it. When he insisted, Ilse ended up admitting that it was true in part.

'I may have been a little distracted lately. Too much going on in my head,' she said, stroking his face.

This will all pass eventually, thought Paul. *We've been going through a lot.*

He suspected there was something else to it, however, something that his mother was hiding. He was still determined to find out the truth about his father's death, but he didn't know where to begin. It would be impossible to approach the von Schroeders, at least while they could rely on the support of the judge. They could have Paul thrown in prison at any moment, and that was a risk he couldn't take, especially not with his mother in the state she was in.

At night the question gnawed at him. At least he could let his thoughts wander without having to worry about waking his mother. They now slept in separate rooms, for the first time in his life. Paul had moved to one on the second floor, towards the rear of the building and smaller than Ilse's, but at least he could enjoy his privacy.

'No girls in the room, Herr Reiner,' the landlady would say at least once a week. And Paul, who had the same imagination and the same needs as any healthy sixteen-year-old boy, found the time to let his thoughts wander in that direction.

Over the months that followed, Germany reinvented itself, just as the Reiners had done. A new government signed the Treaty of Versailles in late June 1919, signalling Germany's acceptance of sole responsibility for the war, and committing to colossal sums in economic reparation. On the streets, the humiliation to which the Allies were subjecting the country produced a buzz of peaceful indignation, but on the whole people breathed more easily for a time. In mid-August, a new constitution was ratified.

Paul began to feel that his life was falling back into some order. A precarious order, but order nonetheless. Gradually, he began to forget the mystery surrounding his father's death, whether because of the difficulty of the task, his fear of confronting it, or his growing obligation to take care of Ilse.

One day, however, in the middle of a morning rest – the very time of day when he'd gone to ask for work – Klaus pushed away his empty beer mug, balled up the sandwich wrapper, and brought the young man back down to earth.

'You seem like a smart kid, Paul. How come you're not studying?'

'Just because of ... life, the war, people,' he said, shrugging his shoulders.

'There's nothing to be done about life, or the war, but people ... you can always strike back at people, Paul.' The coalman exhaled a cloud of bluish smoke. 'Are you the type to strike back?'

All of a sudden Paul felt frustrated and powerless.

'And what if you know that someone's struck you, but you don't know who it is, or what they've done?'

'Well, then you leave no stone unturned until you've found out.'

12

All was quiet in Munich.

In a luxurious building on the east bank of the Isar, however, a gentle murmuring could be heard. Not loud enough to wake the house's inhabitants, just a muffled sound coming from a room that overlooked the square.

The room was old fashioned, childish, ill suited to the age of its owner. She had abandoned it five years earlier, and hadn't yet had time to change the wallpaper; the bookcases were filled with dolls and the bed had a pink canopy. But on a night like this one, her vulnerable heart was grateful for the objects that took her back to the security of a long-lost world. Her nature cursed itself for having regressed so far in its independence and resolve.

The muffled sound was crying, smothered in a pillow.

On the bed was a letter, only the opening paragraphs visible amid the tangle of bedsheets.

Columbus, Ohio, April 7th 1920

Dearest Alys,

I hope that you are well. You can't imagine how much we miss you, as the dancing season is due to start in only two weeks! This year we girls will be able to go together, without our fathers, but with a chaperone. At least we'll be able to go to more than one dance a month!

The big news of the year, however, is that my brother Prescott is engaged to a girl from out east, Dotty Walker. Everyone is talking about the fortune her father, George Herbert Walker, has, and what a good couple they make. Mother couldn't be happier about the wedding. If only you could be here as it will be the first wedding in the family and you're one of us.

The tears rolled slowly down Alys's face. With her right arm she clung to a doll, but then she suddenly hurled it to the other side of the room when she realised what she was doing.

I am a woman. A woman.

Slowly, the same hand that had thrown the doll groped blindly for the hem of her nightdress between her thighs, and pulled it upwards. The other hand struggled with the elastic of her panties, opening a space for the right hand to slip in, against the smooth skin of her stomach.

Slowly, she began to move.

She thought about Prescott, or at least what she remembered of him; they were together under the oak bed in the house in Columbus, and he was whispering as he embraced her. His body was hot and sweaty. But when she looked up she discovered that the boy wasn't dark skinned and strong like Prescott, but fair and thin. Wrapped in her reverie, she was unable to recognise his face.

Her hands moved faster, and the muffled sound of crying faded and ceased, then started again.

But it was no longer crying.

13

It happened so quickly that not even destiny could have prepared him for it.

'Damn you, Paul, where the hell have you been?'

Paul had arrived at Prinzregentenplatz with a full cart. Klaus was in a foul mood, as he always was when they worked the wealthy areas. The traffic was terrible. The cars and trams waged an endless war against beer-sellers' wagons, handcarts piloted by crafty delivery men and even workers' bicycles. Policemen crossed the square every ten minutes, trying to impose order on chaos, their faces inscrutable beneath their leather helmets. They had already warned the coalmen twice that they should hurry up with the unloading, if they didn't want to get an enormous fine.

The coalmen certainly couldn't afford that. Although that month, December 1920, had brought them many orders, encephalomyelitis had carried away two of the horses only a fortnight earlier and they had had to replace them. Many tears had been shed by Hulbert, for those animals were his life, and as he had no family, he even slept with them in the stables. Klaus had spent the last pfennig of his savings on the new horses and any unexpected expense could now ruin him.

It was no wonder, then, that on that afternoon the coalman started yelling at Paul the moment the cart came round the corner.

'There was a huge snarl-up on the bridge.'

'I don't give a damn! Get down here and help us with the load before those vultures come back.'

Paul jumped down from the driver's seat and started lugging baskets. It took much less effort now, though, at sixteen, almost seventeen, his development was still far from complete. He was rather thin, but his arms and legs were pure sinew.

With only five or six baskets left to unload, the coalmen sped up as they heard the rhythmic, impatient clip-clop of the policemen's horses.

'They're coming!' yelled Klaus.

Paul descended with his final load almost running, dropped it into the coal cellar, the sweat pouring down his forehead, then ran back up the stairs to the street. Just as he emerged, an object struck him full in the face.

For a moment the world around him froze. Paul noticed only that his body spun in the air for half a second, his feet trying to find purchase on the slippery steps. He flailed and then fell backwards. He didn't have time to feel any pain, because the darkness had already closed over him.

Ten seconds earlier, Alys and Manfred Tannenbaum had come into the square, after a walk round a nearby park. The girl had wanted to take her brother for a bit of a run around before the earth became too frozen. The first snows had fallen that night and although they hadn't yet settled, the boy would soon be facing three or four weeks when he couldn't stretch his legs as he might like.

Manfred was savouring these last moments of freedom as best he could. The previous day he had retrieved his old football from his wardrobe, and was now kicking it along and bouncing it off the walls, under the reproachful stares of passers-by. In other circumstances Alys would have scowled at them – she couldn't bear people who thought children were a nuisance – but that day she felt mournful and insecure. Lost in thought, her eyes fixated on the small clouds her breath made in the freezing air, she was paying little attention to Manfred, except to make sure he picked up the ball when crossing the road.

Just a few metres before the door to their home, the boy noticed the gaping cellar doors and, imagining that they were the goalmouth in the Grünwalder stadium, he kicked with all his might. The ball, which was made from extremely tough leather, traced a perfect arc before hitting a man square in the face. This man vanished down the stairs.

'Manfred, be careful!'

Alys's angry shout became a scream when she realised the ball had hit someone. Her brother stood frozen on the pavement, terrified. She ran to the cellar door, but one of the victim's colleagues, a short man wearing a shapeless hat, had already run to his aid.

'Damn it! I always knew that stupid idiot would have a fall,' said another of the coalmen, a larger man. He was still standing by the cart, wringing his hands and glancing anxiously towards the corner of Possartstrasse.

Alys stopped at the top of the cellar steps, but she didn't dare descend. For a few awful seconds, she looked down into the rectangle of darkness, but then a figure appeared, as though the colour black had suddenly assumed human form. It was the coalman's colleague, the one who had run past Alys, and he was carrying the fallen man.

'Holy God, he's only a child . . .'

The injured man's left arm was hanging down at a strange angle, and his trousers and jacket were torn. There were wounds to his head and forearms, and the blood on his face mingled with the coal dust in thick brown streaks. His eyes were shut, and he didn't react when the other man laid him on the ground and tried to wipe the blood away with a grimy piece of cloth.

I hope he's just unconscious, Alys thought, squatting down and taking his hand.

'What's he called?' Alys asked the man in the hat.

The man shrugged, pointed to his throat and shook his head. Alys understood.

'Can you hear me?' she asked, fearing he might be deaf as well as mute. 'We have to help him!'

The man in the hat ignored her and turned towards the coal carts, opening his eyes as wide as saucers. The other coalman, the older one, had got up on to the driver's seat of the first cart, the one that was full, and was desperately trying to find the reins. He cracked his whip, tracing a clumsy figure-of-eight in the air. The two horses started up with a snort.

'Let's go, Hulbert!'

The man in the hat hesitated for a moment. He took a step towards the other cart, but seemed to think better of it and turned. He put the bloodstained cloth in Alys's hands, then he walked away and followed the old man's example.

'Wait! You can't leave him here!' she shouted, outraged at the men's behaviour.

She kicked the ground. Enraged, furious and helpless.

14

The most complicated part for Alys was not convincing the policemen to let her tend to the sick man in her home, but overcoming Doris's resistance to letting him in. She had to shout at her almost as loudly as she'd had to shout at Manfred to get him to move himself for God's sake and go and find help. Finally her brother had obeyed and two servants had cleared a path through the circle of spectators and loaded the young man into the lift.

'Miss Alys, you know that Sir doesn't like having strangers in the house, especially when he's not here. I'm firmly against this.'

The young coal-bearer hung limp and unconscious between the servants, who were too old to be able to bear his weight for much longer. They were on the landing of the staircase, and the housekeeper was blocking the door.

'We can't leave him here, Doris. We will have to send for a doctor.'

'It's not our responsibility.'

'It is. The accident was Manfred's fault,' she said, pointing at the boy, who was standing pale faced beside her, holding the ball very far from his body, as though he feared it might injure someone else.

'I've said no. There are hospitals for . . . for people like him.'

'He'll be better looked after here.'

Doris stared at her, as though she couldn't believe what she was hearing. Then she twisted her mouth into a condescending smile. She knew exactly what to say to enrage Alys, and she chose her words carefully.

'Fräulein Alys, you're too young to . . .'

So it's back to this, thought Alys, feeling her face colour with rage and shame. *Well, this time it's not going to work.*

'Doris, with all due respect, get out of the way.'

She moved towards the door and pushed it with both hands. The housekeeper tried to shut it, but she was too late, and the wood struck her shoulder as it swung open. She fell on her backside on the entrance-hall rug, watching powerlessly as the Tannenbaum children led the two servants into the house. The latter avoided her gaze, and Doris was convinced they were trying not to laugh.

'This is not how things are done. I shall tell your father,' she said, furious.

'You don't have to worry about that, Doris. When he comes back from Dachau tomorrow I'll tell him myself,' replied Alys, without glancing back.

Deep down, she wasn't as confident as her words seemed to suggest. She knew that there would be problems with her father, but at that moment she was determined not to allow the housekeeper to get her own way.

'Close your eyes. I don't want to get iodine in them.'

Alys tiptoed into the guest room, trying not to interrupt the doctor, who was cleaning the injured man's forehead. Doris was standing angrily in the corner of the room, constantly clearing her throat, or tapping her feet to show her impatience. When Alys came in, she redoubled her efforts. Alys ignored her and looked at the young coal-bearer stretched out on the bed.

The mattress is completely ruined, she thought. At that moment her eyes met the man's and she recognised him.

The waiter from the party! No, it can't be him!

But it was, because she saw him open his eyes wide and raise his eyebrows. More than a year had passed, but she still remembered him. And suddenly she realised who the fair-haired boy was, who had slipped into her fantasies when she tried to visualise Prescott. She noticed Doris glaring at her, so she faked a yawn and opened the bedroom door. Using it as a screen between her and the housekeeper, she looked at Paul and brought a finger to her lips.

'How is he?' Alys asked, when at last the doctor came out into the corridor.

He was a skinny man with bulging eyes who had been in charge of the Tannenbaums' care since before Alys was born. When her mother had died of influenza, the girl had spent many sleepless nights, hating him for not having saved her, though now his strange appearance produced in her only a shiver, like that of a stethoscope on skin.

'His left arm's broken, though it seems like a clean break. I've put a splint and bandages on him. He should be all right in six weeks or so. Try to stop him moving it.'

'What about his head?'

'The other injuries are superficial though he's bled a lot. He must have scraped himself against the edge of the steps. I've disinfected the wound on his forehead, though he should have a good bath as soon as possible.'

'Can he leave straight away, Doctor?'

The doctor nodded a greeting to Doris, who had just closed the door behind him.

'I'd recommend that he stay here tonight. Well, goodbye,' said the doctor, pulling his hat on firmly.

'We'll see to that, Doctor. Thank you very much,' said Alys, bidding him goodbye and throwing Doris a challenging stare.

Paul twisted in the bathtub, uncomfortable. He had to keep his left arm out of the water so as not to get the bandages wet. With his body covered in bruises, there was no position that didn't make some part of him hurt. He surveyed the room, stunned by the luxury that surrounded him. Baron von Schroeder's mansion, though it was in one of the most highly prized areas in Munich, didn't have the amenities this apartment had, beginning with hot water that flowed straight from the tap. Paul had usually been the one to carry hot water from the kitchen each time someone in the family wanted to take a bath, which was a daily occurrence. And there was just no comparison between the bathroom in which he found himself now and the cupboard with a washstand and basin in the boarding-house.

So this is her house. I thought I'd never see her again. It's a pity she's ashamed of me, he thought.

'That water's very black.'

Paul looked up, startled. Alys was at the bathroom door, an amused expression on her face. Although the bathtub came almost to his shoulders and the water was covered in a greyish lather, the young man couldn't help blushing.

'What are you doing here?'

'Redressing the balance,' she said, smiling at Paul's feeble efforts to cover himself up with one hand. 'I owed you for having rescued me.'

'Bearing in mind that it was your brother's ball that knocked me down those stairs, I'd say you still owe me one.'

Alys didn't reply. She looked at him carefully, focusing on his shoulders and the pronounced muscles of his sinewy arms. Without the coal dust, his skin was very fair.

I wonder if it would be soft. It certainly looks it, thought Alys.

'Anyhow, thanks, Alys,' said Paul, taking her silence to be a mute reproach.

'You remember my name.'

Now it was Paul's turn to be silent. The shine in Alys's eyes was striking, and he had to look away.

'You've bulked up quite a bit,' she continued, after a pause.

'It's those baskets. They weigh a ton, but carrying them about makes you stronger.'

'How did you end up selling coal?'

'It's a long story.'

She took a stool from the corner of the bathroom and sat down close to him.

'Tell me. We have time.'

'Aren't you afraid they'll catch you here?'

'I went to bed half an hour ago. The housekeeper checked on me. But it wasn't difficult to sneak past her.'

Paul picked up the bar of soap and began turning it around in his hand. The lather was disappearing.

'After the party I had a nasty argument with my aunt.'

'Because of your cousin?'

'It was because of something that happened many years ago, something to do with my father. My mother told me he'd died in a shipwreck, but on the day of the party I learned that she'd been lying to me for years.'

'It's something adults do,' Alys said with a sigh.

'They threw us out, me and my mother. The job was the best I could get.'

'You were lucky, I suppose.'

'You call this luck?' said Paul, wincing. 'Working from dawn till dusk, with nothing to look forward to except a few pfennigs in your pocket. Some luck!'

'You have a job, you have your independence, your self-respect. That's something,' she replied, upset.

'I would swap it for some of this,' he said, gesturing around him.

'You have no idea what I mean, Paul, do you?'

'More than you think,' he spat, unable to contain himself. 'You have beauty and intelligence and you spoil it all by pretending to be unhappy, a rebel, spending more time moaning about your luxurious position and worrying about what other people think of you than taking risks and fighting for what you really want.'

He fell silent, suddenly conscious of everything he'd said, and saw the emotion dancing in her eyes. He opened his mouth to excuse himself, but thought that it would only make things worse.

Alys slowly got up from the stool. For a moment Paul thought she was going to leave, but this was just the first of many times he would fail to interpret her feelings correctly over the years. She came over to the bathtub, knelt down beside it and, leaning over the water, she kissed him on the lips. At first Paul froze, but soon he began to respond.

Alys drew back and stared at him. Paul understood where her beauty lay: it was in the glimmer of challenge that blazed in her eyes. He leaned his body forward and kissed her, but this time he opened his mouth slightly. Alys responded with her tongue, shy at first, then eager. After a while she broke away.

They looked at each other again, then she dipped her whole arm into the water.

'What are you doing?' asked Paul, hoarsely.

'Taking risks.'

The water was colder than she expected.

The first thing she touched was his belly, which was as smooth and firm as a board. She caressed the line of his muscles without taking her eyes off his, without caring that the dirty water was soaking the sleeve of her dress. She brushed her hand past the pubic hair and against his penis, which was as hard as a rod. Paul gave a moan and closed his eyes.

'Did I hurt you?'

'No.' He swallowed. 'Not at all.'

She closed her fingers around his penis. It was much thicker than she'd imagined; her experience was limited to the engravings in the magazines her father kept in his desk. Sometimes she would slip out of her room at night to leaf through them, her heart beating, full of fear, in case she was discovered there, crouching by the window, reading by the light of the moon. The stories that accompanied the pictures had a language of their own, both laughable and teasing, filled with extravagant adjectives.

The emotions she'd felt then paled in comparison to what she was experiencing as she caressed Paul. This was real.

'Don't stop,' he said in a voice that seemed alien, strange.

No one has ever done this to him before, thought Alys, proud and excited.

She wanted to undress and get into the bathtub with Paul, to take him inside her. She checked that his eyes were still closed and slipped a hand under her skirt, caressing herself slowly.

Then she heard the door.

15

Alys jumped to her feet at once and backed away from Paul, but it was too late. Her father had entered the bathroom. He barely looked at her – he didn't need to. The sleeve of her dress was completely soaked, and even a man of Josef Tannenbaum's limited imagination could get some idea of what had been happening only a moment before.

'Go to your room.'

'But Papa . . .' she stammered.

'Now!'

Alys burst into tears and ran out of the room. On the way she almost tripped over Doris, who flashed her a triumphant smile.

'As you can see, Fräulein, your father came home earlier than expected. Isn't that marvellous?'

Paul felt totally defenceless, sitting there naked in the rapidly cooling water. As Tannenbaum approached, he tried to get to his feet, but the businessman gripped his shoulder cruelly. Though he was shorter than Paul, he was stronger than his chubby appearance suggested, and Paul found it impossible to get purchase on the slippery tub.

Tannenbaum sat down on the stool where Alys had been seated only a few minutes earlier. He didn't lessen his grip on Paul's shoulder for a moment, and Paul was afraid that he would suddenly decide to push him down and hold his head under the water.

'What's your name, coalman?'

'Paul Reiner.'

'You're not a Jew, Reiner, are you?'

'No, sir.'

'Now pay attention,' said Tannenbaum, his tone softening, like a trainer speaking to the last dog in the litter, the slowest to learn its tricks. 'My daughter is heir to a large fortune, she's from a class far above your own. You're just a piece of shit that's got stuck to her shoe. Understand?'

Paul didn't reply. He managed to overcome his shame and stared back, his teeth clenched in fury. At that moment there was no one in the world he hated more than this man.

'Of course you don't understand,' Tannenbaum said, releasing his shoulder. 'Well, at least I returned before she did something stupid.'

His hand went to his wallet, and he drew out an enormous fistful of banknotes. He folded them carefully and placed them on the marble washbasin.

'This is for the trouble caused by Manfred's ball. And now you can go.'

Tannenbaum headed for the door, but before he left he looked at Paul one last time.

'Of course, Reiner, though you probably wouldn't care, I've spent this afternoon with my daughter's future father-in-law, finalising the details of her wedding. In the spring she will marry an aristocrat.'

You're lucky, Paul, you have your independence, she'd said to him.

'Does Alys know?' he asked.

Tannenbaum gave a snort of derision.

'Never say her name again.'

Paul got out of the bathtub and dressed, hardly bothering to dry himself. He didn't care if he caught pneumonia. He took the wad of banknotes from the sink and went into the bedroom, where Doris was watching him from across the room.

'Allow me to show you to the door.'

'Don't trouble yourself,' the young man replied, turning into the corridor. The front door was clearly visible at the far end.

'Oh, we wouldn't want you to pocket anything by accident,' the housekeeper said with a mocking grin.

'Give this back to your master, ma'am. Tell him I don't need it,' Paul replied, his voice cracking as he held out the banknotes.

He almost ran to the exit, even though Doris was no longer watching him. She was looking at the money and a crafty smile flashed across her face.

16

The following weeks were a struggle for Paul. When he showed his face back at the stables he had to endure the forced apologies of Klaus, who had escaped a fine but still bore the remorse of having left the young man in the lurch. At least this mitigated his anger at Paul's broken arm.

'The middle of winter, and only me and poor Hulbert to do the unloading, with all the orders we have. It's a tragedy.'

Paul refrained from mentioning that they only had so many orders thanks to his scheme and the second cart. He didn't feel like talking much, and he sank into a silence every bit as deep as Hulbert's, freezing his backside off for long hours on the driver's seat, his thoughts elsewhere.

Once he tried to return to Prinzregentenplatz, when he thought Herr Tannenbaum wouldn't be there, but a servant slammed the door in his face. He slipped various notes to Alys through the letterbox, asking her to meet him in a nearby café, but she never turned up. And on Sundays, the only day when he could reach the place at a reasonable hour and walk by the gate, she never appeared. A policeman did – doubtless instructed by Josef – who advised Paul not to return to the neigh-bourhood if he didn't want to end up picking his teeth off the pavement.

Increasingly Paul closed in on himself, and the few times he and his mother crossed paths at the boarding-house, they barely said a word. He ate little, hardly slept, and drove the cart like an automaton, paying no attention to his surroundings. On one occasion the back wheel of the cart narrowly missed a tram. As he endured the curses of the passengers – who shouted that he could have killed them all – Paul told himself he had to do something to escape the thick storm clouds of melancholy that floated around inside his head.

It was not surprising he didn't notice the figure watching him one afternoon on Frauenstrasse. The stranger approached the cart slowly at first, to get a closer look, trying to keep out of Paul's line of sight. The man jotted down notes in a booklet he carried in his pocket, carefully writing the name Klaus Graf. Now that Paul had more time and a healthy arm, the sideboards of the cart were always clean and the letters visible, which went some way to dampening the coalman's anger. Finally the observer sat down in a nearby beer hall until the carts had left. It was only then that he approached the estate they had been supplying to make some discreet enquiries.

Jürgen was in an extremely bad mood. He had just received his marks for the first four months of the year, and they were not in the least bit encouraging.

I'll have to get that cretin Kurt to give me private lessons. Maybe he'll do a couple of bits of work for me. I'll ask him to come round to my house and use my typewriter so they won't find out, thought Jürgen.

It was his final year of secondary school, and a place at university was at stake, with all that it entailed. He had no particular interest in doing a degree, but he liked the idea of strutting around campus, parading his baronial title. Even if he didn't actually have it yet.

It'll be full of pretty girls. I'll be fighting them off.

He was in his bedroom fantasising about university girls when the maid – a new one hired by his mother after she'd thrown out the Reiners – called to him from outside the door.

'Young Master Krohn is here to see you, Master Jürgen.'

'Let him in.'

Jürgen greeted his friend with a grunt.

'Just the person I wanted to see. I need you to autograph my report card; if my father sees it he'll fly off the handle. I've spent the whole morning trying to fake his signature, but it doesn't look anything like it,' he said, pointing to the floor, which was covered in scrunched-up bits of paper.

Krohn glanced at the report lying open on the table, and gave a whistle of surprise.

'Well, we have been enjoying ourselves, haven't we?'

'You know Waburg hates me.'

'From what I can tell half of the common room shares his dislike. But let's not worry about your performance at school right now, Jürgen, because I bring you news. You should prepare yourself for the hunt.'

'What are you talking about? What are we hunting?'

Krohn smiled, enjoying in advance the recognition he would earn from his discovery.

'A bird that's flown the nest, my friend. A bird with a broken wing.'

17

Paul had absolutely no idea something was wrong until it was too late.

His day began as usual, with a tram journey from the boarding-house to Klaus Graf's stables on the banks of the Isar. When he arrived it was still dark, and he had to wake Hulbert, pouring down his throat the coffee from his thermos. He and the mute had hit it off after their initial distrust, and Paul really valued those moments before dawn when they harnessed the horses to the carts and headed for the coal stores. There they'd put the cart in the loading bay, where a wide metal pipe would fill the cart in under ten minutes. An employee would take note of how many times the Graf men came in to load up each day, so the total could be settled on a weekly basis. Then Paul and Hulbert would head off towards their first appointment. Klaus would be there, waiting for them, puffing impatiently on his pipe. A simple, exhausting routine.

On reaching the stables, Paul pushed open the door as he did every morning. It was never locked, because there was nothing inside worth stealing apart from the harnesses. Hulbert slept only half a metre from the horses, in a room with a rickety old bed to the right of the animals' stalls.

'Wake up, Hulbert! There's more snow than usual today. We'll have to head out a little early if we want to get to Moosach in time.'

There was no sign of his mute companion, but that was normal. It always took him a while to appear.

Suddenly Paul heard the horses stamping nervously in their stalls and something turned over in his guts, a feeling he'd not experienced in a long time. His lungs felt leaden and there was an acidic taste in his mouth.

Jürgen.

He took a step towards the door, but then stopped. There they were,

83

appearing from every cranny, and he cursed himself for not having seen them earlier. From inside the cupboard where the shovels were kept, the horses' stalls, and underneath the carts. There were seven of them, the same seven who'd pursued him at Jürgen's birthday party. It seemed like an eternity ago. Their faces were broader, harder and they no longer wore their school jackets, but thick sweaters and boots. Clothes better suited to the task.

'You won't be sliding across the marble this time, cousin,' said Jürgen, gesturing contemptuously at the earth floor.

'Hulbert!' Paul cried, desperately.

'Your retarded friend is tied up in his bed. We didn't have to gag him, of course ...' said one of the thugs. The others seemed to find this very funny.

Paul leaped up on to one of the carts as the boys closed in on him. One of them tried to grab his ankle, but Paul lifted his foot just in time and brought it down on the boy's fingers. There was a crunching sound.

'He's broken it! The absolute son of a bitch!'

'Shut up! Half an hour from now this little piece of shit will wish he was in your place,' said Jürgen.

Some of the boys went round to the back of the cart. Out of the corner of his eye Paul saw another grab hold of the driver's seat, meaning to climb on. He sensed the glint of a penknife blade.

He had a sudden flashback to one of the many scenarios he'd invented around the sinking of his father's boat: his father surrounded by enemies on all sides who were attempting to board. He told himself that this cart was his boat.

I'm not going to let them board.

He looked around, desperately seeking something he could use as a weapon, but all that was to hand were the leftover bits of coal scattered around the cart. The pieces were so small he'd have to throw forty or fifty before he'd cause any harm. With his broken arm, the only advantage Paul had was the height of the cart, which put him just at the right level to kick any attackers in the face.

Another boy attempted to sneak round on to the back of the cart, but Paul sensed the trick. The one by the driver's seat took advantage of the momentary distraction and pulled himself up, no doubt preparing to jump on to Paul's back. Moving quickly, Paul unscrewed the lid of the thermos and threw the hot coffee into the face of the boy. It wasn't boiling as it had been an hour before when he'd prepared it on the stove in his bedroom, but it was hot enough to make the lad clasp his hands to his face, scalded. Paul charged at him and pushed him off the cart. He fell on his back, groaning.

'Shit, what are we waiting for? Everyone, get him,' Jürgen called.

Paul saw the gleam of a penknife once more. He spun around, fists in the air, wanting to show them he wasn't afraid, but everyone in the filthy stables knew it was a lie.

Ten hands seized the cart in ten places. Paul stamped his foot down left and right, but in seconds they were all around him. One of the thugs grabbed his left arm, and Paul, trying to get free, felt the fist of another in the face. There was a crunch and an explosion of pain as his nose was broken.

For a moment all he saw was a pulsating red light. He kicked out, missing his cousin Jürgen by miles.

'Hold on to him, Krohn!'

Paul felt them grab him from behind. He tried wriggling out of their grasp but it was useless. In seconds they had pinned his arms back, leaving his face and chest at his cousin's mercy. One of his captors held his neck in an iron grip, forcing Paul to look straight at Jürgen.

'Not running any more, eh?'

Jürgen carefully put his weight on his right leg, then drew his arm back. The blow struck Paul right in the stomach. He felt the air leave his body as though it were a punctured tyre.

'Hit me all you want, Jürgen,' Paul wheezed when he managed to get his breath back. 'It won't stop you being a useless pig.'

Another punch, this time in the face, split an eyebrow in two. His cousin shook his hand and massaged his injured knuckles.

'You see? There are seven of you to one of me, someone's holding me down, and you're still coming off worse than I am,' said Paul.

Jürgen threw himself forward and grabbed his cousin by the hair so hard that Paul thought he'd pull it out.

'You killed Eduard, you son of a bitch.'

'All I did was help him. Which is more than can be said for the rest of you.'

'So, cousin, you're claiming some relationship to the von Schroeders all of a sudden? I thought you'd renounced all that. Wasn't that what you said to the little Jewish slut?'

'Don't call her that.'

Jürgen came even closer, till Paul could feel his breath on his face. His eyes were locked on Paul's, savouring the pain he was about to cause with his words.

'Relax, she's not going to be a slut for much longer. She's going to become respectable now, a lady. The future Baroness von Schroeder.'

Paul knew at once that it was true, it wasn't just his cousin's usual bragging. Bitter pain rose in his stomach, producing a shapeless, desperate cry. Jürgen laughed out loud, his eyes bulging. At last he let go of Paul's hair, and Paul's head dropped down on to his chest.

'Well then, boys, let's give him what he deserves.'

At that moment Paul threw his head back with all his might. The boy behind him had slackened his grip after Jürgen's blows, doubtless believing victory was theirs. The top of Paul's skull struck the thug's face, and he let Paul go, dropping to his knees. The others hurled themselves on to Paul, and they all landed in a tangle on the floor.

Paul flailed, blindly throwing punches. In the middle of the confusion he felt something hard under his fingers and seized it. He tried to get to his feet, and had almost succeeded when Jürgen noticed him and launched himself at his cousin. Instinctively Paul shielded his face, unaware he was still holding the object he'd just picked up.

There was a dreadful scream, then silence.

Paul pulled himself over to the side of the cart. His cousin was on his knees writhing on the floor. From the socket of his right eye protruded the wooden handle of a short knife. Little more than a penknife. The boy had been lucky – if his friends had had the bright idea of bringing something bigger, Jürgen would be dead.

'Get it out! Get it out!' he screamed.

The others watched him paralysed. They didn't want to be there any more. For them, it was no longer a game.

'It hurts! Help me, for fuck's sake!'

Finally one of the thugs managed to get to his feet and approached Jürgen.

'Don't do it,' said Paul, horrified. 'Get him to a hospital and have them remove it.'

The other boy glanced at Paul, his face expressionless. It was almost as though he wasn't there, or wasn't in control of his actions. He approached Jürgen and placed his hand on the handle of the penknife.

As he gripped it, however, Jürgen gave a sudden jerk in the opposite direction and the blade of the penknife gouged out much of his eyeball.

Jürgen was suddenly silent and brought his hand to the place where the penknife had been a moment earlier.

'I can't see. Why can't I see?'

Then he fainted.

The boy who had pulled out the penknife stood looking at him dumbly, as the pinkish mass that had been the future baron's right eye slid down the blade to the ground.

'You've got to take him to a hospital!' shouted Paul.

The rest of the gang were getting slowly to their feet, still not quite understanding what had happened to their leader. They had gone to the stable to obtain a simple, crushing victory; instead the unthinkable had happened.

Two of them took Jürgen by the hands and feet and carried him towards the door. The others joined them. Not one of them said a word.

Only the boy with the penknife stayed where he was, looking questioningly at Paul.

'Go on, then, if you dare,' Paul said, praying to heaven that he wouldn't.

The boy opened his hand, dropped the penknife to the ground, and ran outside. Paul watched him leave, and then, finally alone, he started to cry.

18

'I have no intention of doing that.'

'You're my daughter, you'll do as I say.'

'I'm not an object you can buy and sell.'

'This is the greatest opportunity of your life.'

'Of your life, you mean.'

'You're the one who'll be a baroness.'

'You don't know him, Father. He's a pig, a rude, arrogant ...'

'Your mother described me in very similar terms when we first met.'

'Keep her out of this. She would never have ...'

'Wanted the best for you? Tried to secure your happiness?'

'... forced her daughter to marry someone she detests. And a Gentile, what's more.'

'Would you have preferred someone nicer? A starving pauper like your friend the coalman? He's not Jewish either, Alys.'

'At least he's not a bad person.'

'That's what you think.'

'I matter to him.'

'You matter to him to the tune of exactly three thousand marks.'

'What?'

'The day your friend came to visit I left a wad of banknotes on the washbasin. Three thousand marks for his troubles, on the condition he never show up here again.'

'...'

'I know, my child. I know it's hard ...'

'You're lying.'

'I swear to you, Alys, on your mother's grave, that your friend the coalman took the money from the sink. You know I wouldn't joke about something like that.'

'I ...'

'People will always disappoint you, Alys. Come here, give me a hug ...'

'Don't touch me!'

'You'll get over it. And you'll learn to love the son of Baron von Schroeder as your mother ended up loving me.'

'I hate you!'

'Alys! Alys, come back!'

She left two days later, blanketed by the snow and the dim morning light.

She took with her a large suitcase filled with clothes and all the money she was able to get together. It wasn't much, but it would be enough to keep her going for a few months until she could find a decent job. Her absurd, childish plan to return to Prescott, dreamt up at a time when it had seemed normal to travel in first-class compartments and eat her fill of lobster, was a thing of the past. Now she sensed that there was a different Alys out there, one who had to make her own way.

She also took a locket that had belonged to her mother. It contained a photo of Alys and another of Manfred. She had worn it round her neck until the day she died.

Before leaving, Alys paused for a moment at her brother's door. She rested her hand on the doorknob, but did not turn it. She was afraid that seeing Manfred's round, innocent face would diminish her resolve. Her willpower had already proved to be considerably weaker than she had anticipated.

Now it's time to change all that, she thought, going out on to the street.

Her leather boots left dirty tracks in the snow, but the blizzard took care of that, wiping them out as it raged by.

19

On the day he was attacked, Paul and Hulbert showed up at their first delivery an hour late. Herr Graf was white with rage. When he saw Paul's battered face and heard his tale – corroborated with constant nodding from Hulbert, whom Paul had found tied to his own bed, humiliation etched across his face – he sent him home.

The next morning Paul was surprised to find Graf at the stables, a place he almost never visited before the end of the day. Still confused by recent events, he didn't spot the strange look the coalman was giving him.

'Hello, Herr Graf. What are you doing here?' he asked, cautiously.

'Well, I just wanted to make sure that there wouldn't be any more problems. Can you assure me those boys won't be coming back, Paul?'

The young man hesitated for a moment before replying.

'No, sir. I can't.'

'That's what I thought.'

Klaus rummaged in his coat and pulled out a couple of wrinkled, dirty banknotes. He handed them guiltily to Paul.

Paul took them, doing the sums in his head.

'A portion of my monthly salary, including today. Sir, are you dismissing me?'

'I've been thinking about what happened yesterday . . . I don't want any problems, you understand?'

'Of course, sir.'

'You don't seem surprised,' said Klaus, who had deep bags under his eyes, doubtless from a sleepless night trying to decide whether he should dismiss the lad or not.

Paul looked at him, wondering whether to explain the depth of the abyss into which he was being cast by the slim envelope in his hand. He decided against it, because the coalman already knew his plight. He opted instead for irony, which was increasingly becoming his currency.

'This is the second time you've betrayed me, Herr Graf. These things lose their charm the second time around.'

20

'You can't do this to me!'

The baron smiled, and sipped his herbal tea. He was enjoying this situation, and what was worse, he was making no attempt to pretend otherwise. For the first time he could see the possibility of getting his hands on the Jew's money without having to marry off Jürgen.

'My dear Tannenbaum, I don't see how I'm doing anything at all.'

'Precisely!'

'There's no bride, is there?'

'Well, no,' Tannenbaum acknowledged reluctantly.

'So there can't be a wedding. And since the lack of a bride,' he said, clearing his throat, 'is your responsibility, it's reasonable that you should be taking care of the costs.'

Tannenbaum shifted uneasily in his seat, searching for a response. He served himself more tea and half the sugar-bowl.

'I see you take it sweet,' said the baron, arching an eyebrow. The revulsion Josef produced in him had slowly been transformed into a strange fascination, as the balance of power shifted.

'Well, after all, I'm the one who's paid for this sugar.'

The baron responded with a grimace.

'There's no need to be rude.'

'Do you think I'm an idiot, Baron? You told me you'd use the money to set up a factory to manufacture rubber products, like the one you lost five years ago. I believed you, and transferred the vast sum you asked me for. And what do I find two years later? Not only have you *not* set up the factory, but the money's ended up in a portfolio of stocks to which only you have access.'

'They're reliable stocks, Tannenbaum.'

'That's as may be. But I don't trust their keeper. It wouldn't be the first time you'd wagered your family's future on a winning hand.'

Otto's face assumed a look of offence that he couldn't bring himself to feel. Lately he had contracted the gambling fever again, and had spent long nights staring at the leather folder that contained the investments he'd made with Tannenbaum's money. Each one had an instant liquidity clause, which meant that he could convert them into wads of banknotes in little over an hour with only his signature and a stiff penalty. He didn't try to fool himself: he knew why the clause had been included. He knew the risk he was running. He'd started drinking more and more before bed, and the previous week he'd returned to the gaming table.

Not at the Munich Casino – he wasn't that stupid. He had disguised himself in the most modest clothes he could find, and visited an establishment in the Aldstadt. A cellar with sawdust on the floor and whores with more paint on them than you'd find in the Alte Pinakothek. He asked for a glass of Korn and started at a table where the opening play was just two marks. He had five hundred in his pocket, the maximum he would allow himself to squander.

The worst thing possible happened: he won.

Even with those filthy cards that stuck to one another like newlyweds on honeymoon, even with the drunkenness brought on by home-brewed drink and the smoke that stung his eyes, even with the unpleasant smell that hung in the air of that basement, he won. Not a lot, just enough for him to leave the place without a knife in his guts. But he had won, and now the itch for the game came to him more and more frequently.

'I'm afraid that on the matter of the money you'll just have to trust my judgement, Tannenbaum.'

The industrialist gave a sceptical laugh.

'I see that I'm going to be left with no money and no wedding. Though I could always redeem that loan letter you signed for me, Baron.'

Otto gulped. He wouldn't allow anyone to take away the folder in his study drawer. And not for the simple reason that the dividends were gradually paying off his debts.

No.

That folder, the act of stroking it, of imagining what he could do with the money, was the only thing that got him through the long nights.

'As I said before, there's no need to be rude. I promised you a wedding between our families, and that's what you'll get. Bring me the bride and my son will be waiting for her.'

Jürgen hadn't spoken to his mother for three days.

When the baron had gone to collect his son at the hospital a week earlier, he had listened to the young man's profoundly biased tale. He'd been pained at what had happened – *even more than when Eduard had returned so badly mutilated*, Jürgen thought stupidly – but he had refused to involve the police in the matter.

'We mustn't forget that the boys were the ones who brought the penknife,' said Otto, justifying his stance.

But Jürgen knew that his father was lying, and that he was hiding a more important reason. He tried to talk to Brunhilda, but she dodged the subject again and again, confirming his suspicions that they were telling him only part of the truth. Infuriated, Jürgen shut himself away in total silence, believing that this would soften his mother.

Brunhilda suffered, but she did not give in.

Instead she counter-attacked, lavishing her son with attention, bringing him endless presents, sweets and his favourite dishes. It got to the stage when even someone as spoiled, ill mannered and self-centred as Jürgen began to feel suffocated, eager to get out of the house.

So when Krohn came to see Jürgen with one of his usual propositions – that he should come along to a political meeting – Jürgen gave a different reply to normal.

'Let's go,' he said, grabbing his overcoat.

Krohn, who had spent years trying to get Jürgen involved in politics, and who was a member of various nationalist parties, was delighted at his friend's decision.

'I'm sure it'll help take your mind off things,' he said, still ashamed at what had happened in the stables a week earlier, when seven had lost to one.

Jürgen didn't have high expectations. He was still taking sedatives for the pain his injury was causing him, and while they took the tram towards the city centre he nervously touched the bulky bandage he would have to wear for a few more days.

And then a patch for the rest of my life, all because of that wretched pig Paul, he thought, feeling extremely sorry for himself.

To top it all, his cousin had vanished into thin air. Two of his friends had been to spy on the stables and discovered that he no longer worked there. Jürgen suspected there would be no way of tracking Paul down in the short term, and this made his innards burn.

Lost in his hatred and self-pity, the baron's son barely heard what Krohn was saying on their way to the Hofbräuhaus.

'He's an extraordinary speaker. A great man. You'll see, Jürgen.'

Nor did he pay any attention to the magnificent setting, an old beer factory built for the kings of Bavaria more than three centuries earlier, nor to the frescoes on the walls. He sat next to Krohn on one of the benches in the enormous hall, and sipped his beer in gloomy silence.

When the speaker Krohn had enthused about stepped up on to the stage, Jürgen thought his friend had gone crazy. The little man walked as if he had a bee-sting on his arse, and looked nothing like a man with something to say. He exuded everything Jürgen despised, from his haircut and his moustache to his cheap crumpled suit.

Five minutes later, Jürgen was looking around in awe. The throng gathered in the hall, no fewer than a thousand people, stood in total silence. Lips barely parted except to whisper 'well said' or 'he's right'. The crowd's hands did the talking, marking each of the little man's pauses with loud clapping.

Almost against his will, Jürgen began to listen. He could barely understand the subject of the speech, because he lived on the periphery of the world that surrounded him, concerned only for his own amusement. He recognised loose fragments, snippets of phrases his father dropped in during breakfast as he hid behind his newspaper. Curses on the French, the English, the Russians. Complete nonsense, all of it.

Out of that confusion, however, Jürgen began to extract a simple meaning. Not from the words, which he barely understood, but from the emotion in the little man's voice, from his exaggerated gestures, from the clenched fists at the end of each line.

There had been a terrible *injustice.*

Germany had been *stabbed in the back.*

The *Jews* and the *Masons* had held that dagger in Versailles.

Germany was *lost.*

The blame for *poverty*, for *unemployment*, for *the bare feet of German children* fell to the Jews, who controlled the government in Berlin as if it were *an enormous brainless marionette.*

Jürgen, who didn't care in the slightest about the bare feet of German children; who didn't give a damn about Versailles; who never had concern for anyone who wasn't Jürgen von Schroeder, found himself on his feet within fifteen minutes applauding the speaker wildly. Before the speech had ended, he told himself he'd follow this man wherever he went.

After the meeting Krohn excused himself, saying he would be straight back. Jürgen fell into silence, until his friend tapped him on the back. He had brought over the speaker, who was looking poor and dishevelled again, his stare shifty and distrustful. But the baron's heir could no longer see him in that light, and stepped forward to greet him. Krohn said with a smile:

'My dear Jürgen, allow me to introduce you to Adolf Hitler.'

THE ENTERED APPRENTICE
1923

In which the initiate discovers a new reality with new rules

This is the entered apprentice's secret handshake, used so that brother Masons can identify one another as such. It involves squeezing the thumb against the top of the knuckle of the index finger of the person being greeted, who will return the action. Its secret name is BOAZ, from the column that represents the moon in Solomon's Temple. If a Mason has any doubts about another man who is claiming to be a brother Mason, he will ask him to spell this name out. Impostors begin with the letter B, while the true initiate starts with the third letter, thus: A – B – O – Z.

21

'Good afternoon, Frau Schmidt,' said Paul. 'What can I get you?'

The woman cast a quick look around her, trying to give the impression that she was considering her purchase, but the truth was that she'd set her eyes on the sack of potatoes in the hope of finding a price tag. It was useless. Fed up with having to change their prices daily, Paul had started memorising them every morning.

'Two kilos of potatoes, please,' she said, not daring to ask how much.

Paul began to pile the tubers on to the scale. Behind the lady a couple of boys were contemplating the sweets displayed in the window, their hands firmly stuffed in their empty pockets.

'They're sixty thousand marks a kilo,' boomed a rough voice from behind the counter.

The woman barely looked at Herr Ziegler, the owner of the grocer's shop, but her face went red.

'I'm sorry, madam . . . I don't have many potatoes left,' lied Paul. That morning he had worn himself out, piling up sacks and sacks of them out the back. 'A lot of our regular customers are yet to come. Would you mind if I gave you just one kilo?'

Her look of relief was so obvious that Paul had to turn away to hide his smile.

'Fine. I suppose I'll have to make do.'

Paul took a few potatoes from the bag until the scales settled at 1000 grammes. He didn't remove the last one, a particularly large specimen, from the bag completely, but kept it in his hand while he checked the weight, then replaced it as he handed the potatoes over.

The action didn't escape the woman, whose hand shook slightly as she paid and took the bag from the counter. As they were about to leave, Herr Ziegler called her back.

'Just one moment!'

The woman turned, pale.

'Yes?'

'Your son dropped this, madam,' said the shopkeeper, holding out the smallest boy's cap.

The woman murmured her thanks and practically ran out.

Herr Ziegler headed back behind the counter. He adjusted his little round glasses and continued to rub the cans of peas with a soft piece of cloth. The place was spotless, as Paul kept it very clean, and in those days nothing stayed in the store long enough to gather dust.

'I saw you,' said the shopkeeper, without looking up.

Paul took a newspaper out from under the counter and began to leaf through it. They would have no more customers that afternoon, as it was Thursday and most people's wages had dried up several days earlier. But the following day would be hell.

'I know, sir.'

'So why did you pretend?'

'It had to look as if you hadn't noticed I was giving her the potato, sir. Otherwise we'd have to give a free one to everybody.'

'That potato will be coming out of your wages,' said Ziegler, trying to sound threatening.

Paul nodded and buried himself in his reading once again. He had ceased to be afraid of the shopkeeper long ago, not only because he never carried out his threats but also because his gruff exterior was just a front. Paul smiled to himself, remembering that just a minute earlier he'd spotted Ziegler putting a fistful of sweets in the boy's cap.

'I don't know what the hell you find so interesting in those newspapers,' said the shopkeeper, shaking his head.

What Paul had been frantically searching for in the papers for some time now was some way of saving Herr Ziegler's business. If he didn't find one, the shop would be bankrupt within the fortnight.

Suddenly he stopped between two pages of the *Allgemeine Zeitung*. His heart somersaulted. It was right there, an idea, in a small two-column piece, almost ridiculous beside the large banner headlines announcing endless disasters and the possible collapse of the government. He could have skipped straight over it if he hadn't been searching for that very thing.

It was crazy.

It was impossible.

But if it works ... we'll be rich.

It would work. Paul was sure of it. The hardest thing would be to convince Herr Ziegler. An old conservative Prussian like him would never accept such a plan, not even in Paul's wildest dreams. Paul couldn't even imagine how to suggest it.

So I'd better think fast, he said to himself, biting his lip.

22

It had all started with the assassination of Minister Rathenau, a famous Jewish industrialist. The desperation into which Germany sank between 1922 and 1923, when two generations saw their values overturned completely, had begun one morning when three students drew up alongside his car and peppered him with bullets. On 24 June 1922, the terrible seed was sown which, more than two decades later, would result in more than fifty million dead.

Until that day, the Germans had thought that things were already going badly. But from that day, with the whole country transformed into a madhouse, all they wanted was to go back to the way things were before. Rathenau had been in charge of the foreign ministry. At that turbulent time, when Germany was in the hands of its creditors, it was a job that was even more important than the presidency of the republic.

The day Rathenau was killed, Paul wondered whether the students had done it because he was Jewish, because he was a politician, or to try to help Germany come to terms with the disaster of Versailles. The impossible reparation the country would have to pay – until 1984! – was plunging the population into destitution, and Rathenau was the last bastion of common sense.

After his death, the country started printing money simply in order to pay their debts. Did those responsible realise that every mark they printed devalued the rest? They probably did, but what else could they have done?

In June 1922, one mark could buy you two cigarettes; 272 marks, one US dollar. By March 1923, on the same day that Paul carelessly put an extra potato in Frau Schmidt's bag, five thousand marks were needed to buy a cigarette, and twenty thousand to go into a bank and come out with a pristine dollar bill.

Families struggled to keep up as the insanity spiralled. On Fridays, which were payday, the women would be waiting for their husbands at the factory door. Then, all at once, they'd besiege the shops and grocery stores, they'd flood the Viktualienmarkt on Marienplatz, they'd spend the last pfennig of the salary on absolute essentials. They'd return home laden with food and try to eke it out for the rest of the week. Not a lot of business was done in Germany on the other days of the week. Pockets were empty. And on a Thursday night, a BMW production supervisor had the same purchasing power as an old tramp dragging his stumps through the mud under the bridges of the Isar.

There were many who could not bear it.

Those who were old, who lacked imagination, who took too much for granted, they were the ones who suffered the most. Their minds could not cope with all these changes, with this back-to-front world. Many committed suicide. Others wallowed in their poverty.

Others changed.

Paul was one of those who changed.

After Herr Graf had dismissed him, Paul had a terrible month. He barely had time to overcome his anger at Jürgen's attack and the revelation of Alys's fate, or to devote more than a fleeting thought to the mystery of his father's death. Yet again, the need for survival was so acute that he had to suppress his own emotions. But the burning pain often flared up at night, populating his dreams with ghosts. Frequently he could not sleep, and on many mornings, as he tramped through the Munich streets in shabby, snow-filled shoes, he thought about dying.

Sometimes, when he returned to the boarding-house with no job, he'd catch himself looking at the Isar from Prinzregenten Brücke, his eyes empty. He wanted to throw himself into the icy waters, to allow the current to drag his body down to the Danube, and from there to the sea. That fantastical expanse of water which he'd never seen, but where he'd always thought his father had met his end.

On these occasions he had to find a reason not to climb up on the railing and jump. The image of his mother, waiting for him every night at the boarding-house, and the certainty that she wouldn't survive without him, prevented him from extinguishing the fire in his belly once and for all. At other times, it was the fire itself, and the reasons for it, that held him back.

Until at last there was a glimmer of hope. Although it came about through death.

One morning a delivery man collapsed at Paul's feet in the middle of the road. The empty wheelbarrow he'd been pushing tipped over on to its side. The wheels were still spinning as Paul crouched down and tried to help the man up, but he couldn't move. He gasped desperately for air, and his eyes were glassy. Another passer-by approached. He was wearing dark clothes and carried a leather case.

'Make way! I'm a doctor.'

For a while the doctor tried to revive the fallen man, but with no success. Finally he stood up, shaking his head.

'A heart attack, or an embolism. Hard to believe, in someone so young.'

Paul was looking at the dead man's face. He could only have been nineteen years old, maybe less.

Like me, thought Paul.

'Doctor, will you take care of the body?'

'I can't, I've got to get to the hospital. We'll wait for the police.'

When the officers arrived, Paul patiently described what had happened. The doctor corroborated his report.

'Would you mind if I took the wheelbarrow back to its owner?'

The officer glanced at the empty wheelbarrow then looked at Paul long and hard. He didn't like the idea of dragging the cart back to the police station.

'What's your name, pal?'

'Paul Reiner.'

'And why should I trust you, Paul Reiner?'

'Because I've got more to gain by taking this to the owner of the shop than if I try to sell these bits of badly nailed wood on the black market,' said Paul with absolute honesty.

'Very well. Tell him to get in touch with the police station. We'll need to know who his next of kin is. If he hasn't called on us in three hours you'll answer to me.'

The officer gave him a bill they'd found, the neat handwriting indicating the address of the grocer's – a street near the Isartor – with a list of the last things the dead boy had transported.

1/2 kilo of coffee

3 kilos of potatoes

1 bag of lemons

1 can of Kruntz soup

1/4 kilo of salt

2 bottles of corn spirit

When Paul arrived at the shop with the wheelbarrow and asked for the dead boy's job, Herr Ziegler flashed him a distrustful look not dissimilar to the one he gave Paul six months later when the young man explained his plan to save them from ruin.

'We should transform the shop into a bank.'

The shopkeeper dropped the cloth he was using to clean the jam jars. One of them would have shattered on the floor if Paul hadn't managed to catch it mid-flight.

'But what are you talking about? Have you been drinking?' he said, staring at the huge circles under the boy's eyes.

'No, sir,' said Paul, who had been up all night turning the plan round and round in his mind. He'd left his room at dawn and taken up position at the door of the town hall half an hour before it opened. Then he'd run from window to window collecting information about permits, taxes and conditions. He had returned with a thick cardboard file. 'I know it might seem mad, but it's not. Right now, money has no value. Wages go up daily, and we have to calculate our prices every morning.'

'Yes, and that reminds me, this morning I had to do it all on my own,' said the shopkeeper, annoyed. 'You can't imagine how hard it was. And on a Friday! Two hours from now the shop's going to be heaving.'

'I know, sir. And we have to do everything we can to get rid of all the stock today. This afternoon I'm going to talk to several of our customers, offering them merchandise in exchange for work, because the work has to be done on Monday. On Tuesday morning we'll go through a municipal inspection, and on Wednesday we open.'

Ziegler looked as though Paul had asked him to smear his body with jam and walk naked across Marienplatz.

'Absolutely not. This shop has been here for seventy-three years. My great-grandfather started it, and then passed it on to my grandfather, who passed it on to my father, who eventually gave it to me.'

Paul saw the alarm in the shopkeeper's eyes. He knew he was one step away from being fired for insubordination and insanity. So he decided to go all in.

'That's a lovely story, sir. But regrettably, in a fortnight, when someone whose surname isn't Ziegler gets hold of the shop at a creditors' meeting, all that tradition will count for shit.'

The shopkeeper raised an accusing finger, ready to scold Paul for his language, but then remembered the situation he was in and collapsed into a chair. His debts had been accumulating since the beginning of the crisis, debts which, unlike so many others, hadn't simply vanished in a puff of smoke. The positive side of all the madness – for some people – was that those with a mortgage whose interest rates were calculated annually had been able to settle their obligations quickly, given the wild fluctuation of the Deutschmark. Unfortunately, those like Ziegler who had committed a share of their income, not a fixed amount in cash, could only end up losing.

'I don't understand, Paul. How is this going to save my business?'

The young man brought him a glass of water then showed him the cutting from the previous day's newspaper. Paul had read it so many times that the ink had become smudged in places. 'It's an article by a university professor. He says that, at a time like this, when people can't rely on money, we have to look to the past. To the time before money. To bartering.'

'But . . .'

'Please, sir, give me a moment. Unfortunately no one can go around trading a bedside table or three bottles of spirits for other things, and the pawnshops are overflowing. So we have to take refuge in promises. In dividends.'

'I don't understand,' said the shopkeeper, who was beginning to feel dizzy.

'Stocks, Herr Ziegler. The stock exchange will rise out of this. Stocks will replace money. And we'll be selling them.'

Ziegler gave in.

Paul barely slept for the next five nights. Convincing tradesmen – carpenters, plasterers, cabinetmakers – to take products away for free this Friday in exchange for working over the weekend wasn't difficult in the least. In fact some were so grateful that Paul had to offer his handkerchief more than once.

We must be in a real mess, when a sturdy plumber bursts out crying when you offer him a sausage in exchange for an hour's work, he thought.

The main difficulty was the bureaucracy, but even in this respect Paul was lucky. He'd studied the guidelines and regulations the civil servants had brought to his attention until he had clauses coming out of his ears. His biggest fear was that he would come across some phrase that would dash all his hopes to the ground. After scribbling down pages and pages of notes in a little book in which he puzzled out the steps that needed to be taken, the requirements for the creation of ZieglerBank had come down to two:

1) The director had to be a German citizen aged over twenty-one.
2) A guarantee of half a million German marks had to be deposited at the offices of the town hall.

The first was simple: Herr Ziegler would be the director, though it was already quite clear to Paul that he should remain closed away in the office as much as possible. The second ... A year earlier half a million marks would have been an astronomical sum, a way of ensuring that only people who were solvent could start a business that relied on trust. Today half a million marks was a joke.

'Nobody has updated the figure!' cried Paul, leaping around the shop, startling the carpenters, who had already begun to tear the shelves off the walls.

I wonder whether the civil servants wouldn't prefer a couple of hams, thought Paul, amused. *At least they could put them to some use.*

23

The lorry was open, and the men travelling in the back had no protection from the night air.

Almost all of them were silent, focusing on what was about to happen. Their brown shirts barely kept out the cold, but that didn't matter, as they would soon be on the move.

Jürgen crouched down and started beating the metal floor of the lorry with his cudgel. He'd acquired this habit on his first outing, when his comrades still regarded him with some scepticism. The SA, the Nazi Party's 'stormtroopers', was composed of hardened ex-soldiers, people from the lowest classes, who could barely read a paragraph aloud without stammering. Their first response to the appearance of this elegant young man – the son of a baron, no less! – was rejection. And when Jürgen had first used the floor of the lorry as a drum, one of his companions had given him the finger.

'Sending a telegram to the baroness, eh, boy?'

The rest had laughed nastily.

That night he'd felt ashamed. Tonight, however, as he began to strike the floor, all the others were quick to follow him. The rhythm was slow at first, measured, distinct, the blows perfectly synchronised. But as the lorry approached its target, an inn close to the central train station, the pounding grew until it was deafening, a roar of noise that filled them all with adrenalin.

Jürgen smiled. It hadn't been easy to win their trust, but now he felt he had them all in the palm of his hand. When, almost a year earlier, he had first watched Adolf Hitler speak and insisted on a party secretary filling in his membership to the NSDAP then and there, Krohn had been delighted. But when, a few days later, Jürgen had applied to join the SA, that delight had turned to disappointment.

'What the hell do you have in common with those brown gorillas? You're intelligent, you could have a career in politics. And that patch on your eye . . . If you start the appropriate rumours, you could make that your calling card. We can say you lost your eye defending the Ruhr.'

The baron's son paid him no attention. He had joined the SA on impulse, but there was a certain subconscious logic to what he had done. He was attracted to the brutality inherent in the Nazis' paramilitary wing, their pride as a group and the impunity for violence that this offered him. A group into which he hadn't fitted to begin with, and where he had been the target of insults and jibes such as 'Baron Cyclops' and 'One-eyed Pansy'.

Intimidated, Jürgen had put aside the thuggish attitude he'd assumed with his school friends. These were real tough guys, and they'd have closed ranks immediately if he'd tried to gain anything by force. Instead he had won their respect bit by bit, demonstrating his lack of scruples each time they, or their enemy, had a meeting.

A squeal of brakes drowned out the violent sound of the cudgels. The lorry stopped abruptly.

'Get out, get out!'

The Brownshirts crowded together at the back of the lorry. Then twenty pairs of black boots tramped over the wet paving-stones. One of the stormtroopers slipped in a puddle of dirty water, and Jürgen hastened to offer him an arm to help him up. He'd learned that gestures like this would win him points.

The building that stood opposite them had no name, only the word TAVERN painted over the door, with a red Bavarian hat drawn alongside. It was often used as a meeting place by a division of the Communist Party, and at that very moment one such meeting was coming to an end. More than thirty people were inside, listening to a speech. On hearing the squeal of the lorry's brakes a number of them raised their heads, but it was too late. The tavern had no back door.

The Brownshirts entered in ordered ranks, making as much noise as possible. A waiter hid behind the bar, terrified, while the first ones in seized beer glasses and plates from the tables and hurled them at the counter, the mirror above it and the shelves of bottles.

'What are you doing?' asked a short man, presumably the tavern's owner.

'We've come to break up an illegal meeting,' said the head of the SA platoon, stepping forward with an incongruous smile.

'You have no authority!'

The head of the platoon raised his cudgel and hit the man in the stomach. He fell to the ground with a groan. The leader gave him a couple more kicks before turning to his men.

'Fall in!'

Jürgen immediately moved to the front. He always did this, only to take a discreet step back at the crucial moment in order to let someone else lead the charge – or take a bullet or blade. Firearms were now forbidden in Germany – this Germany that had had its teeth removed by the Allies – but many war veterans still had their regulation pistol or a weapon they had taken from the enemy.

In formation, standing shoulder to shoulder, they advanced towards the back of the tavern. The communists, scared out of their wits, began to throw anything they could get their hands on at their enemy. The man marching next to Jürgen was struck full in the face by a glass jug. He staggered, but those marching behind caught him, and another came forward to take his place in the front rank.

'Sons of bitches! Go suck your Führer's cock!' shouted a young man in a leather cap, picking up a bench.

The Brownshirts were less than three metres away, within easy reach of any furniture thrown at them, so Jürgen chose this moment to fake a stumble. A man came forward and joined the front rank.

Just in time. Benches flew across the room, there was a groan and the man who'd just taken Jürgen's place slumped forward, his head split open.

'Ready?' cried the head of the platoon. 'For Hitler and Germany!'

'Hitler and Germany!' the others cried in chorus.

The two groups charged at each other, like children playing some kind of game. Jürgen dodged a giant in mechanic's overalls who was heading towards him, striking his knees as he passed. The mechanic tumbled, and those behind Jürgen began to beat him mercilessly.

Jürgen continued his advance. He jumped over an upturned chair and kicked a table, which smashed against the hip of an old man wearing glasses. He fell to the floor, dragging the table with him. There were still some scribbled bits of paper in his hand, so the baron's son deduced that this must be the speaker they had come to interrupt. He didn't care. He didn't even know the old man's name.

Jürgen went straight over to him, taking care to tread on him with both feet as he made his way towards his real target.

The young man in the leather cap was fending off two Brownshirts using one of the benches. The first of the Brownshirts tried to outflank him, but the young man tipped the bench towards him and managed to get him in the neck, knocking him down. The other Brownshirt lashed out with his cudgel, trying to catch the man unawares, but the young communist ducked and managed to bury his elbow in the Brownshirt's kidney. As the Brownshirt doubled over, contorted with pain, the man broke the bench over his back.

So this one knows how to fight, thought the baron's son.

Normally he would have left the toughest opponents for someone else to deal with, but something about this skinny young man with sunken eyes offended Jürgen.

He looked at Jürgen defiantly.

'Come on then, you Nazi whore. Afraid you'll break a nail?'

Jürgen sucked in his breath, but he was too cunning to allow himself to be affected by the insult and he counter-attacked.

'I'm not surprised you're so keen on the reds, you scrawny little shit. That Marx's beard looks just like your mother's backside.'

The young man's face lit up with rage and, hoisting up the remains of the bench, he charged at Jürgen.

Jürgen had planted himself sideways-on and he waited for the attack. As the man lunged at him, Jürgen moved aside and the communist fell to the floor, losing his cap. Jürgen hit him in the back with his cudgel three times in quick succession, not very hard, but enough to take his breath away while still allowing him to get to his knees. The young man tried to crawl away, which was exactly what Jürgen wanted. He drew back his right leg and kicked hard. The toe-capped boot struck the man's stomach, lifting him more than half a metre off the ground. He fell back, struggling to breathe.

With a smile, Jürgen laid into him viciously. The man's ribs crunched under the blows and when Jürgen stood on his arm it snapped like a dry branch.

Grabbing the young man by the hair, Jürgen forced him to rise.

'Try saying what you said about the Führer now, communist scum!'

'Go to hell!' the boy babbled.

'You still want to say stupid things like that?' shouted Jürgen, incredulous.

Grabbing the boy even more tightly by the hair, he raised his cudgel and aimed it at his victim's mouth.

Once.

Twice.

Three times.

The boy's teeth were nothing but a handful of bloody remains on the tavern's wooden floor and his face was swollen. In an instant the aggression that had fed Jürgen's muscles ceased to flow. Finally he understood why he had chosen that particular man.

There was something of his cousin in him.

He let go of the communist's hair, and watched as he fell limply to the floor.

He doesn't look much like anyone any more, Jürgen thought.

He raised his eyes and saw that all around him the fighting had stopped. The only ones left standing were the Brownshirts, who were watching him with a mixture of approval and fear.

'Let's get out of here!' shouted the head of the platoon.

Back in the lorry, a stormtrooper Jürgen had never seen before, and who hadn't travelled with them, sat down beside him. The baron's son barely looked at his companion. After such a violent episode he would usually sink into a state of melancholic withdrawal, and he didn't like anyone to disturb him. Which was why he snarled with displeasure when the other man spoke to him in a low voice.

'What's your name?'

'Jürgen von Schroeder,' he replied reluctantly.

'So it is you. They told me about you. I came here today specially to meet you. My name's Julius Schreck.'

Jürgen noticed the subtle differences in the man's uniform. He wore an insignia with a skull and crossbones, and a black tie.

'To meet me? Why?'

'I'm setting up a special group . . . people with guts, skill, intelligence. Without any bourgeois scruples.'

'How do you know I have those things?'

'I saw you in action back there. You went about it cleverly, not like the rest of this cannon fodder. And then there's the matter of your family, of course. Having you on our team would give us prestige. It would distinguish us from the riff-raff.'

'What is it you want?'

'I want you to join my *Stosstrupp*. The élite of the SA, who answer only to the Führer.'

24

Ever since spotting Paul at the other end of the cabaret club Alys had been having a terrible night. It was the last place she had expected to find him. She looked again, just to be sure, as the lights and smoke could lead to some confusion, but her eyes had not deceived her.

What the hell is he doing here?

Her first impulse was to hide the Kodak Brownie behind her back, ashamed, but she couldn't maintain that position for long as the camera and flash were too heavy.

Besides, I'm working. Hell, that's something I should feel proud of.

'Hey, nice body! Take my photo, gorgeous!'

Alys smiled, raised the flashbulb – supported on a long stick – and squeezed the trigger so that it went off without her having to use up any film. The two drunks obstructing her view of Paul's tables tumbled sideways. Although she had to recharge the flash with magnesium powder every once in a while, this was still the most efficient way of getting rid of any bother.

A lot of people buzzed around her on nights like this, when she would have to take two or three hundred photos of the customers at the BeldaKlub. Once they had been developed, the owner would choose half a dozen to put up on the wall by the entrance, shots showing customers living it up with the club's dancing-girls. The best photos – according to the owner – were the ones taken in the early hours of the morning, when you could frequently witness the biggest wastrels drinking champagne from the girls' shoes. Alys detested the whole place: the noisy music, the sequinned suits, the provocative songs, the alcohol and the people who consumed it in vast quantity. But it was her job.

She hesitated before approaching Paul. She felt she wasn't looking particularly pretty, in that dark blue second-hand suit with a little hat that didn't quite match, and yet she continued to attract the losers like a magnet. She'd long since come to the conclusion that men loved being in the centre of her lens and she decided to use this fact to break the ice with Paul. She still felt ashamed of the way her father had thrown him out of the house, and a slight unease at the lie she'd been told about him keeping the money.

I'll play a joke on him. I'll approach him with the camera covering my face, I'll take the photo and then I'll reveal to him who I am. I'm sure he'll be pleased.

She set off with a smile.

Eight months earlier Alys had been out on the street looking for work.

Unlike Paul, her search hadn't been desperate, as she had enough money to last her a few months. All the same, it had been tough. The only jobs for women going – called out from street corners or whispered in back rooms – were as prostitutes or mistresses, and that was a path down which Alys wasn't prepared to go under any circumstances.

Not that, and I won't go back home either, she swore.

She thought about travelling to another city. Hamburg, Düsseldorf, Berlin. The news that arrived from those places, however, was as bad as what was happening in Munich, or worse. And there was something – the hope of meeting a certain someone again, perhaps – that held her back. But as her reserves dwindled, Alys increasingly began to despair. Then one afternoon, walking down Agnesstrasse in search of a sewing workshop she had been told about, Alys saw a notice on a shop window.

ASSISTANT REQUIRED

WOMEN NEED NOT APPLY

She didn't even check what sort of business it was. She pushed open the door indignantly and marched up to the only person behind the counter – a thin, older man, with dramatically receding grey hair.

'Afternoon, Fräulein.'

'Good afternoon. I've come about the job.'

The little man looked at her intently.

'Might I hazard a guess that you do actually know how to read, Fräulein?'

'Yes, although I always have difficulty with any nonsense.'

At that, the man's face changed. His mouth creased up in amusement, revealing a pleasant smile, which was followed by a laugh.

'You're hired!'

Alys looked at him, utterly thrown. She'd gone into the place ready to rub the owner's face in his ridiculous sign, and thinking that all she'd achieve would be to make a fool of herself.

'Surprised?'

'Quite surprised, yes.'

'You see, Fräulein ...'

'Alys Tannenbaum.'

'August Muntz,' the man said, with an elegant bow. 'You see, Fräulein Tannenbaum, I put up that sign so that a woman just like you would respond. The job I'm offering requires technical skill, presence of mind, and above all a good deal of insolence and daring. It would appear you possess the last two qualities, and the first can be taught, especially with the benefit of my own experience ...'

'What precisely is it that you want me to do?' asked Alys suspiciously.

'Isn't it obvious?' the man said, gesturing around him. Alys looked at the shop for the first time, and saw that it was a photography studio. 'Take photos.'

While Paul had changed with each job he'd taken on, Alys had been completely transformed by hers. The young woman had instantly fallen in love with photography. She'd never been behind a camera before, but once she had learned the basics she understood there was nothing else she wanted to do with her life. She was particularly fond of the darkroom, where the chemicals were mixed in trays. She couldn't tear her eyes away from the image as it began to appear on the paper, as features and faces became distinct.

She immediately hit it off with the photographer too. Although the sign on the door said 'Muntz and Sons', Alys soon discovered that there were no sons, nor would there ever be. August lived in a flat above the shop with a delicate, pale young man he called 'my nephew Ernst'. Alys spent long evenings playing backgammon with the two of them, and as time went on her smile returned.

There was only one aspect of the job she didn't like, which was precisely what August had hired her for. The owner of a nearby cabaret club – August confessed to Alys that the man had been a former lover of his – had offered a good sum of money to have a photographer on the premises three nights a week.

'He'd like it to be me, of course. But I think it's best if a pretty girl shows up ... one who won't allow herself to be bullied,' said August with a wink.

The club owner was happy. The photos at the entrance to his establishment helped to spread the word about the BeldaKlub until it became one of the highlights of Munich nightlife. It couldn't compare to the likes of Berlin, of course, but in dark times any business based on alcohol and sex is bound to succeed. It was a widely spread rumour that many customers would spend their entire salaries in five frenzied hours before resorting to the trigger, the rope or the bottle of pills.

As she approached Paul, Alys trusted that he wouldn't be one of these customers out for a final fling.

No doubt he's come with a friend. Or out of curiosity, she thought. After all, everyone was coming to the BeldaKlub these days, even if it was only to waste hours sipping a single beer. The barmen were understanding sorts, and they were known to accept engagement rings in exchange for a couple of pints.

As she drew near she held the camera up to her face. There were five people at the table, two men and three women. On the tablecloth were several half-empty or overturned bottles of champagne, and a heap of food that was almost untouched.

'Hey, Paul! You've got to pose for posterity!' said the man standing next to Alys.

Paul looked up. He was wearing a black tuxedo that didn't sit at all well on his shoulders, and a bow tie that was undone and hung down over his shirt. When he spoke his voice was thick and his words slurred.

'Hear that, girls? Put a smile on those faces.'

The two women on either side of Paul were wearing silvery party dresses and hats to match. One of them grabbed him by the chin, forced him to look at her and planted a sloppy French kiss just as the shutter came down. The surprised recipient returned the kiss, and then burst out laughing.

'See? *They* really put a smile on your face!' said his friend, braying with laughter.

Alys was astonished to see this, and the Kodak almost slipped from her hands. She wanted to vomit. This drunk, just another one of the kind she had despised night after night for weeks, was so far from her image of the shy coal-bearer that Alys couldn't believe it was really Paul.

And yet it was.

Through the haze of alcohol, the young man suddenly recognised her and unsteadily got to his feet.

'Alys!'

The man who was with him turned to her and raised his glass.

'You know each other?'

'I thought I knew him,' said Alys, coldly.

'Superb! Then you ought to know that your friend is the most successful banker in Isartor ... We sell more shares than any of the other banks that have been popping up lately! I'm his proud accountant ... Come on, drink a toast with us.'

Alys felt a wave of scorn run through her body. She'd heard all about the new banks. Almost all of those set up in recent months had been established by young people, and a lot of student types came to the club every night to burn away their earnings on champagne and whores before the money lost its value completely.

'When my father told me you'd taken the money I didn't believe him. How wrong I was. Now I can see it's the only thing you're interested in,' she said, turning away.

'Alys, wait ...' stammered the young man, embarrassed. He stumbled around the table and tried to grab her hand.

Alys turned and gave him a slap that rang out like a bell. Although Paul tried to save himself by clutching at the tablecloth, he toppled over and ended up on the floor amid a shower of broken bottles and the laughter of the three chorus-girls.

'By the way,' Alys said as she walked off, 'in that tuxedo you still look like a waiter.'

Paul used the chair to lever himself up, just in time to see Alys's back disappearing into the crowd. His friend the accountant was now leading the girls to the dance-floor. Suddenly an arm grabbed Paul firmly and guided him into the chair.

'Looks like you've rubbed her up the wrong way, eh?'

The man who'd helped him seemed vaguely familiar.

'Who the hell are you?'

'I'm a friend of your father's, Paul. Someone who right now is wondering whether you're worthy of sharing his name.'

'What do you know about my father?'

The man pulled out a card and put it in the inside pocket of Paul's tuxedo.

'Come see me when you've sobered up.'

25

Sebastian Keller /
bookseller / Kaufingerstrasse,
next to St Michael's church

Paul looked up from the card and contemplated the sign above the bookshop, still not understanding what he was doing there.

The shop was just a few steps from Marienplatz, in the tiny heart of Munich. This was where Schwabing's butchers and hawkers gave way to watchmakers, milliners and shops selling walking-sticks. There was even a small cinema close to Keller's establishment that was showing Murnau's *Nosferatu*, more than a year after it had first come out. It was the afternoon, and they must already have been halfway through the second screening. Paul pictured the projectionist in his booth, changing the worn reels of film one by one. He felt sorry for him. He had slipped in to see that film – the first and only film he'd seen – in a cinema close to the boarding-house, when the whole town had been talking about it. He hadn't much liked the ugly copy of Bram Stoker's *Dracula*. For him, the true emotion of the story resided in its words and its silence, in the white that surrounded the black letters on the page. The cinema version seemed rather too simple, like a jigsaw with only two pieces.

Paul entered the bookshop cautiously, but soon forgot his misgivings as he studied the volumes scrupulously arranged on the floor-to-ceiling bookcases and on the large tables beside the window. There was no counter in sight.

He was leafing through a first edition of *Death in Venice* when he heard a voice behind him.

'Thomas Mann's not a bad choice, but I'm sure you've read that one already.'

Paul turned. There was Keller, smiling at him. His hair was completely white, he sported an old-fashioned goatee, and from time to time he would scratch his large ears, drawing even more attention to them. Paul felt that he knew this man, though he was unable to say how.

'Yes, I've read it, but in a hurry. I was lent it by someone staying in the boarding-house where I live. Books don't normally stay in my hands for long, however much I want to reread them.'

'Ah. But don't reread, Paul, you're too young, and people who reread tend to fill themselves with inadequate wisdom too quickly. For now you should read everything you can, as wide a variety as possible. Only when you get to my age will you find that rereading isn't a waste of time.'

Paul took another good look at him. Keller was well past fifty, though his back was as straight as a rod and his body was trim in an old-fashioned three-piece suit. It was his white hair that gave him his venerable appearance, though Paul suspected that in reality it might have been dyed. Suddenly he realised where he'd seen this man before.

'You were at Jürgen's birthday party, four years ago.'

'You have a good memory, Paul.'

'You told me to leave as soon as I could ... that she was waiting outside,' Paul said, sadly.

'I remember you rescuing the girl with absolute clarity, right in the middle of the ballroom. In my day I had my moments too ... And my low points, although I never made as big a mistake as the one I saw you making yesterday, Paul.'

'Don't remind me. How the hell was I supposed to know she was there? It's been two years since I last saw her!'

'Well then, I think the right question here is what the hell were you doing getting yourself as drunk as a sailor?'

Paul shuffled his feet uncomfortably. He was embarrassed to be discussing these things with a complete stranger, but at the same time he experienced a peculiar calm in the bookseller's company.

'Anyway,' Keller went on, 'I don't want to torture you, as the bags under your eyes and your pale face tell me you've tortured yourself enough already.'

'You said you wanted to talk to me about my father,' Paul said, anxiously.

'No, that wasn't what I said. I said you should come and see me.'

'Then why?'

This time it was Keller's turn to remain silent. He led Paul to the window and pointed over to the church of St Michael, just across from the bookshop. A bronze plaque detailing the family tree of the Wittelsbach dynasty stood above the statue of the archangel who gave his name to the building. In the afternoon sun, the statue's shadows were long and threatening.

'Look . . . three and half centuries of splendour. And that's just a short prologue. In 1825 Ludwig the First decided to transform our city into the new Athens. Full of light, space and harmony in its avenues and boulevards. Now look a little lower, Paul.'

At the door to the church beggars had gathered, lining up to receive the soup that the parish distributed at sunset. The queue had only just started to form and already it reached farther than Paul could see from the shop window. He wasn't surprised to spot war veterans, still in their grubby uniforms, which had been forbidden for almost five years now. Nor was he shocked by the appearance of the tramps, whose faces had been imprinted by poverty and drink. What did surprise him was seeing dozens of adult men dressed in worn suits but with their shirts perfectly ironed, all of them with no sign of an overcoat in spite of the strong wind that June evening.

The overcoat of a family man who has to go out every day to find bread for his children, that's always one of the last things to be pawned, thought Paul, nervously moving his hands in his own coat pockets. He'd bought the coat second-hand, surprised to find such good-quality fabric for the price of an average-sized cheese.

Just like the tuxedo.

'Five years after the fall of the monarchy: terror, killings in the streets, hunger, poverty. Which version of Munich do you prefer, lad?'

'The real one, I suppose.'

Keller looked at him, evidently pleased with his response. Paul noticed that his attitude had changed slightly, as though the question had been a test for something much greater still to come.

'I met Hans Reiner many years ago. I don't remember the exact date, but I think it was around 1895, because he came into the bookshop and bought a copy of Verne's *Castle of the Carpathians*, which had just come out.'

'He liked reading, too?' asked Paul, unable to hide his emotion. He knew so little about the man who had given him life that any flicker of resemblance filled him with a mixture of pride and confusion, like the echo of another time. He felt a blind need to trust the bookseller, to extract from his head any trace of the father he had never been able to meet.

'He was a real bookworm! Your father and I talked for a couple of hours that first afternoon. That was a lot of time in those days, as my bookshop was full from opening to closing-time, not deserted like it is now. We discovered common interests, such as poetry. Although he was very intelligent, he was rather slow with words, and he marvelled at what people like Hölderlin and Rilke could do. Once he even asked me to help him with a little poem he'd written for your mother.'

'I remember her telling me about that poem,' said Paul, sadly, 'though she never let me read it.'

'Perhaps it's still in your father's papers?' suggested the bookseller.

'Unfortunately the few possessions we had were left in the house where we used to live. We had to leave in a hurry.'

'A pity. Anyway ... every time he came to Munich we'd spend interesting evenings together. That was how I first came to hear of the Grand Lodge of the Rising Sun.'

'What's that?'

The bookseller lowered his voice.

'Do you know what the Masons are, Paul?'

The young man looked at him in surprise.

'The newspapers say they're a powerful secret sect.'

'Run by Jews who control the fate of the world?' said Keller, his voice full of irony. 'I've heard that story many times, too, Paul. All the more so these days, when people are looking for someone to blame for all the bad things that are happening.'

'So what's the truth?'

'The Masons are a secret society, not a sect, made up of select men who seek enlightenment and the triumph of morality in the world.'

'By select do you mean powerful?'

'No. These men choose themselves. No Mason is allowed to ask a Profane to become a Mason. It's the Profane who has to ask, just as I asked your father to grant me admission to the lodge.'

'My father was a Mason?' asked Paul, astonished.

'Wait a moment,' said Keller. He locked the shop door, flipped the sign to CLOSED and then went to the back room. On his return he showed Paul an old studio photograph. It showed a young Hans Reiner, Keller and three other people Paul didn't recognise, all of them looking fixedly into the camera. Their rigid pose was common to pictures from the beginning of the century, when models had to remain still for at least a minute so the photo didn't blur. One of the men was holding up a strange symbol which Paul remembered having seen years earlier in his uncle's study: a square and a compass facing one another with a big G in the middle.

'Your father was the keeper of the temple of the Grand Lodge of the Rising Sun. The keeper ensures that the door to the temple is closed before the Work can begin ... In the language of the Profane, before beginning the ritual.'

'I thought you said it wasn't a sect.'

'As Masons, we believe in a supernatural being, whom we call the Great Architect of the Universe. That's as far as the dogma goes. Each Mason venerates the Great Architect in whatever way he sees fit. In my lodge there are Jews, Catholics and Protestants, although this isn't talked about openly. There are two subjects that are forbidden in the lodge: religion and politics.'

'Did the lodge have anything to do with my father's death?'

The bookseller paused for a while before answering.

'I don't know very much about his death, except that what you've been told is a lie. The day I saw him for the last time he sent a message to me and we met close to the bookshop. We talked hurriedly, in the middle of the street. He told me he was in danger, and that he feared for your life and your mother's. A fortnight later I heard a rumour that his ship had gone down in the colonies.'

Paul wondered whether he should tell Keller about his cousin's last words, about the night his father had visited the Schroeders' mansion, and the shot Eduard had heard, but he decided against it. He'd given the evidence a great deal of thought, but couldn't find anything conclusive to prove that his uncle had been responsible for his father's disappearance. Deep in his heart he believed there was something to the idea, but until he was quite sure he didn't want to share that burden with anyone.

'He also asked me to give you something when you were old enough. I've been looking for you for months,' Keller went on.

Paul felt his heart somersault.

'What is it?'

'I don't know, Paul.'

'Well, what are you waiting for? Give it to me!' said Paul, almost shouting.

The bookseller shot Paul a cool look to make it clear that he didn't like people giving him orders in his own home.

'Do you think you're worthy of your father's legacy, Paul? The man I saw the other day at the BeldaKlub didn't seem to be any better than a drunken lout.'

Paul opened his mouth to reply, to tell this man about the hunger and cold he'd endured when they were thrown out of the Schroeders' mansion. Of the exhaustion of hauling coal up and down damp staircases. Of the desperation of having nothing, and knowing that in spite of all the barriers you still had to continue your search. Of the tempting call of the Isar's cold waters. But finally he repented, because what he'd suffered did not give him the right to behave as he'd done over the previous weeks.

If anything, it made him even more guilty.

'Herr Keller ... if I belonged to the lodge, would that make me more worthy?'

'Were you to ask for it from the bottom of your heart that would be a start. But I assure you it won't be easy, not even for someone like you.'

Paul swallowed before replying.

'In that case I humbly ask for your help. I want to be a Mason, like my father.'

26

Alys finished moving the paper around in the developing tray then placed it in the fixing solution. Looking at the image made her feel strange. Proud, on the one hand, because of the photograph's technical perfection. That tart's gesture as she held on to Paul. The shine in her eyes, his eyes half closed . . . The details made you feel you could almost touch the scene, but despite her professional pride, the image gnawed at Alys's insides.

Lost in her thoughts inside the darkroom, she barely registered the sound of the bell announcing a new visitor to the shop. She looked up, however, when she heard a familiar voice. She peered through the red glass spyhole, which gave a clear view of the store, and her eyes confirmed what her ears and her heart had told her.

'Good afternoon,' Paul called out again, approaching the counter.

Aware that the business of selling shares could be exceedingly short lived, Paul still lodged in the boarding-house with his mother, so he had taken a long detour in order to call at Muntz and Sons. He had obtained the address of the photographer's studio from one of the workers at the club, having loosened his tongue with a few banknotes.

Under his arm he was carrying a carefully wrapped package. It contained a thick black book, embossed in gold. Sebastian had told him it contained the basics that any Profane should know before becoming a Mason. First Hans Reiner and then Sebastian had been initiated with it. Paul was itching with desire to run his eyes across those lines that his father had also read, but there was something more urgent to be done first.

'We're closed,' the photographer said to Paul.

'Really? I thought there were ten minutes left until closing-time,' said Paul, glancing suspiciously at the clock on the wall.

'To you, we're closed.'

'To me?'

'You're not Paul Reiner, then?'

'How do you know my name?'

'You fit the description. Tall, thin, glassy eyed, handsome as the devil. There were other adjectives too, but best if I don't repeat them.'

There was a crash from the back room. Hearing it, Paul tried to look over the photographer's shoulder.

'Is Alys in there?'

'Must be the cat.'

'That didn't sound like a cat.'

'No, it sounded like an empty developing tray being dropped on the floor. But Alys isn't here, so it must be the cat.'

There was another crash, this time louder.

'There goes another one. Just as well they're made of metal,' said August Muntz, lighting a cigarette with an elegant flourish.

'You'd best go and feed that cat. It seems hungry.'

'Furious, rather.'

'I can understand why,' said Paul, lowering his head.

'Listen, my friend, she did leave something for you.'

The photographer held out a photograph to him, face down. Paul turned it over and saw before his eyes a slightly blurred picture, taken in a park.

'It's a woman asleep on a bench in the Englischer Garten.'

August took a long drag on his cigarette.

'The day she took this photograph ... it was her first outing on her own. I lent her a camera to go round the city looking for an image that would move me. She spent her time walking round a park, like all beginners. Suddenly she spotted this woman sitting on a bench and the woman's stillness appealed to Alys. She took a photo and then went to thank her. The woman didn't reply and when Alys touched her shoulder, she fell to the ground.'

'She was dead,' said Paul, horrified, suddenly understanding the truth of what he was looking at.

'Starved to death,' replied August, taking one final drag then stubbing the cigarette out in an ashtray.

Paul gripped the counter for a few moments, his gaze fixed on the photograph. Eventually he handed it back.

'Thank you for showing me this. Please tell Alys that if she goes to this address the day after tomorrow,' he said, taking a piece of paper and a pencil from the counter and making a note, 'she'll see just how well I've understood.'

A minute after Paul had left, Alys came out of the darkroom.

'I hope you haven't dented those trays. Otherwise you're going to be the one hammering them back into shape.'

'You said too much, August. And that thing with the photo . . . I didn't ask you to give him anything.'

'He's in love with you.'

'How do you know?'

'I know a lot about men in love. Especially how hard it is to find them.'

'Things started off badly between us,' said Alys, shaking her head.

'So? The day begins at midnight, in the middle of darkness. From then on, everything is light.'

27

There was an enormous queue outside ZieglerBank.

The previous night, when she'd gone to bed in the room she rented not far from the studio, Alys had decided that she wasn't going to see Paul. She repeated this to herself as she got ready, as she tried on her collection of hats – which consisted of only two – and as she took a tram she never usually took. She was completely surprised to find herself by the queue for the bank.

As she approached she noticed that there were in fact two queues. One led to the bank, the other to the entrance next door. People were coming out of the second door with smiles on their faces, carrying bags bulging with sausages, bread and enormous stalks of celery.

Paul was in the place next door with another man who was weighing up vegetables and hams and attending to his customers. When he saw Alys, Paul pushed his way through the crowd of people waiting to get into the store.

'The tobacconist's shop next to us had to shut when the business went under. We've reopened it and made it into another grocer's shop for Herr Ziegler. He's a happy man.'

'The people are happy, too, from what I can see.'

'We sell merchandise at cost price, and we sell on credit to all the bank's customers. We're eating up every last pfennig of our profits, but the workers and pensioners, everyone who can't keep up with the ridiculous pace of inflation, are all very grateful to us. Today the dollar's at over three million marks.'

'You're losing a fortune.'

Paul shrugged.

'We'll be giving out soup to those who need it in the evenings, starting next week. It won't be like the Jesuits, because we'll only have enough for five hundred portions, but we've already got a group of volunteers.'

Alys was looking at him, her eyes half closed.

'You're doing all this for me?'

'I'm doing it because I can. Because it's the right thing to do. Because I was struck by the photo of the woman in the park. Because this city's going to hell. And yes, because I behaved like an idiot and I want you to forgive me.'

'I've already forgiven you,' she replied, walking away.

'So why are you going?' he asked, throwing his arms wide in disbelief.

'Because I'm still angry with you!'

Paul was just about to run after her, but Alys turned and smiled at him.

'But you can come and pick me up tomorrow night and see if it's passed.'

28

'Therefore I consider you to be ready to begin this journey on which your worth will be tested. Bend down.'

Paul obeyed, and the man in the suit placed a thick black hood over his head. With a sharp tug he adjusted two leather straps around Paul's neck.

'Can you see anything?'

'No.'

Paul's own voice sounded strange inside the hood and the sounds around him seemed to come from another world.

'There are two holes at the back. If you are short of air, pull it away from your neck slightly.'

'Thank you.'

'Now, hold my left arm tightly with your right arm. We will be covering a great distance together. It is very important that you move forward when I tell you to, without hesitation. There is no need to hurry, but you must listen closely to your instructions. At certain points I will tell you to walk, placing one foot in front of the other. At others, I will tell you to lift your knees to go up or down stairs. Are you ready?'

Paul nodded.

'Answer the questions loudly and clearly.'

'I am ready.'

'Let us begin.'

Paul set off slowly, grateful to be moving at last. He'd spent the previous half-hour answering the questions the man in the suit had put to him, although he had never seen this man before in his life. He knew the answers he ought to give in advance because they were all in the book that Keller had given him, three weeks ago.

'Should I memorise them?' he'd asked the bookseller.

'These formulas are part of the ritual we have to preserve and respect. Soon you will discover that the initiation ceremonies and how they change you are an essential aspect of Masonry.'

'There's more than one?'

'There's one for each of the three degrees: Entered Apprentice, Fellow Craft and Master Mason. There are another thirty above the third degree, but these are honorary degrees you will learn about when it's time.'

'What's your degree, Herr Keller?'

The bookseller ignored his question.

'I want you to read the book and consider its contents closely.'

Paul did. The work recounted the origins of Masonry: the guilds of builders in the Middle Ages and before them the mythical builders of Ancient Egypt.

They all discovered a wisdom inherent in the symbols of construction and Geometry. You must always write this word with an upper-case G, because G is the symbol of the Great Architect of the Universe. How you choose to worship him is up to you. In the lodge, the only stone you will work will be your conscience and whatever you carry in it. Your brothers will give you the tools to do this after initiation . . . if you overcome the four trials.

'Will it be hard?'

'Are you afraid?'

'No. Well, a little.'

'It will be hard,' the bookseller admitted, after a moment. 'But you are brave, and you will be well prepared.'

Paul's bravery had not been called upon so far, although the trials had not yet begun. He had been called to an alley in the Altstadt, the city's old centre, at nine o'clock on a Friday night. From the outside the meeting place looked like an average house although it was perhaps rather neglected. A rusty postbox bearing an illegible name hung beside the doorbell, though the lock seemed new and well oiled. The man in the suit had come to the door alone and led Paul into a hallway containing various pieces of wooden furniture. It was there that Paul was submitted to the first ritual interrogation.

Under the black hood, Paul wondered where Keller might be. He had assumed that the bookseller, the only connection he had with the lodge, would be the person who'd introduce him. Instead he had been met by a complete stranger, and he couldn't help feeling slightly vulnerable as he walked blindly on the arm of a man he'd first met half an hour earlier.

After what seemed an enormous distance – he had gone up and down various flights of stairs and several long corridors – his guide finally came to a stop.

Paul heard three loud knocks then an unknown voice asked: 'Who calls at the door of the temple?'

'A brother bringing a Profane who desires to be initiated into our mysteries.'

'Has he been adequately prepared?'

'He has.'

'What is his name?'

'Paul, the son of Hans Reiner.'

They set off again. Paul noticed that the ground beneath his feet was harder and more slippery, possibly stone or marble. They walked for a long while, although inside the hood time seemed to have a different consistency. At certain points Paul felt – more out of intuition than any real certainty – that they were covering ground they'd covered before, as though they were walking in a circle, then being made to retrace their steps.

His guide stopped again and began to undo the straps of Paul's hood.

Paul blinked when the black cloth was pulled back and he realised that he was standing in a small, cold, low-ceilinged room. The walls were completely covered in limestone, on which could be read disordered phrases, written in different hands and at different heights. Paul recognised different versions of the Masonic commandments.

Meanwhile, the suited man stripped him of metallic objects, including his belt and the buckles of his shoes, which he tore off without a thought. Paul regretted not having remembered to bring different footwear, because now this pair was ruined.

'Are you wearing any gold? Entering the lodge with any precious metal is a grave insult.'

'No, sir,' replied Paul.

'Over there you'll find a pen, paper and ink,' said the man. Then, without another word, he disappeared through the door, shutting it behind him.

A little candle illuminated the table on which the writing implements sat. Beside them was a skull and Paul realised with a shiver that it was real. There were also a number of flasks containing elements that signified change and initiation: bread and water, salt and sulphur, ashes.

He was in the Chamber of Reflection. The place where he was to write his testimony as a Profane. He took up the pen and began to write the ancient formula, which he had not completely understood.

All this is bad. All this symbolism, the repetition ... I have the feeling that it's nothing more than empty words, it has no spirit, he thought.

Suddenly he had a desperate longing to walk along Ludwigstrasse, by the light of the street lamps, with the wind in his face. His fear of the dark, which hadn't abated even in adulthood, had crept up on him inside the hood. In half an hour they would be back to fetch him, and he could simply ask them to let him go.

There was still time to turn back.

But in that case I would never know the truth about my father.

29

The man in the suit returned.

'I'm ready,' said Paul.

He knew nothing of the actual ceremony that was to follow. All he knew was the answers to the questions they asked him, no more than that. And the time had come for the trials.

His guide placed a rope around his neck, then covered his eyes once more. This time he didn't use the black hood, but a blindfold made of the same material, which he tied with three tight knots. Paul was grateful to be able to breathe more easily and his feelings of vulnerability decreased, but only for a moment. Suddenly, the man tugged off Paul's jacket, and tore off the left sleeve of his shirt. He then opened the front of the shirt, leaving Paul's torso exposed. Finally he rolled up the left leg of Paul's trousers and took off the shoe and sock on that foot.

'Let's go.'

They were walking again. Paul had a strange feeling as his naked sole touched the cold floor, which he was now sure was marble.

'Halt!'

He sensed a sharp object at his chest and felt the hair on the back of his neck stand on end.

'Has the aspirant brought his testimony?'

'He has.'

'Let him place it on the end of the sword.'

Paul raised his left hand, in which he held the piece of paper he'd written on in the Chamber. He fixed it carefully on the sharp object.

'Paul Reiner, have you come here of your own free will?'

That voice . . . it's Sebastian Keller! thought Paul.

'Yes.'

'Are you ready to face the trials?'

'I am,' said Paul, unable to suppress a shudder.

From that moment on Paul began to drift in and out of consciousness. He understood the questions, and replied to them, but his fear and inability to see had heightened his other senses so much so that they had taken over. He began to breathe faster.

He was climbing a flight of stairs. He tried to control his anxiety by counting the steps, but he quickly lost count.

'This is where the trial of air begins. Breath is the first thing we receive when we are born,' thundered Keller's voice.

The suited man whispered in his ear:

'You're on a narrow gangway. Stop. Then take one more step, but make it a decisive one or you'll break your neck!'

Paul obeyed. Beneath him the surface of the floor seemed to have changed, from marble to rough wood. Before taking the final step, he wiggled the toes of his bare foot and felt that they were at the edge of the gangway. He wondered how high he might be, and in his mind the number of steps he'd climbed seemed to multiply. He imagined finding himself at the pinnacle of the towers of the Frauenkirche, hearing the pigeons cooing beside him with the bustle of Marienplatz an eternity below.

Do it.

Do it now.

He took a step and lost his balance, falling head first, for what couldn't have been more than a second. His face hit a thick net, and the impact made his teeth clatter. He bit the inside of his cheeks and his mouth filled with the taste of his own blood.

When he recovered, he realised he was clinging to the net. He wanted to pull off the hood to be sure that this was so, that a net had indeed broken his fall. He needed to escape the darkness.

Paul barely had time to register his panic because at once several pairs of hands dragged him from the net and straightened him up. He was back on his feet and walking. Keller's voice announced the next challenge.

'The second trial is the trial of water. It is what we are, what we have come from.'

Paul obeyed when told to lift his feet – first the left, then the right.

He started to shiver. He had stepped into a huge container of cold water, and the liquid reached up over his knees.

Again he heard his guide's whisper in his ear.

'Crouch down. Fill your lungs. Then allow yourself to fall back and stay submerged. Don't move, or try to get out, or you will not have passed the trial.'

The young man bent his knees, curling up as the water covered his scrotum and abdomen. Waves of pain ran up his spine. He breathed in deeply then threw himself backwards.

The water closed over him like a blanket.

At first the dominant sensation was the cold. He had never felt anything like it. His body seemed to solidify, turning to ice, marble or rock.

Then his lungs began to complain.

It began with a rasping groan, then a dry croak and then an urgent, desperate appeal. He inadvertently moved his arm and had to summon all his willpower not to put his hands against the bottom of the container and push up towards the surface, which he knew was so close, like an open door through which he could escape. Just when he thought he couldn't take it a second longer, there was a sharp tug and he found himself out of the water, gasping, filling his chest again.

Again they were walking. He was still soaked through, his hair and clothes dripping. His right foot made a ridiculous sound as the shoe pressed against the floor.

Keller's voice again.

'The third trial is the trial of fire. It is the Creator's spark, and what moves us.'

Then there were hands twisting his body and pushing it forward. Whoever was holding him drew very close, almost as though he wanted to embrace him.

'In front of you there is a circle of fire. Take three steps back to build up momentum. Stretch your arms out in front of you, then take a run and jump forward as far as you can.'

Paul could feel the hot air on his face, drying his skin and hair. He heard a sinister crackling, and in his imagination the burning circle assumed massive dimensions, until it became the mouth of an immense dragon.

As he took three steps back he wondered how he would be able to jump through the flames without being burned alive, and trusted to the dampness of his clothes to protect him. What would be even worse would be if he miscalculated the jump and fell head first into the flames.

I simply have to mark an imaginary line on the floor and jump from there.

He tried to visualise the jump, to imagine himself hurtling through the air as though nothing could hurt him. He tensed his calves, flexed and stretched out his arms. Then he took three running strides forward.

And he jumped.

30

He felt the heat against his hands and face as he was in the air, even the hiss of his shirt as the fire evaporated some of the water. He fell to the floor and started patting his face and chest, looking for signs of any burns. Apart from his bruised elbows and knees, no damage had been done.

This time they didn't even allow him to get to his feet. He was already being lifted up, like a shivering sack, and dragged into a confined space.

'The final trial is the trial of earth, to which we must return.'

There were no words of advice from his guide. He simply heard the sound of a stone blocking the entrance.

He felt around him. He was in a tiny room, not even large enough to stand up in. From his crouching position he could touch three of the walls and, stretching his arm out a little, he could touch the fourth and the ceiling.

Relax, he told himself. *This is the final trial. In a few minutes it'll all be over.*

He was trying to regulate his breathing when suddenly he heard the ceiling start to descend.

'No!'

No sooner had he uttered the word than Paul bit his lip. He wasn't allowed to speak during any of the trials, that was the rule. He wondered fleetingly whether they'd heard him.

He tried to push against the ceiling to halt its descent, but in his position he could gain no leverage against the enormous weight advancing towards him. He pushed with his whole being, but to no avail. The ceiling continued its descent, and soon he had to press his back against the floor.

I have to shout. Tell them to STOP!

Suddenly, as though time itself had stopped, a memory flashed through his mind. A fleeting image from his childhood, of coming home from school with the absolute certainty that he was going to receive a thrashing. Every step he took brought him closer to the thing he feared most. Not once had he turned round. There are choices that are simply no choice at all.

No.

He stopped pushing at the ceiling.

At that moment it began to rise.

'Let the voting begin.'

Paul was back on his feet, hanging on to the guide. The trials were over, but he did not know whether he had passed them. He'd dropped like a stone in the trial of air, not taken a firm step as they'd told him to. He'd moved during the trial of water, even though that was forbidden. And he'd spoken during the trial of earth, which was the most serious fault of all.

He could hear a noise like a can containing a stone being shaken.

He knew from the book that all the current members of the lodge would be making their way to the centre of the temple, where there was a wooden box. Into it they would drop a small ivory ball – white if they gave their assent, black if they wished to reject him. The verdict had to be unanimous. Just one black ball would be enough for him to be led to the exit, his eyes still blindfolded.

The sound of the voting stopped, and was replaced by a loud patter, which ceased almost at once. Paul guessed that someone had tipped the votes out on to a plate or a tray. The results were there for everyone but him to see. Perhaps there would be a solitary black ball that would render all the trials he'd been through meaningless.

'Paul Reiner, the result of the vote is definitive and cannot be appealed,' thundered Keller's voice.

There was a moment of silence.

'You have been admitted into the mysteries of Masonry. Remove his blindfold!'

Paul blinked as his eyes returned to the light. He was struck by a wave of emotions, a wild euphoria. He tried to take the scene in all at once:

The enormous room in which he was standing, with a marble chess-board floor, an altar and two rows of benches lining the walls.

The members of the lodge, almost a hundred formally dressed men wearing elaborate aprons and medals, all standing to applaud him with white-gloved hands.

The equipment from the trials, ridiculously inoffensive once his sight had been restored: a wooden staircase over a net, a bath tub, a couple of men holding torches, a large box with a lid.

Sebastian Keller, standing in the centre beside an altar adorned with a square and a compass, holding a closed book for him to swear upon.

And he, Paul Reiner, placing his left hand on the book, raising his right and swearing never to reveal the secrets of Masonry.

'. . . under no less a penalty than to have my throat cut across, my tongue torn out by the roots, and my body buried in the sands of the sea,' Paul concluded.

He surveyed the hundred anonymous faces around him, and wondered how many of them had known his father.

And if somewhere in their midst was the man who had betrayed him.

31

After the initiation Paul's life went back to normal. That night he'd returned home at dawn. After the ceremony the brother Masons had enjoyed a banquet in an adjacent room which had lasted into the early hours. Sebastian Keller had presided at the feast, because, as Paul learned to his great surprise, he was the Grand Master, occupying the highest position in the lodge.

In spite of his best efforts, Paul hadn't been able to find out anything about his father, so he had decided to let some time go by in order to earn the trust of his fellow Masons before he started asking questions. Instead he devoted his time to Alys.

She had started speaking to him again, and they had even gone out together. They discovered that they had little in common, but surprisingly this difference seemed to bring them closer. Paul listened intently to her account of how she'd escaped from the house to avoid the planned marriage to his cousin. He couldn't help but admire Alys's bravery.

'What will you do next? You're not going to take photos in the club all your life?'

'I like photography. I think I'll try to get work with an international press agency ... They pay good money for photos, though it's very competitive.'

In turn he shared with Alys the story of his previous four years, and how his search for the truth about what had happened to Hans Reiner had become an obsession.

'We make quite a couple ...' said Alys, 'you trying to recover the memory of your father, and me praying never to have to see mine again.'

Paul grinned from ear to ear, but not because of the comparison.

She said 'couple', he thought.

Sadly for Paul, Alys was still smarting from that scene with the girl at the club. When one night he tried to kiss her after walking her back home, she gave him a thump that shook his back teeth.

'Bloody hell,' said Paul, holding his jaw. 'What the devil's wrong with you?'

'Don't even try it.'

'Not if you're going to give me another one of those I won't. You obviously don't hit like a girl,' he said.

Alys smiled and, grabbing hold of him by his lapels, she kissed him. An intense kiss, passionate and fleeting. Then she suddenly pushed him away and disappeared up the stairs, leaving Paul bewildered, his lips hanging half open as he tried to understand what had just happened.

Paul had to fight for each small rapprochement, even on matters that seemed simple and straightforward, such as allowing her to go through doors first – which Alys couldn't bear – or offering to carry a heavy package or to pay the bill after they'd had a beer and a few snacks.

Two weeks after his initiation, Paul went to pick her up at the club at about three in the morning. Walking back to Alys's boarding-house, which wasn't far, he asked her why she minded his displays of gentlemanly behaviour.

'Because I'm perfectly capable of doing these things for myself. I don't need anyone to let me go first or to escort me home.'

'But last Wednesday when I fell asleep and didn't come to fetch you, you flew into a rage.'

'You're so clever in some ways, Paul, and so stupid in others!' she said, waving her arms about. 'You get on my nerves!'

'That makes two of us.'

'So why don't you stop pursuing me?'

'Because I'm afraid of what you'd do if I really did stop.'

Alys looked at him in silence. The brim of her hat cast a shadow across her face, and Paul couldn't tell how she'd reacted to his last comment. He feared the worst. When something made Alys angry, they could go days without speaking.

They reached the door to her boarding-house on Stahlstrasse without exchanging another word. The lack of conversation was emphasised by the tense, hot silence that engulfed the city. Munich was bidding farewell to the hottest September in decades, a little breathing-space in a year of misfortune. The stillness of the streets, the late hour and Alys's mood imbued Paul's heart with a strange melancholy. He felt that she was about to leave him.

'You're very quiet,' she said, searching for her keys in her purse.

'I was the last one to speak.'

'Do you think you can stay just as silent as you go up the stairs? My landlady has very strict rules about men, and the old cow has extremely good hearing.'

'You're inviting me up?' asked Paul, astonished.

'You can stay down here, if you'd rather.'

Paul almost lost his hat running through the doorway.

The building had no lift, and they had to climb three flights of wooden stairs that creaked with every step. Alys stuck close to the wall as she climbed, which was less noisy, but all the same, as they passed the second floor, they heard footsteps inside one of the apartments.

'It's her, the witch! Go on, quickly!'

Paul ran past Alys and reached the landing just before a rectangle of light appeared, outlining Alys's slim figure against the peeling paintwork of the staircase.

'Who's there?' asked a croaky voice.

'Hello, Frau Kasyn.'

'Fräulein Tannenbaum. What an unseemly time to be getting home!'

'It's my work, Frau Kasyn, as you know.'

'I can't say I approve of this sort of behaviour.'

'I don't much approve of the leaks in my bathroom either, Frau Kasyn, but the world isn't a perfect place.'

At that moment Paul moved slightly and the wood groaned under his feet.

'Is there someone up there?' said the housekeeper, outraged.

'Let me check!' replied Alys, racing up the flight of stairs that separated her from Paul and ushering him towards her room. She put the key in the lock and had just managed to get the door open and push Paul inside before the old woman – who had hobbled after her – poked her head up the staircase.

'I'm sure I heard someone. Do you have a man in there?'

'Oh, nothing for you to worry about, Frau Kasyn. It's just a cat,' said Alys, closing the door in her face.

144

'Your trick with the cat works every time, eh?' whispered Paul, putting his arms round her and kissing her long neck. His breath burned. She shivered and felt goose bumps rising up her left side.

'I thought we'd be interrupted again, like that day in the bathtub.'

'Stop talking and kiss me,' he said, holding her shoulders and turning her towards him.

Alys kissed him, rubbing herself against Paul and noticing how his body responded. Paul almost tore his jacket as he peeled it off, trying not to be separated from her lips. Then he tackled her clothes. Alys let him, grateful for each button he managed to undo in their clumsy journey towards the bed. She recovered herself slightly as they fell on to the mattress, her body beneath him.

'Stop.'

Paul stopped abruptly, and looked at her with a shadow of disappointment and surprise on his face. But Alys slipped between his arms and moved on top of him, making him follow her rhythm, and taking over the tedious task of freeing them both from the rest of their clothes. When they were both naked, she ran her finger down his abdomen and closed her hands around his penis. She continued massaging until Paul gave a gentle moan.

'I can't hold on much longer, Alys.'

'Don't move.'

She hurried to her bedside table and took a little case out of a drawer from where she removed a condom. She fitted it with trembling hands, then got on top of him.

'What is it?'

'Nothing,' she replied.

'You're crying.'

Alys hesitated for a moment. To tell him the reason for her tears would be to bare her soul, and she didn't think she could do that, not even at a moment like this.

'It's just that . . .'

'What?'

'That I would have liked to have been your first.'

Paul smiled shyly. His face was in shadow, but she knew straight away that he had blushed.

'You needn't worry about that.'

'So, those girls at the club . . .'

Leaning on his elbows, Paul kissed away her tears and made her look him in the eye.

'You *are* the first.'

With a moan, she took him inside her at last.

32

When he received the envelope from Sebastian Keller, Paul couldn't help shuddering.

The months that had gone by since his admission to the Mason's lodge had been disappointing. At first, there had been something almost romantic about entering the secret society almost blindly, the thrill of adventure. But once the initial euphoria had faded, Paul began to wonder what was the point of it all. For a start, he'd been forbidden to speak at the lodge gatherings until he'd completed three years as an Apprentice. But that wasn't the worst of it – the worst thing was performing the extremely long rituals, which seemed to Paul to be a waste of time.

Stripped of their rituals, the meetings were no more than a series of conferences and debates on Masonic symbolism and its practical application in improving the virtue of the brother Masons. The only part Paul found even vaguely interesting was when the members decided which charities they would donate to with the money gathered at the end of each meeting.

For Paul, the meetings became an onerous duty, which he endured each fortnight in order to get to know the members of the lodge. Even this aim wasn't easy to achieve, as the older Masons, those who undoubtedly would have known his father, sat at different tables in the great dining hall. On occasion he'd tried to get close to Keller, wanting to press the bookseller about his promise to hand over whatever it was his father had left for him. In the lodge Keller treated him with a certain amount of distance, however; in the bookshop he brushed Paul off with convincing but vague excuses.

What he'd never done before was written to him, and Paul knew at once that whatever was in the brown envelope the owner of his boarding-house had given him was the thing he'd been awaiting for so long.

Paul sat on the edge of his bed, his breath laboured. He was sure the envelope would contain a letter from his father. He couldn't hold back his tears when he imagined what must have driven Hans Reiner to compose a missive to his son, then just a few months old, attempting to freeze his voice in time until his son was ready to understand it.

He tried to imagine what his father would want to tell him. Perhaps he would offer wise advice. Perhaps he would embrace him across time.

Perhaps he'll give me clues about the person or people who were going to kill him, Paul thought, his teeth clenched.

With extreme care he tore open the envelope and put his hand inside. In it there was another smaller envelope, white, together with a handwritten note on the back of one of the bookseller's business cards.

Dear Paul:
Congratulations. Hans would be proud. This is what your father left for you. I don't know what it contains, but I hope it will help you.
   S.K.

Paul opened the second envelope and a small sheet of white paper printed in blue fell to the ground. Paul was paralysed between disappointment and amazement as he picked it up and saw what it was.

33

The Metzger pawnshop was a cold place, colder even than the early November air. Paul wiped his feet on the mat before entering, as it was raining continuously outside. He left his umbrella in the stand and looked around curiously. He vaguely recalled the morning, four years ago now, when he and his mother had gone to a shop in Schwabing to pawn his father's watch. That had been a sterile place, with glass shelves and employees wearing ties.

Metzger's looked more like a large sewing-box and smelled of naphthalene. From outside, the shop seemed small and insignificant, but on crossing the threshold its enormous depth was revealed, a place filled to bursting with pieces of furniture, galena crystal radios, porcelain figures and even a golden birdcage. Rust and dust had overwhelmed the various objects that had dropped anchor there for the last time. Astonished, Paul considered a stuffed cat caught in the act of snatching a sparrow in flight. Between the feline's extended leg and the wing of the bird a spider's web had formed.

'This isn't a museum, lad.'

Paul turned, startled. A thin, hollow-faced old man had materialised beside him, wrapped in blue overalls that were too large for his frame, and which accentuated his thinness.

'Are you Metzger?'

'I am. And if whatever you've brought me isn't gold, I don't want it.'

'The truth is I haven't come to pawn anything. I've come to collect something,' replied Paul. He had taken a dislike to this man, and his suspicious behaviour.

A flash of greed crossed the old man's tiny eyes. It was obvious that business wasn't going too well.

'Sorry, lad ... I have twenty people coming in here every day who think their great-grandmother's old copper cameo is worth thousands of marks. But let's see, let's see what you've brought me.'

Paul held out the blue and white piece of paper that he'd found in the envelope the bookseller had sent him. In the top left corner was Metzger's name and address. Paul had rushed there as fast as he could, still recovering from the surprise of not finding a letter inside. On the paper, there were a mere four sets of letters and numbers.

Art. 91231
21 marks

The old man pointed at the slip.

'There's a bit missing. We don't accept damaged slips.'

The top right-hand corner, which should have shown the name of the person who had made the deposit, had been torn off.

'The article number is perfectly readable,' said Paul.

'But we can't hand over objects deposited by our customers to the first person who walks through the door.'

'Whatever it is belonged to my father.'

The old man scratched his chin, pretending to study the slip with interest.

'In any case the number is very low – the article must have been pawned many years ago. I'm sure it will have gone out to auction.'

'I see. And how can we be certain?'

'I suppose if the customer were prepared to recover the article, taking into account inflation ...'

Paul flinched as the moneylender at last showed his hand – it was clear he wanted to get as much out of the transaction as he could. But Paul was resolved to recover the object, whatever the cost.

'Very well.'

'Wait here,' said the other man, with a triumphant smile.

The old man disappeared and returned half a minute later with a moth-eaten cardboard box, marked with a yellowing ticket.

'Here you go, lad.'

Paul held out his hand to take it, but the old man grabbed him tightly by the wrist. The touch of his cold, wrinkled skin was repulsive.

'What the hell are you doing?'

'First the money.'

'First you show me what's inside.'

'I'm not having any of that,' said the old man, shaking his head slowly. 'I'm trusting that you're the legitimate owner of this box, and you're trusting that what's inside is worth the trouble. A double act of faith, as it were.'

Paul wrestled with himself for a few moments, but he knew he had no choice.

'Let go of me.'

Metzger opened his fingers, and Paul dug his hand into the inside pocket of his coat. He took out his wallet.

'How much?'

'Forty million marks.'

It was equivalent to ten dollars at that day's rate, enough to feed a family for many weeks.

'That's a lot of money,' said Paul, pursing his lips.

'Take it or leave it.'

Paul sighed. He had the money on him, as the next day he was supposed to go and make some payments for the bank. He'd have to take it out of his next six months' wages, the little he earned after diverting all the profits from the business to Herr Ziegler's charity shop. To cap it all, share prices had recently been stagnating or falling, and the investors had dwindled, making the queues at the welfare food halls longer each day, with no end to the crisis in sight.

Paul took out the enormous recently printed banknotes. Paper money never grew old in those days. In fact the notes from the previous quarter were already worthless and fuelled Munich's chimneys, as they were cheaper than firewood.

The moneylender snatched the notes from Paul's hand and began to count them slowly, studying them one at a time against the light. Finally he looked at the young man and smiled, showing his missing teeth.

'Satisfied?' Paul asked, sarcastically.

Metzger drew back his hand.

Paul opened the box carefully, raising a cloud of dust that floated around him in the light of the bulb. He lifted out a flat square box, made of smooth dark mahogany. It had no decorations, no varnish, only a clasp that opened when Paul pushed on it. The lid of the box rose slowly and silently, as though nineteen years hadn't passed since the last time it was opened.

Paul felt an icy fear in his heart as he looked at the contents.

'You'd best take care, lad,' said the moneylender, from whose hands the banknotes had disappeared as if by magic. 'You could find yourself in enormous trouble if they find you on the streets with that toy.'

What were you trying to tell me with this, Father?

On a padded red velvet base lay a gleaming pistol and a magazine containing ten bullets.

34

'This had better be important, Metzger. I'm extremely busy. If it's about the fees, better come back some other day.'

Otto von Schroeder was seated by the fireplace of his study, and he didn't offer the pawnbroker a seat or anything to drink. Metzger, obliged to remain standing, hat in hand, contained his fury and contrived a servile tilt of the head and a fake smile.

'The truth is, Herr Baron, I've come about another matter. The money you've invested all these years is about to bear fruit.'

'Has he come back to Munich? Has Nagel come back?' asked the baron, tensing.

'It's more complicated than that, Your Lordship.'

'Well then, don't make me guess. Tell me what it is you want.'

'The truth is, Your Lordship, before conveying this important information I would like to remind you that the objects whose sale I have put on hold for all this time, at great cost to my business ...'

'Get on with it, Metzger.'

'... have increased in value a great deal. Your Lordship promised me an annual sum and in return I was to inform you if Clovis Nagel redeemed any of them. And with all due respect, Your Lordship hasn't paid this year or last.'

The baron lowered his voice.

'Don't you dare blackmail me, Metzger. What I've paid you over two decades more than makes up for the junk you've kept in that dump of yours.'

'What can I say? Your Lordship gave his word, and Your Lordship hasn't kept it. Well then, let us consider our agreement to be concluded. Good afternoon,' said the old man, donning his hat.

'Wait!' said the baron, raising his arm.

The moneylender turned, stifling a smile.

'Yes, Herr Baron?'

'I have no money, Metzger. I'm ruined.'

'You surprise me, Your Lordship!'

'I have treasury bonds, which might come to something if the government pays the dividends or restabilises the economy. Till then they're only worth as much as the paper they're written on.'

The old man looked around him, his eyes narrowed.

'Well then, Your Lordship ... I suppose I could accept as payment that little bronze and marble table you have beside your chair.'

'This is worth much more than your annual fee, Metzger.'

The old man shrugged but said nothing.

'Very well. Talk.'

'You would of course have to guarantee your payments for the years to come, Your Lordship. The embossed silver tea service on that little table would do, I suppose.'

'You're a bastard, Metzger,' said the baron, giving him a look of undisguised hatred.

'Business is business, Herr Baron.'

Otto was silent for a few moments. He saw no other way but to give in to the old man's blackmail.

'You win. For your sake I hope it's worth it,' he said at last.

'Today someone came to redeem one of the objects pawned by your friend.'

'Was it Nagel?'

'No, not unless he's found some way of turning the clock back thirty years. It was a boy.'

'Did he give his name?'

'He was thin, with blue eyes, dark blond hair.'

'Paul ...'

'I've told you, he didn't give his name.'

'And what was it he collected?'

'A black mahogany box containing a pistol.'

The baron leaped from his seat so quickly that it tipped backwards and crashed into the low rail surrounding the fireplace.

'What did you say?' he said, grabbing the moneylender by the throat.

'You're hurting me!'

'Talk, for God's sake, or I'll break your neck this instant.'

'A plain black mahogany box,' replied the old man in a whisper.

'The pistol! Describe it!'

'A Mauser C96 with a broom-handle grip. The wood on the butt wasn't oak, like the original model, but black mahogany, matching the case. A fine weapon.'

'How can this be?' said the baron.

Suddenly weak, he released the moneylender and slumped back into his seat.

Old Metzger straightened up, rubbing his neck.

'Mad. He's gone mad,' he said, hurrying to the door.

The baron didn't notice him go. He remained seated, his head in his hands, consumed by dark thoughts.

35

Ilse was sweeping the corridor when she noticed the shadow of a visitor cast across the floor by the light of the wall lamps. She knew who it was even before raising her head, and she froze.

Holy God, how did you find us?

When she and her son had first arrived at the boarding-house, Ilse had had to work to pay for part of the rent, since what Paul was making carrying coal wasn't enough. Later, when Paul had transformed Ziegler's grocer's shop into a bank, the young man had insisted that they find better lodgings. Ilse had refused. There had been too many changes in her life, and she clung to whatever gave her security.

One of those things was the broom handle. Paul – and the owner of the boarding-house, to whom Ilse wasn't much help – had insisted that she stop working, but she had paid no attention. She needed to feel useful somehow. The silence into which she'd sunk after they'd been expelled from the mansion had initially been the result of anxiety, but later had become a voluntary manifestation of her love for Paul. She avoided conversation with him because she was afraid of his questions. When she spoke, it was of unimportant things, which she tried to invest with all the tenderness she could muster. The rest of the time she simply gazed at him silently, from afar, and grieved over what she had been deprived of.

Which was why her anguish was so intense when she found herself face to face with one of the people responsible for her loss.

'Hello, Ilse.'

She took a step back cautiously.

'What do you want, Otto?'

The baron drummed on the ground with the end of his walking-stick. He wasn't comfortable here, that much was clear, as was the fact that his visit signalled some sinister intent.

'Can we talk somewhere more private?'

'I don't want to go anywhere with you. Say what you have to say and leave.'

The baron snorted in annoyance. Then he gestured scornfully at the mouldy paper on the walls, the uneven floor, and the fading lamps that gave off more shadow than light.

'Look at you, Ilse. Sweeping the corridor in a third-class boarding-house. You should be ashamed of yourself.'

'Sweeping floors is sweeping floors, it makes no difference if it's a mansion or a boarding-house. And there are linoleum floors that are more respectable than marble.'

'Ilse dear, you know that when we took you in you were in a bad way. I wouldn't have wanted . . .'

'Stop right there, Otto. I know whose idea that was. But don't think I'm going to fall for the routine that you're only a puppet. You're the one who's controlled my sister from the very start, making her pay dearly for the mistake she made. And for the things you've done hiding behind that mistake.'

Otto took a step back, shocked at the anger that seethed from Ilse's lips. The monocle fell from his eye, and swung against the front of his overcoat, like a condemned man hanging from a gibbet.

'You surprise me, Ilse. They told me you'd . . .'

Ilse gave a joyless laugh.

'Lost it? Gone crazy? No, Otto. I'm quite sane. I've chosen to remain silent all this time because I'm afraid of what my son might do if he found out the truth.'

'So stop him. Because he's going too far.'

'So that's why you've come,' she said, unable to contain her scorn. 'You're afraid the past will finally catch up with you.'

The baron took a step towards Ilse. Paul's mother moved back against the wall, as Otto brought his face up close to hers.

'Now listen carefully, Ilse. You're the only link there is to that night. If you don't stop him before it's too late, I shall have to break that link.'

'Go on then, Otto,' said Ilse, feigning a bravery she didn't feel, 'kill me. But you should know I've written a letter revealing the whole affair. All of it. If anything happens to me, Paul will receive it.'

'But ... you can't be serious? You can't write that down! What if it falls into the wrong hands?'

Ilse didn't reply. All she did was stare at him. Otto tried to hold her stare, a tall, solid, well-dressed man facing down a fragile woman in ragged clothes who clung to her broom to stop herself from falling.

Finally, the baron gave up.

'It doesn't end here,' said Otto, turning and hurrying out.

36

'You called for me, Father?'

Otto glanced at Jürgen with misgiving. It had been weeks since he'd last seen him, and he still found it hard to identify the uniformed figure standing in his dining room as his son. He was suddenly aware of how Jürgen's shoulders filled the brown shirt, how the red armband with the twisted cross framed his thick biceps, how the black boots increased the young man's stature to the point where he had to duck slightly to go under the door frame. He felt a hint of pride, but at the same time he was overwhelmed by a wave of self-pity. He couldn't help but draw comparisons to himself – Otto was fifty-two, and he felt old and tired.

'You haven't been home for a long time, Jürgen.'

'I have important things to do.'

The baron didn't reply. Though he did understand the Nazis' ideals, he had never really believed in them. Like the great majority of Munich's high society he considered them to be a party with little promise, condemned to become extinct. If they'd come so far, it was only because they were benefiting from a social situation that was so dramatic the underprivileged would believe any extremist prepared to make them wild promises. But at that moment he did not have time for subtleties.

'So much so that you neglect your mother? She's been worried about you. Might we know where you've been sleeping?'

'In SA quarters.'

'This year you were meant to have begun your university studies, two years late!' said Otto, shaking his head. 'It's already November, and you still haven't shown up to a single class.'

'I'm in a position of responsibility.'

Otto watched as the pieces of the image he'd preserved of this ill-mannered adolescent – who not long ago would have hurled a cup on to the floor because the tea was too sweet for him – finally disintegrated. He wondered what the best way of approaching him would be. A lot was riding on Jürgen doing as he was told.

He'd lain awake for several nights, tossing and turning on his mattress, before deciding to call on his son.

'A position of responsibility, you say?'

'I protect the most important man in Germany.'

'The most important man in Germany,' mimicked his father. 'You, the future Baron von Schroeder, hired thug to an obscure Austrian corporal with delusions of grandeur. You must be proud.'

Jürgen flinched as though he'd just been struck.

'You don't understand . . .'

'Enough! I want you to do something important. You're the only person I can trust to do it.'

Jürgen was confused by the change of tack. His reply died on his lips as his curiosity took over.

'What is it?'

'I've found your aunt and your cousin.'

Jürgen didn't respond. He sat down next to his father and took the patch from his eye, revealing the unnatural void beneath the wrinkled skin of his eyelid. He stroked the skin slowly.

'Where?' he asked, his voice cold and distant.

'In a boarding-house in Schwabing. But I forbid you even to think about revenge. We have something much more important to deal with. I want you to go to your aunt's room, search it from top to bottom, and bring me any papers you find. Especially any that are handwritten. Letters, notes, anything.'

'Why?'

'I can't tell you that.'

'You can't tell me? You bring me here, you ask for my help after you've denied me the chance to go after the person who did this to me, the same person who gave my sick brother a pistol so he could blow his brains out. You forbid me all this, and then you expect me to obey you without any explanation!' Jürgen was shouting now.

'You'll do what I tell you to do, unless you want me to cut you off!'

'Go ahead, Father. I've never much cared for debts. There's only one thing left of value and you can't take that away from me. I'll inherit your title whether you like it or not.' Jürgen went out of the dining room, and slammed the door shut behind him. He was about to go out into the street when a voice stopped him.

'Son, wait.'

He turned. Brunhilda was coming down the stairs.

'Mother.'

She went up to him and kissed his cheek. She had to stand on tiptoes to do it. She straightened his black tie and with her fingertips she caressed the place where his right eye had once been. Jürgen, sensing the contact, drew back and pulled down the patch.

'You have to do as your father asks.'

'I . . .'

'You *have* to do what you're told, Jürgen. He'll be proud of you if you do. And so will I.'

Brunhilda kept talking for some time. Her voice was sweet and to Jürgen it conjured up images and feelings he hadn't experienced for a long time. He had always been her favourite. She had always treated him differently, never denied him anything. He wanted to curl up in her lap, as he did when he was a child and summer seemed never ending.

'When?'

'Tomorrow.'

'Tomorrow's the eighth of November, Mother. I can't . . .'

'It has to be tomorrow afternoon. Your father's been watching the boarding-house, and Paul's never there at that time.'

'But I already have plans!'

'Are they more important than your own family, Jürgen?'

Brunhilda brought her hand to his face once more. This time Jürgen didn't recoil.

'I suppose I could do it, if I'm quick.'

'Good boy. And when you've got the papers,' she said, lowering her voice to a whisper, 'bring them to me first. Don't say a word to your father.'

37

From the corner, Alys watched Manfred alighting from the tram. She had taken up her position close to her old house, as she had done every week for the past two years, in order to see her brother for a few moments. Never before had she felt so powerfully the need to approach him, to speak to him, to give up once and for all and return home. She wondered what her father would do if she appeared.

I can't do it, especially like . . . like this. It would be like finally admitting he's right. It would be like dying.

Her gaze followed Manfred, who was turning into a good-looking young man. Unruly hair stuck out from under his cap, his hands were in his pockets and there was sheet music tucked under his arm.

I bet he's still terrible at the piano, thought Alys with a mixture of irritation and regret.

Manfred walked along the pavement and, before reaching the gate to his house, he stopped at the sweet shop. Alys smiled. She'd seen him do this the first time two years ago, when she'd discovered by chance that on Thursdays her brother came back from his piano lessons on public transport instead of in their father's chauffeur-driven Mercedes. Half an hour later Alys had gone into the sweet shop and bribed a shop assistant to give Manfred a packet of toffees with a note inside when he came the following week. She'd hastily scribbled

It's me. Come every Thursday, I'll leave you a note. Ask for Ingrid, give her your reply.
Love you – A.

For the next seven days she waited impatiently, fearful that her brother would not want to answer, or that he was angry because she had left without saying goodbye. His reply, however, was typical of Manfred. As though he'd just seen her ten minutes earlier, his note started with a funny story about the Swiss and the Italians, and ended up telling her things about school and what had happened since he last heard from her. Hearing from her brother again filled Alys with happiness, but there was one line, the last line, that confirmed her worst fears.

Papa is still looking for you.

She ran out of the sweet shop, afraid that someone might recognise her. But in spite of the danger she returned every week, always pulling her hat down to her eyebrows and wearing an overcoat or scarf that disguised her features. She never raised her face towards her father's window, in case he should be looking and recognise her. And each week, however dreadful her own situation, she was comforted by the daily successes, the small victories and defeats in Manfred's life. When he won an athletics medal at the age of twelve, she cried with happiness. When he received a thrashing in the school playground because he'd confronted some children who'd called him 'a filthy Jew', she howled with rage. Insubstantial though they were, those letters bound her to the memory of a happy past.

On that particular Thursday, 8 November, Alys waited slightly less time than usual, fearing that if she stayed around Prinzregentenplatz for very long her doubts would overcome her and she'd go for the easiest – and worst possible – option. She went into the shop, asked for a packet of mint toffees and paid three times the standard price, as usual. She would wait till she was on the tram, but that day she looked immediately for the piece of paper inside the wrapping. There were just five words, but they were enough to make her hands shake.

They've found me out. Run.

She had to stop herself from screaming.
Keep your head down, walk slowly, don't look to the side. Maybe they're not watching the shop.
She opened the door and stepped out into the street. She couldn't help glancing back as she walked away.

Two men in raincoats were following her, less than fifty metres away. One of them, realising she'd seen them, gestured to the other and both picked up the pace.

Shit!

Alys tried to walk as fast as she could without breaking into a run. If she was stopped by a policeman, they would catch up with her, and then she'd be done for. No doubt they were detectives hired by her father, who would make up a story in order to detain her or take her back to the family home. Legally she was not yet an adult – there were still eleven months to go before she turned twenty-one – so she would be completely at her father's mercy.

She crossed the street without stopping to look. A bicycle brushed passed her and the boy riding it lost control and fell to the ground, obstructing Alys's pursuers.

'You crazy or what?' shouted the lad, holding his injured knees.

Alys looked back again, and saw that the two men had managed to cross the road, taking advantage of a break in the traffic. They were less than ten metres away, and quickly gaining ground.

Not far to the tram now.

She cursed her shoes, which had wooden soles that made her skid slightly on the wet pavement. The bag where she kept her camera knocked against her hips, and she clung to the strap, which she wore diagonally across her chest.

It was obvious that she wasn't going to make it unless she could come up with something quickly. She could sense her pursuers right behind her.

It can't happen. Not when I'm so close.

At that moment a group of uniformed schoolboys came round the corner in front of her, led by a master who was accompanying them to the tram stop. The boys, twenty or so of them all lined up together, cut her off from the road. There was nothing for it now but to give up.

Unless . . .

She plunged her left hand into the pocket of her coat until she found the packet of toffees she'd just bought at the sweet shop. She pulled out a good handful and showed them to the boys.

'So, who wants some toffees?'

They all raised their arms at once and started to shout. Alys threw the fistful into the air and dived in between the children, taking advantage of the confusion as they broke ranks. When she was in their midst, she took out another handful, and threw them into the air too. As the boys fought to get the toffees, Alys managed to reach the other side of the group, just in time. The tram rolled along its tracks, sounding its bell as it approached.

Reaching out her hand, Alys grabbed hold of the bar and stepped on to the front of the tram. The driver reduced his speed slightly as she did so. When she was safely aboard the packed vehicle, Alys turned round to look at the street.

Her pursuers were nowhere to be seen.

With a sigh of relief, Alys paid and clung to the bar with trembling hands, quite oblivious to the two figures in hats and raincoats who at that moment were boarding the back of the tram.

Paul was waiting for her on Rosenheimerstrasse, close to the Ludwigs-brücke. When he saw her get off the tram he went to give her a kiss, but he stopped when he saw the concern on her face.

'What's wrong?'

Alys closed her eyes and sank into Paul's strong arms. In the safety of his embrace she did not spot her two pursuers getting off the tram and entering a nearby café.

'I went to get my brother's letter, like I do every Thursday, but I was followed. I won't be able to use that method of contact any more.'

'That's terrible – are you all right?'

Alys hesitated before answering. Should she tell him everything?

It would be so easy to tell him. Just open my mouth and let those two words out. So easy . . . and so impossible.

'Yes, I suppose so. I gave them the slip before I got on the tram.'

'All right, then . . . but I think you ought to cancel tonight,' said Paul.

'I can't, it's my first commission.'

After months of persistence, she had finally come to the attention of the head of photography at the *Munich Allgemeine* newspaper. He had told her to go that evening to the Bürgerbräukeller, a beer hall, fewer than thirty steps from where they were now. The State Commissioner of Bavaria, Gustav von Kahr, would be giving a speech in half an hour. For Alys, the chance to stop spending her nights enslaved in the club and begin making a living from the thing she most enjoyed, pho-tography, was a dream come true.

'But after what's happened ... we could go to your room, cuddle up under the blankets and I'll comfort you ...' Paul whispered seductively in her ear.

'Is that the only thing you can think about?' said Alys, pushing him away.

'I just ...'

'"You just" nothing! Do you realise how important tonight is to me? I've been waiting months for an opportunity like this!'

'Calm down, Alys. You're making a scene.'

'Don't tell me to calm down, you idiot! You're the one who needs a cold shower!'

'Please, Alys. You're exaggerating,' said Paul, failing to understand.

'Exaggerating! That's just what I needed to hear,' she snorted, turning and walking off towards the beer hall.

'Wait! Weren't we going to have a coffee first?'

'Have one yourself!'

'Don't you at least want me to go with you? These political meetings can be dangerous, people get drunk and sometimes arguments break out.'

The moment these words left his mouth, Paul knew he'd put his foot right in it. He wished he could catch them in flight and swallow them back down, but it was too late.

'I don't need you to protect me, Paul,' replied Alys, icily.

'I'm sorry, Alys, I didn't mean ...'

'Good evening, Paul,' she said, joining the crowd of laughing people going inside.

Paul was left alone in the middle of the crowded street, wanting to strangle someone, to scream, to kick the ground and cry, all at the same time.

It was seven in the evening.

38

The hardest thing had been to slip into the boarding-house unnoticed.

The landlady was hanging round the entrance like a bloodhound, with her overalls and broom. Jürgen had had to wait a couple of hours, wandering around the neighbourhood and watching the entrance to the building surreptitiously. He couldn't risk doing so brazenly, as he had to be sure he wouldn't be recognised later. In the bustling street it was unlikely that anyone would pay much attention to a man in a black overcoat and hat walking with a newspaper under his arm.

He'd hidden his cudgel in the folded paper and, fearful that it might fall, he was squeezing it so hard against his armpit that the next day he would have a considerable bruise. Under his civilian clothes he was wearing the brown uniform of the SA, which would certainly have attracted too much attention in an area that was as full of Jews as this one. His cap was in his pocket, and he'd left his boots at the barracks, choosing a pair of sturdy shoes instead.

Finally, after going past many times, he managed to find a breach in the line of defence. The landlady left her broom leaning against the wall and disappeared through a small inner door, perhaps to prepare dinner. Jürgen made the most of this gap to slip into the house and trot up the stairs to the top floor. Having passed various landings and corridors, he found himself outside Ilse Reiner's door.

He knocked.

If she's not there everything would be easier, thought Jürgen, anxious to complete the task as soon as possible and cross over to the east bank of the Isar where the members of the *Stosstrupp* had been told to meet two hours earlier. It was a historic day, and here he was, wasting his time in some intrigue he couldn't have cared less about.

If at least I'd been able to fight Paul . . . that would have been different.

A smile lit up his face. At the same moment his aunt opened the door and looked straight into his eyes. Perhaps she read betrayal and murder in them, perhaps she was simply afraid of Jürgen's presence. But whatever the reason, she reacted by trying to slam the door shut.

Jürgen was quick. He managed to get his left hand there just in time. The door jamb hit his knuckles hard and he stifled a cry of pain, but he had succeeded in his aim. However hard Ilse pushed, her fragile body was powerless against the brutal strength deployed by Jürgen. He leaned his great weight against the door, and both his aunt and the chain protecting her were dispatched on to the floor.

'If you scream I'll kill you, old woman,' said Jürgen, his voice low and serious.

'Have some respect. I'm younger than your mother,' said Ilse from the floor.

Jürgen didn't reply. His knuckles were bleeding – the blow had been harder than it had seemed. He set the newspaper and cudgel on the ground and approached the neatly made bed. He tore off a piece of the sheet and was tying it around his hand when Ilse, believing him to be distracted, opened the door. Just as she was about to make a run for it, Jürgen yanked hard at her dress, pulling her back down.

'Nice try. So now can we talk?'

'You haven't come here to talk.'

'That's true.'

Grabbing her by the hair, he forced her to stand up again and look him in the eye.

'So, Auntie, where are the papers?'

'How typical of the baron,' snorted Ilse. 'Sending you to do what he doesn't dare do himself. Do you know what it is he's sent you to get?'

'You people and your secrets. No, my father hasn't told me anything, he's just asked me to get your papers. Luckily my mother gave me more detail. She said I have to find a letter of yours that's full of lies, and another from your husband.'

'I have no intention of giving you anything.'

'You don't seem to understand what I'm prepared to do, Auntie.'

He took off his overcoat and put it down on a chair. Then he drew out a red-handled hunting knife. The sharp edge gave off a silvery gleam in the light from the oil lamp, which was reflected in his aunt's trembling eyes.

'You wouldn't dare.'

'Oh, I think you'll find I would.'

For all his bravado, the situation was more difficult than Jürgen had imagined. It wasn't like a tavern brawl, where he would allow his instinct and adrenalin to take over, when his body became a savage, brutal machine.

When he took the woman's right arm and held it down on the bedside table, however, he felt barely any horror. A sadness bit into him like the sharp teeth of a saw, scraping the pit of his stomach, and showing as little mercy as he himself showed when he put the knife to his aunt's fingers and removed her index finger in two messy cuts.

Ilse screamed in pain, but Jürgen was ready and covered her mouth with his hand. He wondered where was the excitement violence usually brought, which was what had first attracted him to the SA.

Could it be the lack of challenge? Because this scared old crow was no challenge at all.

The screams stifled under Jürgen's palm had dissolved into inaudible sobbing. He fixed his gaze on the woman's tearful eyes, trying to take the same pleasure in the situation that he'd felt knocking out the teeth of the young communist a few weeks earlier. But no. He gave a resigned sigh.

'Now will you co-operate? This isn't much fun for either of us.'

Ilse nodded hard.

'I'm glad to hear it. Give me what I've asked you for,' he said, releasing her.

She moved away from Jürgen and with hesitant steps walked towards the wardrobe. The mutilated hand that she held against her chest left a growing stain on her cream-coloured dress. She searched among her clothes with her other hand, till she found a small white envelope.

'This is my letter,' she said, holding it out to Jürgen.

The young man took the envelope, the surface of which bore a bloody smudge. His cousin's name was written on the other side. He tore open one end of the envelope and removed five sheets filled with tight, round handwriting.

Jürgen glanced over the first lines, but then was drawn in by what he read. Halfway through the text his eye bulged, and his breathing became agitated. He threw Ilse a suspicious look, unable to believe what he was seeing.

'It's a lie! A filthy lie!' he cried, stepping towards his aunt and holding the knife to her throat.

'It isn't, Jürgen. I'm sorry you had to find out like this,' she said.

'You're sorry? You feel sorry for me, do you? I've just cut off your finger, you old hag! What's to stop me slitting your throat, eh? Tell me it's a lie,' hissed Jürgen, in a cold whisper that made Ilse's hair stand on end.

'I've been a victim of this particular truth for many years. It's part of what has made you into the monster you are.'

'Does *he* know?'

This last question was too much for Ilse. She staggered, dizzy with the emotion and loss of blood, and Jürgen had to catch her.

'Don't you dare faint now, useless old woman!'

There was a washbasin close by. Jürgen threw his aunt on to the bed and tipped some water over her face.

'Enough,' she said weakly.

'Answer me. Does Paul know?'

'No.'

Jürgen allowed her a few moments to recover. A tide of conflicting feelings passed through his head as he reread the letter, this time to the end.

When he finished, he folded the pages up carefully and put them in his pocket. Now he understood why his father had been so insistent in wanting these papers, and why his mother had asked him to bring them to her first.

They wanted to use me. They think I'm an idiot. No one is going to have this letter but me ... and I'll use it at just the right moment. Yes, that's it. When they least expect it ...

But there was something else he needed. He walked slowly towards the bed and leaned over the mattress.

'I want Hans's letter.'

'I haven't got it. I swear to God. Your father's always been looking for it, but I don't have it, I'm not even sure that it exists,' Ilse stammered, clinging to her mutilated hand.

'I don't believe you,' lied Jürgen. Ilse didn't seem capable of hiding anything at that moment, but all the same he wanted to see what reaction his disbelief would provoke. This time he held the knife to her face.

Ilse tried to push his hand away but, with her strength almost gone, it was like a child pushing at a tonne of granite.

'Leave me alone. For God's sake, haven't you done enough to me?'

Jürgen glanced around. Moving away from the bed, he seized the oil lamp from the nearby table and threw it against the wardrobe. The glass shattered, spilling burning kerosene everywhere.

He returned to the bed and, looking Ilse right in the eye, he placed the tip of the knife against her belly. He inhaled.

Then he buried the blade up to the hilt.

'I have now.'

39

After the argument with Alys, Paul was in a foul mood. He chose to ignore the cold and walked home, a decision which would become the biggest regret of his life.

It took Paul almost an hour to walk the seven kilometres that separated the beer hall from the boarding-house. He barely paid any attention to his surroundings, his head lost in the conversation with Alys, imagining things he could have said that would have changed the outcome. One moment he wished he'd been conciliatory, the next he wished he'd replied in a way that wounded her, so that she would know how he felt. Lost in the interminable spiral of love, he didn't notice what was happening till he was just a few steps from the gate.

Then he smelled the smoke and saw people running. A fire engine was parked in front of the building.

'Where do you think you're going?'

Paul looked up. There was a fire on the third floor.

'Oh, Holy God – Mama!'

On the other side of the road a crowd was forming, a mixture of curious bystanders and people from the boarding-house. Paul ran towards them, searching for familiar faces and shouting Ilse's name. Finally he found the landlady, who was sitting on the kerb, her face smeared with soot that was furrowed with tears. Paul shook her.

'My mother! Where is she?'

The landlady started to cry again, unable to look him in the eye.

'No one's escaped from the fourth floor. Oh, if my father, may he rest in peace, could see what's become of his building!'

'And the firemen?'

'They've not gone in yet, but there's nothing they can do. The fire's blocked the stairways.'

'And from the other roof? The one at number twenty-two?'

'Perhaps,' said the landlady, wringing her calloused hands in distress. 'You can jump from there . . .'

Paul didn't hear the end of her sentence because he was already running towards the neighbours' door. An unfriendly policeman was at the door, questioning one of the boarding-house tenants. He frowned when he saw Paul charging towards him.

'And where do you think you're going? We're cleari– Hey!'

Paul shoved the policeman aside, knocking him to the ground.

The building had five floors, one more than the boarding-house. Each was a private dwelling, though they must all have been empty at the time. Paul groped his way up the stairs as the building's electricity had clearly been cut off.

On the top floor he had to stop because he couldn't find the way on to the roof. Then he understood that he'd have to reach up to a trapdoor in the middle of the ceiling. He jumped, trying to grip the handle, but he was still short by a couple of feet. Desperately he looked around for something that might help him, but there was nothing he could use.

I have no choice but to force the door of one of the apartments.

He threw himself against the nearest door, barging it with his shoulder, but he achieved nothing except a sharp pain running down his arm. So he started kicking at the height of the lock, and succeeded in opening the door after half a dozen blows. He grabbed the first thing he could find in the dark entrance hall, which turned out to be a chair. Standing on that, he was able to reach the trapdoor and lower the wooden ladder that led to the flat roof.

Outside, the air was unbreathable. The wind was blowing the smoke in his direction, and Paul had to cover his mouth with his handkerchief. He almost fell into the space between the two buildings – a gap of a little more than a metre. He could barely see the neighbouring roof.

Where the hell do I jump?

He took his keys from his pocket, and threw them ahead of him. There was a sound Paul identified as the impact with stone or wood, and he jumped in that direction.

For a brief moment he felt his body floating in the smoke. Then he fell on to his hands and knees, scraping his palms. At last he'd reached the boarding-house.

Hang on, Mama. I'm here now.

He had to walk with his hands stretched out in front of him until he had cleared the smoky area, which was at the front of the building, closest to the street. Even through his shoes he could feel the intense heat being given off by the roof. Towards the back there was an awning, a legless rocking chair and the thing Paul was searching for desperately.

Access to the next floor down!

He ran towards the door, afraid that it would be locked. His strength was beginning to fail, and his legs felt heavy.

Please, God, don't let the fire have reached her room. Please. Mama, tell me you were smart enough to turn on the tap and to stuff something wet into the cracks round the door.

The door to the stairs was open. There was smoke in the stairwell, but it was bearable. Paul rushed down as fast as he could, but on the penultimate step he tripped over something. He knew he'd only have to make it to the end of the corridor and turn right, and then he'd be at the entrance to his mother's room.

He tried to move forward, but it was impossible. The smoke was a dirty orange colour, there was no air, and the heat of the fire was so intense that he couldn't take another step.

'Mama!' he said, wanting to cry out, but the only thing that came from his mouth was a dry, painful croak.

The patterned wallpaper began to burn beside him, and Paul realised he would soon be surrounded by the fire if he didn't get out quickly. He doubled back as the flames lit up the stairwell. Paul could now see what he'd tripped over, what those dark stains were on the rug.

There on the floor, lying by the bottom step, was his mother. And she was hurt.

'Mama! No!'

He crouched down beside her, searching for a pulse. Ilse seemed to respond.

'Paul,' she whispered.

'You've got to hang on, Mama! I'll get you out of here!'

The young man lifted her small body and ran up the stairs. Stepping outside, he moved as far from the staircase as he could, but the smoke had spread everywhere.

Paul stopped. He couldn't get through the curtain of smoke with his mother in that state, still less jump blindly between two buildings with her in his arms. Nor could they stay where they were. Whole sections of the roof had now fallen in, and sharp red spears were licking at the gaps. The roof would collapse in a matter of minutes.

'You've got to hang on, Mama. I'll get you out of here. I'll take you to hospital and you'll soon get better. I swear. So you've got to hang on.'

'The ground . . .' said Ilse, coughing slightly. 'Put me down.'

Paul knelt and rested her legs on the ground. It was the first time he'd been able to see the state his mother was in. Her dress covered in blood. The finger hacked off her right hand.

'Who did this to you?' he said with a grimace.

The woman could barely speak. Her face was pale, and her lips trembled. She'd dragged herself out of the bedroom in order to escape the flames, leaving a red streak behind her. The injury, which had forced her to crawl on all fours, had paradoxically kept her alive for longer, as in that position her lungs had absorbed less smoke. But by now Ilse Reiner barely had a breath of life left in her.

'Who, Mama?' Paul repeated. 'Was it Jürgen?'

Ilse opened her eyes. They were red and swollen.

'No . . .'

'Who, then? Did you recognise them?'

Ilse raised a trembling hand to her son's face, stroking it gently. The tips of her fingers were cold. Overwhelmed by pain, Paul knew that this would be the last time his mother touched him, and he was afraid.

'It wasn't . . .'

'Who?'

'It wasn't Jürgen.'

'Tell me, Mama. Tell me who. I'll kill them.'

'You shouldn't . . .'

Another attack of coughing cut her short. Ilse's arms fell limply to her sides.

'You shouldn't hurt Jürgen, Paul.'

'Why, Mama?'

His mother was fighting for every breath now, but she was fighting on the inside too. Paul could see the struggle in her eyes. She had to make a huge effort to get air into her lungs. But even more to force these three last words from her heart.

'He's your brother.'

40

Brother.

Sitting on the kerb, close to where the landlady had sat an hour earlier, Paul tried to digest that word. In under thirty minutes his life had been turned upside down twice – first with the death of his mother, and then by the revelation she'd made with her final breath.

When Ilse died, Paul had embraced her and was tempted to allow himself to die, too. To stay where he was until the flames consumed the ground beneath him.

That's life. Running across a roof that's condemned to collapse, thought Paul, drowning in a pain that was as bitter, dark and thick as oil.

Was it fear that kept him on the roof in the moments after his mother's death? Perhaps he was afraid of facing the world alone. Perhaps if her last words had been 'I love you so much', Paul would have let himself die. But Ilse's words had given a completely different meaning to the questions that had tormented Paul all his life.

Was it hatred, the thirst for vengeance, or the need to know that finally made him act? Perhaps a mixture of all three. What is beyond doubt is that Paul gave his mother a final kiss on the forehead then sprinted to the opposite end of the roof.

He nearly fell over the edge, but managed to stop himself in time. Children sometimes played on the building, and Paul wondered how they got back across. He deduced that they probably left a plank of wood lying around somewhere. Paul had no time to look for it amid the smoke, so he took off his overcoat and jacket, reducing his weight for the jump. If he missed, or if the opposite bit of roof collapsed under his weight, Paul would drop five floors. Without thinking too much, he had taken a running jump, blindly confident that he would make it.

Now he was back at ground level, Paul tried to assemble the puzzle in which Jürgen

my brother

had become the most complex piece of all. Could Jürgen really be Ilse's son? Paul didn't think it possible, as only eight months separated their birth dates. Physically it was possible, but Paul was more inclined to believe that Jürgen was Hans and Brunhilda's son. Eduard, with his darker, rounder complexion, had looked nothing like Jürgen, nor were they alike in temperament. Jürgen did, however, resemble Paul. They both had blue eyes and pronounced cheekbones, though Jürgen's hair was darker.

How could my father have slept with Brunhilda? And why did my mother hide it from me all this time? I always knew she wanted to protect me, but why not tell me this? And how am I supposed to find out the truth now without approaching the von Schroeders?

The landlady interrupted Paul's thoughts. She was still sobbing.

'Herr Reiner, the firemen say the fire's under control, but it'll be necessary to demolish the building as it's no longer safe. They've asked me to tell the tenants that they can take turns to go in and fetch some clothes as you'll all have to spend the night elsewhere.'

Like a robot, Paul joined the dozen people who were going to fetch some of their things. He stepped over the hoses that were still pumping arcs of water, walked along the sodden corridors and stairways accompanied by a firemen, and finally reached his room, where he picked out clothes at random and put them into a small bag.

'That's enough,' urged the fireman, who had been waiting uneasily in the doorway. 'We have to go.'

Still dazed, Paul followed him. But a few metres later, a faint idea flickered in his brain, like the edge of a gold coin in a bucket of sand. He turned and ran.

'Hey, listen! We've got to get out!'

Paul ignored the man. He ran into his room and dived under his bed. In the narrow space he struggled to move aside a pile of books he'd put there to hide what was behind.

'I told you to get out! Look, it isn't safe here,' said the fireman, pulling on Paul's legs till his body appeared.

Paul didn't mind. He had what he'd come to get.

A black mahogany box, smooth and plain.

It was 9.30 at night.

Paul took his small bag and ran across town.

If he hadn't been in such a state, he would undoubtedly have noticed that something was going on in Munich, something greater even than his own tragedy. There were more people around than usual for that time of night. The bars and taverns were heaving, and angry voices emerged from inside. Anxious men huddled in groups on street corners, and there wasn't a single policeman in sight.

But Paul paid no attention to what was going on around him, he just wanted to cover the distance that separated him from his goal in as little time as possible. Right now it was the only clue he had. He cursed himself bitterly for not having seen it, for not having worked it out sooner.

Metzger's pawnshop was closed. The doors were thick and solid, so Paul didn't waste any time knocking. Nor in calling out, even though he assumed – correctly – that being an avaricious old man, the money-lender would live on the premises, perhaps in a rickety old bed round the back.

He put his bag down by the door and looked around him for something solid. There were no loose paving stones, but he found a dustbin lid, the size of a small tray. He picked it up and threw it at the shop window, which shattered into a thousand pieces. Paul's heart was jumping out of his chest and pounding in his ears, but he ignored that, too. If anyone called the police they might arrive before he'd got what he'd come for, but then again, they might not.

I hope not, thought Paul. *Otherwise, the next place I'll be going for answers will be the von Schroeders' mansion. Even if my uncle's friends send me to prison for the rest of my life.*

Paul leaped inside. His shoes crunched on the mass of glass shards, a mixture of the bits of broken window and a Bohemian crystal dinner-service that had also been smashed by his projectile.

It was pitch black inside the shop. The only light came from the back room, from where he could hear loud shouts.

'Who's there! I'm calling the police!'

'Go ahead!' Paul shouted back.

A rectangle of light appeared on the floor, throwing into relief the ghostly shapes of the pawnshop wares. Paul stood there in the middle of them, waiting for Metzger to emerge.

'Get out of here, damned Nazis!' shouted the moneylender, appearing in the doorway, his eyes still half closed from sleep.

'I'm not a Nazi, Herr Metzger.'

'Who the hell are you?' He came into the shop and switched on the light, checking that the intruder was alone. 'There's nothing of any value here!'

'Perhaps not, but there's something I need.'

The old man's eyes came into focus at that moment and he recognised Paul.

'What are you ... Oh.'

'I see you remember me.'

'You were here recently,' Metzger babbled.

'Do you always remember all your customers?'

'What the devil do you want? You'll have to pay me for that window!'

'Don't try to change the subject. I want to know who pawned that pistol I retrieved.'

'I don't remember.'

Paul didn't reply. He simply took the weapon from his trouser pocket and pointed it at the old man, who retreated, holding his hands out in front of his body like a shield.

'Don't shoot! I swear to you, I don't remember! It's been almost two decades!'

'Let's suppose I believe you. What about your records?'

'Put the gun down, please ... I can't show you my records, that information is confidential. Please, son, be reasonable ...'

Paul took six steps towards him and raised the gun to shoulder height. The barrel was now only two centimetres from the forehead of the moneylender, who was drenched in sweat.

'Herr Metzger, let me explain. Either you show me the records, or I'll shoot you. It's a simple choice.'

'Very well! Very well!'

His hands still raised, the old man led the way to the back room. They crossed a large storeroom that was filled with spider's webs and was even dustier than the shop itself. Cardboard boxes were stacked from floor to ceiling on rusty metal shelves and the stink of mould and damp was unbearable. But there was something else to that smell, something indefinable and rotten.

'How can you stand this smell, Metzger?'

'Smell? I can't smell anything,' said the old man without turning round.

Paul guessed that the moneylender had got used to the stench, having spent countless years among other people's things. The man had clearly never enjoyed a life of his own and Paul couldn't help feeling some pity for him. He had to banish such thoughts from his head in order to continue gripping his father's pistol with the same sense of purpose.

At the back of the storeroom there was a metal door. Metzger removed some keys from his pocket and opened it. He gestured for Paul to pass.

'You first,' Paul replied.

The old man looked at him curiously, his pupils steady. In his mind Paul imagined him as a dragon protecting his cave of treasure, and he told himself to be more alert than ever. The miser was as dangerous as a cornered rat, and at any moment he could turn and bite.

'Swear you won't steal anything from me.'

'What would be the point of that? Remember I'm the one holding the weapon.'

'Swear it,' the man insisted.

'I swear I won't steal anything from you, Metzger. Tell me what I need to know, and I'll leave you in peace.'

To the right was a wooden bookcase filled with books in black bindings; to the left, an enormous safe. The moneylender immediately positioned himself in front of it, protecting it with his body.

'There you have it,' he said, gesturing Paul towards the bookcase.

'You find it for me.'

'No,' the old man replied, his voice tense. He wasn't prepared to move from his corner.

He's getting bolder. If I push him too much he might jump on me. Damn it, why did I load the gun? I wouldn't have needed it to overpower him.

'At least tell me which volume to look in.'

'It's on the shelf, level with your head, the fourth from the left.'

Without taking his eyes off Metzger, Paul found the book. He removed it carefully and held it out to the moneylender.

'Find the reference.'

'I don't remember the number.'

'91231. Be quick.'

Reluctantly the old man took the book, and gently turned the pages. Paul glanced around the storeroom, afraid that at any moment a group of policemen would turn up to arrest him. He'd already stayed too long.

'Here it is,' said the old man, handing back the book, open at one of the early pages.

There was no record of the date, only a curt '1905 / Week 16'. Paul found the number at the bottom of the page.

'There's just a name. Clovis Nagel. The address isn't there.'

'The customer preferred not to give any more details.'

'Is that legal, Metzger?'

'The law on the matter is confused.'

It wasn't the only entry on which Nagel's name appeared. He was listed in the 'Depositing Customer' column for another ten items.

'I want to see the other items he pawned.'

Relieved to be getting the intruder away from his safe, the money-lender led Paul to one of the bookshelves in the outer storeroom. He took down a cardboard box and showed the contents to Paul.

'Here they are.'

A couple of cheap watches, a gold ring, a silver bracelet ... Paul examined the trinkets but could not understand what linked Nagel's objects. He was beginning to despair; after all the effort he now had even more questions than before.

Why would one man pawn so many objects on the same day? He must have been running away from someone, probably from my father. But if I want to find out any more I'll have to find this man, and a name alone doesn't help much.

'I want to know where to find Nagel.'

'You've already seen, son. I don't have an address ...'

Paul raised his right hand and struck the old man. Metzger fell to the floor and brought his hands to his face. A trickle of blood appeared between his fingers.

'No, please no, don't hit me again!'

Paul had to stop himself from striking the man again. His whole body was filled with a sick energy, an indistinct hatred that had built up over many years, and which had suddenly found a target in the pathetic bleeding figure at his feet.

What am I doing?

Suddenly he felt sick at what he'd done. This had to be brought to an end as soon as possible.

'Talk, Metzger. I know you're hiding something from me.'

'I don't remember him too well. He was a soldier, I could tell from the way he talked. Perhaps a sailor. He said he was going back to South-West Africa, and that he wouldn't be needing any of those things there.'

'What was he like?'

'Rather short, fine features. I don't remember much, please, don't hit me again!'

Short, fine-featured. Eduard described the man who was in the room with my father and my uncle as short with delicate features like a girl's. It could have been Clovis Nagel. And if my father discovered him stealing things on the boat? Perhaps he was a spy. Or had my father asked him to pawn the gun in his name? He knew, of course, that he was in danger.

Feeling as though his head was about to explode, Paul walked out of the storeroom, leaving Metzger snivelling on the floor. He jumped up on to the front window ledge, but suddenly remembered that he'd left his bag beside the door. Fortunately it was still there.

But everything else around him had changed.

Dozens of people filled the streets, in spite of the lateness of the hour. They huddled on the pavement, some moving from one huddle to another, conveying information like bees pollinating flowers. Paul approached the closest group.

'They say the Nazis set fire to a building in Schwabing . . .'

'No, it was the communists . . .'

'They're setting up checkpoints . . .'

Troubled, Paul took one of the men by the arm and drew him aside. 'What's going on?'

The man took a cigarette from his mouth and gave him a crooked smile. He was delighted to find willing ears for the bad news he wanted to pass on.

'Haven't you heard? Hitler and his Nazis are staging a *coup d'état*. It's time for the revolution. At last there will be some changes.'

'You say it's a *coup d'état*?'

'They've forced their way into the Bürgerbräukeller with hundreds of men and they're keeping everyone locked inside, starting with the State Commissioner of Bavaria.'

Paul's heart gave a somersault.

'Alys!'

41

Until the shooting started, Alys had thought the night belonged to her.

The argument with Paul had left a bitter taste in her mouth. She understood that she was madly in love with him, she could see that clearly now. Which was precisely why she was more scared than ever.

She had decided therefore to focus on the task in hand. She entered the main room of the beer hall, which was more than three-quarters full. More than a thousand people were crowding around the tables, and soon there'd be at least another five hundred, as people kept arriving. German flags hung from the wall, barely visible through the tobacco smoke. The room was humid and stifling, which was why those present kept harassing the waitresses, who jostled through the crowds carrying trays with half a dozen beer glasses above their heads, never spilling a drop.

Now that's tough work, thought Alys, grateful again for all that today's opportunity put within her reach.

Elbowing her way through, she managed to find a place at the foot of the speakers' podium. Three or four other photographers had already taken up their position. One looked at Alys in surprise and nudged his companions.

'Be careful, gorgeous. Don't forget to take your finger away from the lens.'

'And you remember to take yours out of your arse, idiot. Your nails are filthy.'

The photographer inspected his fingertips and turned as red as a beetroot. The others cheered.

'Serves you right, Fritz!'

Smiling to herself, Alys found a position where she would have a good view. She tested the light and did a few quick calculations. With a bit of luck she could get a good shot. She began to get excited. Putting that idiot in his place had done her good. Besides, from that day on things were going to change for the better. She'd talk to Paul, they'd face their problems together. And with a new, stable job, she would truly feel fulfilled.

She was still immersed in her daydream when Gustav von Kahr, State Commissioner of Bavaria, climbed on to the stage. She took a number of photos, including one she thought might be rather interesting, in which von Kahr was gesticulating widely.

All of a sudden a commotion broke out at the back of the room. Alys craned her neck to see what was going on, but between the bright lights that surrounded the podium and the wall of people behind her, she couldn't see a thing. The roar of the crowd, together with the thunder of falling tables and chairs, and the smashing of dozens of glasses, was deafening.

Someone emerged from the crowd close to Alys, a sweaty little man wearing a creased raincoat. He pushed aside a man sitting at the table closest to the podium, climbed on to his chair and from there on to the table.

Alys turned her camera towards him, in a single instant capturing the wild stare, the slight trembling of his left hand, the cheap clothes, the pimp's haircut plastered across his forehead, the cruel little moustache, the raised arm and the gun aimed at the ceiling.

She wasn't afraid, and she didn't hesitate. All that went through her head were the words August Muntz had said to her years before.

There are moments in the life of a photographer when a photograph passes in front of you, just a single photograph, which could change your life and the lives of those around you. That's the decisive moment, Alys. You'll see it before it happens. And when it happens, shoot. Don't think, shoot.

She pressed the button just as the man pulled the trigger.

'The national revolution has begun!' the little man shouted in a powerful, grating voice. 'This place is surrounded by six hundred armed men! No one leaves. And if there isn't immediate silence, I'll order my men to stick a machine gun up in the gallery.'

The crowd fell silent, but Alys didn't notice, nor was she alarmed by the Brownshirts who had appeared from all sides.

'I declare the Bavarian government deposed! The police and the army have joined our flag, the swastika – may they hang from every barracks and police station.'

Another feverish cry erupted in the room. There was applause punctuated with boos and shouts of 'Mexico! Mexico!' and 'South America!' Alys was oblivious. The shot was still ringing in her ears, the image of the little man firing was still engraved on her retina; and her mind was stuck on three words.

The decisive moment.

I've done it, she thought.

Squeezing the camera to her chest, Alys dived into the crowd. Right now her only priority was to make it out of there and get to a darkroom. She couldn't exactly remember the name of the man who'd fired the gun, though his face was very familiar ... he was one of the many fanatical anti-Semites who shouted their opinions in the town's taverns.

Ziegler. No ... Hitler. That's it – Hitler. The mad Austrian.

Alys didn't believe this coup stood any chance at all. Who would follow a madman who had declared that he would wipe the Jews from the face of the earth? In the synagogues people were joking about idiots like Hitler. And the image she'd captured with sweat dripping down his forehead and the wild expression in his eyes would put that man in his place.

By which she meant a lunatic asylum.

Alys could barely make any headway through the sea of bodies. People had started shouting again, and some of them were fighting. One man smashed a beer glass on another's head, and the dregs soaked Alys's jacket. It took her almost twenty minutes to reach the other end of the hall, but there she found a wall of Brownshirts armed with rifles and pistols blocking the exit. She tried to talk to them, but the stormtroopers refused to let her through.

Hitler and the dignitaries he'd interrupted had disappeared through a side door. A new speaker had taken his place, and the temperature in the room continued to rise.

With a grim expression, Alys found a spot where she'd be as protected as possible and tried to think of a way to escape.

Three hours later her mood was bordering on desperation. Hitler and his acolytes had given a number of speeches, and the band in the gallery had played '*Deutschland über alles*' more than a dozen times. Alys had tried to move discreetly back into the main hall, in search of a window through which she could climb, but the stormtroopers blocked her path there too. They weren't even allowing people to go to the bathroom, which in such a crowded place, and with the waitresses still serving beer after beer, would soon be a problem. She'd already seen more than one person relieving himself against the back wall.

But hang on – the waitresses!

Struck by a sudden flash of inspiration, Alys approached a service table. She picked up an empty tray, took off her jacket, wrapped it round her camera and held it under the tray. Then she collected a couple of empty beer glasses and headed for the kitchen.

Perhaps they won't see. I'm wearing a white blouse and black skirt just like the waitresses. Perhaps they won't see I'm not wearing an apron. Just as long as they don't notice the jacket under the tray . . . !

Alys passed through the crowd, holding the tray aloft, and had to bite her tongue when a couple of patrons touched her backside. She didn't want to attract attention to herself. As she approached the swinging doors she got behind another waitress, and passed by the SA guards, fortunately without any of them giving her a second glance.

The kitchen was long and very large. The same tense atmosphere reigned in there, though without the tobacco smoke and flags. A couple of waiters were filling glasses with beer while the kitchen-boys and cooks talked to one another by the stoves, under the stern gaze of a couple of Brownshirts, who were again blocking the exit. Both were carrying rifles and pistols.

Shit.

Not knowing quite what to do, Alys realised she couldn't just stand there in the middle of the kitchen. Someone would realise that she wasn't one of the staff and throw her out. She left the glasses in the enormous metal sink and picked up a dirty rag she found near by. She ran it under the tap, soaked it, wrung it out and pretended to be cleaning while she tried to come up with a plan. As she looked around discreetly, an idea occurred to her.

She sidled over to one of the rubbish bins next to the sink. It was full almost to bursting with leftovers. She placed her jacket in it, put the lid on, and picked up the bin. Then she began to walk brazenly towards the door.

'You can't go past, Fräulein,' said one of the Brownshirts.

'I've got to take out the rubbish.'

'Leave it here.'

'But the bins are full. You can't have full rubbish bins inside a kitchen, it's against the law.'

'Don't worry about that, Fräulein, we're the law now. Put the bin back where it was.'

Alys, deciding to gamble everything on a single hand, put the bin down on the floor and folded her arms.

'If you want to move it, move it yourself.'

'I'm telling you to get that thing away from here.'

The young man didn't take his eyes off Alys. The kitchen staff had noticed the scene and were looking at him angrily. As Alys had her back to them, they couldn't tell she wasn't one of them.

'Come on, man, let her past,' the other stormtrooper intervened. 'It's bad enough having to be stuck here in the kitchen. We're going to have to wear these clothes all night and the smell's going to stick to my shirt.'

The one who'd spoken first shrugged and moved aside.

'You go, then. Accompany her to the rubbish container outside and then get back here as quickly as possible.'

Silently cursing, Alys led the way. A narrow door gave on to an even narrower alley. The only light came from a single bulb at the opposite end, closer to the street. The rubbish container was there, surrounded by scrawny cats.

'So . . . have you been working here long, Fräulein?' said the Brownshirt, in a slightly embarrassed tone.

I don't believe it! We're walking down an alley, I'm carrying a rubbish bin, he's carrying a machine gun, and this idiot is making a pass at me!

'You might say I'm new,' replied Alys, pretending to be friendly. 'And what about you, have you been carrying out *coups d'état* for long?'

'No, this is my first,' the man replied seriously, failing to catch her irony.

They reached the rubbish container.

'Right, well, you can go back now. I'll stay and empty the bin.'

'Oh no, Fräulein. You empty the bin, then I've got to accompany you back.'

'I wouldn't want you to have to wait for me.'

'I'd wait for you any time you like. You're lovely . . .'

188

He moved to kiss her. Alys tried to step back but she was trapped between the rubbish container and the Brownshirt.

'No, please,' said Alys.

'Come on, Fräulein . . .'

'Please, no.'

The Brownshirt hesitated, remorseful.

'I'm sorry if I offended you. I just thought . . .'

'Don't worry about it. It's just that I'm already engaged.'

'I'm sorry. He's a lucky man.'

He is?

'Don't worry about it,' repeated Alys, shaken.

'Let me help you with the bin.'

'No!'

Alys tried to pull away the hand of the Brownshirt, who in his confusion let go of the bin. It tumbled over and rolled along the ground. Some of the leftovers scattered in a semicircle, revealing Alys's jacket and its precious cargo.

'What the hell is that?'

The parcel had opened slightly and the lens of the camera was clearly visible. The soldier looked at Alys, who wore a guilty expression. She didn't need to confess.

'Damn slut! You're a communist spy!' said the Brownshirt, feeling for his cudgel.

Before he could grab it, Alys picked up the metal lid of the dustbin and tried to hit the stormtrooper on the head. Seeing the attack coming, he raised his right arm. The lid struck his wrist with a deafening noise.

'Aaargh! That hurt, bitch!'

He snatched the lid with his left hand, throwing it far away. Alys tried to dodge him and run off, but the alley was too narrow. The Nazi grabbed her by the blouse and pulled hard. Alys's body turned, and her shirt tore down one side, exposing her underwear. The Nazi, who'd raised an arm to strike her, froze for a moment, caught between excitement and fury. That look filled the girl's heart with fear.

'Alys!'

She looked towards the entrance to the alley.

Paul was there, in a dreadful state, but he was there all the same. In spite of the cold he was wearing only a sweater. His breathing was ragged and he had a stitch from having run across the city. Half an hour earlier he'd planned to enter the Bürgerbräukeller by the back door, but he hadn't even been able to cross the Ludwigsbrücke, as the Nazis had set up a roadblock.

So he had taken the long way round. He looked for policemen, soldiers, anyone who could answer his questions about what was going on in the beer hall, but all he found were citizens applauding those who had taken part in the coup, or booing them, from a wise distance.

Having crossed to the opposite bank via the Maximiliansbrücke, he started asking the people he met on the street. Finally someone mentioned the alley that led to the kitchens and Paul ran towards it, praying that he'd arrive before it was too late.

He was so surprised to see Alys outside, struggling with the Brownshirt, that instead of launching a surprise attack he announced his arrival like an idiot. When the other man drew his gun, Paul had no choice but to hurl himself forward. His shoulder bashed the Nazi's stomach, knocking him over.

The two of them rolled on the ground, struggling for the weapon. The other man was stronger than Paul, who was also utterly drained by the events of the previous hours. The struggle lasted less than five seconds, at the end of which the other man pushed Paul aside, got to his knees and pointed the gun.

Alys, who had now retrieved the metal dustbin lid, stepped in, pounding the soldier furiously with the lid. The impact rung out through the alley like the crash of cymbals. The Nazi's eyes went blank, but he didn't fall. Alys struck him again, and at last he toppled forward and fell flat on his face.

Paul got up and ran to embrace her, but she pushed him away and crouched down on the ground.

'What's wrong with you? Are you all right?'

Alys stood up, furious. In her hands she held the remains of the camera, which was completely destroyed. During Paul's fight with the Nazi it had been crushed.

'Look.'

'It's broken. Don't worry, we'll buy a better one.'

'You don't understand! There were photos in there!'

'Alys, there's no time for that now. We have to go before his friends come looking for him.'

He tried to take the girl by the hand but she pulled away and ran ahead of him.

42

They didn't look back until they were far from the Bürgerbräukeller. At last they stopped beside the church of St Johannes, whose impressive spire pointed at the night sky like an accusing finger. Paul led Alys to the archway over the main entrance to gain shelter from the cold.

'God, Alys, you have no idea how scared I was,' he said, kissing her on the mouth. She returned the kiss without much conviction.

'What's going on?'

'Nothing.'

'That's not what it looks like to me,' said Paul, annoyed.

'I said it's nothing.'

Paul decided not to pursue the matter. When Alys was in this mood, trying to get her out of it was like trying to escape from quicksand: the more you struggled the deeper you sank.

'Are you all right? Have they hurt you, or . . . anything?'

She shook her head. It was only then that she fully registered Paul's appearance. His shirt stained with blood, his face covered in soot, his bloodshot eyes.

'What's happened to you, Paul?'

'My mother died,' he replied, lowering his head.

As Paul recounted the events of the night, Alys felt sorrow for him and shame at the way she'd treated him. More than once she opened her mouth to ask his forgiveness, but she had never believed in the meaning of that word. It was a disbelief fed by pride.

When he told her his mother's last words, Alys was astonished. She couldn't understand how the brutal, vicious Jürgen could be Paul's brother, and yet deep down it didn't surprise her. Paul had a dark side that flared up at certain moments, like a sudden autumn wind shaking the curtains of a cosy house. And at the same time – though she would rather have died than admit this out loud – she'd seen something in Jürgen's savagery on the night of the party that had unsettled her dreams, because it wasn't quite the disgust he provoked in her rational mind.

When Paul described breaking in to the pawnshop, and how he'd had to hit Metzger to make him talk, Alys began to feel very afraid for him. Everything to do with this business seemed unbearable, and she wanted to distance him from it as quickly as possible, before the mystery consumed him completely.

Paul concluded his tale by recounting his dash to the beer hall.

'And that's all.'

'It's more than enough, I think.'

'What do you mean?'

'You aren't seriously planning to keep digging around, are you? It's obvious there's someone out there who is prepared to do anything to keep the truth hidden.'

'That's precisely the reason to keep digging. It proves someone's responsible for the murder of my father.'

There was a brief pause.

'Of my parents.'

Paul didn't cry. After what had just happened, his body was begging him to cry, his soul needed him to and his heart was overflowing with tears. But Paul kept it all inside, forming a small shell around his heart. Perhaps some ridiculous sense of manhood wouldn't allow him to show his feelings in front of the woman he loved. Perhaps it was this that ignited what happened moments later.

'Paul, you should give up,' said Alys, increasingly alarmed.

'I have no intention of doing that.'

'But you have no proof. No clues.'

'I have a name: Clovis Nagel. I have a place: South-West Africa.'

'South-West Africa is a very big place.'

'I'll start at Windhoek. A white man shouldn't be hard to spot over there.'

'South-West Africa is very big ... and very far away,' repeated Alys, emphasising every word.

'I have to do it. I'll leave on the first boat.'

'So that's it?'

'Yes, Alys. Haven't you listened to a word I've said since we met? Don't you realise how important it is for me to find out what happened nineteen years ago? And now ... now this.'

For a moment Alys contemplated stopping him. Explaining how much she'd miss him, how much she needed him. How much she'd fallen in love with him. But pride stilled her tongue. Just as it prevented her from telling Paul the truth about her own behaviour over the last few days.

'So go, then, Paul. Do whatever you have to do.'

Paul looked at her, utterly bewildered. The icy tone of her voice made him feel as though his heart had been torn out and buried in the snow.

'Alys ...'

'Go straight away. Leave now.'

'Alys, please!'

'Leave, I'm telling you.'

Paul seemed on the verge of tears, and she prayed that he would cry, that he'd change his mind and tell her he loved her and that his love for her was more important than a search that had brought him nothing but pain and death. Perhaps Paul was waiting for something similar, or perhaps he was just trying to record Alys's face in his memory. For long, bitter years she would curse herself for the haughtiness that overcame her, just as Paul would blame himself for not having taken the tram back to the boarding-house before his mother was stabbed.

Or for having turned round and walked away.

'You know what? I'm glad. This way you won't burst into my dreams and trample all over them,' said Alys, throwing to her feet the broken bits of the camera she had been clinging to until that moment. 'Since I met you only bad things have happened to me. I want you out of my life, Paul.'

Paul hesitated for a moment, and then, without looking back, said, 'So be it.'

Alys remained in the church doorway for several minutes, fighting a silent battle against her tears. Suddenly a figure emerged from the darkness, from the same direction in which Paul had disappeared. Alys tried to collect herself and put a smile on her face.

He's coming back. He's understood, and he's coming back, she thought, taking a step towards the figure.

But the street lights revealed that the person approaching was a man in a grey raincoat and hat. Too late, Alys realised it was one of the men who had followed her that afternoon.

She turned to run, but as she did she saw his companion, who had come round the corner and was less than three metres away. She tried to escape, but the two men lunged at her and caught her by the waist.

'Your father's looking for you, Fräulein Tannenbaum.'

Alys struggled in vain. There was nothing she could do.

A car emerged from a nearby street and one of her father's gorillas opened the door. The other pushed her towards it and tried to force her head down.

'You'd best be careful with me, imbeciles,' said Alys, with a look of scorn. 'I'm pregnant.'

43

Elizabeth Bay, 28 August 1933

Dear Alys,

I've lost count of how many times I've written to you. At a rate of once a month it must be more than a hundred letters, all of them unanswered.

I don't know if they're reaching you and you've decided to forget me. Or perhaps you've moved house and not left a forwarding address. This one will go to your father's house. I write to you there every once in a while, even though I know that it is useless. I remain hopeful that one of these will somehow get past your father. In any case, I shall keep writing to you. These letters have become my only contact with my former life.

I want to begin, as always, by asking you to forgive me for the way I left. I've recalled that night ten years ago so many times, and I know I shouldn't have behaved in the way I did. I'm sorry I shattered your dreams. Each day I've prayed for you to be able to realise your dream of being a press photographer, and I hope that over these years you've succeeded.

Life in the colonies isn't simple. Ever since Germany lost these lands South Africa has controlled the mandate over the former German territory. We aren't welcome here, though they tolerate us.

There aren't many jobs going. I work in farms and in the diamond mines for a few weeks at a time. When I've saved a bit of money I travel the country in search of Clovis Nagel. It's not an easy task. I've found traces of him in the villages of the Orange River basin. One time I visited a mine site that he'd just left. I missed him by only a few minutes.

I also followed a tip-off that led me north, to the Waterburg peninsula. There I met a strange, proud tribe, the Herero. I spent some months with them, and they taught me how to hunt and gather in the desert. I fell sick with a fever, and for a long time I was very weak, but they took care of me. I've learned a lot from these people, besides physical skills. They are exceptional. They live in the shadow of death, every day a constant struggle to find water and adapt their lives to the pressures from the white men.

I'm out of paper, this is the last piece of a batch I bought from a peddler on the road to Swakopmund. Tomorrow I'm heading back there, in search of new leads. I'll go on foot, as I've run out of money, so my search will have to be a brief one. The hardest thing about being here, apart from the lack of news about you, is the time it takes me to earn my living. I've often been on the point of giving it all up. However, I don't mean to give up. Sooner or later I'll find him.

I think about you, about what has happened over these past ten years. I hope you are well and happy. If you decide to write to me, write to the Windhoek post office. The address is on the envelope.

Once again, forgive me.

I love you,

PAUL

THE FELLOW CRAFT
1934

In which the initiate learns that the path cannot be taken alone

The secret handshake of the Fellow Craft degree involves pressing hard
on the knuckle of the middle finger, and ends when the brother Mason
returns an identical greeting. The secret name of this handshake is
JACHIN, from the column representing the sun in Solomon's Temple.
Again there is a trick to the spelling-out, which must be given thus:
A – J – C – H – I – N.

44

Jürgen was admiring himself in the mirror.

He tugged lightly at his lapels, decorated with a skull and the insignia of the SS. He never tired of looking at himself in his new uniform. Walter Heck's design and the excellent workmanship of tailor Hugo Boss, highly celebrated in the society press, inspired reverence in everyone who saw it. When Jürgen walked down the street, children would stand to attention and raise their arm in salute. The previous week a couple of old ladies had stopped him and told him how lovely it was to see strong, healthy young men getting Germany back on track. They asked whether he'd lost his eye fighting the communists. Pleased by this, Jürgen had helped them carry their shopping bags to a nearby doorway.

At that moment there was a knock at the door.

'Come in.'

'You look good,' said his mother, coming into the large bedroom.

'I know.'

'Are you eating with us today?'

'I don't think so, Mama. I've been called to a meeting at the Security Service.'

'No doubt they want to recommend you for a promotion. You've been an *Untersturmführer* for too long now.'

Jürgen nodded cheerfully and picked up his cap.

'The car's waiting for you at the door. I'll tell Cook to prepare something for you in case you're back early.'

'Thanks, Mama,' said Jürgen, kissing Brunhilda on the forehead. He went out into the corridor, his black boots echoing loudly on the marble steps. A maid was waiting with his overcoat in the entrance hall. Ever since Otto and his cards had disappeared from their lives eleven years earlier, their economic situation had gradually been improving. An army of servants was once again attending to the day-to-day running of the mansion, though Jürgen was now head of the household.

'Will you be coming back for dinner, sir?'

Jürgen inhaled sharply when he heard her use that mode of address. It always happened whenever he was nervous and unsettled, as he was that morning. The most trivial of details disturbed his icy exterior and exposed the storm of conflicts that raged inside him.

'The baroness will give you instructions.'

Soon they'll start addressing me by my proper title, he thought as he stepped out on to the street. His hands were shaking slightly. Fortunately he had folded his overcoat over his arm, so the driver did not notice when he opened the door for him.

In the past, Jürgen had been able to channel his impulses through violence, but since the Nazi Party's election victories the previous year, the undesirable factions had become more cautious. Every day Jürgen found it harder to control himself. On the journey he tried to breathe slowly. He didn't want to arrive agitated and nervous.

Especially if I'm going to be promoted, as Mama says.

'Frankly, my dear von Schroeder, you give me grave doubts.'

'Doubts, sir?'

'Doubts concerning your loyalty.'

Jürgen noticed his hand had started to shake again and he had to squeeze his knuckles hard to get it under control.

The meeting room was completely empty apart from Reinhard Heydrich and himself. The head of the Security Service, the intelligence organ of the Nazi Party, was a tall man with a clear brow, just a couple of months older than Jürgen. In spite of his youth he'd become one of the most powerful men in Germany. His organisation was tasked with discovering threats – real or imaginary – to the party. Jürgen had heard that on the day they interviewed him for the job, Himmler had asked Heydrich how he would organise a Nazi intelligence agency and Heydrich had replied with a rehash of all the spy novels he'd ever read. The Security Service was already feared throughout Germany – though whether this owed more to cheap fiction or innate talent was unclear.

'Why do you say that, sir?'

Heydrich put his hand on a folder in front of him, which bore Jürgen's name.

'You started out in the SA during the early days of the movement. That's fine, it's interesting. Surprising, though, that someone of your ... lineage should ask specifically for a place in an SA battalion. And then there are the recurring episodes of violence reported by your superiors. I've consulted a psychologist about you ...'

He's consulted a psychologist about me!

'... and he suggests that you might have a serious personality disorder. Still, that's not a crime in itself, though it might' – he emphasised the 'might' with a half-smile and a raise of his eyebrows – 'be a handicap. But now we come to the thing that most concerns me. You were called – like the rest of the *Stosstrupp* – to attend the special event at the Bürgerbräukeller on 8 November 1923. However, you never turned up.'

Heydrich paused, allowing his last words to float in the air. Jürgen began to sweat. After the election victories, the Nazis had begun, slowly and systematically, to take vengeance on anyone who'd obstructed the 1923 uprising, thus delaying Hitler's rise to power by a year. For months, Jürgen had lived in fear that someone would point the finger at him.

Heydrich continued, his tone now menacing.

'According to your superior you did not report to the location of the meeting as you were required to do. However, it would seem that – and I quote – "Stormtrooper Jürgen von Schroeder was with a squadron of 10th Company on the night of 8 November. His shirt was soaked in blood and he claimed to have been attacked by a number of communists, and that the blood was from one of them, a man he had stabbed. He requested to join the squadron, which was controlled by a police commissioner from the Schwabing district, until the coup was over." Is this correct?'

'Down to the last comma, sir.'

'Right. That must be what the investigating commission thought, since they awarded you the party's gold insignia and the medal of the Blood Order,' said Heydrich, pointing to Jürgen's chest.

The party's gold insignia was one of the most sought-after decorations in Germany. It was made up of a Nazi flag shaped into a circle, surrounded by a laurel wreath in gold. It distinguished those members of the party who had signed up before Hitler's victory in 1933. Until that day, the Nazis had had to recruit people to join their ranks. From that day on, endless queues formed at the party's headquarters. Not everybody was granted the privilege.

As for the Blood Order, it was the most valuable medal in the Reich. The only people to wear it were those who had taken part in the 1923 *coup d'état*, which had come to a tragic end with the death of sixteen Nazis at the hands of the police. It was a decoration even Heydrich didn't wear.

'I do wonder,' continued the head of the Security Service, tapping his lips with the edge of the file, 'whether we oughtn't to open a commission of inquiry into you, my friend.'

'That wouldn't be necessary, sir,' said Jürgen, in a whisper, knowing just how brief and decisive commissions of inquiry tended to be in those days.

'No? The most recent reports say you have been somewhat "cool in the carrying out of your duty", that there's "a lack of involvement" ... Shall I go on?'

'That's because I've been kept off the streets, sir!'

'It's possible, then, that other people are concerned about you?'

'I assure you, sir, my commitment is absolute.'

'Well then, there is one way you can regain the trust of this office.'

Finally the penny dropped. Heydrich had summoned Jürgen with a proposition in mind. He wanted something from him, and that was why he'd piled on such pressure from the start. He probably had no idea what Jürgen had been doing that night in 1923, but what Heydrich did or didn't know didn't matter. His word was law.

'I'll do anything, sir,' Jürgen said, already a little calmer.

'Well then, Jürgen. I can call you Jürgen, can't I?'

'Of course, sir,' he said, swallowing his anger that the other man was not returning the courtesy.

'Have you heard about Freemasonry, Jürgen?'

'Of course. My father was a member of a lodge when he was young. I think he soon tired of it.'

Heydrich nodded. It didn't come as a surprise to him, and Jürgen deduced that he'd already known.

'Since we took power the Masons have been ... actively discouraged.'

'I know, sir,' said Jürgen, smiling at the euphemism. In *Mein Kampf*, a book every German had read – and had on show at home if they knew what was good for them – Hitler had pronounced his visceral hatred of Masonry.

'A good number of the lodges have dissolved voluntarily or reorganised. Those particular lodges were of little significance to us, as they were all Prussian, with Aryan members and nationalist tendencies. Since they have dissolved voluntarily and handed over their membership lists no measures have been taken against them ... for the moment.'

'I gather, then, that some lodges are still troubling you, sir?'

'It is quite clear to us that many lodges have remained active, the so-called "humanitarian" lodges. The bulk of their members are of a liberal bent, Jews, that sort of thing ...'

'Why don't you simply ban them, sir?'

'Jürgen, Jürgen,' said Heydrich in a patronising tone, 'that would only hinder their activity, at best. As long as they retain a scrap of hope they would continue to meet and talk about their compasses and squares and all that Judaic rubbish. What I want is each of their names on a little fourteen-by-seven card.'

Heydrich's little cards were famous throughout the party. A vast room next to his office in Berlin stored information on those considered 'undesirable' by the party: communists, homosexuals, Jews, Masons, and generally anyone inclined to comment that the Führer seemed a little tired in his speech today. Whenever someone was denounced, a new card would join the other tens of thousands. The fate of those who appeared on the cards was as yet unknown.

'If Masonry were banned, they'd simply go underground like rats.'

'Precisely!' said Heydrich, smacking his hand down on the desk. He leaned in towards Jürgen and said in a confidential tone: 'Tell me, do you know why we want the names of this rabble?'

'Because Masonry is a puppet of the international Jewish conspiracy. It's well known that bankers like Rothschild and ...'

A huge guffaw interrupted Jürgen's impassioned speech. Seeing the face of the baron's son fall, the head of security restrained himself.

'Don't parrot the *Volkischer Beobachter* editorials back to me, Jürgen. I helped write them myself.'

'But sir, the Führer says ...'

'I have to wonder how far the dagger that took your eye went in, my friend,' said Heydrich, studying his features.

205

'Sir, there's no need to be offensive,' said Jürgen, furious and confused.

Heydrich flashed an ominous smile.

'You're full of spirit, Jürgen. But that passion must be governed by reason. Do me a favour, don't become one of those sheep bleating at demonstrations. Allow me to give you a little lesson in our history.' He stood up and began to walk round the large table. 'In 1917 the Bolsheviks dissolved all the lodges in Russia. In 1919 Bela Kun got rid of all the Masons in Hungary. In 1925 Primo de Rivera banned lodges in Spain. That year Mussolini did the same in Italy. His blackshirts dragged the Masons out of bed in the middle of the night and beat them to death in the streets. An instructive example, don't you think?'

Jürgen nodded, surprised. He knew nothing about this.

'As you can see,' Heydrich continued, 'the first act of any strong government that intends to remain in power is to get rid of – among others – the Masons. Not because they're following orders about some hypothetical Jewish conspiracy. They do it because people who think for themselves cause a great deal of trouble.'

'What exactly do you want from me, sir?'

'I want you to infiltrate the Masons. I'll give you good enough contacts. You're an aristocrat, and your father belonged to a lodge some years back so they'll accept you without too much fuss. Your aim will be to get hold of the list of members. I want the name of every Mason in Bavaria.'

'Will I have carte blanche, sir?'

'Unless you hear anything to the contrary, yes. Wait here a moment.'

Heydrich walked to the door, opened it and barked a couple of instructions to an adjutant sitting on a bench in the corridor. The subordinate clicked his heels and returned a few moments later with another young man dressed in outdoor clothes.

'Come in, Adolf, come in. My dear Jürgen, allow me to introduce you to Adolf Eichmann. He's a very promising young man who's working at our Dachau camp.'

'A pleasure,' said Jürgen, holding out his hand.

'Likewise.'

'Adolf has requested to join my office, and I'm inclined to make the move easy for him, but first I'd like him to work alongside you for a few months. All the information you obtain you'll deliver to him, and he will be responsible for making sense of it. And when you complete this task I believe I will be able to send you to Berlin, on a mission of greater magnitude.'

45

I've seen him. I'm sure of it, thought Clovis, elbowing his way out of the tavern.

It was a July night and already his shirt was drenched with sweat. But the heat didn't bother him too much. He had learned to overcome it in the desert, when he first discovered that Reiner was following him. He had had to abandon a promising diamond mine in the Orange River basin in order to throw Reiner off the scent. He had left behind the last of his excavation materials, taking only essentials with him. At the top of a low ridge, rifle in hand, he had seen Paul's face for the first time and put his finger on the trigger. Afraid that he might miss, he had slid over to the other side of the hill, like a snake in tall grass.

He'd then lost Paul for several months, until he'd been forced to flee again, this time from a whorehouse in Johannesburg. That time Reiner had spotted him first, but from afar. When their eyes met, Clovis had been stupid enough to show his fear. He knew at once that the cold, hard shine in Reiner's eyes was the look of the hunter memorising the shape of his prey. He managed to escape through a secret back door, and even had time to go back to the dump of a hotel where he was lodged and throw his clothes into a suitcase.

It was three years before Clovis Nagel grew tired of feeling Reiner's breath on the back of his neck. He couldn't sleep without a weapon under his pillow. He couldn't walk around without turning to check whether he was being followed. And he didn't stay in any one place longer than a few weeks, for fear that one night he might awake to the steely shine of those blue eyes, watching him from behind the barrel of a revolver.

Finally he gave up. Without funds he couldn't run for ever, and the money the baron had given him had run out long ago. He started writing to the baron, but not one of his letters was answered, so Clovis boarded a boat bound for Hamburg. Back in Germany, on his way to Munich, he had felt momentarily relieved. For the first three days he was convinced that he had given Reiner the slip. Until one night he went into a tavern close to the train station and recognised Paul's face amid the throng of customers.

A knot formed in Clovis's stomach, and he fled.

As he ran as fast as his short legs would carry him, he realised the dreadful mistake he had made. He'd travelled to Germany without any firearms because he was afraid of being stopped at customs. He still hadn't had time to get hold of anything, and now all he had to defend himself with was his flick-knife.

He removed it from his pocket as he ran down the street. He wove in and out of the cones of light cast by the street lamps, running from one to the next as though they were islands of salvation, until he realised that if Reiner was following him he was making things too easy for him. He turned right down a darker side street that ran parallel to the train tracks. A train was approaching, rattling along on its way to the station. Clovis didn't see it, but he could smell the smoke from the chimney and feel the vibration in the ground.

A sound came from the other end of the side street. The ex-marine was startled and bit his tongue. He started running again, his heart almost leaping out of his mouth. He could taste blood, an ill omen of what he knew would happen if the other man caught up with him.

Clovis came to a dead end. Unable to go any farther, he hid behind a pile of wooden crates that smelled of rotting fish. Flies buzzed around him, settling on his face and hands. He tried to wave them away, but another noise and a shadow at the entrance to the alley made him freeze. He tried to slow his breathing.

The shadow became the silhouette of a man. Clovis couldn't make out his face, but there was no need. He knew perfectly well who it was.

Unable to stand the situation any longer, he lunged towards the end of the alley, knocking over the pile of wooden crates. A couple of rats ran terrified between his legs. Clovis followed them blindly, and saw them disappear through a half-open door that he had gone straight past in the darkness. He found himself in a dark corridor and took out his cigarette lighter to get his bearings. He allowed himself a couple of seconds of light before tearing off again, but at the end of the corridor he tripped and fell, grazing his hands against some damp cement steps. Not daring to use the lighter, he picked himself up and started to climb, ever alert to the slightest sound behind him.

He climbed for what seemed like an eternity. Finally his feet alighted upon a stretch of flat ground and he dared to flick on his lighter. The trembling yellow light revealed that he was in another corridor, at the end of which was a door. He pushed it and it wasn't locked.

I've thrown him off the scent at last. This looks like an abandoned warehouse. I'll spend a couple of hours here, till I'm sure he's not following me, Clovis thought, his breathing returning to normal.

'Good evening, Clovis,' said a voice behind him.

Clovis turned, pressing the button on his flick-knife. The blade jumped out with a barely audible click, and Clovis threw himself, his arm extended, towards the figure waiting by the door. It was like trying to touch a moonbeam. The figure stepped aside, and the steel blade missed by almost half a metre, fixing itself in the wall. Clovis tried to prise it out, but had barely managed to remove the filthy plaster before a blow knocked him to the ground.

'Make yourself comfortable. We're going to be here for a while.'

The voice came out of the darkness. Clovis tried to get up, but a hand pushed him back down. Suddenly a white ray split the gloom in two. His pursuer had turned on a flashlight. He pointed it at his own face.

'Does this face look familiar to you?'

Clovis studied Paul Reiner at length.

'You don't look like him,' said Clovis. His voice was hard and tired.

Reiner pointed the flashlight at Clovis, who put his left hand over his eyes, to shield himself from the glare.

'Point that thing somewhere else!'

'I'll do whatever I want. We're playing by my rules now.'

The beam of light moved from Clovis's face to Paul's right hand. He was holding his father's Mauser C96.

'Very well, Reiner. You're in charge.'

'I'm glad we're in agreement.'

Clovis moved his hand to his pocket. Paul took a threatening step towards him, but the ex-marine pulled out a packet of cigarettes and held it up to the light. He also took out some matches, which he carried in case his lighter fuel ran out. There were only two left.

'You've made my life impossible, Reiner,' he said, lighting a filterless cigarette.

'I know a bit about ruined lives myself. You destroyed mine.'

Clovis laughed, a deranged sound, as out of place in that situation as a priest in a brothel.

'Are you amused by your imminent death, Clovis?' asked Paul.

The laugh caught in Clovis's throat. If Paul's voice had been angry, Clovis wouldn't have felt so frightened. But his tone had been casual, calm. Clovis was sure Paul was smiling in the darkness.

'Easy, there. Let's just see . . .'

'We're not going to see anything. I want you to tell me how you killed my father, and why.'

'I didn't kill him.'

'No, of course you didn't. That's why you've been on the run for twenty-nine years.'

'It wasn't me, I swear it!'

'So who, then?'

Clovis paused for a few moments. He was afraid that if he answered, the young man would simply shoot him. The name was the only card he held, and he had to play it.

'I'll tell you if you promise to let me go.'

The only response was the sound of a hammer being cocked in the darkness.

'No, Reiner!' screamed Clovis. 'Listen, it's not just about *who* killed your father. What good would it do you, knowing that? What matters is what happened before. The *why*.'

There were a few moments of silence.

'Go on, then. I'm listening.'

46

'It all started on 11 August 1904. Before that day we'd spent a couple of wonderful weeks in Swakopmund. The beer wasn't bad by African standards, the weather wasn't too hot, and the girls were very obliging. We'd just returned from Hamburg and Captain Reiner had named me his first lieutenant. Our boat was due to spend a few months patrolling the coast of the colonies, in the hope of striking fear into the English.'

'But it wasn't the English who were the problem?'

'No ... The natives had revolted a few months earlier. A new general had arrived to take over command and he was the biggest son of a bitch, the most sadistic bastard I've ever set eyes on. His name was Lothar von Trotta. He started putting pressure on the natives. He was under orders from Berlin to come to some kind of political agreement with them, but he didn't care about that in the least. He said the natives were subhuman, monkeys who'd dropped down from the trees and learned to use rifles only by imitation. He hounded them until the others showed up in Waterburg, and there we all were, those of us from Swakopmund and Windhoek, weapons in hand, cursing our filthy luck.'

'You won.'

'They outnumbered us three to one, but they didn't know how to fight like an army. More than three thousand fell, and we took all their livestock and weapons. Then ...'

The ex-marine lit another cigarette from the stub of the previous one. By the light of the torch his face had lost all expression.

'Von Trotta ordered you to advance,' said Paul, encouraging him to continue.

'I'm sure you've been told this story, but no one who wasn't there knows what it was really like. We pushed them into the desert. No water, no food. We told them not to come back. We poisoned every well within a radius of hundreds of kilometres, and gave them no warning. The ones who'd been in hiding, or who'd turned back to fetch water, they were the first warning they got. The others ... more than twenty-five thousand, mainly women, children and old people, made their way into the Omaheke. I don't want to imagine what became of them.'

'They died, Clovis. No one crosses the Omaheke without water. The only people who survived were a few Herero tribes to the north.'

'We were given leave. Your father and I wanted to get as far away from Windhoek as possible. We stole horses and headed south. I don't remember the exact route we took, because the first few days we were so drunk that we barely knew our own names. I remember that we passed through Kolmanskop, and that a telegram from von Trotta was waiting for your father there, saying his leave was over and ordering him to return to Windhoek. Your father tore the telegram up and said he would never return. It had all affected him too deeply.'

'It really did affect him?' said Paul. Clovis could hear the anxiety in his voice, and knew he'd found a chink in his opponent's armour.

'It did, both of us. We carried on getting drunk and riding along, trying to get away from all the horror. We had no idea where we were heading. One morning we reached an isolated farm in the Orange River basin. A family of German colonists lived there, and the devil take me if the father wasn't the stupidest bastard I'd ever met. There was a stream on their property, and the girls kept complaining that it was full of little pebbles and that when they went to bathe it hurt their feet. The father had taken those little pebbles out one by one and piled them up round the back of the house, 'to make a pebbled path', he said. Except that they weren't pebbles.'

'They were diamonds,' said Paul, who, after years of working in the mines, knew that this mistake had happened more than once. Before they are cut and polished, certain kinds of diamond look so coarse that people often confuse them with translucent stones.

'There were some as fat as pigeons' eggs, son. Others were small and white, and there was even a pink one, this big,' he said, holding his fist up to the beam of light. 'In those days you could find them in the Orange quite easily, though you ran the risk of government inspectors shooting you if you were caught prowling too close to the site, and there was never any shortage of dead bodies drying out in the sun at crossroads, under the sign "diamond thief". Well, there were lots of

213

diamonds in the Orange, but I never saw as many in one place as we did in that farm. Never.'

'What did the man say when he found out?'

'Like I said, he was stupid. All he was interested in was his Bible and his crops, and he never let any of his family go down to the city. They didn't have any visitors either, as they lived in the middle of nowhere. Which was just as well, because anyone with half a brain would have known straight away what those stones were. Your father saw the pile of diamonds while they were showing us around the property and he elbowed me in the ribs – just in time, because I was about to say something stupid, hang me if that's not the truth. The family took us in without asking any questions. Your father was in a foul mood at dinner. He said he wanted to go to sleep, that he was tired, but when the farmer and his wife offered us their room your father insisted on sleeping in the living room under some blankets.'

'So you could get up in the middle of the night.'

'Which is precisely what we did. There was a trunk next to the fireplace containing the family's trinkets. We tipped them out on to the floor, careful not to make a sound, Then went round the back and put the stones in the trunk. Believe me, though the trunk was big the stones still filled three-quarters of it. We put a blanket on top of them, and then lifted the trunk up on to the small covered wagon the father used for getting supplies. It would all have gone perfectly if it hadn't been for the damned dog that slept outside. As we hitched our own horses to the wagon and moved off we ran over its tail. Fuck me, how that damned animal howled! The farmer was up, shotgun in hand. Though he may have been stupid he wasn't completely daft, and our wonderfully invent- ive explanations did no good at all, because he had suspected we were up to no good. Your father had to draw that pistol, the same one you're pointing at me, and shoot off his head.'

'You're lying,' said Paul. The beam of light was shaking slightly.

'No, son, may a lightning bolt strike me down this minute if I'm not telling you the truth. He killed the man, he killed him good, and I had to gee up the horses because the mother and the two daughters came out on to the porch and started screaming. We hadn't gone fifteen kilometres when your father told me to stop and ordered me to get out of the cart. I told him he was crazy, and I don't think I was wrong. All that violence and alcohol had made him a shadow of his former self.

Killing the farmer was the final straw. It didn't matter, he had his gun and I'd lost mine one drunken night, so to hell with it, I said, and I got off.'

'What would you have done if you'd had a gun, Clovis?'

'I'd have shot him,' replied the ex-marine, without a second thought. He had an idea about how he could turn the situation to his advantage.

I just need to lead him to the right place.

'So what happened?' said Paul. His voice was less confident now.

'I had no idea what to do, so I went on along the track that led back to the town. Your father had cleared off in the early hours of the morning and it was past noon when he returned, except now he didn't have the wagon, only our horses. He told me he'd buried the trunk in a place only he knew, and that we'd be back to collect it when things had calmed down.'

'He didn't trust you.'

'Of course he didn't. And he was right. We left the road, as we were afraid the wife and children of the dead colonist might put out the alert. We headed north, sleeping out in the open, which wasn't comfortable, especially as your father talked in his sleep and shouted a great deal. He couldn't get that farmer out of his head. And so it went on till we arrived back in Swakopmund, and learned that we were both wanted for desertion, and that your father had lost the command of his boat. If the business with the diamonds hadn't got in the way, your father would doubtless have given himself up, but we were scared that they'd link us to what had happened in the Orange basin, so we remained on the run. We escaped the military police by the skin of our teeth by stowing away on a boat headed for Germany. One way or another we managed to get back in one piece.'

'Was that when you approached the baron?'

'Hans was obsessed with going back to the Orange for the trunk, and so was I. We spent a few days at the baron's mansion, in hiding. Your father told him everything, and the baron went crazy . . . just like your father had, just like everyone did. He wanted to know the precise location, but Hans refused to tell. The baron was bankrupt and didn't have the money needed to finance a trip back to find the trunk, so Hans signed some papers in which he transferred the house in which you and your mother lived, together with a small business the two of them owned. Your father assumed the baron would sell them to raise funds for recovering the trunk. Neither of us could do it as by then we were wanted men in Germany too.'

'And the night of his death, what happened?'

'There was a fierce argument. A lot of money, four people shouting. Your father ended up with a bullet in his guts.'

'How did it happen?'

Carefully, Clovis took out the packet of cigarettes and the little box of matches. He took the last match and lit it carefully. Then he lit a cigarette and exhaled the smoke towards the beam of the torch.

'Why are you so interested, Paul? Why do you care so much about the life of a murderer?'

'Don't call my father that!'

Come on now . . . a little closer.

'No? What would you call what we did in Waterburg? What he did to the farmer? He blew his head off, he let him have it right here,' he said, touching his forehead.

'I'm telling you to shut up!'

With a cry of rage, Paul came forward and raised his right arm to strike Clovis. With a skilful movement Clovis threw the lit cigarette in his eyes. Paul jerked back, instinctively protecting his face, and this bought Clovis enough time to jump up and run out, playing his final card, a desperate last attempt.

He won't shoot me in the back.

'Wait, you bastard!'

Especially if he doesn't know who fired the shot.

Paul was chasing after him. Dodging in and out of the torchlight, Clovis ran towards the back of the warehouse, trying to escape the way his pursuer had come in. He could make out a little door next to a window with blacked-out glass. He picked up his pace and had almost reached the door when his feet got tangled in a piece of rubbish.

He fell headlong, and was trying to get to his feet when Paul caught up with him and grabbed his jacket. Clovis tried to hit Paul, but he missed and staggered dangerously towards the window.

'No!' Paul shouted as he lunged at Clovis once more.

Struggling to recover his balance, the ex-marine reached out his arms towards Paul. His fingers brushed those of the young man for a moment before he keeled over and smashed against the window. The old glass gave way like paper, and Clovis's body fell through the opening and disappeared into the darkness.

There was a short cry and then a dry thud.

Paul leaned out through the window and pointed the torch at the ground. Ten metres below him, Clovis's body lay in the middle of a growing pool of blood.

47

Jürgen wrinkled up his nose as he entered the asylum. The place stank of piss and dirt, poorly disguised by the smell of disinfectant.

He had to ask a nurse for directions, as this was the first time he'd been to visit Otto since they had put him there eleven years earlier. The woman, perched behind a desk, was reading a magazine with a bored expression on her face, and her feet dangled free of her white clogs. On seeing the brand new *Obersturmführer* appear before her, the nurse stood up and raised her right arm so quickly that the cigarette she had been smoking fell from her lips. She insisted on accompanying him in person.

'Aren't you afraid one of them will escape?' asked Jürgen as they walked down the corridors, gesturing towards the old men wandering aimlessly near the entrance.

'It does happen sometimes, mainly when I've gone to the bathroom. It doesn't matter, though, because the man from the kiosk on the corner usually brings them back.'

The nurse left him at the door to the baron's room.

'He's in here, sir, all settled in and comfy. He even has a window. Heil Hitler!' she added, just before leaving.

Jürgen returned the salute reluctantly, pleased to see her go. He wanted to savour this moment by himself.

The door to the room was open, and Otto was slumped in a wheel-chair next to the window, asleep. A thread of drool dripped on to his chest, trailing across his dressing-gown and the old monocle on its gold chain, the glass of which now seemed to be cracked. Jürgen remembered how different his father had looked the day after the *coup d'état*. How furious he had been that it had failed, even though he'd not contributed anything to it himself.

Jürgen had briefly been detained and interrogated, though long before it was all over he'd had the good sense to change his blood-soaked brown shirt for a clean one, and he wasn't carrying a firearm. There were no repercussions for him, nor for anyone else. Even Hitler spent only nine months in prison.

Jürgen had returned home, as the SA barracks had been shut down and the organisation dissolved. He had spent several days locked in his room, ignoring his mother's attempts to find out what had happened with Ilse Reiner, and calculating how best to make use of the letter he had stolen from Paul's mother.

My brother's mother, he repeated to himself, confused.

Finally he had ordered photostat copies of the letter and one morning after breakfast, he presented one to his mother and one to his father.

'What the hell is this?' said the baron, receiving the sheets of paper.

'You know perfectly well, Otto.'

'Jürgen! Show more respect!' said his mother, horrified.

'After what I've read here, there's no reason why I should.'

'Where is the original?' asked Otto, his voice hoarse.

'Somewhere safe.'

'Bring it here!'

'I have no intention of doing that. These are just a few of the copies. I've sent the others to the newspapers and police headquarters.'

'You've done what?' shouted Otto, coming round the table. He tried to raise his fist to strike Jürgen, but his body didn't seem to respond. Jürgen and his mother watched dumbstruck as the baron lowered his arm and tried to raise it again without any success.

'I can't see. Why can't I see?' asked Otto.

He staggered forward, dragging the breakfast tablecloth with him as he fell. Cutlery, plates and cups tumbled over, scattering their contents, but the baron didn't seem to notice as he lay motionless on the floor. All that could be heard in the dining room were the screams of the maid, who had just entered holding a tray of freshly made toast.

As he stood at the door to the room, Jürgen couldn't suppress a bitter grin as he recalled the ingenuity he'd shown back then. The doctor said that the baron had suffered a stroke that had deprived him of the power of speech, and the use of his legs.

'With the excesses this man has indulged in during his life, I'm not surprised. I don't expect he'll last more than six months,' said the medic, putting away his instruments in a leather bag. Which was lucky, because he was spared seeing the cruel smile that had flashed across Jürgen's face when he heard the diagnosis.

And here you are, eleven years later.

He went in now without making a sound, and brought a chair over to sit opposite the invalid. The light from the window may have looked like an idyllic sunbeam, but it was nothing more than the sun's reflection on the bare white wall of the building opposite, the only view from the baron's room.

Bored of waiting for him to wake up, Jürgen cleared his throat several times. The baron blinked and finally lifted his head. He stared at Jürgen, but if he felt any surprise or fear his eyes didn't show it. Jürgen contained his disappointment.

'You know, Otto? For a long time I tried very hard to win your approval. Of course, that didn't matter to you in the slightest. You only cared about Eduard.'

He paused slightly, waiting for some reaction, some movement, anything. All he received was the same stare as before, alert but frozen.

'It was a huge relief to learn you weren't my father. I was suddenly free to hate the disgusting cuckold swine who had ignored me all my life.'

The insults didn't produce the slightest effect either.

'Then you had the attack, and finally left me and my mother in peace. But of course, like everything you've done in your life, you didn't finish it. I've given you too much leeway, waiting for you to correct this mistake, and I've been thinking for some time about how to get rid of you. And now, how convenient ... someone appears who could save me the trouble.'

He took the newspaper he had been carrying under his arm and held it in front of the old man's face, close enough that he could read it. Meanwhile he recited the contents of the article from memory. He had read it over and over that night, anticipating the moment when the old man would see it.

Munich (Editorial). The police have finally been able to identify the body found last week in an alley close to the Hauptbahnhof. It is the body of former marine lieutenant Clovis Nagel, who since 1904 had an outstanding summons to a court-martial for having deserted his post during a mission to South-West Africa. Although he had returned to the country under a false name, the authorities were able to identify him from the large number of tattoos covering his torso. There are no further details regarding the circumstances surrounding his death, which as our readers will recall happened following a fall from a great height, possibly as a result of being pushed. The police have reminded the public that anyone who had contact with Nagel is under suspicion, and request that those with information should make themselves known to the authorities immediately.

'Paul's back – isn't that superb news?'

A glimmer of fear flickered in the baron's eyes. It lasted only a few seconds, but Jürgen savoured the moment as though it were the great humiliation his twisted mind had envisaged.

He got up and walked over to the bathroom. He took a glass and half-filled it under the tap. Then he sat down next to the baron once more.

'You know he'll come for you now. And I don't imagine you want to see your name in the headlines, isn't that right, Otto?'

Jürgen took a metal box no bigger than a postage stamp from his pocket. He opened it and extracted a small green pill, which he left on the table.

'There's a new branch of the SS that's experimenting with these lovely things. We have agents all over the world, people who at any given moment might have to disappear silently and painlessly,' said the young man, omitting to mention that the painlessness had not yet been achieved. 'Spare us the shame, Otto.'

He picked up his cap and pulled it firmly back on his head, then walked over to the door. When he reached it he turned and saw Otto groping towards the tablet. His father held the pill between his fingers, his face still as blank as it had been throughout. Then the hand rose to his mouth so slowly that the movement was almost imperceptible.

Jürgen left. For a moment he was tempted to stay and watch, but it was better to stick to the plan and avoid potential problems.

From tomorrow, the staff will address me as Baron von Schroeder. And when my brother comes looking for answers, he'll have to ask me.

48

Two weeks after Nagel's death, Paul finally dared to go back outside.

The sound of the ex-marine's body hitting the ground had echoed in his mind the whole time he'd spent closed away in the room he'd rented in a Schwabing boarding-house. He had tried going back to the old building he'd shared with his mother, but it was now a private apartment block.

That wasn't the only thing that had changed in Munich during his absence. The streets were cleaner and there were no longer groups of the unemployed loitering on street corners. The queues outside churches and employment offices had disappeared, and people didn't have to lug around two suitcases of small banknotes every time they wanted to buy bread. There were no bloody tavern brawls. The enormous columns of notices, which could be found on the main roads, had other things to report. Previously they had been packed with news of political meetings, fiery manifestos and dozens of 'Wanted for Theft' posters. Now they announced peaceful things such as meetings of horticultural societies.

In place of all these omens of doom Paul found that the prophecy had been fulfilled. Everywhere he went he saw groups of boys wearing red swastika armbands. Passers-by had to raise their arm and shout 'Heil Hitler!' if they didn't want to risk being tapped on the shoulder by a couple of plainclothes agents with an order to come along with them. A few, the minority, scurried off into doorways to escape the salute, but that solution wasn't always possible, and sooner or later everyone had to raise their arm.

Everywhere you looked, people were displaying the disturbing black spider of the swastika, whether as a tiepin, an armband or on a kerchief tied around their neck. They were sold at tram stops and kiosks alongside tickets and newspapers. This burst of patriotism had come since the end of June, when dozens of SA leaders were killed in the middle of the night for 'betraying the Fatherland'. With this action Hitler had sent out a double message – that nobody was safe and that in Germany he was the only person in charge. Fear was etched on every face, however much people tried to hide it.

The walk through the city brought Paul some small measure of relief, although this was at the cost of the concern he felt for the direction Germany was heading in.

'You want a tiepin, sir?' a young lad called, after having looked him up and down. The boy was wearing a long leather sash showcasing several models, everything from the simple twisted cross to an eagle holding the Nazi crest.

Paul shook his head and walked on.

'You'd do well to wear one, sir. An excellent sign of your support for our glorious Führer,' the boy insisted, running along behind him. Seeing that Paul wasn't giving in, he stuck out his tongue and went in search of new prey.

I'll die before I wear that symbol, thought Paul.

His mind plunged back into the feverish, nervous state it had been in since Nagel's death. The story of the man who had been his father's first lieutenant had besieged him with doubts, not only about how to continue his investigation but also about the nature of that search. If he were to believe Nagel, Hans Reiner had lived a life that was complex and twisted, and he had committed a crime for money.

Of course, Nagel was not the most trustworthy of sources. But in spite of that the song he'd sung was not out of tune with the note that had always sounded in Paul's heart when he thought about the father he had never known.

As he looked at the calm, clear nightmare into which Germany was plunging so enthusiastically, Paul wondered whether he wasn't finally waking up.

Last week I turned thirty, he thought bitterly as he walked along the bank of the Isar, where couples gathered on benches, *and I've wasted more than a third of my life looking for a father who might not have been worth the effort. I left the person I loved, and have found nothing but sadness and sacrifice in exchange.*

Perhaps that was why he had idealised Hans in his daydreams – because he needed to make up for the dark reality he guessed at in Ilse's silences.

He realised all of a sudden that he was saying goodbye to Munich once again. The only thought in his head was a desire to leave, to get away from Germany and return to Africa, the place where, although he had not been happy, he had at least been able to find a part of his soul.

But I have come so far ... how can I allow myself to give up now?

The problem was twofold. He also had no idea how to continue. Nagel's death had eliminated not only his hopes but also the last concrete clue he had. He wished that his mother had confided in him more, as then she might still be alive.

I could go and find Jürgen ... talk to him about what my mother told me before she died. Maybe he knows something.

After a while he rejected that idea. He had had his fill of the von Schroeders, and in all likelihood Jürgen still hated him for what had happened in the coalman's stables. He doubted that time had done anything to appease his anger. And if he were to approach Jürgen, with no proof at all, and tell him he had reason to believe they might be brothers, his reaction would surely be terrible. Nor could he imagine trying to talk to the baron or Brunhilda. No, this alley was a dead end.

It's over. I'm leaving.

His erratic journey brought him to Marienplatz. He decided to pay one last visit to Sebastian Keller before leaving the city for good. On his way, he wondered whether the bookshop was still open, or whether its owner had succumbed to the crisis in the twenties like so many other businesses.

His fears proved unfounded. The place looked just as it had always done, neat and tidy, with its generous window displays offering a careful selection of classic German poetry. Paul barely paused before going in, and Keller immediately poked his head round the back-room door, just as he had done that first day in 1923.

'Paul! Dear God, what a surprise!'

The bookseller held out his hand, a warm smile on his face. It was as though time had barely passed. He still dyed his hair white, and he wore new gold-framed glasses, but apart from that, and the odd wrinkle around his eyes, he still exuded the same aura of wisdom and tranquillity.

'Good afternoon, Herr Keller.'

'But this is such a pleasure, Paul! Where have you been hiding yourself all this time? We'd given you up for lost ... I read in the papers about the fire at the boarding-house and feared you had died there too. You could have written!'

Somewhat ashamed, Paul apologised for having remained silent all those years. Contrary to his custom, Keller closed the bookshop and took the young man into the back room, where they spent a couple of hours drinking tea and talking about the old days. Paul recounted his travels in Africa, the various jobs he had done and his experiences in different cultures.

'You've had some real adventures ... Karl May whom you so admire would have liked to have found himself in your shoes.'

'I suppose so ... though novels are a completely different matter,' said Paul with a bitter smile, thinking about Nagel's tragic end.

'And what about Masonry, Paul? Have you kept in touch with any lodge during this time?'

'No, sir.'

'Well then, when all's said and done the essence of our Brotherhood is order. As it happens there's a meeting tonight. You must come along, I won't take no for an answer. You can resume your work where you left off,' said Keller, patting him on the shoulder.

Reluctantly, Paul accepted.

49

That night, back in the temple, Paul felt the familiar sense of artifice and boredom that had swamped him years earlier when he had started attending Masonic meetings. The place was full to bursting with more than a hundred people in attendance.

At an opportune moment, Keller, who was still Grand Master of the Lodge of the Rising Sun, stood up and introduced Paul to his brother Masons. Many of them already knew him, but at least ten members greeted him for the first time.

Apart from when Keller addressed him directly, Paul spent much of the meeting lost in thought. Until near the end, when one of the older brothers – someone by the name of Furst – got up to introduce a subject that was not on that day's agenda.

'Most Venerable Grand Master, a group of brothers and I have been discussing the current situation.'

'What are you referring to, Brother Furst?'

'To the worrying shadow Nazism is casting over Masonry.'

'Brother, you know the rules. No politics in the temple.'

'But the Grand Master will agree with me that the news from Berlin and Hamburg is worrying. Many lodges there have dissolved of their own free will. Here in Bavaria there are none of the Prussian lodges left.'

'So are you proposing the dissolution of this lodge, Brother Furst?'

'Certainly not. But I believe the time may be right to take measures that others have taken in order to ensure their permanence.'

'And what are these measures?'

'The first would be to cut off our links with brotherhoods outside Germany.'

This statement was followed by a lot of murmuring. Masonry was traditionally an international movement, and the more links a lodge had, the more it was respected.

'Silence, please. When the brother has finished, everyone will be able to give their own thoughts on the matter.'

'The second would be to rename our society. Other lodges in Berlin have changed their name to "Order of the Teutonic Knights".'

This set off another wave of grumbling. Changing the name of the order was simply not acceptable.

'And finally I think we should discharge from the lodge – honourably – those brothers who place our survival at risk.'

'And which brothers would those be?'

Furst cleared his throat before continuing, visibly uncomfortable.

'The brothers who are Jewish, of course.'

Paul leaped up from his seat. He tried to take the floor to speak, but the temple had become a pandemonium of shouts and curses. The commotion lasted for several minutes, with everyone trying to speak at once. Several times Keller struck his lectern with the mace, which he had seldom had occasion to use.

'Order, order! We will speak one at a time, or I shall have to dissolve the meeting!'

Tempers cooled a little, and speakers took the floor in support of or to reject the proposal. Paul counted the number of people weighing in, and was surprised to discover there was an even split between the two positions. He tried to think of something to contribute that would sound coherent. He urgently wished to convey how unfair he found the whole discussion.

Finally Keller gestured to him with the mace. Paul stood up.

'Brothers, this is the first time I've spoken in this lodge. It may well be the last. I've been astonished by the discussion provoked by Brother Furst's proposal, and what most astonishes me isn't your opinions on the subject but the mere fact that we've had to discuss it at all.'

There were mutterings of approval.

'I'm not Jewish. I have Aryan blood running through my veins, or at least I think I have. The truth is, I'm not altogether sure of what I am, or who I am. I arrived in this noble institution following in the footsteps of my father, with no other objective than to find out about myself. Certain circumstances in my life have kept me far away from you for a long time, but when I came back I never imagined things would be so different. Within these walls we are supposedly in pursuit of enlighten-ment. So can you explain to me, brothers, why this institution would discriminate against people for anything other than their actions, just or unjust?'

There were more murmurs of assent. Paul saw Furst rise from his seat.

'Brother, you *have* been away a long time and you don't know what's happening in Germany!'

'You're right. We are living through a dark time. But in such times we have to cling strongly to what we believe.'

'What's at stake here is the survival of the lodge!'

'Yes, but at what cost?'

'If we have to . . .'

'Brother Furst, if you were crossing the desert and you saw the sun was getting stronger and your canteen was getting empty, would you piss in it to stop it running out?'

The roof of the temple quaked with the outburst of laughter. Furst was losing the match, and he seethed with rage.

'And to think that these are the words of the outcast son of a deserter,' he exclaimed, furious.

Paul took the blow as best he could. He squeezed hard on the back of the chair in front of him until his knuckles turned white.

I must control myself, or he will have won.

'Most Venerable Grand Master, are you going to allow Brother Furst to expose my statement to this crossfire?'

'Brother Reiner is right. Stick to the rules of debate.'

Furst nodded with a wide smile that put Paul on the alert.

'Delighted. In that case I ask you to withdraw the floor from Brother Reiner.'

'What? On what grounds?' said Paul, trying not to shout.

'Do you deny that you only attended the lodge's meetings for a few months before your disappearance?'

Paul became flustered.

'No, I don't deny it, but . . .'

'So you haven't reached the degree of Fellow Craft, and you do not have the right to contribute to meetings,' Furst interrupted.

'I've been an Apprentice for more than eleven years. The degree of Fellow Craft is gained automatically after three years.'

'Yes, but only if you attend the Works regularly. Otherwise you have to be approved by a majority of the brothers. So you have no right to speak in this debate,' said Furst, unable to hide his satisfaction.

Paul looked around for support. Every face looked back at him in silence. Even Keller, who had seemed to want to help him moments earlier, was quiet.

'Very well. If that's the prevailing spirit, I renounce my membership of the lodge.'

Paul stood and left the bench, walking towards the lectern occupied by Keller. He removed his apron and gloves and threw them at the Grand Master's feet.

'I'm not proud of these symbols any more.'

'And nor am I!'

One of the others present, a man by the name of Joachim Hirsch, stood up. Hirsch was Jewish, Paul recalled. He too threw the symbols down at the foot of the lectern.

'I'm not going to wait for a vote on whether or not I should be expelled from a lodge I've belonged to for twenty years. I'd prefer to leave,' he said, standing at Paul's side.

Hearing this, many others stood up. Most of them were Jewish, though there were a few, Paul noticed with satisfaction, who were clearly just as indignant as he was. Within a minute more than thirty aprons had piled up on the chequered marble. The scene was chaotic.

'That's enough!' shouted Keller, beating the mace in a vain attempt to make himself heard. 'If my position allowed it, I'd throw this apron down, too. Let us respect those who have taken this decision.'

The group of dissidents began to leave the temple. Paul was one of the last to go, and he left with his head held high, though it grieved him. Although being a member of the lodge had never been particularly to his taste, it hurt him to see how such a group of intelligent, cultured people could be split apart by fear and intolerance.

He walked in silence towards the entrance hall. Some of the dissidents had gathered in a huddle, though most had collected their hats and were making their way out into the street in groups of two or three so as not to attract attention. Paul was preparing to do the same when he felt someone touch his back.

'Please allow me to shake your hand' – it was Hirsch, the man who had thrown his apron in after Paul. 'Thank you so much for setting an example – if you hadn't done what you did I wouldn't have dared do it myself.'

'No need to thank me. I just couldn't bear to see the injustice of it all.'

'If only more people were like you, Reiner, Germany wouldn't be in the mess she's in today. Let's just hope it's only a passing ill wind.'

'People are scared,' said Paul, with a shrug.

'I'm not surprised. Three or four weeks ago the Gestapo got the power to act extrajudicially.'

'What do you mean?'

'They can detain anyone they like, even for something as simple as "walking suspiciously".'

'But that's ridiculous!' said Paul, astonished.

'There's more,' said another of the men who was about to leave; 'after a few days the family receives a notification.'

'Or they're called in to identify the body,' added a third gloomily. 'It's already happened to an acquaintance of mine, and the list is growing. Krickstein, Cohen, Tannenbaum . . .'

When he heard that last name Paul's heart leaped.

'Wait, did you say Tannenbaum? Which Tannenbaum?'

'Josef Tannenbaum, the industrialist. Do you know him?'

'Sort of. You could say I'm . . . a friend of the family.'

'Then I'm sorry to have to tell you that Josef Tannenbaum is dead. The funeral is being held tomorrow morning.'

50

'Rain should be compulsory at funerals,' said Manfred.

Alys didn't reply. She just took his hand and squeezed it.

He's right, she thought, looking around her. The white gravestones shone under the morning sun, creating an atmosphere of serenity completely at odds with her state of mind.

Alys, who knew so little of her own emotions, and who so often fell victim to this emotional blindness, did not quite know what she was feeling that day. Ever since he had summoned them back from Ohio fifteen years earlier she had hated her father from the depths of her soul. Over time her hatred had acquired a variety of shades. At first it was tainted with the indignant hue of the angry adolescent who is always being contradicted. From there it progressed to scorn when she saw her father in all his egotism and greed, a businessman prepared to do anything in order to prosper. Last came the evasive, skittish hatred of a woman afraid of becoming dependent.

Ever since her father's henchmen had caught her on that fateful night in 1923 Alys's hatred towards him had been transformed into cold animosity of the purest kind. Emotionally drained after her break-up with Paul, Alys had stripped her relationship with her father of all passion, focusing on it from a rational point of view. He – it was best to refer to that person as *he*, it hurt less – was ill. He didn't understand that she had to be free to live her own life. He wanted to marry her off to someone she despised.

He wanted to kill the child she carried in her belly.

Alys had had to fight with all her strength to prevent it. Her father had slapped her, had called her a filthy whore and worse.

'You're not having it. The baron will never accept a pregnant whore as a bride for his son.'

So much the better, thought Alys. She withdrew into herself, roundly refusing to have an abortion, and informed the scandalised servants that she was pregnant.

'I have witnesses. If you make me lose it I'll turn you in, you bastard,' she told him with a self-possession and certainty she'd never felt before.

'Thank heavens your mother isn't alive to see her daughter like this.'

'Like what? Sold to the highest bidder by her father?'

Josef found himself obliged to go to the von Schroeders' mansion and confess the truth to the baron. With an expression of poorly feigned sorrow, the baron informed him that obviously, under such conditions, the agreement would have to be annulled.

Alys never spoke to Josef again after the fateful afternoon when he returned from his meeting with the in-law who wasn't to be, seething with fury and humiliation. An hour after his return, Doris, the house-keeper, came to inform her that she was to leave immediately.

'The master will allow you to take a suitcase of clothes with you if you need them.' The tone of her voice left no doubt as to her feelings on the matter.

'Tell the master thank you very much but I don't need anything from him,' said Alys.

She walked towards the door, but before leaving she turned back.

'By the way, Doris ... Try not to steal the suitcase and say I've taken it with me, like you did with the money my father left on the sink.'

Her words punctured the housekeeper's supercilious attitude. She turned red and began to gasp.

'Now you listen here, I can assure you I ...'

The young woman left, cutting off the end of the sentence with a slam of the door.

Despite being on her own, despite everything that had happened to her, despite the vast responsibility that was growing inside her, the look of outrage on Doris's face had made Alys smile. The first smile since Paul had left her.

Or was I the one who forced him to leave me?

She spent the next eleven years trying to work out the answer to that question.

*

When Paul showed up on the tree-lined path in the cemetery the question answered itself. Alys saw him approach and move to one side, waiting as the priest said the prayer for the dead.

Alys completely forgot about the twenty people surrounding the coffin, a wooden box empty but for an urn containing Josef's ashes. She forgot that she had received the ashes by post, along with a note from the Gestapo saying her father had been arrested for sedition and had died 'trying to escape'. She forgot that he was being buried under a cross and not a star, as he had died a Catholic in a country of Catholics who cast their votes for Hitler. She forgot her own confusion and fear, for in the middle of all this, one certainty appeared now before her eyes like a lighthouse in a storm.

It was my fault. I was the one who pushed you away, Paul. Who hid the truth from you and didn't allow you to make your own choice. And damn you, I'm still as in love with you as I was the first time I saw you fifteen years ago, when you were wearing that ridiculous waiter's apron.

She wanted to run to him, but thought that if she did she might lose him for ever. And even though she had matured a great deal since becoming a mother, her feet were still shackled by pride.

I have to approach him slowly. Find out where he's been, what he's done. If he still feels anything . . .

The funeral ended. She and Manfred received the guests' condolences. Paul was the last in the line and approached them with a cautious look.

'Good morning. Thank you for coming,' said Manfred, holding out his hand, not recognising him.

'I share your sorrow,' replied Paul.

'Did you know my father?'

'A little. My name is Paul Reiner.'

Manfred dropped Paul's hand as though it had burned him.

'What are you doing here? You think you can appear back in her life just like that? After eleven years without a word?'

'I wrote dozens of letters, and never received a reply to any of them,' Paul said, flustered.

'That doesn't change what you did.'

Don't tell him! Alys shouted inwardly.

'It's all right, Manfred,' she said, laying a hand on his shoulder. 'You go home.'

'Are you sure?' he asked, looking at Paul.

'Yes.'

'All right. I'll go home and see if . . .'

'Fine,' she interrupted him before he could say the name. 'I'll be along soon.'

With a final spiteful glance at Paul, Manfred pulled on his hat and left. Alys turned along the central pathway of the cemetery, walking in silence with Paul at her side. Their eye contact had been brief but intense and painful, so she preferred not to have to look at him just yet.

'So you've come back.'

'I came back last week, pursuing a lead, but it turned out badly. Yesterday I met an acquaintance of your father's who told me about his death. I hope you were able to grow closer over the years.'

'Sometimes distance is the best thing.'

'I understand.'

Why would I say a thing like that? Now he'll think I was talking about him. What do I say now?

'And what about your travels, Paul? Did you find what you were looking for?'

'No.'

Say you were wrong to leave, damn you. Say you were wrong and I'll admit my mistake and you'll admit yours, and then I'll fall into your arms again. Say it!

'Actually, I've decided to give up,' Paul went on. 'I've reached a dead end. I have no family, I have no money, I have no profession, I don't even have a country to return to, because this place is not Germany.'

She stopped and turned to look at him closely for the first time. She was surprised to see that his face hadn't changed much. His features had hardened, there were deep circles under his eyes and he had put on some weight, but he was still Paul. Her Paul.

'You really wrote to me?'

'Many times. I sent letters to your address at the boarding-house, and also to your father's house.'

Another reason to be grateful to my father.

'And so . . . what are you going to do?' she said. Her lips and her voice were trembling but she couldn't stop them. Perhaps her body was sending a message she didn't dare articulate. When Paul replied there was also emotion in his voice.

'I'd considered going back to Africa, Alys. But when I heard about what had happened to your father, I thought . . .'

'What?'

'Don't take this the wrong way, but I'd like to talk to you in different surroundings, with more time, tell you about what's happened over the years.'

'That's not a good idea,' she forced herself to say.

'Alys, I know I have no right to come back into your life whenever I feel like it. I . . . Leaving that time was a big mistake, it was a huge mistake, and I'm ashamed of it. It's taken a while for me to realise that, and all I ask is that we sit down and have a coffee together one day.'

And if I were to tell you that you have a son, Paul? A gorgeous boy with sky-blue eyes just like yours, blond and stubborn like his father? What would you do, Paul? And if I were to let you into our lives and then it didn't work out? However much I want you, however much my body and my soul want to be with you, I can't allow you to hurt him.

'I need a little time to think about it.'

He smiled and small wrinkles Alys had never seen before clustered around his eyes.

'I'll be waiting,' said Paul, holding out a little piece of paper with his address. 'As long as you need me to.'

Alys took the note and their fingers brushed against one another.

'All right, Paul. But I can't promise anything. Go now.'

Slightly hurt at the brusque dismissal, Paul left without another word.

As he disappeared down the path, Alys prayed he wouldn't turn round and see how much she was shaking.

51

'Well, well. It looks like the rat has taken the bait,' said Jürgen, gripping his binoculars tightly. From his vantage point, on a hillock eight metres from Josef's grave, he could see Paul making his way up the queue to offer condolences to the Tannenbaums. He recognised him instantly. 'Was I right, Adolf?'

'You were right, sir,' said Eichmann, a little uncomfortable at this deviation from the programme. In the six months he had been working with Jürgen, the newly minted baron had managed to penetrate a number of lodges thanks to his title, his superficial charm and a number of fake credentials supplied by the Lodge of the Prussian Sword. The Grand Master of that lodge, a recalcitrant nationalist and acquaintance of Heydrich's, supported the Nazis with every inch of his being. He had unscrupulously granted Jürgen the degree of Master and given him an intensive course on how to pass as an experienced Mason. Then he had written letters of recommendation to the Grand Masters of the humanitarian lodges, urging their collaboration 'to weather the current political storm'.

Visiting a different lodge each week, Jürgen had managed to obtain the names of more than three thousand members. Heydrich was ecstatic at the progress, and Eichmann too, as he saw his dream of escaping his grim employment in Dachau coming ever closer. He hadn't minded typing up notecards for Heydrich in his free time, or even the occasional weekend trip with Jürgen to cities near by, such as Augsburg, Ingoldstadt or Stuttgart. But the obsession that had awoken in Jürgen over the last few days worried him a great deal. The man thought of almost nothing but this Paul Reiner. He hadn't even explained what part Reiner played in the mission Heydrich had charged them with, he'd said only that he wanted to find him.

'I was right,' repeated Jürgen, more to himself than to his nervous companion. 'She's the key.'

He adjusted the lenses of the binoculars. Using them wasn't easy for Jürgen, having only one eye, and he had to lower them every once in a while. He shifted a little and the image of Alys appeared in his field of vision. She was very beautiful, more mature than the last time he'd seen her. He looked at the way her black short-sleeved blouse emphasised her breasts, and adjusted the binoculars to get a better look.

If only my father hadn't turned her down. What a terrible humiliation it would have been for this little tart to have to marry me and do anything I wanted . . . Jürgen fantasised. He had an erection, and had to put his hand in his pocket to arrange himself discreetly so that Eichmann wouldn't notice.

On second thoughts it's better like this. Marrying a Jew would have been fatal to my career in the SS. And this way I can kill two birds with one stone. Luring Paul in, and having her. She'll learn soon enough. Oh yes, the whore will learn soon enough.

'Shall we continue as planned, sir?' said Eichmann.

'Yes, Adolf. Follow him. I want to know where he's lodging.'

'And then? We turn him in to the Gestapo?'

With Alys's father it had been so very easy. One call to an *Obersturmführer* he knew, ten minutes' conversation, and four men had removed the insolent Jew from his Prinzregentenplatz apartment, giving no explanation. The plan had worked out perfectly. Now Paul had come to the funeral, just as Jürgen was sure he would.

It would be so simple to do it all again . . . find out where he slept, send over a patrol, then head to the cellars of the Witelsbacher palace, the Gestapo's headquarters in Munich. To go into the padded cell – padded not to stop people hurting themselves, but to muffle the screams – sit down in front of him and watch him die. Perhaps he could even bring the Jew and rape her right in front of Paul, enjoy her while Paul struggled desperately to free himself from his bonds.

But he had to think of his career. He didn't want people talking about his cruelty, especially now he was becoming better known. On the back of his title, and his achievements, he was so close to promotion, and a ticket to Berlin to work side by side with Heydrich.

And then there was also his desire to confront Paul man to man. Pay the little shit back for all the pain he'd caused without hiding behind the machinery of the state.

There has to be a better way.

Suddenly he knew what he wanted to do, and his lips twisted into a cruel smile.

'Excuse me, sir,' Eichmann insisted, thinking he hadn't heard. 'I was asking if we will be turning Reiner in?'

'No, Adolf. This will require a more personal touch.'

52

'I'm home!'

Returning from the cemetery, Alys walked into the small apartment and readied herself for the usual wild charge from Julian. But this time he didn't appear.

'Hello?' she called, puzzled.

'We're in the studio, Mama!'

Alys made her way down the narrow corridor. There were only three bedrooms. Hers, the smallest, was as bare as a wardrobe. Manfred's was almost exactly the same size, except that her brother's was always piled high with technical manuals, strange books in English and a stack of notes from the engineering course he had completed the previous year and which he always said he was going to throw away. Manfred had lived with them since he started university, and the arguments with his father had intensified. It was supposedly a temporary arrangement, but they'd lived together for so long now that Alys couldn't imagine juggling her career as a photographer and looking after Julian without the help he gave her. Nor did he have much opportunity for advancement, because in spite of his excellent degree, job interviews always ended with the same phrase: 'It's such a shame you're a Jew.' The only money coming into the household was what Alys made selling photos, and it was getting harder to pay the rent.

The 'studio' was what in normal homes would have been the living room. Alys's developing equipment had taken it over completely. The window had been covered in black sheets, and the only light bulb was red.

Alys knocked on the door.

'Come in, Mama! We're just finishing!'

The table was covered in developing trays. Half a dozen lines of pegs ran from wall to wall, clasping photos left out to dry. Alys ran over to kiss Julian and Manfred.

'Are you all right?' her brother asked.

She made a gesture to say that they would talk later. She hadn't told Julian where they were going when they left him with a neighbour. The boy had never been allowed to get to know his grandfather in life, nor would his death provide the boy with an inheritance. In fact the entirety of Josef's estate – much depleted in recent years, since his business had lost momentum – had gone to a cultural foundation.

The last wishes of a man who once said he was doing it all for his family, thought Alys as she listened to her father's lawyer. *Well, I have no intention of telling Julian about his grandfather's death. At least we'll spare him that unpleasantness.*

'What's that? I don't remember taking those photos.'

'Looks like Julian's been using your old Kodak, sis.'

'Really? Last I remember, the shutter was jammed.'

'Uncle Manfred fixed it for me,' replied Julian, with a guilty smile.

'Telltale!' said Manfred, giving him a playful shove. 'Well, it was that or let him loose on your Leica.'

'I'd have skinned you alive, Manfred,' said Alys, feigning annoyance. No photographer likes a child's sticky little fingers anywhere near their camera, but both she and her brother couldn't refuse Julian a thing. Ever since he had learned to speak he'd always got his way, but still, he was the most sensitive and affectionate of the three.

Alys approached the photos and checked whether the earliest ones were ready to handle. She took one and held it up. It was a close-up of Manfred's desk lamp, with a pile of books next to it. The photo was exceptionally accomplished, with the cone of light half-illuminating the titles and excellent contrast. It was slightly out of focus, no doubt the product of Julian's unsteady hands on the shutter-release. A beginner's mistake.

And he's only ten. When he grows up he'll be a great photographer, she thought proudly.

She glanced over at her son, who was watching her intently, desperate to hear her opinion. Alys pretended not to notice.

'What do you think, Mama?'

'About what?'

'About the photo.'

'It's a little shaky. But you chose the aperture and depth very well. Next time you want to do a still life without much light, use the tripod.'

'Yes, Mama,' said Julian, grinning from ear to ear.

The little pest knows I'm drawing attention to his mistakes on purpose, she thought, unable to stop herself smiling in turn. Ever since Julian's birth, her nature had sweetened considerably. She ruffled his blond hair, which always made him laugh.

'So, Julian, what would you say to a picnic in the park with Uncle Manfred?'

'Today? Will you let me take the Kodak?'

'If you promise to be careful,' said Alys, resigned.

'Of course I will! The park, the park!'

'But first go to your room and change.'

Julian raced out, and Manfred remained, watching his sister in silence. Under the red light that obscured her expression, he couldn't tell what she was thinking. Alys meanwhile had taken Paul's piece of paper out of her pocket and was staring at it as though the half-dozen words might transform themselves into the man himself.

'He gave you his address?' asked Manfred, reading over her shoulder. 'To cap it all, it's a boarding-house. Please ...'

'He might mean well, Manfred,' she said, defensively.

'I don't understand you, sis. You haven't heard a word from him in years, for all you knew he was dead, or worse. And now suddenly he shows up ...'

'You know how I feel about him.'

'You should have thought about that earlier.'

Her face contorted.

Thanks for that, Manfred. As though I haven't regretted it enough.

'I'm sorry,' said Manfred, seeing he had upset her. He stroked her shoulder affectionately. 'I didn't mean it. You're free to do whatever you want. I just don't want you to get hurt.'

'I've got to try.'

They were both silent for a few moments. They could hear the sound of things being tossed on to the floor in the boy's room.

'Have you thought about how you're going to tell Julian?'

'I have no idea. Little by little, I guess.'

'How so, little by little, Alys? Will you show him a leg first, and say, "this is your father's leg"? And the next day, an arm. Look, you've got

241

to do it all at once, you'll have to admit you've been lying to him all his life. No one's saying it won't be hard.'

'I know,' she said pensively.

Another noise thundered through the wall, louder than the previous one.

'I'm ready!' shouted Julian from the other side of the door.

'You two had best go on ahead,' said Alys. 'I'll make some sandwiches and we'll meet in half an hour by the fountain.'

When they had left, Alys tried to put her thoughts, and the battlefield of Julian's bedroom, into some sort of order. She gave up when she realised she was matching up different-coloured socks.

She went over to the little kitchen and put some fruit, cheese and jam sandwiches and a bottle of juice into a basket. She was trying to decide whether to take one beer or two when she heard the doorbell.

They must have forgotten something, she thought. *It's better this way, we can all go together.*

She opened the front door.

'You really are so forgetf . . .'

The last word became a gasp. Anyone would have reacted the same way to the sight of an SS uniform.

But there was another dimension to Alys's alarm: she recognised the person wearing it.

'So did you miss me, my Jewish whore?' said Jürgen, with a smile.

53

When he heard the knock at his door, Paul had a half-eaten apple in one hand and a newspaper in the other. He hadn't touched the food his landlady had brought him, as the emotion of his meeting with Alys had unsettled his stomach. He was forcing himself to chew the fruit to calm his nerves.

On hearing the sound, Paul stood up, dropped the newspaper and took the gun from under his pillow. Holding it behind his back, he opened the door. It was his landlady again.

'Herr Reiner, there are two people here who want to see you,' she said with a concerned expression.

She stepped aside. In the middle of the corridor stood Manfred Tannenbaum, holding the hand of a frightened boy who clung to a worn football as though it were a lifebelt. Paul stared at the child, and his heart somersaulted. The dark blond hair, the pronounced features, the dimple in his chin and blue eyes. The way he looked at Paul, afraid but not avoiding his eyes.

'Is this . . .?' he stammered, seeking confirmation he didn't need, as his heart had told him everything.

The other man nodded, and for the third time in Paul's life everything he thought he knew imploded in an instant.

'Oh God – what have I done?'

Ten minutes later, Paul and Manfred were watching the boy attack the sausage and boiled potatoes that his father had been unable to eat. Both were silent, Manfred recovering from the effects of finding his home empty when he went back to fetch Alys, and Paul from the tremendous shock of seeing his son for the first time.

'Are you my father?' the boy had said as he led them through to the bedroom.

Paul and Manfred were aghast.

'Why do you say that, Julian?'

Without replying to his uncle, the boy grabbed Paul's arm, forcing him to crouch down so they were face to face. He ran his fingertips around his father's features, exploring them as though merely looking were not enough. Paul closed his eyes, trying to hold back tears.

'I look like you,' said Julian at last.

'Yes, son. You do. Very much so.'

'Could I have something to eat? I'm hungry,' said the boy, pointing to the tray.

'Of course,' said Paul, suppressing the need to hug him. He didn't dare get too close, because he understood that the boy must also be in shock.

'Go and wash your face and hands – go on.' Manfred pushed the child affectionately towards the bathroom.

'What happened?' asked Paul.

'We were going on a picnic. Julian and I went ahead to wait for his mother, but she didn't show up so we returned home. Just as we were coming round the corner, a neighbour told us that a man in an SS uniform had taken Alys away. We didn't dare go back, in case they were waiting for us, and we had nowhere else to go.'

Paul went over to the cupboard and from the bottom of a suitcase took a little gold-topped bottle. With a twist of his wrist he broke the seal and held it out to Manfred, who took a long swig and started to cough.

'Not so fast, or you'll be singing before too long . . .'

'Damn, that burns. What the hell is it?'

'It's called *krügsle*. It's distilled by the German colonists in Windhoek. The bottle was a present from a friend. I was saving it for a special occasion.'

'Thank you,' said Manfred, handing it back. 'I'm sorry you had to find out this way, but . . .'

Julian came back from the bathroom and dug into his lunch. The two men sat in silence till he had finished. The boy even ate the rest of Paul's apple.

'I need to talk to Herr Reiner alone,' Manfred said.

The boy folded his arms.

'I'm not going anywhere. The Nazis have taken Mama away, and I want to know what you're talking about.'

'Julian . . .'

Paul placed his hand on Manfred's shoulder and gave him a questioning look. Manfred shrugged.

'Very well, then.'

Paul turned towards the boy and tried to force a smile. To be sitting there looking at the small version of his own face was a painful reminder of his last night in Munich, back in 1923. Of the terrible, selfish decision he had taken, leaving Alys without at least trying to understand why she had told him to leave her, leaving without putting up a fight. Now the pieces were falling into place, and Paul understood the serious mistake he had made.

I've lived my whole life without a father. Blaming him and those who killed him for his absence. I swore a thousand times that if I had a child I would never, never let him grow up without me.

'Julian, my name is Paul Reiner,' he said, holding out his hand.

The boy returned the handshake.

'I know, Uncle Manfred told me.'

'And did he also tell you I didn't know I had a son?'

Julian shook his head, silent.

'Alys and I always told him his father was dead,' said Manfred, avoiding his gaze.

This was too much for Paul. He felt the pain of all those nights when he'd lain awake, imagining his father as a hero, now projected on to Julian. Fantasies built on a lie. He wondered what dreams this boy must have conjured in those moments before he fell asleep. He couldn't bear it any longer. He ran over, lifted his son from the chair and hugged him tight. Manfred stood up, wanting to protect Julian, but he stopped when he saw that Julian, his fists clenched and tears in his eyes, was hugging his father back.

'Where have you been?'

'Forgive me, Julian. Forgive me.'

54

When their emotions had calmed a little, Manfred told them that when Julian was old enough to ask about his father, Alys had decided to tell him he was dead. After all, no one had heard from Paul for a long time.

'I don't know if it was the right decision. I was just a teenager at the time, but your mother did think long and hard about it.'

Julian sat listening to his explanation, his expression serious. When Manfred had finished he turned to Paul, who tried to explain his long absence, though the story was as hard to tell as it was difficult to believe. And yet Julian, in spite of his sadness, seemed to understand the situation and only interrupted his father to ask the occasional question.

He's a smart lad, with nerves of steel. His world has just been turned upside down, and he's not crying, not stamping his feet or calling for his mother like many other children would do.

'So you spent all these years trying to find the person who hurt your father?' asked the boy.

Paul nodded. 'Yes, but it was a mistake. I never should have left Alys, because I love her very much.'

'I understand. I'd look everywhere for someone who had hurt my family too,' replied Julian in a low voice that seemed strange for someone his age.

Which brought them back to Alys. Manfred told Paul what little he knew about his sister's disappearance.

'It's happening more and more frequently,' he said, looking at his nephew out of the corner of his eye. He didn't want to blurt out what had happened to Josef Tannenbaum – the boy had suffered enough. 'No one does anything to stop it.'

'Is there anyone we can go to?'

'Who?' said Manfred, throwing up his hands in despair. 'They didn't leave a report, or a search warrant, or a list of charges. Nothing! Just an empty space. And if we show up at the Gestapo headquarters . . . Well, you can guess. We'd have to be accompanied by an army of lawyers and journalists, and I worry even that wouldn't be enough. The whole country is in these people's hands, and the worst thing is that nobody noticed until it was too late.'

They went on talking for a long while. Outside, dusk was hung over the Munich streets like a grey blanket, and the street lamps were coming on. Tired from so much emotion, Julian was giving his leather ball desultory kicks. He ended up putting it down and falling asleep on top of the bedspread. The ball rolled towards the feet of his uncle, who picked it up and showed it to Paul.

'Familiar?'

'No.'

'It's the ball I hit you on the head with all those years ago.'

Paul smiled at the recollection of his tumble down the stairs and the chain of events that had led to him to fall in love with Alys.

'It's thanks to this ball that Julian exists.'

'That's what my sister said. When I was old enough to confront my father and resume contact with Alys, she asked for the ball. I had to rescue it from a storeroom, and we gave it to Julian on his fifth birthday. I think that was the last time I saw my father,' he recalled bitterly. 'Paul, I . . .'

He was interrupted by a knock at the door. Alarmed, Paul gestured for him to be quiet and got up to fetch the gun, which he had put away in the cupboard. It was the landlady again.

'Herr Reiner, there's a call for you.'

Paul and Manfred exchanged a curious look. Nobody knew Paul was staying there but Alys.

'Did they say who they were?'

The woman shrugged.

'They said something about Fräulein Tannenbaum. I didn't ask anything else.'

'Thank you, Frau Frink. Just give me a moment, I'll get my jacket,' said Paul, leaving the door ajar.

'It might be a trick,' said Manfred, holding on to his arm.

'I know.'

Paul approached the young engineer and put the gun in his hand.

'I don't know how to use this,' said Manfred, frightened.

'You have to keep it for me. If I don't come back, look in the suitcase. There's a false bottom under the zip where you'll find a little money. It's not much, but it's all I have. Take Julian and get out of the country.'

Paul followed the landlady down the stairs. The woman was bursting with curiosity. The mysterious tenant who had spent two weeks locked in his room was now causing a commotion, receiving strange visitors and even stranger telephone calls.

'There it is, Herr Reiner,' she said to him, pointing towards the telephone halfway along the corridor. 'Perhaps afterwards you would all like to eat something in the kitchen. On the house.'

'Thank you, Frau Frink,' said Paul, picking up the receiver. 'Paul Reiner here.'

'Good evening, little brother.'

When he heard who it was Paul shivered. A voice deep inside had told him that Jürgen might have something to do with Alys's disappearance, but he had stifled his fears. Now the clock turned back fifteen years, to the night of the party, when he had stood surrounded by Jürgen's friends, alone and defenceless. He wanted to yell, but he had to force the words out.

'Where is she, Jürgen?' he said, squeezing his hand into a fist.

'I raped her, Paul. I hurt her. I hit her very hard, several times. Now she's somewhere she'll never escape from ever again.'

Amid his fury and pain, Paul clung to a tiny hope. Alys was alive!

'You still there, little brother?'

'I'm going to kill you, you son of a bitch.'

'Perhaps. The truth is, that's the only way out for you and I, isn't it? Our fates have both been hanging from the same thread for years, but that thread is very fine – and eventually one of us has to fall.'

'What do you want?'

'I want us to meet.'

It was a trap. It *had* to be a trap.

'First, I want you to let Alys go.'

248

'Sorry, Paul. I can't promise you that. I want us to meet, just you and I, somewhere quiet where we can settle this once and for all, without anyone interfering.'

'Why don't you just send your gorillas over and be done with it?'

'Don't think that hasn't occurred to me. But it would be too easy.'

'And what's in it for me, if I go?'

'Nothing, because I'm going to kill you. And if by any chance you're the one left standing, Alys will die. If you die, Alys dies too. Whatever happens she's going to die.'

'Then you can rot in hell, you son of a bitch.'

'Now, now, not so fast. Listen to this: "My dear son. Colon. There isn't a right way to begin this letter. The truth is, this is only one of the many attempts I've made ... "'

'What the hell is that, Jürgen?'

'A letter, five sheets of tracing-paper. Your mother had very neat handwriting for a kitchen maid, you know that? Dreadful style, but the contents are extremely illuminating. Come and find me, and I'll give it to you.'

Paul banged his forehead against the black dial of the telephone in frustration. He had no option but to give in.

'Little brother ... You haven't hung up, have you?'

'No, Jürgen. I'm still here.'

'Well then?'

'You win.'

Jürgen gave a triumphant laugh.

'You'll see a black Mercedes parked outside your boarding-house. Tell the driver I sent you. He has instructions to give you the keys and tell you where I am. Come alone, no guns.'

'OK. And Jürgen ...'

'Yes, little brother?'

'You might find I'm not so easy to kill.'

The line went dead. Paul ran to the door, almost knocking over his landlady. The limousine was waiting outside, totally out of place in such an area. A liveried chauffeur got out as he approached.

'I'm Paul Reiner. Jürgen von Schroeder sent me.'

The man opened the door.

'Go ahead, sir. The keys are in the ignition.'

'Where am I meant to go?'

'Herr Baron didn't give me an actual address, sir. He said only that you should go to the place where thanks to you he had to start wearing an eye-patch. He said you would understand.'

ᴛʜᴇ ᴍᴀsᴛᴇʀ ᴍᴀsᴏɴ
1934

Where the hero triumphs when he accepts his own death

The secret handshake of the Master Mason is the most complex of the three degrees. Commonly known as 'the lion's claw', the thumb and little finger are used as a grip, while the other three press against the inside of the brother Mason's wrist. Historically this was done with the body in a particular position, known as the five points of fellowship – foot to foot, knee to knee, chest to chest, a hand on the other's back and cheeks touching. This practice was abandoned in the twentieth century. The secret name of this handshake is MAHABONE, and the special way of spelling it out is by dividing it into three syllables: MA – HA – BONE.

55

The wheels squealed slightly as the car came to a stop. Paul studied the alley through the windscreen. A light rain had started. In the darkness it would barely have been possible to see, were it not for the yellow cone of light projected by a solitary street lamp.

After a couple of minutes Paul finally emerged from the car. It had been fourteen years since he'd set foot in that alley by the bank of the Isar. It smelled as bad as ever, of wet peat, rotting fish and damp. At this time of night the only sound was that of his own footsteps echoing on the pavement.

He reached the stable door. It seemed nothing had changed. The peeling dark green stains that spattered the wood were perhaps a little larger than in the days when Paul used to cross the threshold each morning. The hinges still gave the same high-pitched screech as they opened, and the door still got stuck halfway and required a shove to open it completely.

Paul went in. A bare bulb hung from the ceiling. The stalls, earth floor and the coalman's cart.

And on it, Jürgen, with a pistol in his hand.

'Hello, little brother. Close the door and put your hands up.'

Jürgen was wearing only the black trousers and boots of his uniform. From the waist up he was naked, apart from his eye-patch.

'We said no firearms,' Paul replied, raising his arms cautiously.

'Lift up your shirt,' said Jürgen, gesturing with the gun while Paul obeyed his orders. 'Slowly. That's it – very good. Now turn around. Good. Looks like you've played by the rules, Paul. So I shall play by them too.'

He removed the magazine from the gun and set it on the wood that separated off the horses' stalls. There must have been a bullet left in the chamber, however, and the barrel was still pointing at Paul.

'Is this place as you remember it? I do hope so. Your friend the coalman's business went bust five years ago, so I was able to get my hands on these stables for a pittance. I hoped you'd come back one day.'

'Where's Alys, Jürgen?'

His brother licked his lips before replying.

'Ah, the Jewish whore. Have you heard of Dachau, brother?'

Paul nodded slowly. People didn't talk about the Dachau camp much, but everything they did say was bad.

'I'm sure she'll be very comfortable there. At least she seemed happy enough when my friend Eichmann took her there this afternoon.'

'You're a disgusting swine, Jürgen.'

'What can I say? You don't know how to protect your women, brother.'

Paul staggered as though he'd been struck. Now he understood the truth.

'You killed her, didn't you? You killed my mother.'

Jürgen sneered. 'Fuck, it's taken you a long time to figure that out.'

'I was with her before she died. She . . . she told me it wasn't you.'

'What do you expect? She lied to protect you with her final breath. But there are no lies in here, Paul,' said Jürgen, holding up Ilse Reiner's letter. 'You have the whole story here, from beginning to end.'

'Are you going to give it to me?' said Paul, looking anxiously at the sheets of paper.

'No. I've told you already, there's absolutely no possibility of you winning. I'm going to kill you myself, little brother. But if by any chance a thunderbolt from heaven strikes me down . . . well, here it is.'

Jürgen leaned over and impaled the letter onto a loose nail sticking out of the wall.

'Take off your jacket and shirt, Paul.'

Paul obeyed, throwing the pieces of clothing on to the floor. His bare torso was no longer that of a weedy, skeletal adolescent. Powerful muscles bulged under his dark skin, which was criss-crossed with little scars.

'Satisfied?'

'Well, well . . . Looks like someone's been taking his vitamins,' said Jürgen. 'I wonder if I shouldn't just shoot you and save myself the trouble.'

'So do it, Jürgen. You've always been a coward.'

'Don't even think of calling me that, little brother.'

'Seven against one? Knives against bare hands? What would you call that, *little brother?*'

With a gesture of rage Jürgen hurled the gun down and picked up a hunting knife from the driver's seat of the cart.

'Yours is over there, Paul,' he said, gesturing towards the other end. 'Let's get this over with.'

Paul approached the cart. Fourteen years earlier he had been the one standing up there, defending himself against a band of thugs.

It was my boat. My father's boat, attacked by pirates. Now the roles have changed so much I don't know who's the good guy and who's the bad guy.

He approached the back of the cart. There he found another knife, with a red handle, identical to the one held by his brother. He took it in his right hand, pointing the blade up, just as the Herero had taught him. Jürgen's was pointing down, which would hinder his arm movements.

I may be stronger now, but he's a lot stronger than me – I will have to tire him out, not let him push me to the ground or back me up against the sides of the cart. Use his blind right side.

'Who's a chicken now, brother?' said Jürgen, beckoning to him.

Paul rested his free hand on the side of the cart, and hoisted himself up. Now they were standing face to face for the first time since Jürgen had been left blind in one eye.

'There's no need for us to do this, Jürgen. We could . . .'

His brother didn't hear him. Raising the knife, Jürgen tried to slash at Paul's face, missing by millimetres as Paul ducked to the right. He almost fell off the cart, and had to break his fall by grabbing on to one of the sides. He kicked out, hitting his brother's ankle. Jürgen tottered backwards, giving Paul time to straighten up.

The two men were now facing each other, standing two steps apart. Paul put his weight on his left leg, a gesture Jürgen took to mean he was going to jab towards the other side. Trying to pre-empt this, Jürgen attacked on the left, just as Paul had hoped. As Jürgen's arm surged forward, Paul ducked down and slashed upwards. Not with too much force, just enough to slice him with the edge of the blade. Jürgen screamed but instead of pulling back, as Paul had expected, he punched Paul twice in the side.

They both backed off momentarily.

'The first blood is mine. Let's see whose is spilled last,' said Jürgen.

Paul didn't reply. The punches had robbed him of breath, and he didn't want his brother to notice. He needed a few seconds to recover, but he wasn't going to get them. Jürgen rushed towards him, his knife held at shoulder height, in a lethal version of the ridiculous Nazi salute. At the last moment, he twisted to the left and traced a short straight slash across Paul's chest. With no space to retreat Paul had to jump off the cart, but couldn't dodge another cut that marked him from his left nipple to his sternum.

As his feet hit the ground he forced himself to ignore the pain and rolled under the cart to avoid an assault from Jürgen, who had already jumped down after him. He emerged on the other side and immediately tried to get back up on to the cart, but Jürgen had anticipated his move and was back up there himself. He was now running towards Paul, ready to skewer him the moment he set foot on the timbers, so Paul had to drop back.

Jürgen made the most of the situation by using the driver's seat to launch himself at Paul, holding the knife out in front of him. As he tried to dodge the attack, Paul tripped. He fell, and that would have been the end of him but for the fact that the cart's shafts were in the way and his brother had to crouch down under the thick slabs of wood. Paul made the most of the opportunity by giving Jürgen a kick in the face, catching him full in the mouth.

Paul turned and tried to wriggle away from Jürgen's reach. Wild with rage, and with blood frothing from his lips, Jürgen managed to grab him by an ankle, but he lost his grip when his brother kicked back and struck his arm.

Panting for breath, Paul managed to get to his feet, almost at the same time as Jürgen. Jürgen bent down, picked up a bucket of wood chips and hurled it at Paul. The bucket hit him square in the chest.

With a cry of triumph, Jürgen surged at Paul. Still stunned by the blow from the bucket, Paul was knocked over and the two of them tumbled to the floor. Jürgen attempted to slit Paul's throat with the edge of his blade but Paul used his own arms as protection. He knew he couldn't last long like this, however. His brother was almost twenty kilos heavier than him, and besides, he was the one on top. Sooner or later Paul's arms would give way and the steel would slit his jugular.

'You're done for, little brother,' screamed Jürgen, spattering Paul's face with blood.

'The hell I am.'

Summoning all his strength, Paul brought his knee up hard against Jürgen's side, and Jürgen toppled over. Immediately he threw himself back on top of Paul. His left hand gripped Paul by the neck, and his right tried to free itself from Paul's grip as he attempted to keep the knife away from his throat.

Too late he noticed that he had lost sight of the hand in which Paul was holding his own knife. He glanced down and saw the tip of Paul's blade grazing his abdomen. He looked up again, fear etched on his face.

'You can't kill me. If you kill me, Alys dies.'

'That's where you're wrong, *little brother*. If you die, Alys will live.'

Hearing that, Jürgen desperately tried to free his right hand. He succeeded and raised his knife to plunge it into Paul's throat, but the movement seemed to happen in slow motion and by the time Jürgen's arm came down there was no strength left in it.

Paul's knife was buried up to the hilt in his belly.

56

Jürgen collapsed. Utterly exhausted, Paul lay spread out beside him, on his back. The two young men's laboured breathing mingled then faded. After a minute Paul was better; Jürgen was dead.

With great difficulty Paul managed to get to his feet. He had several broken ribs, superficial cuts all over his body and a much uglier one across his chest. He had to find help as soon as possible.

He climbed over Jürgen's body to reach his clothes. He tore his shirtsleeves, and improvised some bandages to bind the wounds on his forearms. They were immediately soaked with blood, but that was the least of his worries. Fortunately his jacket was dark, which would help to hide the damage.

He went out into the alley. As he opened the door, he didn't notice a figure slipping off into the shadows on the right-hand side. Paul walked straight past, oblivious to the presence of the person watching him, so close he could have touched him if he'd stretched out an arm.

He reached the car. As he sat behind the wheel he felt an intense pain in his chest, as though a giant hand were crushing it.

I hope my lung isn't punctured.

He started the engine, trying to forget about the pain. He didn't have far to go. On the way, he'd noticed a cheap hotel, probably the place his brother had called from. It was a little over six hundred metres from the stables.

The employee behind the counter paled when Paul came in.

I can't look too good if someone's afraid of me in a dump like this.

'Do you have a telephone?'

'On that wall over there, sir.'

The telephone was old, but it worked. The landlady of the boarding-house answered on the sixth ring and seemed to be wide awake in spite of the unreasonable hour. She usually stayed up late, listening to music and serials on her wireless.

'Yes?'

'Frau Frink, this is Herr Reiner. I'd like to speak to Herr Tannenbaum.'

'Herr Reiner! I was very worried about you, I was wondering what you were doing out at this time. And with those people still in your room ...'

'I'm fine, Frau Frink. Could I ...'

'Yes, yes, of course. Herr Tannenbaum. Right away.'

The wait seemed to go on for ever. Paul turned towards the counter, and noticed that the receptionist was studying him attentively over the top of the *Volkischer Beobachter*.

Just what I need. A Nazi sympathiser.

He lowered his gaze and realised that blood was still dripping from his right arm, trickling down his hands and forming a strange pattern on the wooden floor. He raised his arm to stop the dripping, and tried to wipe the stain with the soles of his shoes.

He turned round. The receptionist hadn't taken his eyes off him. If he spotted anything suspicious he would most likely alert the Gestapo the moment Paul stepped out of the hotel. And then it would all be over. Paul would have no way of explaining his injuries, nor the fact that he was driving a car belonging to the baron. The body would be found in a matter of days if Paul didn't dispose of it immediately, as some tramp would doubtless notice the stench.

Pick up the phone, Manfred. Pick up, for God's sake.

Finally he heard Alys's brother's voice, filled with anxiety.

'Paul, is that you?'

'It's me.'

'Where the hell have you been? I ...'

'Listen carefully, Manfred. If you ever want to see your sister again, you must listen. I need you to help me.'

'Where are you?' asked Manfred, his voice serious.

Paul gave him the address of the warehouse.

'Get a cab to bring you here. But don't come directly. First stop at a chemist's and pick up gauze, bandages, alcohol and thread for stitching up wounds. And anti-inflammatories – that's very important. And bring my suitcase with all my things. Don't worry about Frau Frink, I've already ...'

Here he had to pause. The tiredness and loss of blood were making him feel dizzy. He had to rest against the telephone to stop himself from falling.

'Paul?'

'I've paid her two months in advance.'

'OK, Paul.'

'Hurry, Manfred.'

He hung up and walked towards the door. As he passed the receptionist he gave a quick, spasmodic version of the Nazi salute. The receptionist responded with an enthusiastic *Heil Hitler!*, rattling the pictures on the walls. Walking towards Paul, he opened the front door for him and was surprised to see the luxury Mercedes parked outside.

'Nice car.'

'It's not bad.'

'Had it long?'

'A couple of months. It's second-hand.'

For God's sake, don't call the police ... You haven't seen anything but a respectable worker stopping to make a call.

He felt the employee's suspicious gaze on the back of his neck as he got into the car. He had to grit his teeth to stop himself crying out with the pain as he sat down.

Everything is normal, he thought, focusing all his senses on starting the engine without fainting. *Go back to your paper. Go back to your quiet night. You don't want to get mixed up with the police.*

The receptionist kept his eyes on the Mercedes until it turned the corner, but Paul couldn't be sure whether he was just admiring the bodywork or making a mental note of the licence plate.

When he arrived at the stables Paul allowed himself to slump forward on to the steering wheel, his strength gone.

He was awoken by knocking on the window. Manfred's face was peering down at him with concern. Beside him was another smaller face.

Julian.

My son.

In his memory, the next few minutes were a jumble of disconnected scenes. Manfred dragging him from the car into the stables. Washing his wounds and sewing them up. Stinging pain. Julian offering him a bottle of water. Him drinking for what seemed like an eternity, unable to quench his thirst. And then silence again.

When he eventually opened his eyes, Manfred and Julian were sitting on the cart, watching him.

'What's he doing here?' said Paul, hoarsely.

'What should I have done with him? I couldn't leave him alone in the boarding-house!'

'What we have to do tonight isn't work for children.'

Julian climbed down from the cart and ran over to hug him.

'We were worried.'

'Thank you for coming to rescue me,' said Paul, ruffling his hair.

'Mama does that to me too,' said the boy.

'We're going to go get her, Julian. I promise.'

He rose and went to clean himself up in the small washroom out the back. It was little more than a bucket – now covered in spider's webs – positioned under a tap, and an old mirror covered in scratches.

Paul studied his reflection carefully. Both his forearms and his whole torso were bandaged. On his left side, blood was straining against the white fabric.

'Your injuries are nasty. You have no idea how much you screamed when I put on the antiseptic,' said Manfred, who had come to the door.

'I don't remember a thing.'

'Who's the dead man?'

'He's the man who took Alys.'

'Julian, put that knife back down!' shouted Manfred, who had been glancing over his shoulder every few seconds.

'I'm sorry he had to see the body.'

'He's a brave boy. He held your hand the whole time I was working and I can assure you it wasn't pretty. I'm an engineer, not a doctor.'

Paul shook his head, trying to clear it.

'You'll have to go out and buy some sulphonamide. What time is it?'

'Seven a.m.'

'Let's rest for a bit. Tonight we'll go and get your sister.'

'Where is she?'

'Dachau.'

Manfred opened his eyes wide, and swallowed.

'You know what Dachau is, Paul?'

'It's one of those camps the Nazis magicked up out of nowhere to house their political enemies. Basically an open-air prison.'

'You've just got back to these shores, and it shows,' said Manfred, shaking his head. 'Officially, these places are wonderful summer camps for unruly or undisciplined children. But if you believe the few decent journalists who are still around, places like Dachau are a living hell.'

Manfred then described the horror that was hidden only a few kilometres from the city. A few months ago an article had appeared in various German magazines in which Dachau was described as a low security prison, with groups of well-fed, well-dressed inmates smiling at the camera. The photos had been taken so that they could be distributed internationally, but the reality that lay behind them was very different. Dachau was a place to which anyone who bothered the Nazis was condemned. A place where guard dogs howled through night, surrounded by electric fences and the sweeping glare of searchlights.

'They don't provide information on anyone held there. And nobody ever escapes, you can be sure of that.'

'Alys won't have to escape.'

Paul outlined a rough plan. Just a dozen phrases, but enough that by the end of the explanation Manfred was even more worried than before.

'There are a million things that could go wrong.'

'But it could also work.'

'And the moon could be green when it rises tonight.'

'Look, are you going to help me save your sister or not?'

Manfred looked at Julian, who had got back up on to the cart and was kicking his ball against its sides.

'I suppose so,' he said, with a sigh.

'So, go and rest for a while. When you wake up, you're going to help me kill Paul Reiner.'

When he saw Manfred and Julian sprawled on the ground, trying to rest, Paul realised just how exhausted he was. There was still one thing left for him to do, however, before he could get some sleep.

At the other end of the stables, his mother's letter was still attached to the nail.

Again Paul had to step over Jürgen's body, but this time it was much more of an ordeal. He spent several minutes looking at his brother, his missing eye, the increasing paleness of his skin as the blood accumulated in his lower parts, the symmetry of his body felled by the knife that had cut into his abdomen. In spite of the fact that this person had caused him nothing but suffering, he couldn't help feeling a profound sorrow.

Things should have been different, he thought, finally daring to step through the wall of air that seemed to solidify above the body.

With the utmost care he pulled the letter from the nail.

He was tired but, all the same, the emotion he felt when he opened the letter was almost overwhelming.

57

My dear son:

There isn't a right way to begin this letter. The truth is, this is only one of several attempts I've made over the last four or five months. After a while – an interval that gets shorter each time – I have to pick up my pencil and try to write it all over again. I always hope you aren't in the boarding-house when I burn the previous version and scatter the ashes out of the window. Then I set to the task, this poor substitute for what I need to do, which is tell you the truth.

Your father. When you were small you used to ask me about him. I would brush you off with vague answers, or kept my mouth shut, because I was afraid. In those days our lives depended on the charity of the von Schroeders, and I was too weak to look for an alternative. If only I'd ... but no, ignore me. My life is full of if only's and I grew tired of feeling regret a long time ago.

It's also been a long time since you stopped asking me about your father. In a way this has worried me even more than your tireless interest in him when you were small, because I know how obsessed with him you still are. I know how hard you find it to sleep at nights, and I know that the thing you want most is to know what happened.

Which is why I have to remain silent. My mind does not work all that well, and occasionally I lose track of time, or the sense of where I am, and I only hope that in those moments of confusion I don't give away the location of this letter. The rest of the time, when I'm lucid, all I feel is fear – fear that the day you learn the truth you will rush to confront those responsible for Hans's death.

Yes, Paul, your father didn't die in a shipwreck as we told you, something you guessed not long before we were thrown out of the baron's home. That would have been an apt death for him, all the same.

Hans Reiner was born in Hamburg, in 1876, though his family moved to Munich when he was still a boy. He ended up loving both cities, but the sea was his only real passion.

He was an ambitious man. He wanted to be a captain, and he succeeded. He was already a captain when we met at a dance, around the turn of this century. I don't remember the date exactly, I think it was late 1902, but I can't be sure. He asked me to dance, and I said yes. It was a waltz. By the time the music had finished, I was hopelessly in love with him.

He courted me, between sea voyages, and ended up making Munich his permanent home just to please me, however inconvenient this was for him professionally. The day he walked into my parents' house to ask your grandfather for my hand was the happiest day of my life. My father was a big, genial man, but that day he was very solemn, and even shed a tear. It's sad that you never had the chance to meet him, you would have liked him very much.

My father said we would have a party to celebrate, a big engagement party in the traditional style. A whole weekend, with dozens of guests and a fine banquet.

Our little home wasn't suitable, so my father asked my sister's permission to hold the event at the baron's country house in Herrsching. In those days your uncle's enthusiasm for gambling was still under control, and he had several properties scattered across Bavaria. Brunhilda agreed, more in order to stay on good terms with my mother than for any other reason.

When we were little, my sister and I were never that close. She was more interested in boys, dances and fancy outfits than I was. I preferred to stay at home with my parents. I was still playing with dolls when Brunhilda went on her first date.

She's not a bad person, Paul. She never was, only selfish and spoilt. When she married the baron, a couple of years before I met your father, she was the happiest woman in the world. What made her change? I don't know. Boredom perhaps, or your uncle's infidelity. He was a self-confessed womaniser, something she had never noticed before, having been dazzled by his money and his title. Later, however, it became too obvious for her not to notice. She had a son with him, which I had never expected. Eduard was a sweet-natured, solitary child, who grew up in the care of maids and wet-nurses. His mother never paid him much attention because the boy had not served his purpose – to keep the baron on a short leash and away from his tarts.

Let's go back to the weekend of the party. At noon on the Friday the guests started to arrive. I was ecstatic, walking with my sister in the sun and waiting for your father to arrive to introduce them to each other. At last he appeared, in his military jacket, white gloves, captain's cap, and carrying a dress sword. He was dressed as he would have to be for the engagement on the Saturday night, and he said he'd done it to impress me. It made me laugh.

But when I introduced him to Brunhilda, something odd happened. Your father took her hand and held it for a little longer than was proper or appropriate. And she seemed bewildered, as though struck by a bolt of lightning. At the time I thought – fool that I was – that it was just embarrassment, but Brunhilda had never displayed even a hint of that emotion in her life.

Your father had just returned from a mission to Africa. He had brought me an exotic perfume used by the natives in the colonies, made with sandalwood and molasses, I believe. It had a strong and very distinctive scent, but was also delicate and lovely. I clapped like a fool. I was delighted with it, and I promised him I would wear it for the engagement celebrations.

That night, while we were all asleep, Brunhilda let herself into your father's bedroom. The room was completely dark, and Brunhilda was naked under her dressing-gown, wearing only the perfume your father had given me. Without a sound she got into bed, and made love to him. I still find it difficult to write these words, Paul, even now that twenty years have passed.

Your father, believing I had wanted to give him an advance on our wedding night, didn't resist. At least that was what he told me the following day, as I looked him in the eye.

He swore to me, and swore again, that he hadn't noticed anything until it was all over and Brunhilda spoke for the first time. She told him she loved him and asked him to run away with her. Your father threw her out of the room and the next morning he took me aside and told me what had happened.

'We can cancel the wedding if you want to,' he said.

'No,' I replied. 'I love you, and I'll marry you if you swear to me that you truly had no idea it was my sister.'

Your father swore again, and I believed him. After all these years I'm not sure what to think, but there is too much bitterness in my heart now.

The engagement went ahead, as did the wedding in Munich three months later. By then it was easy to make out your aunt's swollen belly under the red lace dress she wore, and everyone was happy except for me, because I knew all too well whose child it was.

Finally the baron found out too. Not from me. I never confronted my sister or reproached her for what she had done, because I am a coward. Nor did I tell anyone what I knew. But it had to come out sooner or later, and Brunhilda probably threw it in the baron's face during an argument about one of his affairs. I don't know for certain, but the fact is he found out, and this was partly to blame for what happened later.

I too fell pregnant soon afterwards, and you came into the world while your father was on what would be his final mission to Africa. The letters he wrote to me were increasingly dark, and for some reason – I don't know why exactly – he felt less and less proud of the job he was doing.

One day he stopped writing altogether. The next letter I received was from the Imperial Navy, informing me that my husband had deserted, and that I had a duty to notify the authorities if I heard from him.

I cried bitterly. I still don't know what prompted him to desert, nor do I want to know. I learned too many things about Hans Reiner after his death, things that do not fit at all with the portrait I'd made of him. That was why I never spoke to you about your father, because he was not a role model, or someone to be proud of.

Towards the end of 1904 your father returned to Munich without my knowledge. He came back secretly, with his first lieutenant, a man by the name of Nagel, who had accompanied him everywhere. Instead of coming home, he went to seek refuge at the baron's mansion. From there he sent me a brief note, and this is exactly what it said:

'Dear Ilse: I've made a terrible mistake, and I'm trying to fix it. I've asked your brother-in-law for help, and another good friend. They might be able to save me. Sometimes the greatest treasure is hidden in the same place as the greatest destruction, or at least I've always thought so. With love, Hans.'

I've never understood what your father meant by those words. I read the note over and over again, though I burned it a few hours after it arrived, for fear it might fall into the wrong hands.

As for your father's death, all I know is that he was staying at the von Schroeders' mansion and one night there was a fierce argument after which he was dead. His body was thrown off a bridge into the Isar under the cover of darkness.

I don't know who killed your father. Your aunt told me what I'm telling you here, almost to the word, though she was not present when it happened. She told me with tears in her eyes, and I knew that she was still in love with him.

The boy Brunhilda gave birth to, Jürgen, was the spitting image of your father. The love and unhealthy devotion his mother always showed him were hardly surprising. His wasn't the only life to be thrown off course that dreadful night.

Defenceless and scared, I accepted Otto's proposal that I should go and live with them. For him it was at once an expiation for what had been done to Hans and a way of punishing Brunhilda, reminding her who it was that Hans had preferred. For Brunhilda it became her own way of punishing me for having stolen the man she'd taken a fancy to, even though this man had never belonged to her.

And for me it was a way of surviving. Your father had left me nothing but his debts, when the government deigned to pronounce him dead some years later, although his body never turned up. So you and I lived in that mansion, which contained nothing but hatred.

There is one other thing. To me, Jürgen has never been anything less than your brother, because although he was conceived in Brunhilda's womb I have considered him my son. I have never been able to show him affection, but he is a part of your father, a man I loved with all my soul. Seeing him every day, even for a few moments, has been like having my Hans back with me again.

My cowardice and selfishness have shaped your life, Paul. I never wanted your father's death to affect you too. I tried to lie to you and hide the facts so that when you were older you wouldn't go out in search of some ridiculous vengeance. Do not do that – please.

If this is the letter that ends up in your hands, which I doubt, I want you to know that I love you very much, and all I have tried to do through my actions is to protect you. Forgive me.

Your mother who loves you,

ILSE REINER

58

When he had finished reading his mother's words, Paul cried for a long time.

He shed tears for Ilse, who had suffered her entire life because of love, and who, out of love, had made mistakes. He shed tears for Jürgen, who had been born into the worst possible situation. He shed tears for himself, for the boy who had cried for a father who hadn't deserved it.

As he fell asleep he was overcome by a strange sense of peace, a feeling he didn't recall ever having experienced before. Whatever the outcome of the madness they were about to attempt in a few hours' time, he had achieved his goal.

Manfred woke him, tapping him gently on the back. Julian was a few metres away, eating a sausage sandwich.

'It's seven p.m.'

'Why did you let me sleep for so long?'

'You needed the rest. In the meantime I went shopping. I've brought everything you said. The towels, a steel spoon, the shovel, everything.'

'So let's begin.'

Manfred made Paul take the sulphonamide to stop his wounds becoming infected, then the two of them sent Julian to the car.

'Can I start it?' the boy asked.

'Don't even think about it!' shouted Manfred.

He and Paul then stripped the dead man of his trousers and boots and dressed him in Paul's clothes. They tucked Paul's documents into the jacket pocket. Then they dug a deep hole in the floor and buried him.

'This'll confuse them for a while, I hope. I don't think they'll find him for a few weeks, and by then there won't be much of him left,' said Paul.

Jürgen's uniform was hanging from a nail in the stalls. Paul was more or less the same height as his brother, though Jürgen was stockier. With the bulky bandages Paul was wearing around his arms and chest, the uniform sat reasonably well. The boots were tight, but the rest fitted.

'That uniform fits you like glove. The thing that's never going to wash is this.'

Manfred showed him Jürgen's identity card. It was in a little leather wallet, together with his Nazi Party card and an SS card. The similarity between Jürgen and Paul had increased over the years. Both had a strong jaw, blue eyes and similar features. Jürgen's hair was darker, but they could solve that with the hair grease Manfred had bought. Paul could easily pass for Jürgen, except for one small detail, which Manfred was pointing to on the card. In the section about 'distinguishing features' were clearly written the words *Right eye missing*.

'A patch isn't going to be enough, Paul. If they ask you to lift it . . .'

'I know, Manfred. That's why I need your help.'

Manfred looked at him in complete amazement.

'You're not thinking of . . .'

'I've got to do it.'

'But it's madness!'

'Just like the rest of the plan. And this is its weakest point.'

Finally Manfred agreed. Paul sat on the driver's seat of the cart, towels covering his chest as though he were at the barber's.

'Ready?'

'Wait,' said Manfred, who seemed terrified. 'Let's go over it again one more time to be sure there are no mistakes.'

'I'm going to put the spoon at the edge of my right eyelid, and pull my eye out by its roots. While I'm taking it out you have to put the antiseptics and then the gauze on me. All right?'

Manfred nodded. He was so scared he could barely speak.

'Ready?' Paul asked again.

'Ready.'

Ten seconds later, there was nothing but screaming.

By eleven that night, Paul had taken almost an entire packet of aspirin, leaving himself two more. The wound had stopped bleeding, and

Manfred disinfected it every fifteen minutes, putting on fresh gauze each time.

Julian, who had come back in a few hours earlier, alarmed at the shouts, found his father holding his head in his hands and howling at the top of his lungs, while his uncle screamed hysterically for him to get out. He'd gone back and shut himself away in the Mercedes, then burst into tears.

When everything had calmed down, Manfred went out to fetch his nephew and explain the plan. On seeing Paul, Julian asked: 'Are you doing all this just for my mother?' There was something like reverence in his voice.

'And for you, Julian. Because I want us to be together.'

The boy didn't answer, but he clung tightly to Paul's arm, and still hadn't let go when Paul decided it was time for them to leave. He climbed into the back seat of the car with Julian and Manfred drove the sixteen kilometres that separated them from the camp with a tense expression on his face. It took them almost an hour to get there, as Manfred barely knew how to drive and the car kept stalling.

'When we get there the car mustn't stall, under any circumstances, Manfred,' said Paul, concerned.

'I'll do what I can.'

As they approached the city of Dachau, Paul noticed a dramatic change compared to Munich. Even in the darkness, the poverty in this city was evident. The pavements were badly maintained and dirty, the traffic signs pockmarked, the façades of the buildings old and peeling.

'What a sad place,' said Paul.

'Of all the places they could have taken Alys, this is definitely the worst.'

'Why do you say that?'

'Our father owned the gunpowder factory that used to be situated in this city.'

Paul was about to tell Manfred that his own mother had worked in that munitions factory and that she'd been dismissed, but found he was too tired to start the conversation.

'The really ironic thing is that my father sold the land to the Nazis. And they built the camp on it.'

*

Finally they saw a yellow sign with black letters informing them that the camp was eight hundred metres away.

'Stop, Manfred. Turn round slowly and go back a bit.'

Manfred did as he was told, and they backtracked as far as a small building that looked like a gamekeeper's hut, though it seemed to have been deserted for some time.

'Julian, listen very carefully,' said Paul, holding the boy by his shoulders and forcing him to look him in the eye. 'Your uncle and I are going to go into the camp to try to get your mother out. But you can't come with us. I want you to get out of the car now with my suitcase and to wait round the back of this building. Hide yourself away as best you can, don't talk to anyone and don't come out, unless you hear me or your uncle calling you, understand?'

Julian nodded, his lips quivering.

'Brave boy,' said Paul, giving him a hug.

'And what if you don't come back?'

'Don't even think about that, Julian. We will.'

With Julian installed in his hiding-place, Paul and Manfred got back in the car.

'Why didn't you tell him what to do if we don't come back?' asked Manfred.

'Because he's an intelligent child. He'll look in the suitcase, he'll take the money and leave the rest. Anyway, I don't have anyone to send him to. How does the wound look?' he said, turning on the reading light and pulling away the gauze.

'It's swollen, but not too badly. The lid isn't too red. Does it hurt?'

'Like hell.'

Paul looked at himself in the rear-view mirror. Where previously there had been a eyeball, there was now a patch of wrinkled skin. A little thread of blood trickled from the corner of his eye, like a scarlet tear.

'It's got to look old, for fuck's sake.'

'They might not ask you to take the patch off.'

'Thanks for reminding me.'

He took the patch from his pocket and put it on, throwing the pieces of gauze out of the window into a ditch. When he looked at himself in the mirror again, a shiver went down his spine.

The person looking back at him was Jürgen.

He glanced at the Nazi armband on his left arm.

I remember I once thought I'd rather die than wear this symbol, thought Paul. *Today Paul Reiner is dead. I am now Jürgen von Schroeder.*

He got out of the passenger seat and moved into the back, trying to remember what his brother was like, his contemptuous air, his arrogant manner. The way he projected his voice as though it were an extension of himself, trying to make everyone else feel inferior.

I can do it, said Paul to himself. *We shall see . . .*

'Start her up, Manfred. We mustn't waste any more time.'

59

ARBEIT MACHT FREI

Those were the words written in iron letters over the gate of the camp. The words, however, were no more than bars in another form. None of the people in there would earn their freedom through work.

When the Mercedes stopped at the entrance, a sleepy guard in a black uniform came out of a sentry-box, briefly shone his flashlight into the car and gestured for them to pass. The gates opened at once.

'That was simple,' whispered Manfred.

'Ever known a prison that was hard to get into? The difficult part tends to be getting out,' Paul replied.

The gate was fully open, but the car didn't move.

'What the hell's wrong with you? Don't just stop here.'

'I don't know where to go, Paul,' replied Manfred, his hands clenched on the steering-wheel.

'Shit.'

Paul opened his window and gestured to the guard to approach. He ran over to the car.

'Yes, sir?'

'Corporal, I have a splitting headache. Please explain to my idiot driver how to get to whomever is in charge here. I'm bringing orders from Munich.'

'At the moment the only people are in the guardhouse, sir.'

'Well then, go on, Corporal. This idiot and I don't speak the same language.'

The guard gave instructions to Manfred, who didn't have to fake his expression of anger.

'You didn't overdo things a little?'

'If you'd ever seen my brother talking to the staff ... this would be him on one of his good days.'

Manfred drove the car around a fenced-off area which seemed to give off a strange acrid odour that they could smell even with the windows closed. On the other side they could see the dark shape of numerous huts. The only movement came from a group of prisoners who were running around a floodlit post, each of them with their right foot tied to the ankle of the one behind. When one person fell, at least four or five would go down with them.

'Come on, dogs! You'll keep going till you've done ten circuits in a row without stumbling!' shouted a guard, waving a stick in the air with which he beat any prisoner who fell.

'There's no place like home,' said Manfred, his voice sombre.

'Good God, I can't believe Alys has ended up in a place like this.'

'Well if we don't succeed, you and I will end up here too. That is, if they don't shoot us instead.'

The car stopped in front of a low white building, the floodlit door of which was being guarded by another couple of soldiers. Paul had his hand on the door handle when Manfred stopped him.

'What are you doing?' he whispered. 'I have to open the door for you!'

Paul caught himself just in time. His headache and sense of disorientation had grown worse in the past few minutes, and he was struggling to get his thoughts in order. He felt a stab of fear at what he was about to do. For a moment he was tempted to tell Manfred to turn around and get away from that place as quickly as possible.

I can't do that to Alys. Or to Julian, or to myself. I have to go in ... whatever happens.

The car door was opened. Paul put one foot on the cement ground and stuck out his head, and the two soldiers instantly stood to attention and raised their arms. Paul got out of the Mercedes and returned the salute.

'At ease,' he said, as he went through the door.

The guardhouse consisted of a small office-like room with three or four neat desks, each one with a tiny Nazi flag next to the pencil-holder, and a portrait of the Führer as the only decoration on the walls. Close to the door was a long table, like a counter, manned by a single sour-faced official. He straightened up when he saw Paul come in.

'Heil Hitler!'

'Heil Hitler!' replied Paul, studying the room carefully. At the back there was a window overlooking what seemed to be a sort of common room. Through the glass he could see about ten soldiers playing cards amid a cloud of smoke.

'Good evening, Herr Obersturmführer,' said the official. 'What can I do for you at this time of night?'

'I'm here on urgent business. I have to take a female prisoner back with me to Munich for ... for interrogation.'

'Certainly, sir. And the name?'

'Alys Tannenbaum.'

'Ah, the one they brought in yesterday. We don't have many women here, no more than fifty, you know. It's a shame she's being taken away. She's one of the few who's ... not bad,' he said with a lascivious smile.

'You mean for a Jew?'

The man behind the counter gulped at the threat in Paul's voice.

'Of course, sir, not bad for a Jew.'

'Of course. Well then, what are you waiting for? Fetch her!'

'Straight away, sir. Can I see the transfer order, sir?'

Paul, whose arms were crossed behind his back, clenched his fists tightly. He had prepared his answer to this question. If his little speech worked, they would get Alys out, jump into the car, and leave the place as free as the wind. If not there would be a telephone call, possibly more than one. In less than half an hour he and Manfred would be the camp's guests of honour.

'Now listen carefully, Herr ...'

'Faber, sir. Gustav Faber.'

'Listen, Herr Faber. Two hours ago I was in bed with this delightful girl from Frankfurt I'd been chasing for days. Days! Suddenly the telephone rang and you know who it was?'

'No, sir.'

Paul leaned over the counter and lowered his voice discreetly.

'It was Reinhard Heydrich, the great man himself. He said to me, "Jürgen, my good man, bring me that Jewish girl we sent to Dachau yesterday, because it turns out we didn't get enough out of her." And I said to him, "Can't someone else go?" And he said to me, "No, because I want you to work on her on the way. Frighten her with that special method of yours." So I got into my car and here I am. Anything to do a favour for a friend. But that doesn't mean I'm not in a foul mood. So get the Jewish whore out here as quick as you like, so I can get back to my little friend before she's fallen asleep.'

'Sir, I'm sorry, but ...'

'Herr Faber, do you know who I am?'

'No, sir.'

'I'm Baron von Schroeder.'

At that the little man's face changed.

'Why didn't you say so before, sir? I'm a good friend of Adolf Eichmann's. He's told me a lot about you' – he lowered his voice – 'and I know the two of you are working on a special job for Herr Heydrich. Anyway, don't you worry, I'll sort this out.'

He got up, walked over to the common room and summoned one of the soldiers, who was clearly annoyed at having his game interrupted. After a few moments the man disappeared through a door that was out of Paul's sight.

In the meantime Faber returned. He took a purple form out from under the counter and started to fill it in.

'May I have your ID? I need to take down your SS number.'

Paul held out the leather wallet.

'It's all here. Make it quick.'

Faber removed the identity card and looked at the photo for a few moments. Paul watched him closely. He saw a shadow of doubt cross the official's face, as he looked up at him and then back down at the photo. He had to do something. Distract him, give him the *coup de grâce* that removed any doubt.

'What's the matter, you can't find it? Need me to cast my eye over it?'

When the official looked at him, confused, Paul lifted the patch for a moment and gave an unpleasant laugh.

'No ... no, sir. I'm just making a note of it now.'

He returned the leather wallet to Paul.

'Sir, I hope you don't mind me mentioning this, but ... there's blood in your eye-socket.'

'Oh, thank you, Herr Faber. The doctor is draining the tissue that has formed over the years. He says he can put in a glass eye. In the meantime I'm at the mercy of his instruments. Anyway ...'

'It's all set, sir. Look, they're bringing her over now.'

A door opened behind Paul, and he heard footsteps. Paul didn't turn to look at Alys just yet, for fear that his face would betray even the slightest emotion, or worse, that she would recognise him. It was only when she was standing next to him that he dared to give her a quick sideways glance.

Alys, dressed in a sort of coarse grey smock, had her head bowed, her eyes on the floor. She was barefoot, and her hands were cuffed.

Don't think about how she is, thought Paul. *Just think about how to get her out of here alive.*

'Well, if that is all . . .'

'Yes, sir. Sign here, and here, please.'

The fake baron took the pen and was careful to make his scribble illegible. Then he took Alys by the arm and turned, dragging her along with him.

'Just one last thing, sir?

Paul turned again.

'What the hell is it now?' he shouted, exasperated.

'I'll have to call Herr Eichmann to authorise the prisoner's departure, since he was the one who signed her in.'

Terrified, Paul tried to find something to say.

'You think it's necessary to wake our friend Adolf for such a trivial matter?'

'It won't take a minute, sir,' said the official. He was already holding the telephone.

60

We're done for, thought Paul.

A bead of sweat formed on his forehead, ran down over his eyebrows and slipped into the socket of his good eye. Paul blinked discreetly, but more drops were already forming. It was very hot in the guardroom, especially where Paul was standing, directly below the bulb that lit the entrance. Jürgen's cap, which was tight on him, was not helping.

They mustn't see that I'm nervous.

'Herr Eichmann?'

Faber's strident voice echoed round the room. He was one of those people who spoke louder when he was on the telephone to make it easier for the cables to carry his voice.

'I'm sorry to trouble you at this time. I have Baron von Schroeder here, he's come to collect the prisoner who ...'

The pauses in the conversation were a relief to Paul's ears, but a torture for his nerves, and he would have given anything to hear the other side. 'Right. Yes, indeed. Yes, I understand.'

At that moment the official looked up at Paul, his face very solemn. Paul held his gaze as a new drop of sweat traced the path of the first.

'Yes, sir. Understood. I'll do that.'

He hung up, slowly.

'Herr Baron?'

'What's going on?'

'Would you mind waiting here for a moment? I'll be right back.'

'Very well, but make it quick!'

Faber went back out of the door that led to the common room. Through the glass Paul saw him approach one of the soldiers, who in turn went over to his colleagues.

They've found us out. They've found Jürgen's body and now they're going to arrest us. The only reason they haven't attacked as yet is because they want to take us alive. Well, that's not going to happen.

Paul was completely terrified. Paradoxically the pain in his head had lessened, doubtless because of the rivers of adrenalin racing through his veins. More than anything, he was conscious of the touch of his hand against Alys's skin. She hadn't looked up since she came in. At the far end of the room, the soldier who had brought her was waiting, impatiently tapping the floor.

If they come for us, the last thing I'll do will be to kiss her.

The official came back in, now accompanied by two other soldiers. Paul turned to face them, forcing Alys to do the same.

'Herr Baron?'

'Yes?'

'I've spoken to Herr Eichmann and he's given me some surprising news. I had to share it with the other soldiers. These men want to talk to you.'

The two who had come from the common room stepped forward.

'Please, allow me to shake your hand, sir, on behalf of the whole company.'

'Permission granted, Corporal,' Paul managed to say, astonished.

'It's an honour to meet an authentic Old Fighter, sir,' said the soldier, pointing to the small medal on Paul's chest. An eagle in mid-flight, its wings spread, holding a laurel wreath. The Blood Order.

Paul, who hadn't the vaguest idea what the medal signified, merely nodded and shook hands with the soldiers and the official.

'Was that when you lost your eye, sir?' Faber asked him with a smile.

An alarm bell rang in Paul's head. This could be a trap. But he had no idea what the soldier was getting at, nor how to reply.

What the hell would Jürgen tell people? Would he say it was an accident during a silly fight in his youth, or would he pretend his injury was something it wasn't?

The soldiers and the official watched him, hanging on his words.

'My whole life has been dedicated to the Führer, gentlemen. And my body too.'

'So you were injured during the coup of '23?' Faber pressed him.

He knew Jürgen had lost his eye before that, and he wouldn't have dared tell such an obvious lie. So the answer was no. But what explanation would he have given?

'I fear not, gentlemen. It was a hunting accident.'

The soldiers seemed a little disappointed, but the official was still smiling.

So perhaps it wasn't a trap after all, thought Paul, relieved.

'So are we done with the social niceties, Herr Faber?'

'Actually no, sir. Herr Eichmann told me to give you this,' he said, holding out a small box. 'It's the news I was talking about.'

Paul took the box from the official's hand and opened it. Inside was a typed sheet and something wrapped in brown paper.

My dear friend,

Congratulations on your excellent performance. I feel you have more than completed the task I charged you with. We will begin to act on the evidence you have gathered very shortly. I also have the honour of conveying to you the personal gratitude of the Führer. He asked me about you, and when I told him you already wore the Blood Order and the party's gold insignia on your chest, he wondered what special honour we could grant you. We talked for a few minutes and then the Führer came up with this brilliant joke. He's a man with a fine sense of humour, so much so he had this made by his personal jeweller.

Come to Berlin as soon as you can. I have great plans for you.

Cordially yours,

REINHARD HEYDRICH

Understanding nothing of what he had just read, Paul unwrapped the object. It was a gold emblem of a two-headed eagle on a Teutonic cross diamond. The proportions weren't right, and the materials a deliberate and insulting parody, but all the same Paul recognised the symbol immediately.

It was the emblem of a 32nd Degree Mason.

Jürgen, what have you done?

'Gentlemen,' said Faber, gesturing towards him, 'a round of applause for Baron von Schroeder, a man who – according to Herr Eichmann – has completed a task so important to the Reich that the Führer himself had a unique decoration created specially for him.'

The soldiers applauded, while a confused Paul made his way outside with the prisoner. The official accompanied them, opening the door for him. He put something in Paul's hand.

'The keys to the handcuffs, sir.'

'Thank you, Faber.'

'It's been an honour, sir.'

As the car neared the exit, Manfred turned round slightly, his face drenched in sweat.

'What the hell took you so long?'

'Later, Manfred. Not till we're out of here,' whispered Paul.

His hands searched for Alys's, and she squeezed him back, in silence. They remained like that until they had got through the gates.

'Alys,' he said at last, taking her chin, 'you can relax. It's only us.'

Finally she looked up. She was covered in bruises.

'I knew it was you the moment you grabbed my arm. Oh, Paul, I've been so afraid,' she said, resting her head on his chest.

'Are you all right?' said Manfred.

'Yes,' she replied weakly.

'Did that bastard do anything to you?' her brother asked. Paul hadn't told him that Jürgen had boasted of having raped Alys brutally.

She hesitated for a few moments before answering, and when she did she avoided Paul's gaze.

'No.'

No one will ever know, Alys, thought Paul. *And I'll never let you find out that I know.*

'That's just as well. In any case, you'll be pleased to know that Paul killed the son of a bitch. You don't know how far this man has gone to get you out of there.'

Alys looked at Paul, and suddenly she understood what the plan had entailed, just how much he had sacrificed. She raised her hands, still cuffed, and lifted off the patch.

'Paul!' she cried, holding back a sob. She put her arms around him.

'Hush . . . don't say a thing.'

Manfred swerved off the road and parked next to the gamekeeper's hut. Paul took advantage of the moment to remove Alys's handcuffs.

'Let's go and fetch him together. He'll get such a surprise.'

'Fetch who?' she asked, surprised.

'Our son, Alys. He's hiding behind the hut.'

'Julian? You brought Julian here? Are you both crazy?' she shouted.

'We didn't have a choice,' Paul protested. 'The last few hours have been terrible.'

She didn't hear him, because she was already getting out of the car and running towards the hut.

'Julian, Julian darling, it's Mama! Where are you?'

Paul and Manfred rushed after her, afraid that she would fall and hurt herself. They bumped into Alys at the corner of the hut, which stood bathed in the glare of the headlamps like a last bastion of light before the darkness of the forest. Alys had stopped in her tracks, terrified, her eyes wide.

'What's going on, Alys?' said Paul.

'What's going on, my friend,' said a voice from the gloom, 'is that the three of you will really have to behave yourselves if you know what's good for this little fellow.'

Paul stifled a cry of rage as a figure took a few steps towards the headlamps; just enough so that they could recognise him and see what he was doing.

It was Sebastian Keller. And what was he doing was pointing a gun at Julian's head.

61

'Keller!'

'Hello, Paul. The uniform suits you.'

'Mama!' cried Julian, utterly terrified. The old bookseller had his left arm around the boy's neck; the other hand was pointing the gun. 'I'm sorry, he surprised me. Then he saw the suitcase and took out the gun ...'

'Julian, darling,' said Alys, calmly. 'Don't worry about that now. I ...'

'Silence, everyone,' shouted Keller. 'This is a private matter between me and Paul.'

'You heard what he said,' said Paul.

He tried to nudge Alys and Manfred out of Keller's line of fire, but the bookseller stopped him, squeezing Julian's neck even tighter.

'Stay where you are, Paul. It would be better for the boy if you were to stand behind Fräulein Tannenbaum.'

'You're a rat, Keller. Only a cowardly rat would hide behind a defence-less child.'

The bookseller began to step backwards, burying himself in the shadows once more until they could only hear his voice.

'I'm sorry, Paul. Believe me, I am sorry. But I don't want to end up like Clovis and your brother.'

'But how ...'

'How did I know? I've been following you since you walked into my bookshop three days ago. And the last twenty-four hours have been very informative. But I'm tired now and I'd like to get some sleep, so just give me what I'm asking for and I'll release your son.'

'Who the hell is this lunatic, Paul?' said Manfred.

'The man who killed my father.'

The surprise was clear in Keller's voice.

'Well, now ... so you aren't as naive as you seem.'

Paul stepped forward, positioning himself between Alys and Manfred.

'When I read the note from my mother she said he was with her brother-in-law, Nagel, and a third person, "a friend". That's when I realised you've been manipulating me from the very beginning.'

'That night your father called me to intercede on his behalf with certain powerful people. He wanted the murder he had committed in the colonies and his desertion to disappear. It was complicated, though your uncle and I might have been able to make it happen. In exchange he offered us ten per cent of the stones. Ten per cent!'

'So you killed him.'

'It was an accident. We were having an argument. He drew the gun, I threw myself at him ... what does it matter?'

'Except it did matter, didn't it, Keller?'

'We expected to find the treasure map in his papers, but there was no map. We knew he'd sent an envelope to your mother, and we thought she'd kept it, that one day ... But years passed and it never came to light.'

'Because he never sent her any map, Keller.'

Then Paul understood. The last piece of the jigsaw slotted into place.

'Have you found it, Paul? Don't lie to me, I can read you like a book.'

Paul looked around before answering. The situation couldn't have been any worse. Keller had Julian, and the three of them were unarmed. With the car headlights trained on them, they would make perfect target practice for the man hidden in the shadows. And even if Paul decided to attack and Keller turned the gun away from the boy's head, he would have a perfect shot at Paul's body.

I have to distract him. But how?

The only thing that occurred to him was to tell Keller the truth.

'My father didn't give you an envelope for me, did he?'

Keller guffawed scornfully.

'Paul, your father was one of the biggest bastards I've ever clapped eyes on. He was a philanderer, a liar and a coward, though he was fun to be with too. We had some good times together, but the only person Hans ever worried about was himself. I made up the story about the envelope just to get you going, to see if you could stir things up a bit after all these years. When you retrieved the Mauser, Paul, you retrieved the gun that killed your father. Which in case you hadn't noticed is the same gun I'm pointing at Julian's head.'

'And all this time . . .'

'Yes, all this time I've been waiting to get my hands on the prize. I'm fifty-nine, Paul. I've got another ten good years ahead of me, with any luck. And I'm sure that a trunk full of diamonds will liven up my retirement. So tell me where the map is, because I know you know.'

'It's in my suitcase.'

'No it's not. I've searched it from top to bottom.'

'I'm telling you, that's where it is.'

There were a few seconds of silence.

'Very well,' said Keller, at last. 'This is what we're going to do. Fräulein Tannenbaum will take a few steps towards me and she will follow my instructions. She will drag the suitcase into the light and then you will crouch down and show me where the map is. Is that clear?'

Paul nodded.

'I repeat, is that clear?' Keller insisted, raising his voice.

'Alys,' said Paul.

'Yes, it's clear,' she said in a steady voice, stepping forward.

Concerned by her tone, Paul caught her arm.

'Alys, don't do anything silly.'

'She won't, Paul. Don't you worry,' said Keller.

Alys freed her arm. There was something in the way she walked, in her apparent passivity, in the way she entered the shadows without revealing the tiniest hint of emotion, that made Paul's heart constrict. All of a sudden he felt a desperate certainty that it had all been useless. That in a few minutes there would be four loud bangs, four bodies laid out on a bed of pine needles, four sets of dead, cold eyes contemplating the dark silhouette of the trees.

Alys was too horrified by Julian's predicament to try anything. She followed Keller's short, dry instructions to the letter, and immediately reappeared in the illuminated area, walking backwards and dragging an open suitcase full of clothes.

Paul crouched down and began to rummage through the tangle of his belongings.

'Be very careful what you're doing,' said Keller.

Paul didn't reply. He had found what he was looking for, the clue to which his father's words had led him.

287

Sometimes the greatest treasure is hidden in the same place as the greatest destruction.

The mahogany box where his father kept his pistol.

With slow movements and keeping his hands in sight, Paul opened it. He stuck his fingers into the fine red felt lining and yanked hard. The cloth tore away with a ripping sound, revealing a little square of paper. On it were various drawings and numbers, handwritten in India ink.

'Well, Keller? How does it feel to know the map was under your nose all these years?' he said, holding up the piece of paper.

There was another silence. Paul would have given anything to have seen the disappointment that must have been crossing the old bookseller's face.

'Very well,' said Keller hoarsely. 'Now give the paper to Alys, and let her approach me very slowly.'

Paul calmly put the map in his trouser pocket.

'No.'

'Did you not hear what I said?'

'I said no.'

'Paul, do what he's telling you!' said Alys.

'This man killed my father.'

'And he's going to kill our son!'

'You have to do as he says, Paul,' urged Manfred.

'Very well,' said Paul, putting his hand back in the pocket and retrieving the note. 'In that case ...'

With a quick movement he crumpled it up, put it in his mouth, and started to chew.

'Nooooo!'

Keller's cry of rage echoed through the forest. The old bookseller stepped out of the shadows, dragging Julian with him, the gun still pointed at his skull. But as he approached Paul he trained it on Paul's chest.

'Damned son of a bitch!'

Come a little closer, thought Paul, getting ready to jump.

'You had no right!'

Keller stopped, still out of Paul's reach.

Closer!

He began to squeeze the trigger. Paul tensed the muscles in his legs.

'Those diamonds were mine!'

That last word was transformed into a high-pitched, shapeless scream. The bullet left the gun, but Keller's arm had jolted upwards. He let go of Julian and spun around strangely, as though he were trying to reach something behind him. As he twisted, the light revealed a strange red-handled appendage in his back.

The hunting knife that, twenty-four hours earlier, had fallen from Jürgen von Schroeder's hand.

Julian had kept the knife in his belt all this time, waiting for a moment when the gun was no longer pointing at his head. He had stuck the blade in with as much force as he could, but at a strange angle so he hadn't done much more than give him a superficial wound. Howling in pain, Keller aimed at the boy's head.

Paul chose that moment to leap and his shoulder struck Keller's waist. The bookseller toppled to the ground and tried to roll over, but Paul was already sitting on top of him, pinning his arms down with his knees and punching his face again and again.

He lashed out at the bookseller more than two dozen times, not noticing the pain in his hands – which the following day would be completely swollen – or his grazed knuckles. His conscience disappeared and the only thing that mattered to Paul was the pain he was causing. He didn't stop until he couldn't cause any more.

'Paul. That's enough,' said Manfred, putting his hand on his shoulder. 'He's dead.'

Paul turned. Julian was in his mother's arms, his head buried in her chest. He prayed to God that his son hadn't seen what he had just done. He removed Jürgen's jacket, which was soaked in Keller's blood, and went over to hug Julian.

'Are you all right?'

'I'm sorry I disobeyed what you said about the knife,' said the boy, starting to cry.

'You were very brave, Julian. And you saved our lives.'

'Really?'

'Really. Now we have to go,' he said, heading towards the car. 'Someone might have heard the shot.'

Alys and Julian got in the back, and Paul settled in the passenger seat. Manfred started the engine and they returned to the road.

*

'There's one thing I want to know, Paul,' whispered Manfred, breaking the silence half an hour later, as Alys and Julian lay asleep in each other's arms.

'What's that?'

'Did that little piece of paper really lead to a trunk full of diamonds?'

'I believe it did. Buried somewhere in South-West Africa.'

'I see,' said Manfred, disappointed.

'Would you have liked to look for it?'

'We have to leave Germany. Going in search of treasure wouldn't be such a bad idea. Shame you swallowed it.'

'The truth is,' said Paul, removing the map from his pocket, 'what I swallowed was a note awarding my brother a medal. Though, given the circumstances, I'm not sure he'd mind.'

Epilogue

The Straits of Gibraltar
12 March 1940

As the waves struck the improvised craft Paul began to worry. The crossing should have been straightforward, just a few miles across a calm sea, under the cover of night.

Then everything became complicated.

Not that anything had been easy over the past few years, of course. They had escaped Germany across the Austrian border without too many setbacks, and had reached South Africa in early 1935.

It was a time of new beginnings. The smile returned to Alys's face, and she went back to being the strong, stubborn woman she always used to be. Julian's terrible fear of the dark began to abate. And Manfred developed a strong friendship with his brother-in-law, especially because Paul let him win at chess.

The search for Hans Reiner's treasure proved to be more complicated than it might at first have seemed. Paul went back to work in a diamond mine for several months, now accompanied by Manfred, who, thanks to his qualification as an engineer, became Paul's boss. Alys in turn wasted no time in becoming the unofficial photographer for every social event under the Mandate.

Between them, they managed to save up enough money to buy a small farm in the Orange River basin, the same one from which Hans and Nagel had stolen the diamonds thirty-two years earlier. The property had changed hands several times over the previous three decades, and many said it was cursed. A number of people warned Paul that he'd be throwing away his money if he bought the place.

'I'm not superstitious,' he said. 'And I've a hunch that my luck might change.'

They were discreet about it. They let several months go by before they started looking for the diamonds. Then one night, in the summer of 1936, the four of them set off under the light of a full moon. They knew the adjoining lands perfectly, having walked through them Sunday after Sunday with picnic baskets, pretending to be going on an outing.

Hans's map was surprisingly precise, as might have been expected from a man who had spent half his life hunched over navigational charts. He had drawn a ravine and the course of a stream, and a rock shaped like an arrowhead at the place where they met. Thirty steps north of the rock, they began to dig. The earth was soft, and it didn't take them long to find the chest. Manfred whistled in disbelief when they opened it and saw the coarse stones beneath the light of their torches. Julian started playing with them, and Alys danced a lively foxtrot with Paul, with no music other than that of the crickets in the ravine.

Three months later they celebrated their wedding in the town church. Six months after that Paul showed up at the gemmological appraisal office and said that he'd found a couple of stones in the stream on his land. He had taken some of the smaller ones and watched, with his heart in his mouth, as the valuer examined them against the light, rubbed them on a piece of felt and smoothed his moustache – all those unnecessary elements of sorcery that experts perform to make themselves seem important.

'They're quite good quality. If I were you I'd buy a sieve and start to drain that place, lad. I'll buy whatever you bring me.'

They continued to 'remove' diamonds from the stream for two years. In the spring of 1939, Alys learned that the situation in Europe was turning very ugly.

'The South Africans are on the side of the English. Soon we won't be welcome in the colonies.'

Paul understood that the time had come to leave. They sold a bigger batch of stones than usual – so many that the appraiser had to call the mine administrator to send him cash – and one night they left without saying goodbye to anyone, bringing only a few personal effects and five horses.

They had taken an important decision about what to do with the money. They headed north, to the Waterburg peninsula. That was where the Herero survivors lived, the people whom his father had tried to eradicate and with whom Paul had lived for a long time during his first stay in Africa. When Paul rode back into the village, the medicine man greeted him with a song of welcome.

'Paul Mahaleba has returned, Paul the white hunter,' he said, waving his feathered wand.

Paul went straight over to speak to the chief and handed him a huge pouch containing three-quarters of what they had made from the sale of the diamonds.

'This is for the Herero. To return the dignity to your people.'

'You are the one who recovers his dignity through this act, Paul Mahaleba,' the medicine man stated. 'But your gift shall be welcome among our people.'

Paul nodded humbly at the wisdom of those words.

They spent several wonderful months in the village, helping as best they could to restore it to what it had once been. Until the day Alys heard the terrible news from one of the traders who passed through Windhoek from time to time.

'War has broken out in Europe.'

'We have done enough here,' said Paul, pensively, looking at his son. 'Now it's time to think about Julian. He's fifteen, and he needs a normal life, somewhere with a future.'

Which was how they came to begin their long pilgrimage towards the far side of the Atlantic. First to Mauritania by boat, then on to French Morocco, from where they had been forced to escape when the borders closed to anyone who didn't have a visa. This was a formality not easy to accomplish for a Jewish woman without papers or a man who was officially dead and who had no other identification but the old card belonging to a vanished SS officer.

After speaking to a number of refugees, Paul decided to attempt the crossing to Portugal from a place on the outskirts of Tangier.

'It won't be hard. Conditions are good, and it's only thirteen miles.'

The sea loves to contradict the foolish words of men who are over-confident, and that night a storm blew up. They fought against it for a long time, and Paul even tied his family to the raft, so that the waves could not rip them away from the pathetic craft they'd bought for an arm and a leg from a crook in Tangiers.

If the Spanish patrol had not appeared just in time, the four of them would undoubtedly have drowned.

Ironically Paul was more frightened in the hold than during his spectacular attempt to board, when he had hung against the side of the patrol boat for seconds that seemed never ending. Once on board, they were all afraid that they would be taken to Cadiz, from where they could easily be dispatched back to Germany. Paul cursed himself not having tried to learn even a few words of Spanish.

His plan had been to get to a beach east of Tarifa, where apparently someone would be waiting for them, a contact of the crook who'd sold them the craft. This man was to take them across to Portugal in a lorry. But they never got the chance to find out whether he turned up.

Paul spent many hours in the hold trying to come up with a solution. His fingers brushed against the secret pocket in his shirt where he had hidden a dozen diamonds, the last of Hans Reiner's treasure. Alys, Manfred and Julian each carried a similar consignment in their clothes. Perhaps if they bribed the crew with a handful . . .

Paul was extremely surprised when the Spanish captain took them out of the hold in the middle of the night, gave them a rowing boat and pointed them towards the Portuguese coast.

By the light of the lantern on deck, Paul examined the face of this man, who must have been his age. The same age his father had been when he died, and the same profession. Paul wondered how things would have turned out if his father had not been a murderer, if he himself hadn't spend the best part of his youth trying to find out who'd killed him.

He rummaged in his clothes and took out the only memento he still had of that time. The fruit of Hans's wickedness, the emblem of his brother's treachery.

Perhaps things would have been different for Jürgen if his father had been an honourable man, he thought.

Paul wondered how he might make this Spaniard understand. He put the emblem in his hand and repeated two simple words.

'Betrayal,' he said, touching his own chest with his index finger. 'Salvation,' he said, touching the chest of the Spaniard.

Perhaps some day the captain would meet someone who could explain to him what the two words meant.

He jumped on to the little boat, and the four of them began to row. Within a few minutes they could hear the water lapping against the bank, and the boat scraped lightly against the gravel of the riverbed.

They were in Portugal.

He looked around before getting out of the boat, just to make sure that there was no danger, but he could see none.

It's strange, thought Paul, *since I pulled out my eye I have to keep turning my head to see what's happening around me.*

And yet I see everything much more clearly now.

Santiago de Compostela, June 2008

Author's Note

The novel, dear reader, is over now, but the story of the traitor's emblem is not quite finished, and that deserves an explanation.

Three years ago, when I first met Juan Carlos González, I never imagined the course our friendship would take. At that time he was already running a famous bookshop in Vigo, which I shall not name so as to preserve its intimacy. One afternoon I told him – very roughly – the plot of the novel I was researching at the time, and which could have been the book you are holding in your hands now. That's what would have happened, if he hadn't opened his mouth and said:

'Do you want me to tell you a story that really deserves to be turned into a novel?'

I nodded, politely resigned. If I had ten cents for each time I've heard that line I could take my family out for a nice dinner.

But this time was different.

This time it was true.

Juan Carlos told me the story of how the patrol boat on which his father had served had saved four mysterious Germans from drowning in the Straits, and how one of them paid him back with a gold emblem. His story went farther than mine, as his father and the man who had given him the emblem did meet again, though five thousand miles away and twenty years later. But that's another story, and perhaps one day I'll find myself wanting to tell you that one, too.

When I said goodbye to Juan Carlos, before getting into the car with a good journalist friend of mine, Moncho Paz, I told both of them that, though it was a good story, it would never be enough to sustain a whole novel. When I arrived home I told the story to my wife, Katuxa.

'I can tell you're going to change your mind,' she said, shaking her head.

'It's impossible to write a story with only those elements. There's no human interest, no conflict. It's just an anecdote. Besides, I've already finalised the paperwork for { . . . }.'

'Trust me . . . you'll write this one,' said Katuxa with the patronising certainty that makes me love her and hate her so very much.

I've discovered – thanks to her – that when I insist on how little I want something or how little something interests me, everyone around me immediately knows that it is the only thing on my mind. So I spent the next ten weeks trying to demonstrate to everyone how wrong they were.

I was, of course, the last person to understand that the only one who was wrong was me.

Fortunately, by then, I had already read a hundred books and taken a thousand pages of notes. Most important of all were the following two paragraphs:

The masons were the object of persecution during the Nazi dictatorship in Germany: more than eighty thousand of them died in the concentration camps. An ancient Masonic legend claims that the fall of all the lodges was the fault of one single mason, who sold all the others out to the Nazis.

As payment, they say that Hitler commissioned his personal goldsmith to make a gold cross, a mocking replica of the brass medal of the treacherous 32nd Degree Mason. In it, the goldsmith set a very special diamond, which had been part of an unmatched set of diamonds that had belonged to Hitler's niece – and lover – Geli Raubal.

Could Juan Carlos González's chunky gold object really be the famous traitor's emblem? We don't know for sure, but the way it was made and the evaluation carried out on it by independent experts suggest that this is possible. This is in addition to the fact that Juan Carlos has received offers of vast sums from distinguished Masons who have come to learn of the object's existence 'by chance'.

Whether legend or truth, I suddenly understood that this story would indeed be enough to sustain a novel. It was lacking one essential component, however, which was why anyone should commit such an act of betrayal. That is where my story parts company with the legend, and enters the souls of Paul, Jürgen and Alys, who, as they fight against the sins of their fathers, commit a number of sins of their own. Eventually, as in all good stories, the characters and their problems end up devouring the premise from which they sprung.

I have no doubt that – as Paul says towards the end of the novel – Masonry is extremely dull. Which is why the Masons' ceremonies have been drastically curtailed on the altar of storytelling (so that the reader doesn't fall asleep).

There were three sources of inspiration for *The Traitor's Emblem*. The first was Juan Carlos González's own story, his emblem and the legend. The second was the autobiographical writings of Sebastian Haffner and Viktor Klemperer, who helped me penetrate the hugely complex mentality of Germany between the wars. And the third, Alexandre Dumas's novel *The Count of Monte Cristo*, which mine does not even remotely resemble (to my misfortune), but which starts off from the same idea, of a need for vengeance that has lain dormant for decades.

There is one final inspiration, which is predominantly for my female readers. The character of Alys is my way of expanding the feelings contained in the song 'Who's Gonna Ride Your Wild Horses', one of the best songs from the greatest rock band of all time – U2.

Germany between the wars was where the figure of the independent woman first appeared in Europe – sexually liberated, with equality of opportunity, or reasonably close, given the circumstances. She attained this position herself, though there were many who tried to place obstacles in her way.

It was the first time that this light shone, a light that should never be allowed to go out.